COFFEE CRASH

a novel

by Steve Hoffenberg

"Like" the book at www.facebook.com/coffeecrash
Twitter follow the author @SteveHoffenberg
Tweet about *Coffee Crash* with hashtag #CoffeeCrash
See more about *Coffee Crash* and the author at
www.stevehoffenberg.com

"Don't Sue Me" (a.k.a. Disclaimers)

The author assumes no liability for any distress, either emotional or intestinal, that the reader may experience reading this book.

This is a work of fiction. The events and persons depicted herein are entirely fictitious. Any resemblance of characters to real persons, living or dead, is purely coincidental. Any names of real persons, places, companies or products mentioned herein are used in a fictitious manner. The fictional group Curators Of The Earth has no relation to and is in no way based upon the real Brazilian environmental sustainability group Curadores da Terra.

This book contains no paid products placements. Any brands or products mentioned herein were selected solely for their suitability to the characters and situations, and do not constitute endorsements by the author.

The brief chapter-opening quotations are used for commentary, illustration, satire and/or parody.

Opinions expressed by characters in this work do not represent those of the author.

Acknowledgments

The author gratefully acknowledges the assistance of many people in creating this work, including those who edited or commented on various drafts: Charles LeCompte, Annette Schwartz, Marty Sterman, Lynell & George Stromberg, Dana Chandler, and Kristy Holch.

The author especially thanks Marina Amaral for her assistance with Portuguese translations and Brazilian cultural questions.

This book is dedicated to the illusion of safety that was still intact on September 10, 2001

Part I:
Café Americano

Prologue

"You haven't seen a tree until you've seen its shadow from the sky."
Amelia Earhart (1897–1937)

~~~~~

JULY 18, 2013

Dr. Paul Mendonça shouted, "Miguel? *Tudo bem?* Are you OK?"

Paul couldn't tell if the other man had heard him. Miguel was wearing a headset, and with the loud background noise, direct conversation was difficult.

Miguel's arms and legs were shaking, and his neck was arched, pointing his head upward. Within seconds Miguel's shaking became more intense, then suddenly it stopped, as if he had lost consciousness or perhaps even had died. Paul waved a hand in front of Miguel's open eyes, noting the lack of response.

Paul snatched the handheld microphone from the center console. He pushed its button, and called out, "*Socorro!* Help! SOS!" Then he remembered the more proper distress call, "Mayday, mayday, mayday! *Declarando emergência!*" After repeating the distress call several times without hearing a reply, he glanced with dismay at the numerous buttons and knobs on the stack of radio gear in the instrument panel. Scanning all the other controls and gauges of the Cessna Skyhawk, he muttered, "*Bosta*. Shit. I wish I'd learned how to fly a plane."

Paul dropped the microphone and grabbed the handles of the co-pilot's yoke in front of his seat. Looking through the windshield at the treetops passing below, he released his left hand from the yoke to kiss his gold wedding band. *I hope I get to see you again, Fabiana,* he thought. *And I hope you get to see my Sweet Surprise.*

Chapter 1

"Imagine a hungry puppy coming to a corner where he has to choose between turning left toward a plate of dry fish bones abandoned by the cat, and turning right toward a dish of his favorite juicy hamburger. Naturally, he feels (and is) quite free to make up his mind which way to go, though it takes only one sniff to decide him... For the puppy is free to *do* what he wants although not free to *want* what he wants..."

Guy Murchie, from *The Seven Mysteries of Life*, 1978

~~~~~

AUGUST 4, 2013

Samuel Decker stood in front of a restroom mirror, noting his morose appearance on what should have been a happy occasion. *It's such a pity that Ellen didn't live to see this day,* he thought. *If only the cancer had waited a few more years.*

He placed his hands under the faucet, although he had to move them in and out several times before the sensor turned on the water. *And what about the newlyweds? With the outrageous prices of real estate, how will they ever afford to buy a home? That kind of money doesn't grow on trees.*

He put a hand under the automatic paper towel dispenser, and the machine yielded about six inches of material. *What kind of world is this to bring grandkids into anyway? Full of crime, drugs, and guns, and that's just in the schools.*

He waited a few seconds for the little red light on the dispenser to indicate it was ready to feed out more paper. *And what have I done with my measly little life? The greatest so-called accomplishment of my career has been to enable corporate conglomerates to keep selling candy bars. And without Ellen here to share it with anymore, why do I even bother?*

Decker wandered out of the restroom back into the reception hall.

"There you are," he heard his older daughter Evelyn's voice. "Are you OK, dad?"

He looked at her, standing pretty in her pale yellow bridesmaid's dress. "I'm fine, dear. I was just thinking."

"Come on. Everyone's gathering outside for the send-off." Evelyn brushed off the lapels of his tuxedo, and she clutched his arm as they walked out the front door of the reception hall into the early evening heat in Newton, Massachusetts, a suburb west of Boston.

A few minutes later, the newlywed couple emerged from the building accompanied by tossed bird seed from the cheering attendees. The bride, Decker's younger daughter Suzanne, threw the bouquet into the hands of a waiting maiden. Decker gave her one last kiss on the cheek, then she and her new husband Eric climbed into a white stretch limousine. The limo pulled away trailing white balloons and streamers of white crepe paper.

The wedding guests said their good-byes, then dispersed to their cars in the parking lot, the younger ones bound for an after-party at a nightclub in downtown Boston.

Still on the sidewalk in front of the reception hall, Decker was ready to head home after the emotionally draining experience. Evelyn tapped him on the arm, and she pointed to a group of two men and a woman standing across the street, all dressed in gray business suits. Decker remained in place, and the three stepped off the curb, headed his way. The trim, 30-ish woman with long black hair and prominent cheekbones looked familiar to Decker, although he couldn't remember from where.

The older man, with graying temples and olive skin, reached out a hand to shake. "Professor Decker, my name is Roberto Duarte." The origin of his accent was foreign to Decker. "I'm sorry to be disturbing you on this joyous occasion, but we have come a very long way just to see you."

"What can I do for you, Mr. Duarte?"

"I'm Chief Executive Officer of Delcese Agricola, the second largest grower of coffee beans in Brazil. We have a major problem, and we're hoping you can help us."

Decker turned to Evelyn and said, "Honey, you should go ahead to that party for you twenty-somethings. It appears I have business."

"OK. Bye, dad. I'll talk to you tomorrow." She hugged him then walked away.

Decker turned back to the uninvited but not unwelcome guests. "I'd be happy to consult with your company, Mr. Duarte. But are you aware that my bean experience is with cacao, not coffee?"

"Yes, of course. I'll allow my associate to elaborate. This is Dr. Wendy Westphal."

"I'm pleased to meet you," she said, extending a hand. "Or perhaps I should say I'm pleased to see you again. When I was a graduate student in organic chemistry at MIT, I attended a lecture you gave at Tufts about your applied research on cacao fungus. Your work in Ivory Coast saved thousands of jobs and tens of millions of dollars. We need similar help, Dr. Decker."

"I prefer to go by Mister Decker. Around Boston, if someone hears you're a doctor at Tufts, they start asking medical questions. But you can call me Sam."

"I'll get right to the point, Sam." She pulled a tablet computer out of her briefcase. She brought up a photo image on its display.

Decker put on a pair of reading glasses from his jacket pocket. The image on the screen showed a branch of a leafy tree, bearing numerous clusters of round reddish-purple berries. The green leaves had a bright red growth all over them.

"Once a given coffee tree is infected," Westphal said, "all of its leaves and cherries become engulfed."

She swiped the screen with a fingertip to show the next picture. It was a close-up of coffee cherries, the exteriors of which were covered with the red growth, although the appearance of the disease was less distinguishable from the natural color of the fruits.

"The surface looks wet," Decker commented.

"Initially, the fungus draws moisture from inside the plant out to the surface, then it dries out in a few days."

The next photo showed infected coffee cherries cracked open.

"You can see here," Westphal explained, pointing to portions of the image with her pinkie finger, "how the pulp is desiccated, and how the pairs of beans within each cherry have rotted, disintegrating inside the parchment layer."

"Does it only infect trees that are laden with fruit?"

"No. Harvested trees are just as susceptible. It attacks the leaves first, then it spreads all over the plants. And it spreads like wildfire. Here's a photo micrograph of the fungus itself."

She handed the tablet to Decker. The image, taken with a laser scanning microscope, showed a forest of red stalk-like structures with numerous yellow balls on each of their ends.

Decker studied the picture only a few inches in front of his reading glasses, then he said, "All the doohickeys on the thingamabobs..." He paused. "Sorry, I've had a few glasses of champagne." He cleared his throat. "The multitude of spores on each of the hyphae all appear uniform in size, that is, no separate macroconidia and microconidia. If it's spreading quickly it must sporulate asexually. And I'm assuming it's totally autoecious, completing its full life cycle on a single species, and maybe even its repeating stage on the same plant." He handed the tablet back to Westphal. "It looks like you've got a prolific critter."

Duarte said, "As bad as that seems, Mr. Decker, the situation is worse. This fungus first appeared a couple of weeks ago in our largest plantation and since then has infected nearly every coffee tree there.

Two days ago, it appeared in the fields at our corporate headquarters. Yesterday, we detected the first instance of it in our fields in another region. We were only halfway through our annual harvest when the outbreak started. We've accelerated harvesting as fast as possible to attempt to remove the remaining healthy cherries before they become infected, but we can't harvest as fast as the disease is spreading. About one quarter of this year's coffee crop could be ruined. And, unlike most cases of common coffee leaf rust, this organism is killing the trees that it infects. Unless we can stop its spread soon, we're at risk of losing the whole of our crop for the next three to four years, which is how long it would take for newly planted trees to bear fruit, and up to five years to reach full production yield."

"I see this is indeed a calamity in the making for your company," Decker said. "But why come all this way to recruit me? There must be many scientists in Brazil who are far more familiar than I am with such diseases of the coffee plant."

"Several reasons," Duarte replied. "First, this pathogen appears to be a previously unknown species of fungus. Second, according to Dr. Westphal, some of its biological characteristics resemble the cocoa pod rot of your expertise. And third..." Duarte made eye contact with the other man, who thus far had been out of the conversation. "Forgive me, Mr. Decker. This is Ramon Costa, my Chief of Security."

They shook hands, Decker feeling Costa's powerful grip and noting a large blotch of port-wine birthmark on the left side of his neck. Decker wondered if his title was a euphemism for bodyguard.

Duarte explained, "Mr. Costa heads the entire team responsible for securing all the assets of Delcese, including personnel, intellectual property, and physical facilities."

Costa reached into his inner jacket pocket and retrieved a folded sheet of paper. He spoke in a deep voice with a thick accent. "I found thish one in Englizh."

Costa unfolded the paper and handed it to Duarte, who handed it to Decker. It was an obituary printed from the website of *Tea & Coffee Trade Journal*, with a photo of a man standing next to a coffee plant. The text read:

> Paul Mendonça, Ph.D., 57
> Prominent coffee scientist Dr. Paul Mendonça died July 18th in the crash of a private aircraft in Brazil. Mendonça was renowned for his research in breeding disease-resistant varieties of coffee plants.
> Mendonça was born in Miami to Brazilian immigrant parents who owned a coffee importing business. Educated at the University of Arizona, his career then burgeoned at the University of Hawaii, where

for more than a decade he conducted extensive experiments on plant diseases, especially those affecting Kona coffee trees. Twelve years ago he moved into the private sector as Chief Scientist and Vice President of Research for Delcese Agricola, one of Brazil's largest coffee growers.

Dr. Mendonça leaves behind his wife, Dr. Fabiana Munhoz of Brazil; and his mother, Mrs. Isabela Mendonça, residing in Florida.

"An unfortunate tragedy," Decker said with genuine concern. Then he added, "I met Dr. Mendonça at an international conference years ago, and I was impressed with his passion for science. But how does his death relate to me?"

Westphal responded, "Dr. Mendonça's recent notes contained several specific references to your work..."

"...therefore," Duarte continued, "you, Mr. Decker, are a natural choice to help with our urgent problem."

"I may be able to help you out in the short term," Decker said, "although I'm not looking for a new full-time job, especially one so far away from my family." He motioned to the emptied reception hall.

"Of course, Mr. Decker," Duarte said. "We're merely seeking you on a consulting basis. Millions of kilograms of our coffee beans are at risk right this moment. Wendy and our other staff scientists are quite competent, but they're overwhelmed by how fast this disease is spreading and would benefit greatly from your experience. It was Wendy who suggested that we approach you. Mr. Costa will ensure you have complete cooperation from all employees of the company. And if payment is a concern, you might want to check your mobile."

Decker took the mobile phone from his jacket pocket. A pop up message on the screen from Bank of America stated, "You have a pending wire transfer." He tapped on the message to reveal a transfer from Banco Bradesco S.A. in the amount of US$20,000 to be credited the next business day. In all of Decker's years of consulting to supplement his professor's salary, never before had a client sent payment prior to him accepting an assignment, and he wondered how they had obtained his bank account information.

Duarte continued, "That payment is for your first week of service, which would require your presence in Brazil. If you're willing and able to continue past that time, more would be forthcoming. I hear from Wendy that real estate prices in the Boston area are far out of reach for many young families. Perhaps your newlywed daughter and her husband could use such funds to assist with a down payment on a home."

Making sure he wasn't misrepresenting himself, Decker said, "I don't speak a word of Portuguese."

"That's not a problem. Most of our managers and technical staff are fluent in English."

"I'm not much of a coffee aficionado. My coffeemaker takes those little K-Cup thingies."

Becoming edgy, Duarte said, "Mr. Decker, I don't need another expert coffee *drinker*. I need an expert scientist who can help solve my company's problem."

Decker reached out a hand to shake. "Very well, Mr. Duarte. When do we leave Beantown for Brazil?"

Duarte asked something in Portuguese to Westphal. She replied several sentences to him, which Decker initially assumed related to travel details, but he realized otherwise when she used the English phrase "baked beans."

Duarte nodded at Westphal, then he turned back toward Decker. "If we hurry, we can still catch a plane to Newark in time to make tonight's *corujão*, what you'd call the red-eye flight, to São Paulo. We took the liberty of making reservations. If our car brings you home, can you get packed in twenty minutes?"

"It might take me that long just to find my passport," Decker said as they scurried toward the black limousine waiting across the street, "and I'll have to dig into the spare closet to find enough clean underwear for a week on short notice. Do I need a visa to get into Brazil?"

"Mr. Costa has already taken care of that. We have friends in high places. You'll need certification of inoculation against yellow fever, although I imagine you already have that from your travels in Africa."

Sitting in the opposing rear seats of the limo, Costa extracted from his briefcase a formal letter and handed it to Decker.

Decker was surprised to see that the letter included an embossed official seal and a flourished signature by Evandro Aguiar, Ambassador of the Federative Republic of Brazil to the United States of America. He was even more surprised to see that the text of the letter contained his own name, including full middle name, and his passport number. "I don't even know my passport number. How'd you get this letter, on a Sunday no less? And how'd you get my bank account number?"

Duarte explained, "Before we left Brazil, Mr. Costa made a phone call to the embassy. When we landed in Boston, a courier was waiting for us with the letter and your other information. Until he became Ambassador, *Senhor* Aguiar was a member of the Board of Directors of our company. Mr. Costa also has a prior relationship with him."

Decker thought about the letter, the bank payment, and the airline reservation, then asked, "What if I'd already been occupied with another consulting job?"

"The latest update on your LinkedIn profile indicated that you're available immediately for contract assignments."

"I often post that, in case an interesting opportunity comes up, which this seems to be." Then another thought occurred to Decker. "What if I simply hadn't been interested?"

Duarte replied, "You're a scientist, Mr. Decker. Would you have preferred to remain here and work on your lesson plans for next semester?"

The other two just grinned.

Chapter 2

~~~~~

For the short flight to Newark, Decker and Westphal sat on one side in the first class cabin, with Duarte and Costa across the aisle. The United Airlines plane lifted off from Logan Airport over the Boston Harbor islands.

As the plane climbed toward its cruising altitude, Decker asked Westphal, "Which fungicides have you tried?"

She replied, "E-F-T-W-G."

"I'm not familiar with that one."

"It's a term that Dr. Mendonça used," she explained. "It means, pardon my French, Every F-ing Thing We Got. But nothing we've tried has stopped the progress of our red menace."

"Do you know how it's being disseminated?"

"Like most fungi, it can be moisture-borne, but the dissemination of this one is more complex. It's the dry season now in São Paulo State, so it's unusual to have a fungal infection start this time of year. This organism draws its moisture from the plants themselves, which ultimately kills them. As the surface of the fungus dries out, its spores readily detach. We think the spores are transported onward by wind."

"Have you tested the distribution under wet ambient conditions?"

"We set one infected field under irrigation sprinklers, simulating heavy rain. We completely flooded another field. In both cases, the atmospheric moisture reduced the rate at which the fungus extracted moisture from the plants, but it accelerated the subsequent distribution. The water carried the spores right on to other plants."

"How about under extremely arid conditions?"

"We set up an infrared heating system around an infected patch to see if the lack of ambient moisture would halt the infection. The fungus just sucked moisture out of the plants faster, killing them more quickly. Even worse, the spores also detached from the surface more quickly. Most of our attempts to slow its spread have sped it up."

"When a tree gets infected, how long before it's fully engulfed?"

"The spores germinate within a few hours of contacting a coffee tree, and the whole tree becomes engulfed in only one or two days. It's remarkable how fast this stuff grows."

"It's like it was designed to..." Decker stopped mid-sentence.

"What's that?"

"Never mind." Decker glimpsed across the aisle at Duarte.

"And," Westphal continued, "it may have additional distribution mechanisms that we haven't identified yet."

"What makes you think that?"

"Mr. Duarte mentioned earlier that we just detected the fungus at one of our plantations in another region. That's in the State of Paraná hundreds of kilometers from the site where we first discovered this fungus. And it's upwind from prevailing breezes over the last few weeks. No way the spores could have been blown there from the first plantation."

Decker shifted the topic of his questions. "Had Dr. Mendonça seen the fungus at the first plantation?"

"We don't know for sure. We suspect that he had spotted an early infestation of it, and we think he was in the act of inspecting it from the air when the plane crashed."

"How do you know that? Was it in his notes? Did he tell someone? Or did someone else survive the crash?"

"The only other person in the plane when it crashed was the pilot. He hasn't been able to say anything. He's been in a coma. The reason we think Dr. Mendonça was inspecting an early infestation is because the field where the plane crashed is the first field that was infected."

Decker turned his whole body to face Westphal directly. "Are you sure that the fungus was in the field *before* the plane crashed?"

"We don't have a way to know for certain. No one else saw the fungus in the field until the day after the crash, but there's no indication that it came from the plane. The plantation manager inspected everything inside the plane after the crash, and he didn't find any sample plates or other containers with fungus, or any cuttings from infected plants, for example. I also went through all the items from the plane myself when they got sent back to our headquarters. There wasn't anything that could have initiated the infection. I even had the men's clothing sent from the hospital to our headquarters, and I didn't find anything on the clothes."

"How about something on the exterior of the plane?"

"The plantation manager examined the plane's exterior and didn't find anything that could have been a source. The only explanation our scientists can think of that fits all the evidence is that the fungus must have been in the field before the plane crashed."

÷

While changing gates at Newark Liberty International Airport, the group stopped in a Bright Cup Café on the concourse.

As they stepped up to the counter, Duarte said, "Ladies first."

Westphal ordered a Double Ristretto. Decker ordered a cup of Sumatran Gold, then he momentarily felt embarrassed that he hadn't ordered a Brazilian variety in the presence of his new client. Duarte ordered a Jamaican Blue Mountain.

Decker asked, "Not a Brazilian coffee, sir?"

Duarte waved a hand toward the menu board behind the counter. "I consume the finest beans that Brazil has to offer when I'm home. I like to sample the world's variety when I travel. We don't have such a vast selection back in Brazil."

Costa ordered a House Decaf. While a barista prepared the drinks in bright yellow cups, the Brazilian security man sneered at the faux rainforest motif of the North American coffee shop chain and the company's logo of a parrot perched on the rim of a coffee cup.

"Stupid phony bird," Costa blurted out, regarding the brightly colored life-size plastic parrot sitting atop the cash register with a $39.99 price tag dangling from its foot.

The barista nonchalantly touched a button on the back of the Squawkie toy, and the bird squawked back in a high pitched voice, "Stupid phony bird. Stupid phony bird."

Costa barked, "What the hell?"

The bird echoed, "What the hell? What the hell?"

"It seems," Duarte said, "that the phony bird is not so stupid."

Costa told the barista he wanted to buy one. To pay for the toy, Costa tapped his mobile handset on the Near Field Communications spot on the cash register, then he carried the Squawkie's box onward to the gate.

÷

In the business class cabin of the Boeing 767, Decker took the window seat, and Duarte sat down next to him. After the plane had taken off, Duarte opened his briefcase and pulled out two sheets of paper, placing them on the tray table in front of Decker. Duarte said, "I'm certain you understand the need for this."

Decker scanned the Mutual Confidentiality And Non-Disclosure Agreement, or NDA for short. "Of course," he said.

Both men signed and dated both copies, then Decker slid one into his briefcase.

"Now that we've dispensed with that formality," Duarte said, "I have a few questions for you, Sam."

"Fire away, Mr. Duarte."

"Tell me the details of how you halted the cocoa fungus in Ivory Coast. And please, call me Roberto."

Decker leaned forward in his seat. "For as long as people have been cultivating *Theobroma cacao*, those trees have been susceptible to the disease *Phytophthora megakarya*, commonly called cocoa pod rot. For the past century, the standard treatment for the disease had been copper-based pesticide sprays. Unfortunately, the infestation in Ivory Coast was no longer being suppressed by such agents. Overuse of the sprays in the region had created a survival-of-the-fungi most able to withstand the pesticide. Other researchers had devised an alternative potassium-based treatment that successfully halted the fungus by stimulating the natural immune response of the cacao. Unfortunately, that treatment left behind toxic residual compounds that killed a substantial portion of the cacao trees, so the farmers were reluctant to apply the potassium treatment. Without an effective non-detrimental treatment, the pod rot became a threat to propagate itself to all the cocoa growers throughout the African continent."

"And your solution?"

"My solution, Roberto, was simple in theory, although difficult to accomplish. In short, I genetically engineered a new 'good guy' fungus that had two significant characteristics. First, it blocked the 'bad guy' fungus from attaching itself to the plant by preoccupying the chemical sites where the harmful fungus would normally invade, while not itself penetrating into the cocoa pods and rotting out the beans. Second, it fed off residual compounds in the cacao plants, preventing deleterious effects of the potassium-based treatment, such that *that* treatment could be applied innocuously. Once they were widely implemented, the one-two punch of my 'good guy' fungus and the potassium treatment then brought the 'bad guy' fungus to a screeching halt in less than a month. As an article in *The New York Times* later put it, 'the world became safe again for chocolate bars and hot cocoa.'"

"That's a fascinating solution." Duarte's face lit up. "Not only did it solve the immediate problem, but it did so without having to breed or plant new trees. Therefore, it didn't take years to recover."

Decker added, "And, the cacao trees and beans aren't genetically modified organisms. No protests from the granola eaters, at least not the ones that put chocolate chips in their gorp."

"Brilliant!" Duarte said, although he had no idea what the word *gorp* meant.

"Furthermore," Decker continued, "that solution has had an interesting side effect. It created a symbiotic relationship between the cacao trees and the engineered fungus. The trees provide freely habitable sites for the fungus, and the fungus cleanses the trees of toxic compounds. Even years later both are now thriving on their own, without any further direct application of either the potassium treatment or the 'good guy' fungus. The solution appears to be self-perpetuating."

"Now I can understand more clearly why Wendy recommended you for our situation. Does your 'good guy' fungus have a name?"

"I call it Marion."

"Named after a wife or daughter, perhaps?"

Decker chuckled. "The name is in memory of actor John Wayne, whose real first name was Marion. He always played the good guy."

"How long did it take you to solve that cacao problem?"

"About eight months, which was faster than most other experts said it could be done."

"I'm afraid, Sam, that at the rate our fungus is progressing, we won't have the luxury of anywhere near that much time. We need a solution in days or weeks, not months." Duarte sighed, then he offered, "What questions can I answer for you?"

"For starters, I'd like to understand more about what Dr. Mendonça's job entailed. Exactly what research was he doing?"

"When I first hired Paul over a decade ago, his primary mission was to oversee our selective breeding and hybridization program, to improve the quality of our arabica coffee trees and to reduce the incidence of disease. Over the years, the scope of the program expanded along with Paul's staff of researchers. He began using genetic engineering techniques to achieve a wide range of specific characteristics. He and his team created new species variants that grew better in open sunlight and with less fertilizer, and that could grow at lower elevations, to make our large scale plantation methods more economically viable. He created trees that produced consistently sized and shaped cherries both from limb to limb and from year to year, so we could optimize the functionality of the mechanical harvesting equipment. He created arabica trees that began producing harvestable cherries in only three years instead of four, and produced more cherries per tree, to enhance productivity and profitability."

"And most recently?"

"Paul had been working on three major projects. First, he was attempting to create a tree that produced beans very low in caffeine, a naturally un-caffeinated coffee."

"Was he having success in that effort?"

"Partially. He engineered a tree based on the Bourbon cultivar, but containing one third the caffeine. Unfortunately, its cup taste has been dismal. The source cultivar was named after the former French colony called Bourbon Island. To express their disapproval of this new plant, our in-house cuppers—the coffee tasters—jokingly refer to it as Boursin."

"Like the smelly cheese?"

Duarte nodded. "Second, and somewhat counter to the first, Paul was experimenting to improve the flavor of our beans. You're probably not aware, but Brazilian beans have long held a reputation for being less than excellent in taste compared to premium beans from several other nations, such as Colombia. Among coffee connoisseurs, Brazilian beans receive little respect, and therefore garner relatively low prices. Granted, our arabica beans are considered a step above robustas from Vietnam and elsewhere, but even to make such a comparison is a backhanded compliment to those of us who have dedicated our careers to producing quality Brazilian coffee. Paul's efforts in this direction held promise in two ways: higher contract prices for our beans on the commodities markets, and a better drinking experience for the public."

"Any progress in that direction?"

"Over the years, Paul had been experimenting with variants of the Typica cultivar. Instead of trying to improve the flavor of an existing high productivity plant, he started with a cultivar that already had well-regarded taste but low productivity. He attempted to improve its suitability for our high volume production methods, but he was having little success in that effort. Then, several years ago while on vacation hiking with his wife in remote mountains, he discovered a wild patch of unusual coffee plants. He filled his backpack for the return hike with cuttings and more than ten kilograms of cherries. The cup taste of the beans turned out to be marvelous, and he started a program to nurse seedlings for cultivation. He planted those seedlings two years ago in one of his experimental fields. We won't know their productivity for another year or two."

"Interesting find."

Duarte added, "It's even more interesting. Those coffee trees he found in the mountains turned out to be a distinct new species, not a subspecies of *Coffea arabica* or the robusta plant *Coffea canephora*. That was a surprise because as far as anyone knows, the *Coffea* genus isn't native to the Americas. Paul was stumped by the plant's origin."

Decker commented, "It seems improbable that any coffee plant native to Brazil wouldn't have been discovered before. On the other hand, nearly all mutations are detrimental rather than beneficial. It's a one-in-a-million chance that a mutated coffee plant would produce beans that taste better than the species it mutated from. I can see why he was stumped."

"Paul once told me he couldn't have genetically engineered plants to produce beans that tasted as good as those wild ones. He named this new species *Coffea gracinha*. In Portuguese, one of the meanings of the word *gracinha* is 'sweet.'"

"He chose the name because the beans taste sweet, I presume?" Decker pointed to his own tongue.

"The word for that kind of sweetness would be *doce*. *Gracinha* means sweet as in to be very pleasant. He named the new species in honor of his wife, Fabiana. *Gracinha* was his term of endearment for her, like 'sweetie.'"

"Touching," Decker said, thinking of his own late wife. "And the third project he was working on?"

"The third area of Paul's recent research was creating hardier plants, more able to withstand both disease and climatic extremes. Numerous times over the nearly three centuries of coffee growing in Brazil, abnormal frosts or devastating organisms have wiped out substantial portions of our crops, creating not only economic difficulties, but domestic political turmoil and international political tensions. We agricultural companies desire stability above all: stability of our crops, stability of our prices, and stability of our markets."

"And had Paul been making progress in that effort?"

"He already had been quite successful, particularly with disease resistance. In fact, the coffee trees that we now grow in the majority of Delcese's fields are a variant Paul genetically engineered six years ago based on the Timor cultivar. He named his hardy new cultivar Isabela, in honor of his mother, who lives in a retirement home in Miami at the age of ninety-two. With the Isabela coffee variant, the yield is high, the cup taste is respectable, and up until a few weeks ago it had proven to be completely free of diseases, even when we had tried to infect some of our experimental plots. Isabela is patented and exclusive to Delcese. But the spread of the new fungus isn't limited to the Isabela fields. All of our arabica variants have succumbed. Prior to Paul's death, his most recent work had involved continuing improvements to Isabela, to further enhance flavor."

Decker asked, "Is it possible Dr. Mendonça had become aware of a potential genetic flaw in the Isabela cultivar?"

"I suppose it's possible, but that wouldn't explain how the new fungus has infected our other coffee variants."

"Unless the new fungus has mutated already, enabling a jump to the others." Decker made a mental note to ask Westphal if she had crosschecked different samples of the new fungus against each other.

Duarte asked, "Wouldn't it be more likely that the opposite had occurred? That another fungus which affects the other varieties mutated into this new pest and became able to infect Isabela?"

"Perhaps."

Decker gazed out the window into the blackness of the night sky. His mind attempted to arrange pieces of the jigsaw puzzle into relative positions, but he did not yet possess enough of the pieces to create a coherent picture. His eyelids floated down, and he drifted off to sleep for much of the remainder of the nine hour flight.

Chapter 3

"You don't see people rushing off to see people do tricks with butterflies, do you?"

Tiger handler Roy Horn (of Las Vegas duo Siegfried and Roy), after the showman was seriously injured by one of his performing tigers in 2003

~~~~~

AUGUST 5

The *becak* tricycle rickshaw rolled past Pasar Burung Ngasem, the bustling Bird Market in the city of Yogyakarta on the island of Java in Indonesia. The *becak*'s passenger, Eddy Zeger, frowned with shame at the sight of the thousands of stalls filled with crudely caged exotic birds, as well as squirrels, rabbits, and other animals for sale as pets or even as food, right here in his home city. He looked away to the distant north at the 2,900-meter-high volcanic cone of Mt. Merapi.

From the saddle behind the passenger's seat, the driver under the coolie hat pedaled the rig through streets teeming with pedestrians, other *becaks*, and exhaust-spewing motor scooters.

The *becak* stopped at a corner on Jalan Prawirotaman, a major thoroughfare in the southern section of the city. The slim 36-year-old passenger paid the driver, then walked down the side street to the entrance of a building. Over the doorway, a large purple sign with ornate yellow lettering read, "Kraton Kupu Kupu: The Butterfly Palace of Java."

From the nearly 30 degree Centigrade heat, Zeger passed through the doorway into the air-conditioned lobby of the tourist attraction. He walked through the gift shop, with its cash register sporting small signs reading in English, "We're sorry, but our butterflies are not for sale," and in Javanese, "Yogya residents receive 15% discount off admissions and merchandise." He greeted employees and a few of the customers, "*Sugeng siang*" in Javanese, and other customers, "*Konnichiwa*" and "Good afternoon." He walked past the museum exhibit areas containing static displays, video monitors, and recorded audio narrations. He continued past the pedestal sign informing guests that guided tours began on the hour. He walked through the first set of glass doors into the transition hallway, then through the second set of glass doors into the temperature- and humidity-controlled expanse of the 10-meter-high octagonal main butterfly habitat.

In the vast room, numerous skylights illuminated thousands of tropical plants in dozens of families from throughout Indonesia and Southeast Asia, including: citrus-bearing *Rutaceae*; leafy *Sapindaceae*; and flowering *Umbelliferae* and *Annonaceae*.

The main attraction, of course, was the diverse population of butterflies, hundreds of them, freely flitting about, or sipping flower nectar through their unfurled proboscises, or occasionally perching on the outstretched fingers of enchanted children. (Posted signs gave visitors explicit instructions on this, the only acceptable technique for touching the butterflies, or, more accurately, allowing the butterflies to touch them.)

The butterfly species list, printed in handout form for the visitors, included, among others:

- stately Golden Birdwing, *Troides aeacus*
- feather-like Pierid, *Cepora celebensis*
- eye-opening Great Orange Tip, *Hebomoia glaucippe*
- black and white Checkered Swallowtail, *Papilio demoleus*
- enticingly named Chocolate Royal, *Remelana jangala*
- black and green Tailed Jay, *Graphium agamemnon*
- bright yellow Delia, *Delias belisama nakula*

The most prized species of the lot was the mammoth, bright green, black-edged Goliath Birdwing, *Ornithoptera goliath*, with a wingspan of 25 centimeters (10 inches). That species, however, was kept in an adjacent room, where the nearly 100 specimens were visible from the main habitat only through an observation window. Zeger kept them isolated for several reasons he had learned during his early years in business. First, the wings of *O. goliath* produced a mildly poisonous, powdery substance that irritated human skin. Second, the sheer size of these butterflies made them irresistible for children to chase after, touch, and inevitably damage. And third, their rarity made them prime candidates for less-scrupled visitors to attempt to capture and sneak out of the building.

Additional isolation rooms observable from windows in the main habitat contained the pre-metamorphosis development areas for egg laying, larva hatching, caterpillar feeding, and pupa cocooning.

As was his custom upon arriving every day, Zeger stood dead center in the main habitat, gazing around at his personal creation, a perpetual domain for the world's most marvelous creatures.

It's not much compared to the Earth's greater glory, he thought, *but it's the best that I can do for now... until I'm ready to execute my grand plan.*

~~~~~

Zeger's family traced its local lineage back to wealthy Dutch spice traders in the 1700s, before the region became the colony called Dutch East Indies. (During World War II, the Japanese army ousted Dutch authorities, and after the war the archipelago declared itself the nation of Indonesia.)

When Eddy Zeger completed high school in 1994, his parents wanted him to study international business at a European university. Instead, he stayed in Yogyakarta, enrolling at Gadjah Mada University (GMU), where he earned a *Sarjana* (Bachelor's) degree in biology.

Upon graduation from GMU in 1998, Zeger loaded a backpack and bought a round-the-world plane ticket. Starting in New Zealand, he spent three months tramping (hiking) the south island's national parks during the mild winter, then he hung out with hip young way-farers in Queenstown. Through connections he made while there, he signed on as a deckhand for a month on a marine biology research vessel studying sharks near the Great Barrier Reef off the northeast coast of Australia.

Next, he flew to Tokyo, where he immersed himself for several weeks in that city's hyperkinetic lifestyle both daytime and nighttime. Then he trekked on foot out of the dense metropolitan sprawl on a four day, 100 kilometer pilgrimage to the magnificent looming cone of Mt. Fuji. Once there, he climbed the great peak in two days. He spent the overnight with hundreds of fellow hikers in the Taishi-kan mountain lodge, befriending a young Englishman who lived in Hong Kong.

In India, he wandered through the squalor of Mumbai's streets, and he spent a two week silent retreat at an ashram in Rishikesh in the foothills of the Himalayas.

He made the circuit of European museums and cultural institutions, then went to Amsterdam to stay with relatives for the Christmas holiday. There, he saw on television a 10th anniversary replay of the 1988 speech by Queen Beatrix to Parliament in which she insisted that Holland, one of the world's most densely populated nations, become a model of environmental concern at all levels from agriculture to industry to consumer habits.

In Rotterdam, the world's largest seaport, Zeger boarded a cargo ship as a paying passenger bound for Santos, Brazil. Traveling overland through the Brazilian States of São Paulo, Mato Grosso do Sul, Mato Grosso, and Amazonas, he saw vast stretches of jungle deforested to make way for industrialized cattle grazing. He met a group of eight amiable travelers from across Europe, and in the city of Manaus they jointly hired a *gaiola* riverboat, aboard which they watched the shores of the Amazon River pass by on the way downstream. The *gaiola* broke down en route, and they spent two days in Santarém for engine repairs before continuing on to Belém, near the mouth of the great river.

Zeger accompanied a Swiss couple when they flew into San José, Costa Rica, and the three of them toured the large variety of ecological reserves in the tiny nation. On his own, he then purchased a used car and drove north.

In Nicaragua, Zeger met two former Contra rebels, with whom he had dinner and sympathetic conversation. He drove onward through Honduras into Guatemala, where he got lost in the mountains during a rainstorm and inadvertently encountered a coffee farm near the town of Barillas. The English-speaking farm owners, interested in hearing tales of his worldly travels, offered him meals and a bed for the night. The next day, he saw that bird species were plentiful around the farm, but the more plentiful indigenous workers handpicked the berries for long hours and lived in poor conditions.

Zeger drove across the border into Mexico, and he spent a week among the ancient Mayan ruin sites in the Yucatán peninsula. He was transfixed by the massive Temple of Kukulkan at Chichen Itza. But what fascinated him most was how the population of a thriving civilization seemed to have vanished, leaving the structures abandoned for reasons that experts still debated. He read a guidebook article in which the author theorized that overpopulation and its consequent resource depletion were the major factors.

When he arrived in Mexico City, Zeger remained obsessed by memories of the Mayan ruins, and he couldn't help but imagine how the city would look if all its inhabitants were to vanish. The thought was both deeply disturbing and oddly appealing.

Zeger sold the used car in Mexico City to a dealer who paid a lowball price with a wad of U.S. currency. Zeger had not seen many U.S. bills in person before, so he was concerned that they might be counterfeit, but they were accepted wherever he used them on the next leg of his journey.

He flew out of Mexico City, with a connection in Guadalajara, to Las Vegas.

Upon deplaning through the jetway into the terminal at McCarran International Airport, after more than nine months of traveling across the globe, the first thing he encountered on his first visit to the United States of America was a row of slot machines blaring out, "Wheel of fortune!" It made a lasting first impression.

He spent a day walking The Strip, gawking with incredulity at the neon casinos, the showgirl-laden billboards, and the nonstop bustle.

That evening on the sidewalk, he thought of the Temple of Kukulkan when he stared at the enormous vacant structure of the newly built Venetian Hotel, externally completed but not yet open for business.

Zeger rented a car and drove across the desert plain away from the Vegas glitz, beginning a monthlong tour well ahead of the peak summer crowds. He camped and hiked through the great national parks of Grand Canyon, Zion, Bryce Canyon, Arches, Yellowstone, and Yosemite. The grandeur of the experience was both awe-inspiring and mind-numbing, but its most potent effect was to leave him with a sense of geologic time scales in which mankind's existence was only a brief blip.

Zeger drove to San Francisco. He rode the cable cars, and rented a bicycle that he pedaled across the Golden Gate Bridge. In Chinatown, he ate the only meal of the entire trip that reminded him of the food back home.

He flew on to New York City, where he took in the museums and Broadway shows. On his third evening there, strolling the sidewalks of Manhattan, he was mugged and beaten up by three youths who stole his wallet and wristwatch. His glimpse from the ground of them running away formed a lasting last impression of the U.S.

The next day, he caught the first Cathay Pacific flight from JFK Airport to Hong Kong, connecting to Jakarta then home to Yogyakarta.

Unsure what he wanted to do for a career, Zeger brushed aside his parents' suggestion that he join the family's hardwood furniture export business. Instead, he searched for a graduate educational program that matched both his old interests and his new experiences. He found it in the Department of Natural Resource Sciences at McGill University in Montréal, Canada. The program included courses in Wildlife Biology, Entomology, and Renewable Resources, with an optional semester of field research in Latin America. He was accepted for admission to begin in the winter term. He spent the intervening months studying Spanish and Portuguese languages, enhancing the exposure to each during his travels. He also refreshed himself in French for practical purposes to live in Québec province, although the campus courses were taught in English.

Montréal was less than 100 kilometers from the New York State and Vermont borders, but Zeger never again set foot on U.S. soil.

After studying for a year on campus, he spent three months in Panama at the Smithsonian Tropical Research Institute, which he devoted to Paleoecology, the examination of tropical ecosystems' biological and climatic changes over geologic time periods. Another year in Montréal, and he was awarded a Master of Science degree. He elected not to continue on for a Ph.D. because it would have required him to narrow his focus more than he cared to do.

Zeger returned home to Yogyakarta with a vision to establish a climate-controlled facility for systematic study of Java's entomological species. He began in a small greenhouse with experiments breeding butterflies under varied environmental conditions. His intention was to investigate how climatic changes affected proper development of young Lepidoptera, and how well the adult creatures could withstand such changes. One day he looked up and saw a group of children with their noses pressed to the greenhouse glass. The kids pleaded with him to let them inside. Soon more children showed up, sometimes dragging along their parents, and as word spread, Zeger found himself spending more time with his visitors than with his creatures.

Thus arose for him the concept of Kraton Kupu Kupu. He had heard of similar places during his travels, although he hadn't visited one. He would not have anticipated that such a business could be successful in Yogyakarta, which was not known for being a family vacation destination. Nevertheless, his experience outweighed his own logic, and he brought the idea to fruition.

To Zeger, the first irony of The Butterfly Palace of Java was that his enterprise became more profitable than his parents' furniture export business, which had fallen on hard times. When logging of tropical hardwoods had become publicized as destructive to native forests and ecosystems, the prices skyrocketed due to a shortage of available logs, and the furniture fell out of favor with Western consumers. Zeger regarded the hardwood price increases to be more significant to the foreigners than the ecological impacts, although he ignored the fact that ecological concerns were the catalyst for the reduction in logging. Rather than convert the business to handling cheaper but still popular rattan furniture, which was a crowded field with thin profit margins, his parents sold the business to a larger firm. With the proceeds, they purchased a successful small hotel in the Yogyakarta business district.

The second irony of Kraton Kupu Kupu was that it offered Zeger frequent opportunities to observe human beings interacting in a positive fashion with natural fauna and flora. He still harbored the belief that the presence of mankind upon the planet—no matter how well intentioned any individuals might be—was destroying the plant and animal life. Yet he knew that even the wealthiest person in the world could never control enough of the planet's land to single-handedly prevent the impending destruction of the environment at the hands of *Homo sapiens*.

~~~~~

Zeger stepped from the main butterfly habitat through a doorway marked in English, "Private, Employees Only," and he ascended the stairway to the administrative area on the floor above the gift shop and museum. In a cramped office with a window overlooking a side alley, a small young man with the dark skin of a native Indonesian sat at a desk, staring at a computer screen and typing away on a keyboard.

Zeger asked, "Any word from Brazil last night, Brother Pyrrhus?"

Jarma Pukartra replied, "Yes, Brother Goliath, one brief email message. I'll call up the decoded version." He clicked the mouse, then he lowered his voice. "It reads, 'goliath, u.c. marching on. still clear on dr. m., cleobaea.'"

"This unintended consequence will draw attention," Zeger said. "It could pose a greater risk to exposing us than Dr. Mendonça himself would have. But for now, I can't think of any action we can take that will improve our situation. Post a signal for Sister Cleobaea to maintain a holding pattern."

Pukartra called up the source files for the Kraton Kupu Kupu website. On the gallery page for the orange and black striped Tiger Queen (*Lycorea cleobaea*), he added a small animated graphic of a pink butterfly flying in circles.

Chapter 4

~~~~~

Decker looked out the airplane window at the far-reaching sprawl of São Paulo, a serious contender for largest urban area in the world. *It must cover hundreds of square miles,* he thought, *or rather square kilometers.*

Inside the terminal at Guarulhos International Airport, Decker's letter from the Brazilian Ambassador enabled him to pass through *Imigração* without a hitch.

At Westphal's direction he stopped at an automatic teller machine to procure some *reais* (plural of *real*, the Brazilian unit of currency).

She said, "This is the last ATM you're likely to see for a while, but you won't need much cash where we're going. And Brazilians usually tell foreign visitors to be careful of pickpockets, but that won't be a problem where we're going."

The four travelers transferred to the general aviation area of the airport, where they approached a waiting helicopter on the tarmac.

Decker asked Duarte, "Your company own this copter?"

"We own a one-quarter fractional share. We also own two small planes outright for transportation between the plantations. Although I suppose we're down to one now."

Decker, Westphal, and Duarte climbed into the rear passenger bench of the helicopter in the universal boy-girl-boy order of mixed gender vehicular seating. Decker had to smile at the incongruous site of Costa holding the phony bird box on his lap while occupying the front passenger seat of a much larger phony bird.

The helicopter headed north from the city of São Paulo into São Paulo State. Decker noted that the inland terrain was flatter than the rugged coastal area, at least for the first 100 kilometers. The helicopter banked westward over the city of Campinas, and a few minutes later the pampas below began tilting upward. Beyond the smaller city of Piracicaba, Decker pointed down at lush green farm fields.

"Sugarcane," Westphal mouthed silently at him, not wanting to compete with the engine noise.

The helicopter continued for another 50 kilometers into a region called The Highlands, where the waters of the Rio Piracicaba became brown and broad. Then the copter veered north, away from the river.

Decker soon spotted their destination, a complex of a dozen buildings surrounded by at least ten square kilometers of cultivated land. The farm fields were of two distinct types: partially harvested sugarcane tracts like those near Piracicaba, covering about three quarters of the area; and neatly spaced rows of small trees, which Decker recognized as coffee from his previous trips to Ivory Coast. It struck him as odd that the coffee fields occupied the smaller portion of land at the corporate headquarters of a major coffee grower. More significantly, he saw that plants in some of the coffee fields were tinted red.

On the ground, the travelers got onto an electric cart. Costa drove, stopping the cart in front of an immaculate two-story white building reminiscent of a Georgia Southern mansion. A sign on the lawn identified it as *Residência dos Visitantes*.

"Take an hour or so to freshen up, Mr. Decker," Duarte said, "and we'll have someone pick you up."

÷

Decker showered, then while shaving, he paused to examine his appearance in the mirror. Appraising the lines on his face, he thought, *Wrinkles add character.*

He put on khaki pants and a short-sleeved button down shirt, informed that dress at Delcese was casual. Noting the condition of his just-unpacked attire, he thought, *Yep, wrinkles add character.*

An hour after he had arrived, Decker heard a knock on his door. A tall, svelte black woman in her late-20's wore navy blue coveralls with "Delcese Agricola" embroidered in red script lettering over the chest pocket. Her hair was in rows of braids the size of licorice sticks.

"Hello, sir. Welcome to *Sede de Delcese Agricola*, our corporate headquarters." Her English bore a British accent. "My name is Lucinda Vivan, but everyone just calls me Lucy. I'll be your guide and translator during your stay."

"Pleased to meet you, Lucy. I'm Sam Decker." Attempting to localize her accent, he asked, "Birmingham?"

"Manchester, sir." She led him out of the room. "It's a pleasure to have a preeminent boffin such as yourself here. I've been instructed to get you a quick lunch, give you a tour of our facilities, then bring you to a briefing at two o'clock where you'll meet with the senior scientists. Follow me, please."

Outside they boarded a cart. "Don't worry, Mr. Decker. I'll keep you on the right side of the road." She drove to a brick building half a kilometer away. "This is the Employee Services Center. It has a fully equipped gymnasium, a health care center for the workers, and a cafeteria where you'll have most of your meals. I'll issue you an ID card that will give you access twenty-four seven."

Inside the building she led him into the queue of office workers in the cafeteria. He selected a hot meal plate of roast pork, rice, and green cabbage, and she took a bowl of a meat stew. He stood perplexed in front of the drink case until Lucy suggested he try a can of Guaraná Antarctica soda. She picked for herself a Kero Coco coconut water, which came in a flexible pouch.

The cashier scanned the bar code on Lucy's ID card for their payment. "*Obrigada* [Thank you]," the cashier said.

Seated at a table, Decker asked Lucy, "How'd you come to Brazil?"

"My father grew up here," she explained. "He and my mother met in the U.K., where she ran a tea shop, and he imported tea and spices. After I graduated from high school, my parents got divorced. My dad moved back here to the homeland and became a coffee broker in São Paulo. I wanted to see more of Brazil beyond the few visits I had as a child, so I came along for what I thought would be a couple months' stay. I loved it so much that I attended university here, and six years after that I'm still here."

Reaching for the salt shaker on the table, Decker pointed to an unlabeled glass jar of dark brown liquid that was between the salt and pepper.

"It's *melaço*. Molasses," Lucy said. "As a by-product from the local sugar refinery, it's plentiful around here. Some of the workers use it to add flavor to the cafeteria gruel."

He salted his pork. "Is your mother still in Manchester?"

"No. After she remarried, she and her new husband moved to the States. They live in the Boston area, by the way."

"Really, what part?"

"In Cambridge. The name reminded them of the U.K."

"What part of Cambridge?"

"Their house is on Hampshire Street. That name also reminded them of the U.K."

"What part of Hampshire Street?" he asked, stifling a laugh.

"Near a place called Inman Square. Why?"

"They must live within a block or two of me."

"*Mundo pequeno*," she commented. "Small world."

÷

"The entire compound," Lucy explained as she drove the cart, "gets about forty percent of its electric power from the solar panels on the roofs of the buildings. With the frequent rain in the climate here much of the year, there isn't enough sunlight to go off the grid entirely, but our solar power usage is exemplary nonetheless." She pointed to a lime green school bus. "That's one of the bio-buses. They shuttle workers around the further parts of the compound and farm fields. During the week, they make daily trips to Piracicaba for workers who live in that area. On the weekends, one of them will take migrant workers into Campinas. For national holidays, we'll even send one all the way to São Paulo. They run on bio-diesel fuel made out of used vegetable oil from the cafeteria blended with an alcohol distilled from the sugarcane. In the tropical climate here, the diesel engines don't require any modifications to run on the stuff." She pointed to a three-story building. "Migratory laborers for this compound stay in the dormitory."

"Can I take a look in the dorm?"

Lucy checked her watch. "We've got time. I don't see why not."

She drove the cart up near the door. The radio-frequency ID reader detected the proximity of her ID card, and the door unlocked automatically.

Lucy proceeded inside, but Decker stopped just outside the door. He put on his glasses, then he got down on his hands and knees to inspect the doormat from a few inches away.

Inside the dormitory, he surveyed one of the bunkrooms: beds all neatly made with white sheets and olive drab wool blankets; footlockers at the ends of the beds; upright lockers at one end of the room; coat racks along the walls; vinyl flooring. He poked his head under one of the beds. He looked around in the bathroom.

When they emerged from the building, Decker said, "That wasn't what I expected."

"How's that, sir?"

"The housing I've seen for migratory farm labor is much more... shall we say 'rustic' than this. Dilapidated shacks. Dirt floors or rough wooden planks. No running water. Maybe an outhouse. Maybe not. Frankly, this place is nicer than the housing I've seen for most farm workers in the States."

"This compound is our flagship, our corporate headquarters, so it's something of a showpiece. When Mr. Duarte took over fourteen years ago, before my time here, he instituted a program to modernize the entire Sede facility. But most of our other plantations are indeed more rustic." After a moment she added, "Mr. Duarte is quite progressive, sir. He's done far more than just what looks good for show."

Back in the cart, she pointed out the Executive Residence. "The senior execs have apartments there where they sometimes stay during the week, but they all go home to their families on the weekends." She drove them along the edge of the sugarcane fields. "After your meeting this afternoon, I'll take you into the coffee fields to see the fungus up close. Fortunately, it doesn't affect the sugarcane."

"How come there's so much sugarcane growing here and not that much coffee?"

"Our elevation of seven hundred meters is fairly low for arabica coffee trees to thrive. The bulk of our coffee is grown in *fazendas*—that's Portuguese for plantations—further up in the hills above a thousand meters elevation. Most are open sun plantations like this one, where we machine harvest. One of our smaller farms is above fifteen hundred meters, where we hand pick our premium shade-grown beans. Soil and climatic conditions on this plantation, though, are optimal for *cana de açúcar*. The harvested sugarcane is loaded onto railroad cars at the east end of the complex, and is taken to a huge crushing and refining mill in the town of Costa Pinto near Piracicaba. The mill turns it into a variety of products, including table sugar and the fuel alcohol we use in the bio-buses. The smell of a sugar mill is rather pungent, so it's just as well that it's off site. All our coffee cherries, on the other hand, need to be processed on the premises at each plantation, such as here..."

She pulled up the cart in front of a single-story building about 50 meters a side. Inside was an assortment of processing equipment. She led Decker to one end of the floor.

"The coffee cherries start here," she said, raising her voice against the clamor of the machinery. She reached into a wooden crate, took out a handful of the red berries, and handed them to Decker.

He squeezed them with his fingertips. "They're softer than they look."

Lucy pointed to a long machine with trenches of flowing water carrying cherries between small chutes and rotating drums. "The cherries go through this pulping machine that presses the beans out of the skin. The beans are then conveyed to the tanks here." She walked him over to huge open vats full of beans soaking in water. "At Delcese, we still do this part the old fashioned way, by fermentation instead of by machine. Fermentation loosens the slimy mucilage that covers the beans. The beans sit in the tanks for one to two days, after which they're run through troughs to separate out the mucilage. Then they're moved to the drying patio out here." She walked him to an open door.

Outside was a vast cement slab, over which an open-sided frame held a clear plastic roof. A layer of coffee beans covered almost the entire slab. A worker rode along the slab on a low-slung recumbent bicycle that had the pedals out in front. The back of the contraption was dragging a two-meter-wide notched rake, shifting and stirring the beans as it moved.

"The beans are partially dried out here," Lucy continued, "for two or three days, depending on the ambient humidity. At Delcese, we encourage innovation at all levels. The drying patio workers previously raked the beans by hand, a slow and tedious process. One of them thought up the bicycle idea and even cobbled together the first proto-type himself. It proved more efficient at exposing new bean surfaces to the air, and drying time was reduced by twenty percent."

She walked him back inside the building to a large machine with horizontal drums that were slowly turning. "After patio drying, the final drying stage is done in these mechanical dryers to achieve the optimum moisture content in the beans for flavor retention and mold resistance during storage. Here at Sede, as fuel to fire these dryers we burn the green tops that are cut off of our harvested sugarcane."

She pointed toward a window at the rear of the building. "After drying, the beans are stored in those silos out back for one to two months, still in the parchment layer that encases each bean. We call that storage time *repouso*, which means 'rest.' It allows residual mois-ture to be evenly distributed within each bean, which helps achieve uniform roasting. After resting, the beans are brought back in and put through a milling process to remove the parchment layer." She pointed to a broad machine that wasn't running.

She took him by the elbow and walked him to another machine. It was two meters high, with three vertical chutes from which narrow streams of coffee beans were flying down at high speed. "This sorting machine scans every bean and separates out the undesirables: unripe, broken, and blackened beans, not to mention, insects, stones, and any other junk that doesn't belong in a coffee cup. And finally, the beans are loaded into those burlap sacks for storage and transport. Sixty kilograms per sack. We move the sacks by rail to our giant warehouse in the seaport of Santos, from where they're shipped to fill orders. Nearly sixty percent of our beans go to North America, thirty percent to Europe, and ten percent to Asia. Only a couple of percent stay here in country."

She reached into an open burlap sack and lifted out a handful of the greenish-brown beans, still wrapped in their final protective layer, a thin silver membrane. "At this stage, the unroasted beans are called green coffee." She rubbed a few of the beans to remove their silver skins. "The thin skin becomes chaff waste when the beans are roasted." She dropped the naked beans into his hands.

Decker fondled the beans vacantly for a few moments. He looked around the building at all the equipment. Then he looked at Lucy and said, "This seems to be an awful lot of work and a highly complicated process, just to produce a beverage that doesn't even taste that good unless it's loaded with cream and sugar."

She laughed and replied, "Follow me, sir."

They got back in the cart, and she drove them to a two-story brick office building. Beds of pink orchids lined the walkway to the entrance. "This is the Administration Building, where most of the office and lab work happens."

She walked him past the reception desk, into a windowless room the size of a closet. She directed him to sit in the chair and look into the lens. Two minutes later he had a digitally printed and laminated photo ID card, which he clipped to his belt.

They walked up the staircase in the lobby to the second floor. Lucy directed him to stop in front of an internal glass window, looking onto a large room outfitted with chemistry equipment and scientific instruments, staffed by people in blue lab coats.

"This is the main lab area. We have a few dozen scientists, lab technicians and research assistants who work here. A bio-containment room is off the back over there, where they handle potentially infectious materials like the fungus and various bacteria. Since we don't work with anything that's especially hazardous to humans, we only need Biosafety Level Two instead of a higher level."

Continuing the tour, Lucy walked Decker further down the hall to another observation window.

"This is the cupping room, where the coffee is taste-tested and graded. Our timing is fortuitous. You have the opportunity to watch *Senhor* Mosta, our most distinguished cupper, at work. Those small metal cylinders along the back wall are miniature roasters."

Inside the room, a gray-haired gentleman in a blue lab coat checked the state of the beans in the roasters using a long metal scoop.

Lucy continued, "When beans are roasted, they absorb heat then crack audibly when they let it out. Each bean can crack multiple times. When we roast here for cupping, we usually remove the beans before they crack a second time. A lot of large commercial roasting companies let the beans crack twice to produce a dark roast with stronger cup taste, but that overpowers the delicate flavors of many beans."

Lucy and Decker watched as *Senhor* Mosta emptied the contents of a roaster into a steel bin. He poured the beans from the bin into a grinder, set the bin underneath the machine, adjusted a knob, and pressed a button. He carried the bin of ground coffee to a circular table in the center of the room. Around the table were three stools, each alongside a tiny round sink like those for spitting out rinse water in a dentist's office. On the table in front of one of the seating positions, six porcelain cups were arranged in a triangular formation: three, two, one. *Senhor* Mosta measured two heaping spoonfuls of ground coffee into each cup. He sat down on a stool and leaned over the table. He placed his nose several centimeters above each of the cups for a few seconds, then he made a series of notations on a sheet of paper.

"That's the fragrance test," Lucy quietly informed Decker, being careful not to disturb the master at work, even though he was on the other side of a thick plate glass window.

Retrieving a large kettle from a stove along the back wall, *Senhor* Mosta poured hot water into each cup. A minute later he sat back down and leaned low over the table again. Using a spoon to press down the grounds then lift the liquid closer to his nose, he repeated the sniffing process, rinsing the spoon in a bowl of water between cups. He made another series of notations on the paper.

"With the hot water, it becomes the aroma test."

What happened next occurred so quickly that Decker barely saw it for the first cup, but by the last cup, he was able to comprehend the sequence. Again leaning low at the table, *Senhor* Mosta took a spoonful of liquid from a cup. He rapidly slurped from the spoon, then he turned and let the liquid just fall out of his mouth into the sink, as though he was flooding drool. The slurping sound was so loud and high pitched that Decker could hear it through the glass. The entire process for all six cups lasted no more than 15 seconds. *Senhor* Mosta wiped his chin on a napkin, then made another series of notations, taking more time than the actual tasting process.

Decker said, "That's one of the most bizarre things I've ever witnessed."

"Bizarre, perhaps, but it's the most important part of the cupping test, when he actually tastes the coffee."

"Why does he slurp it like that?"

"It spreads the coffee over the entire tongue and palate."

"How come he doesn't swallow the coffee."

"With the number of cups he tastes," Lucy explained, "he has to spit it out or else he'd never get any sleep. He grades the coffee in each cup for flavor, acidity, body, and aftertaste."

"How can he possibly distinguish all those characteristics with each sample in his mouth for less than a second?"

"*Senhor* Mosta has been tasting coffee since before *you* were born, sir."

When the cupping session was complete, Lucy knocked on the cupping room door, then entered. She spoke to the man, pointing to Decker in the window. *Senhor* Mosta went to one of the roasters. He scooped some beans into a paper bag and handed it to her.

÷

Lucy led Decker into a large conference room on the second floor. The room had full-length, floor-to-ceiling windows overlooking the plantation fields. She directed him to a chair at the far side of the table, while she continued on to a counter at the end.

"The others will be joining us soon," she said, checking her watch.

She poured the beans from the paper bag into a small grinder, and after a quick whir, she dumped the ground coffee into a drip brewer. She set a thermal carafe under the spout, then pressed the red button on the front of the machine. When the coffee ceased dripping, she poured a mug and handed it to Decker without any cream or sugar.

Decker held the mug under his nose and sniffed. He pondered the complex aroma. He blew on the coffee's surface several times to cool it down. He raised the mug to his lips and took a tiny sip. He savored the liquid on his tongue, then he took another sip.

"This is tasty coffee." After a few more sips, he added, "I've never had coffee this good before."

Lucy said, "Few people have ever tasted coffee from cream-of-the-crop beans freshly roasted to their peak of flavor by a true master of the craft."

Decker extracted a laptop computer from his briefcase, and he started typing notes on topics he wanted to discuss in the meeting. A few minutes later, Lucy poured him a refill.

Chapter 5

"Dontopedalogy is the science of opening your mouth and putting your foot in it, a science which I have practiced for a good many years."

Prince Philip, the Duke of Edinburgh, 1960

~~~~~

While Decker used the restroom, others filed into the conference room. Several poured themselves mugs of Lucy's freshly brewed coffee. Westphal sat on one side of Decker's seat, and Lucy sat on the other.

When Decker returned, Westphal whispered to him, "Although Dr. Mendonça was technically in charge of our entire research effort, the last few years many of his projects were separate from the rest of our department's activities. Dr. Mendonça was something of a loner. At Mr. Duarte's direction, I took on the staff management role."

Duarte stood at the head of the table and introduced everyone, sounding more formal than was necessary. As he spoke, each new face in turn got up, walked over to Decker, shook hands, and exchanged business cards.

"Starting with the lady, *Doutora* Simone Horton, Biochemistry; *Doutor* Mauricio Santini, Genetic Engineering; *Doutor* Tiago Nestor, Horticulture; *Doutor* Pedro Ribiero, Selective Breeding and Hybridization; *Doutor* Frank Caison, Plant Pathology; *Doutor* Rafael Tosca, Pesticides and Fertilizers; and *Senhor* Tomás Manling, Laboratory Manager. And in case any of you don't know her, this is *Senhorita* Lucy Vivan. For the sake of our guest, we'll conduct the meeting in English. Lucy can assist in translations where necessary. *Doutora* Westphal..."

Westphal stood up to address the group. "I'd like to welcome our guest, Mr. Samuel Decker, Distinguished Professor of Microbiology and Molecular Biology at Tufts University near Boston, and thank him for taking the time to join us such a long way from home. I've briefed Mr. Decker on many aspects of what we know about this infestation, so we can start by letting him set the agenda and ask questions."

Decker remained seated and began, "Thank you, Wendy. From what I know so far, I see four main questions that we want to answer, each of which may lead to additional questions." He counted with his fingers. "First, where did this fungus come from? Second, how is it spreading? Third, how do we stop it from further spreading? And fourth, how do we prevent further outbreaks in the future? That last question can wait until we've coped with the emergency at hand. Starting with the first question, where the fungus came from..." Decker paused. *I might as well kick things off by dropping a bomb*, he thought. "Is it possible that Dr. Mendonça engineered this fungus?"

A flurry of Portuguese comments flew around the room.

Lucy leaned over to Decker and whispered, "They're not too happy with your question. They're saying, 'How dare he accuse Dr. Mendonça of such treachery?' and, 'An insult to a dead man!'"

Decker thought, *My first Brazilian faux pas. Probably won't be my last.* "Please, please," he continued, motioning with his hands to simmer down, "allow me to elaborate. I assure everyone I meant no disrespect to the deceased doctor. On the contrary, only a supremely talented researcher would even attempt to create such an organism..."

Coming to Decker's defense, Dr. Santini spoke up, "I had already considered that question, Mr. Decker, and yes, it's theoretically possible that Dr. Mendonça could have engineered this fungus. We've got all the necessary equipment here for both agrobacterium and biolistic methods of gene transfer. And Dr. Mendonça had the technical know-how to do it. However, in pondering such a possibility, I bump into the inevitable question: Why? What reason would he have had to create such a pestilence?"

Decker explained, "When Dr. Westphal briefed me on this fungus, it sounded like a nearly perfect destructive organism: it spreads easily and rapidly, and it causes a lot of damage. And I thought to myself, if I wanted to design a destructive fungus, I'd want it to turn out something like this."

Santini repeated his argument, "But why would you want to make such a thing?"

"At this point, I don't have an answer."

Westphal said, "Both myself and Dr. Ribiero have reviewed Dr. Mendonça's notes and records. We haven't encountered any about him engineering a new fungus, although he referenced some of your work in that regard. And even if he had done so, I can't imagine why he would have released it in a production field rather than in one of his experimental fields."

"We don't need to dwell further on this question for the moment," Decker said, "but I'd like all of you to keep the possibility in mind as we go forward. Now, let's consider the alternatives. Dr. Santini, have you been able to work up a full genetic profile of this fungus yet?"

"We're about eighty percent complete with that process, although it's complicated by the fact that some of the ribosomal RNA sequences are not contained in our database of known fungal sequences."

"Do you know if samples of the fungus taken from different plantations are identical?"

"Thus far, they appear to be the same, but I won't know with any more certainty until the full genetic sequencing is complete."

"Do you know of other specific fungi that match closely enough that they could have mutated into this one?"

"One or two are, as you Americans say, in the ball park."

"However," Dr. Nestor chimed in, "we had no established infection of other fungi in the fields at the time that this one broke out."

"Except..." It was Dr. Ribiero.

"Doctor?"

Ribiero explained, "Except for the experimental fields, the hectare plots out in the distant forest, where Dr. Mendonça tested cultivars and disease treatments. I think that one of those fields was actively infected with conventional coffee leaf rust."

Nestor said, "But those fields are quite isolated, and they're downwind from the first known incidence of this new fungus. I don't see how they could have infected the fields at Fazenda Fiorva."

Decker said, "Which is an excellent segue..." He paused while he typed some notes on his laptop.

A few of the others looked at Lucy, uncertain of Decker's last word, which was only familiar to them as a wheeled device for personal locomotion.

"*Transição*," Lucy said quietly.

Decker continued, "...to the next question of how the fungus is spreading. I've seen evidence that field workers are tracking around spores, such as at the dormitory."

Dr. Nestor responded, "I agree, but that's been after the fact of primary infection."

"It certainly isn't helping matters."

"I understand." Nestor entered a note on his tablet. "I already instructed the field supervisors to have workers change boots in the field, leaving potentially contaminated footwear and other clothing within each zone. But not all the workers comply."

Duarte spoke up for the first time. "I'll handle the worker compliance issue." He wrote himself a note.

Decker said, "I've been told this fungus has now appeared upwind in the Paraná region. Is it possible that some workers or equipment have carried the fungus to fields there?"

Nestor replied, "We haven't transferred any personnel or equipment to Fazenda Madrigal in Paraná since the first outbreak began at Fazenda Fiorva."

"How about workers traveling to the area on their days off to visit friends or relatives?"

Lucy responded, "After the appearance in Paraná, I checked with the bio-bus drivers, who chat with the workers on the way to and from town. The drivers weren't aware of anyone from here that has traveled to the region."

Decker said, "Which reminds me of my next point. Lucy told me earlier that the sugarcane harvest from this plantation is sent to an outside mill for processing. Have any cane shipments gone out since the coffee fungus appeared here at Sede, or maybe just before? That could be spreading around spores to other areas."

"We had already finished the sugarcane harvest for this season when the fungus appeared here," Nestor replied. "I don't think any shipments have gone out since then, but I'll double-check. The sugarcane still standing here won't get harvested until next year. It takes two years to grow, so we alternate fields for each year's harvest."

Next, *Doutora* Horton described several of her experiments, "Altering the pH of the soil or the ambient moisture, at least within ranges that the coffee plants can tolerate, doesn't hinder the fungus."

Decker asked, "How about outside the ranges the plants can tolerate? Not that we would implement such a treatment on a mass scale, but it would be useful to know the effect on the fungus."

Horton tapped herself a note on her mobile handset.

"Now, on to our next big question," Decker continued, "How do we stop further spreading? In that regard, what are you doing with the cherries from the infected plants?"

"They're still in place on the trees," Nestor replied. "We've stopped harvesting any infected zones. We don't want to contaminate the equipment."

Caison added, "And we don't want to further disturb the fungus until we understand more about it. Perhaps after all the trees die, the remaining fungus might die on its own. If so, that would simplify a portion of the cleanup effort."

Decker asked, "Have you considered incineration?"

"Yes," Caison replied. "We've already tested that, uprooting and burning some infected plants. The fungus did not survive the burn."

Tosca commented, "All we have to do to save our coffee crop is burn down all the fields."

Decker responded, "Unless we can answer our first two questions, where it came from, and how it's spreading, even that might not be sufficient. Mr. Manling, how many scientists and technicians are on your staff?"

"Thirty-four. Normally about half are devoted to sugarcane, but I have temporarily reallocated the resources so that all but three of the staff are now working on this coffee problem."

"I'd like to meet the lab staff. Given the large number, I can start by meeting them all as a group."

Manling asked, "What are your objections?"

"Objectives," Lucy corrected.

"In the large companies I've seen over the course of my consulting work," Decker explained, "the staff scientists and lab technicians perform most of the field research tasks, such as collecting samples and monitoring treatment responses, while the professional thinkers like us spend most of our time indoors, reading reports, writing memos, and sitting in meetings such as this one. The staff people are our best eyes and ears. They might have noticed things they haven't mentioned, because they didn't think they were relevant, or because they didn't think anyone was interested, or because they didn't even think they were worth thinking about. Likewise, the farm laborers might have information that turns out to be crucial to solving the problem."

"I can set up a meeting for first thing tomorrow morning," Manling offered.

"How about this afternoon?" Decker motioned to Duarte. "Your CEO has lit a fire under my butt."

"*Um fogo sob sua bunda*," Lucy translated the idiom.

Duarte nodded.

Manling checked the time on his mobile phone. "Let's make it at three-thirty."

Decker looked out across the room. "OK. I think that does it for now, unless anyone has anything else they'd like to add." Silence and shakes of heads. "I'd like us to hold this meeting every day, same time, same place, for daily progress reports."

Westphal said, "We've already been doing that, Sam."

"Then, let's carry on."

Chapter 6

~~~~~

The Delcese lab staff was assembled in a classroom normally used for field worker training. At the front stood Decker, Duarte, Westphal, Manling, Nestor, Tosca, and Lucy Vivan.

Manling said to Decker, "We've got twenty-six of the staff here. One is out sick today. The rest are either out in the fields here or at our other plantations."

Duarte began to address the group in Portuguese.

Lucy translated for Decker, "He says, 'I'm sure you are all aware of the challenge this new fungus poses to our coffee crop. To assist in our efforts to overcome this challenge, we have engaged Professor Samuel Decker from Tufts University...'"

÷

Near the rear of the room, a young technician sporting a blond buzz cut and an earring, Felix Mina, leaned over to the middle-aged woman sitting on his left, Martina Hasse.

"See," Felix said, "I told you they were bringing in a consultant who would waste our time in meetings."

"Shhh," Hasse returned.

÷

"...and I have assured the professor that you will all give him your utmost cooperation." Duarte motioned to Decker.

Decker began, "I appreciate the time you've all taken out of your busy schedules to come to this meeting on such short notice." He paused for Lucy to translate.

Lucy spoke in Portuguese, but instead of stopping after the one sentence, she continued speaking for over a minute. While she talked, Decker looked at the faces of the staff to see who was paying attention.

When Lucy stopped, she turned to Decker and explained, "I told them that you want to know if they've seen anything that might give us clues about the origins of this fungus, how it's spreading, and how we might stop it. Any change they might have noticed either immediately before or after the fungus appeared. Anything at all, no matter how insignificant it might seem."

Decker said, "Thank you, Lucy."

Manling prompted the attendees, "Does anyone have anything that might be useful?"

÷

Felix snickered to himself. *They needed to hire a guy to come all the way from the States to ask us if we've seen anything?*

÷

A man in the front row raised his hand, speaking in Portuguese, "I've noticed that when a tree gets infected, the fungus appears on the south side first, an hour or two before it shows up on the north side."

Lucy translated for Decker, then he nodded and said to the room, "That's a good example of the type of observation I'm looking for. It would indicate some preference for..." He considered being in the southern hemisphere. "...the shady side of the tree, which might lead us to some useful paths to investigate. Or maybe it's related to prevailing wind direction." Decker turned to the others standing in the front of the room. "Did any of you previously know that?"

They all shook their heads.

Decker turned back to the man in the front row. "Thank you. *Obrigada.*"

Everyone laughed, although Decker didn't understand why.

Lucy leaned over to him. "I say *obriga-DA.*" She used a hand to puff up her hair as though she was a fashion model. She pointed to him. "You say *obriga-DO.*"

Everyone laughed again.

Great, Decker thought, *my second Brazilian faux pas. So much for decorum. Maybe it'll loosen them up.*

÷

Felix whispered to Martina Hasse, "*Esse cara é um panaca.*" This guy's a dork.

÷

Manling pointed. "*Senhor* Mina, do you have anything to contribute to the group discussion?"

"Not at this time, sir," Felix replied, squirming like an embarrassed schoolboy, an impression enhanced by the classroom setting.

Manling asked, "Anyone else?"

A woman raised her hand. "I've noticed that when I breathe on the fungus, its color changes. From the bright red it picks up a purplish tint for a few seconds."

After Lucy translated for Decker, he commented, "Could be from the moisture or the heat or, more likely, the carbon dioxide. Good observation. *Obriga-DO.*"

÷

Felix whispered a goad at Hasse, "Do you know the old saying about the definition of a consultant?"

"Shhh," she admonished him again.

÷

Manling asked, "Other observations?"

No one responded.

÷

Felix continued whispering while Hasse frowned in his direction. "A consultant is just a pompous bird who swoops in, shits all over everything, then flies away."

÷

Decker said, "That will do it for now." He held up his hand in the OK sign. "OK, everybody, thank you..."

Everyone laughed.

Lucy grabbed Decker's hand to lower it. She shielded one hand with the other, then discretely showed him a raised middle finger.

Brazilian faux pas number three, he thought.

÷

Hasse suddenly turned to Felix. "What did you just say?"

"*Nada.*"

"No, no. Say it again."

Felix whispered, aware that several others now were listening in. "Uh, I said, 'A consultant is just a... bird who swoops in...'"

Hasse yelled out, "*Espera!* Wait!"

Manling pointed to her. "*Senhora* Hasse?"

"*Uma ave!* A bird!" She broke into rapid-fire Portuguese. When she stopped, it was followed by a couple of Portuguese comments from others in the room.

Lucy summarized for Decker. "*Senhora* Hasse says that a few days ago, she saw a bird that she's never seen before, a parrot. She saw it in the coffee fields here at Sede. She says she's a birdwatcher, and she thinks the parrot was new to this territory. And she says she saw it eating coffee cherries."

"Parrots don't eat coffee cherries," someone retorted in English.

Hasse insisted, "*Este fez!* This one did!"

Decker told Manling that he wanted the woman to stay, but the other staff could be dismissed.

÷

On the way out the door, Felix said in a hushed voice to the woman who had been seated on his opposite side, "Martina is such a *nerd*," using the word adopted directly from English to Portuguese.

That woman, Larissa Júnior (pronounced "ZHOO-nee-or"), looked back at him and replied, "The English have a more appropriate phrase: goody-two-shoes."

÷

Martina Hasse remained in her classroom chair, daunted to be facing the senior staff at the front of the room. She was a short, overweight woman in her late-40's, with graying hair and horn-rimmed bifocals.

Decker asked, "Can you explain exactly what you saw?"

Hasse replied in English with a hint of a German accent. "I saw a large parrot, a macaw. It was blue with a red crest, and both red and blue tail feathers. It was perched in a coffee tree near the back of the plantation, and it was pecking on coffee cherries. The closest thing I'd seen to it before was a macaw near Iguaçu Falls, but that one didn't have as much blue coloration. This species, I'd never seen before, even in my birding books."

"You only saw it once?"

"With all the overtime we've been working because of the fungus, I haven't had any spare time to go out and look more. When I get a chance, I was planning to try to find this parrot again and photograph it so I could show it to my birding club."

"Had you ever before seen birds eating coffee cherries here?"

Hasse glanced at Duarte and the others, then she said, "Pardon me for being candid, but the style of production-oriented open sun monoculture we employ here is a poor environment for birds. Shade-grown coffee, by comparison, provides an excellent bird habitat. The diversity of growth under the canopy offers a wealth of insects and plants for the birds to feed on, and plentiful nesting opportunities. On the larger plantations, the insecticides and herbicides we use to protect the coffee plants destroy the habitat. I see very few birds of any kind on this plantation."

Decker asked, "Do birds eat coffee cherries in shade-growing regions?"

"I've heard there's a species of bush tanager in Mexico that eats coffee cherries," Hasse replied, "but I don't know any parrots that do."

Dr. Nestor added, "When I was visiting a small farm in Uganda years ago, they told me that they would occasionally see a type of parrot eating the coffee cherries. I never saw it myself, but they called it a *Jardim* parrot, a Garden parrot, or something like that."

Decker asked, "Has anyone ever seen a bird eating coffee cherries at this plantation before?"

Heads shook all around.

Decker addressed Hasse. "*Senhora*, this is very important. You might have identified an upwind distribution mechanism. This bird and others of its kind might be spreading the fungus on their wings or their claws, or by carrying parts of infected cherries, or even through their digestive systems. The coffee tree where you saw this bird, was it infected with the fungus?"

Hasse replied, "The tree didn't appear to be infected, at least not then. I haven't been back out to the same spot since. As I said before, I haven't had time with all the extra hours we've been putting in."

"Can you take me to the spot?"

"Yes, of course."

"One last question, *senhora*. Do parrots migrate?"

"Not in the way you probably mean it. Most parrot species are semi-nomadic. They wander around, but it's within a limited range. They don't fly away hundreds or thousands of kilometers with the change of seasons."

"At least that might limit the distribution," Decker noted, "if this bird is a carrier."

÷

Lucy drove the cart with Hasse in the front passenger seat and Decker and Nestor in the rear. They rode along the edge of the sugarcane, headed for the back fields of coffee.

"I'm not positive," Hasse said, "that I can identify the exact tree, but I'm sure of the area. It will be right around this corner here at the end of the sugarcane."

Lucy stopped the cart about 10 meters into the coffee field.

Nestor looked at the rows of coffee trees each three to four meters in height, all fully infected with fungus. "I think, *Senhora* Hasse, the exact tree is no longer important."

Lucy said, "There's a fungus among us."

"In this case," Decker responded, "it's the other way around. We are among the fungus."

÷

Decker and Lucy walked down the second floor hallway back in the Administration Building. He asked, "Lucy, when you're not escorting guests around the premises, what exactly is your job here?"

"I work in the Security Department, sir." She looked down at her coveralls. "I don't wear the *Segurança* uniform when escorting guests."

"Do your responsibilities include spying on me for Mr. Costa?"

"My responsibilities do include reporting to Mr. Duarte and Mr. Costa anything of significance that might happen while I'm with you, although I'd hardly call that spying. We're both working on behalf of the same company and pursuing the same interests, are we not?"

These guys are more shrewd than I had anticipated, Decker thought. "Tomorrow morning," he said, "I'd like to see the plantation where the fungus first appeared."

"I'll arrange it. We'll take a small plane. It's about forty minutes by air, instead of several hours driving on unimproved roads."

"You can't get there from here."

"Sir?"

"It's a saying we have back where I grew up in Maine."

"But you can get there from here."

"I know. It means it's hard to get to."

"But it's easy to get to the plantation if you take a plane."

"I know. It's hard to explain." Then he asked, "Do you have a camera here? In my hurry to pack for this trip, I neglected to bring one. All I've got is the one in my phone."

"We've got one in the Security Department. I'll bring it along tomorrow."

They arrived at the door to Westphal's office.

Decker said to Westphal, "I'd like to review Dr. Mendonça's notes and records."

Westphal looked at her watch. "Lucy, you can call it a day. I'll take Mr. Decker from here."

Lucy said to Decker, "I'll pick you up at your room bright and early at seven thirty AM, sir."

"By the way, Lucy," Westphal added, "We'll need Mr. Decker's ID card programmed to give him access to Dr. Mendonça's office."

Lucy responded, "It already is."

÷

Westphal walked Decker to Mendonça's office, only three doors away. Inside the office, piles of papers covered the entire surface of Mendonça's desk. Westphal picked up from the top of a pile two lab notebooks with black and white speckled covers. She handed them to Decker, "You can start with these. They're his most recent field notes, at least the most recent ones we could find. Most of the other scientists here have switched to electronic note taking, but Dr. Mendonça still preferred handwriting."

Decker put on his reading glasses and flipped through the notebooks. *At least his notes are mostly in English,* he thought. *And his handwriting is more legible than my own.*

Westphal suggested, "Why don't you take those back to your room this evening? They'll keep you occupied for as long as you can stay awake. You can take a look at the files on his computer another time."

"All right."

Westphal closed the office door behind them. "Mr. Duarte has a formal dinner planned for us with the senior staff tomorrow evening, once we've had a chance to catch up on our sleep. Do you want to hit the cafeteria to grab a bite to eat now?"

"I'm not too hungry at the moment. I think I lost my appetite when I saw the coffee field this afternoon."

Westphal stopped in her office and retrieved a black gym bag. Decker looked at her inquisitively.

"It's for jiu-jitsu class," she explained.

"Like in those mixed martial arts fights I've seen on TV?"

"Sort of, but we practice straight jiu-jitsu, not MMA. Nobody gets beaten up, and nobody bleeds, unless you count the occasional scrape from mat burn. Up in the States, they call it BJJ, for Brazilian Jiu-Jitsu, but down here, it's just JJ. Our own Mr. Ramon Costa was once runner up in the São Paulo State JJ championships. Monday through Thursday evenings, he teaches a free class, open to all Delcese employees including the field laborers. I find that it helps release job stress when you get to throw around your co-workers. Care to come along?"

"I've never done any martial arts."

"You could just watch at first."

"I could use some exercise. You guys have a fitness center over in the Services Building, right?"

"Yes."

"I think I'll go for a run on the treadmill. Maybe I'll check out the jiu-jitsu another day."

Westphal and Decker stopped at his guest room, where he tossed the notebooks on the bed and picked up his gym clothes, then they walked over to the Services Building.

Inside, she showed him a workout studio on the first floor. "This is the JJ Room."

He looked into the studio through the glass door. Two dozen people of varying sizes and builds were warming up and stretching out on blue mats over the hardwood floor. About two-thirds of the participants were wearing casual sweat clothes. The rest were wearing the traditional Japanese martial arts outfit known as a *gi*, heavy white cotton pants and matching jacket tied with an *obi* waist belt of a color indicative of skill level. Mirrors lined the entire front wall, and waist-high wooden rails ran along the side walls.

Decker recognized a particular woman in the studio as one of the attendees in his meeting with the lab staff. She was in her mid-30s, tall, with straight blond hair pulled back in a ponytail. Her face was attractive but gaunt, with traces of past adolescent pockmarks on the skin. She stretched a long leg on the wooden rail, exhibiting her fit physique through the sleeveless athletic shirt atop her *gi* pants.

Decker said to Westphal, "That woman has the build of a dancer."

"Larissa? She's an exercise fanatic. I see her heading out jogging almost every day at lunchtime. She's a swimmer and a rock climber, too, and she kicks my butt at jiu-jitsu." Westphal pointed Decker to the men's locker room and the fitness center down the hall. "I'd better get changed for class," she said. "See you tomorrow. I trust you can find your way back to the Visitors' Residence on your own."

÷

The fitness room was unoccupied, but well-equipped with weight machines, treadmills, and stationary bikes. Decker turned on the TV on the wall and switched channels until he found CNN in English. He jogged for 30 minutes on a treadmill, then he attempted to stretch for a few minutes, although his aging muscles were stiff. *I'm not ready for rigor mortis yet*, he thought, *not for a few more decades*.

After showering in the locker room, he walked past the JJ Room and peeked in at the squirming bodies paired up on the mats, men with men and women with women. *Where I come from*, he thought, *they call that wrestling*. Then he saw one woman put her arm around another's neck in a choke hold. After unsuccessfully struggling to escape, the victim tapped three times on the arm, signaling her submission. *But that part ain't wrestling*.

÷

Back in his room at the Visitor's Residence, Decker booted up his laptop and responded to emails from friends and relatives who had attended the previous day's wedding. He wondered, *Was it really only yesterday?*

He shut down the computer, then he opened one of Dr. Mendonça's notebooks.

÷ ÷ ÷ ÷ ÷

Three hours later, a woman ducked into the business center room in a hotel in the resort town of Águas de São Pedro. She sat down at a computer terminal and composed an email message.

÷

Two hours after that, at The Butterfly Palace of Java, Pukartra read a message aloud from a computer screen, "goliath, new man has large nose. he might sniff us out. advise course of action. cleo."

Zeger said, "We need to lay low until this other thing blows over. I'm concerned that Cleobaea may jeopardize Operation Sweet Surprise if she gets too anxious over all the attention elsewhere at Delcese right now. Signal her to keep cool."

In the source files for the Kraton Kupu Kupu website, on the page for *Lycorea cleobaea*, Pukartra changed the graphic of the circling pink butterfly to a static blue one.

Chapter 7

"Coffee makes it possible to get out of bed, but chocolate makes it worthwhile."

Anonymous

~~~~~

AUGUST 6

At 7:00AM, a man sat alone in a booth at the rear of a small café in downtown Campinas, eating breakfast and sipping the insipid swill that passed for coffee within much of Brazil. *With all the beans grown around here*, he thought, *couldn't we keep at least some of the good ones for local consumption?*

Alexandre Werner was reviewing a pocket-sized spiral-bound pad with his handwritten notes from the various news stories he had in progress: a student protest over tuition hikes at UNICAMP; construction underway on a new industrial park south of the city; and the son of the police chief of Itatiba arrested for drunk driving.

Two men in shabby farm workers' clothes sat down on stools at the end of the counter nearest to Werner. He looked up briefly, adjusting his rimless glasses and brushing away the blond hair fallen across his face. The men chatted with each other as they surveyed the menu. Werner overheard them talking about catching the bus south to see their sister who lived in Santos. Then their conversation shifted to the work in the fields, mentioning *grãos de café*, coffee beans. Werner kept perusing his notes, but he looked up again when he heard one of the men emphatically use the word *ferrugem*. Rust.

Werner got up and sat down next to the men.

"*Oi, pessoal.* [Hi, folks.] I couldn't help but overhear that you're on your way to Santos. I grew up there in São Vicente, right along Gonzaguinha beach..."

Twenty minutes later, Werner crossed the street to talk to his editor in the newsroom of *Correio Popular* (*Popular Mail*), the main newspaper in the city of Campinas, albeit with a modest daily circulation of fewer than 50,000 copies.

÷÷÷÷

In the rear of a coffee field at Sede de Delcese Agricola, Martina Hasse put down the backpack containing her gear. She assembled her collapsible stool and set up the well-worn Gitzo tripod. She unpacked the Nikkor 500mm f/4 telephoto lens, a sizable piece 400 millimeters (15 inches) long, weighing three kilograms (over six pounds). She called the lens her *canhão* (cannon), a curious nickname given the similarity to a different camera brand. Ordinarily she wouldn't have been able to afford such a lens, but she had picked it up used on VivaStreet.com.br (a Brazilian equivalent to Craigslist) for a bargain price because the barrel was dinged and the front element had a scratch across it. She screwed the mounting bracket of the lens onto the tripod head. She unpacked an old Nikon F3 SLR 35mm film camera body, and she attached the body to the rear of the much larger lens. She loaded the camera body with a roll of Fujichrome Provia slide film.

She laid out the remaining items for her day in the field: vintage Leica Trinovid binoculars, also purchased used; BPA-free plastic water bottle; and the books *Aves de Brasil* (*Birds of Brazil*), *Ornitologia Brasileira* (*Brazilian Ornithology*), *The Birds of Southern Brazil*, and *Os Papagaios de Brasil* (*The Parrots of Brazil*).

I can't believe I'm getting paid to do this, she thought. *I'm getting paid to go birding.*

She picked up the binoculars and commenced scanning the coffee trees for signs of avian life.

÷ ÷ ÷ ÷ ÷

Decker awoke to a knock on the door. He opened his eyes in the daylight, squinting at the red LED clock: 7:32.

"Just a moment," he called out.

He closed the notebook that had fallen off his chest, and he swung his feet out of bed, still wearing the street clothes he had changed into the previous night after showering at the fitness center. He opened the door to see Lucy standing in uniform, holding two large paper cups, no lids, with steamy brown liquid.

"Good morning, Mr. Decker," she said, handing him a cup. "This is from beans culled at Fazenda Fiorva, where we're headed today. You look like you just woke up, sir."

He took a sip from the cup. "Yeah, give me a couple of minutes. Pretty good coffee." He took another sip. "Not quite as..." He searched for the precise word. "...piquant as the pot you made for me yesterday."

"We'll make a master cupper out of you, sir. Yesterday's was from our shade-grown *sítio* [site] way up in the mountains. This is Isabela, our standard production grade, similar to what you might buy in a grocery store back home, only a much fresher roast, of course."

÷

Lucy drove the cart up to the hangar. A small, high-winged Cessna plane was out on the paved runway, with the pilot standing next to it.

Getting out of the cart, Lucy pointed to the coffee cup in Decker's hand. "You'd better finish that before we climb aboard. The ride's a little bumpy for open drinks."

Lucy introduced Decker to the pilot, Carlos, in Portuguese, then she said, "The only English that Carlos knows is flying terminology."

Decker offered Lucy the front co-pilot's seat in the four-seater, out of both courtesy and his general unease at flying in small, turbulence-prone aircraft, particularly in light of Dr. Mendonça's recent demise.

"You go ahead and sit up there, sir," she responded. "You'll get a better view."

When they were seated and belted in, Carlos held up packets of ear plugs. Decker shook his head. Carlos put on a headset and made some comments in Portuguese over the radio.

Rolling down the runway, Decker was careful not to touch the co-pilot's control yoke on his side of the plane. He turned back to Lucy and shouted over the engine noise, "If we were in the U.K., would this side be the pilot's seat?"

"Got me. Never flew in a small plane back there."

Within a few minutes the plane was headed northwest, and the terrain beneath it shifted from cultivated plains to forested hillsides, with the broad surface of the Rio Piracicaba still visible to the south.

Decker noted few roads below the airplane, and those that were visible ran along the valleys, while the plane's flight path cut perpendicular across the ridge lines.

÷÷÷÷÷

Werner stood on the street alongside his beat-up Volkswagen Beetle, a Type 1 (old-style) version built in 1992 in Puebla, Mexico. He considered it doubly ironic that the original "people's car," a worldwide symbol of personal freedom and independence, initially had been commissioned by Adolf Hitler, based on a design *der Führer* had copied from a Jewish engineer named Josef Ganz.

Werner eyed the patches of *ferrugem* in the green paint along the edges of the Beetle's fender wells. He climbed into the car and drove northwest out of Campinas, headed for the hills beyond Piracicaba.

÷÷÷÷÷

The plane veered north, and Decker spotted the *fazenda* in the distance. The coffee fields were collectively much larger than those at Delcese headquarters, but the buildings were smaller and less modern. He directed Lucy to take an aerial photo.

Carlos made a brief statement in Portuguese over his headset, then the plane descended toward the dirt airstrip at the near edge of the complex.

After the bumpy landing, Carlos taxied the plane to the front of the hangar, where they disembarked. Visible inside the hangar was the wreckage of a small plane, the same model as the one in which they had just arrived. The front end of the wreck was crushed in and the propeller was gone, but otherwise it was remarkably intact.

"Dr. Mendonça's fateful flight," Lucy said.

Decker commented, "If I had known we would see the damaged airplane, I might have opted for us to drive here."

Carlos evidently understood that they were discussing the plane. He told them in Portuguese, which Lucy translated for Decker, "Investigators from the *Departamento de Aviaçao Civil* examined the plane where it had crashed, looking for signs of mechanical malfunction. Their initial investigation was inconclusive because the plane's engine was damaged by the impact of the crash. The investigators instructed the farm manager to move it into the hangar for safekeeping and further examination at a later date. Carlos says the pilot, Miguel, was a good friend of his, so he's pained to look at the plane, but he's glad that Miguel is still alive."

A short, rotund man emerged from the farmhouse and walked over to them. "Welcome to Fazenda Fiorva," he said in accented English, extending a hand to Decker. "I'm Eduardo Mabro, the manager of this plantation."

"I'm Sam Decker. Pleased to meet you, Eduardo. Has Lucy briefed you on my objective in coming here?"

Mabro replied, "Yes, *Senhorita* Vivan told me you're the scientist brought in by *Senhor* Duarte to fix the fungus. You wish to examine the place where we first saw it."

"Yes, please."

"I'll take you to the worker who spotted it. Carlos can wait in the farmhouse until you're ready to return."

÷

Mabro drove them along the coffee fields in an old Ford pickup truck. Every tree in the fields appeared to be infected with the fungus. Decker indicated to Lucy to take photos.

"As you can see, *Senhor* Decker," Mabro stated flatly, "the whole of Fazenda Fiorva is now consumed by the red fungus. Our remaining crop is lost, and all of our coffee trees are dying or already dead. I had to let go many of the farm workers for the season because there is nothing for them to harvest. Combined with the death of *Doutor* Mendonça in the airplane, the workers called the fungus *o Sangue de Cristo*, the Blood of Christ, as though God had sent this plague to cleanse their sins. I know you can't help this plantation this year, but I hope you can prevent all our other plantations from the same fate, and perhaps you can fix things so we can plant new seedlings soon. But even then, it will be several years before we have a new harvest here."

"I'll do my best, Eduardo. Have any of the workers that you let go moved on to Paraná?"

"Not that I know of, but I wouldn't necessarily know. If it's important, I can check."

"Please do."

They got out of truck along the edge of a field, where a man was waiting for them.

Mabro said, "This is Jose [pronounced 'zho-ZEH'] Carvalho. He's the supervisor of the workers in this field. At least he was the supervisor when we had workers for him to supervise. Now, he's the only employee I still have in this section."

Jose's left arm was in a sling. Decker extended a hand. Jose took off his baseball cap and tucked it into the sling, then shook hands.

Decker said to Mabro, "Please ask him to describe how he discovered the fungus on the trees."

Mabro translated the inquiry to Jose, then the response. "He says that early in the morning when he came into this field, he saw red spots on the lower branches of one of the trees. It was just a few spots on some of the leaves. He went to the other side of the field to run a harvesting machine with a few of the workers. When he came back to this side later in the morning, he saw that many of the trees were then covered in red patches. When he saw that, he took some clippings and brought them back to the farmhouse for me to examine."

"And when you saw the clippings, Eduardo?"

"The patches were brighter red than coffee leaf rust. They were unlike any plant disease I'd seen before. I sealed the samples in plastic bags and sent them down to Sede for testing. I came out to the field with Jose about three hours later. By the time I saw it, more than a hectare was infected. I wouldn't have believed that any plant disease could infect a field so quickly."

"Ask Jose how much further it spread the next day."

Hearing the translation, Jose answered and pointed across the field one way, then perpendicular. "He says that by the middle of the next day, trees were infected about two hundred meters in each direction. Another day later, another few hundred meters."

"The first clippings of the fungus that Jose brought to you, were those coffee cherries already showing signs of desiccation?"

"The first clippings were only leaves, no cherries. The tree they came from was harvested."

Decker looked at the trees in front of them. "These trees still have cherries. Rotted cherries, but coffee cherries nonetheless. Is this the field where he first saw the fungus?"

Mabro translated the question to Jose. The field worker walked them 50 meters down the row and pointed to a tree with no remaining cherries. "That's the first tree he saw it on."

Decker looked confused. "The first tree he saw infected was one of the last ones harvested?" *That must be significant,* Decker thought, *but it's unclear how if both types got infected. Perhaps the harvesting machine churned up some dormant spores.* "Did he stop harvesting because he saw the red spots?"

Jose shook his head speaking to Mabro. "He says that no, he had stopped harvesting there the day before, because of the plane crash." Jose pointed further down the row, where several trees were knocked over and a patch of dirt was plowed up.

Decker gaped at the spot. "That's the exact place where Dr. Mendonça's plane crashed?" He turned and looked back at the first tree only 10 meters away. "And the first place Jose saw the fungus was right there a day later?"

Jose gave further description, making overhead motions with his good arm, then pointing to his arm in the sling.

Lucy translated the gist of his comments. "Jose stopped harvesting because he jumped off the harvesting machine when he saw the incoming airplane. That's how he broke his collarbone."

Decker turned to Mabro. "How long did the wreckage of the plane remain here in the field?"

"We left the plane where it crashed for two days while aviation officials examined it. The day after that, we moved it into the hangar."

Decker thought, *Aviation investigators might have tracked around spores to other regions.* He looked back at the first infected tree. "Eduardo, Dr. Westphal told me you didn't find anything to indicate that the fungus came from the airplane."

"That's correct. I examined the exterior of the plane and all the men's possessions in the plane. I didn't find anything that could have been a source of the fungus. The only explanation I could think of is that *Doutor* Mendonça might have seen a developing problem from the air and asked Miguel to fly low to get a closer look, and that's when the plane crashed."

Decker asked, "Did it rain here after the plane crashed but before it was moved into the hangar?"

"No. This is the dry season."

"Let's go back to the hangar. Have Jose come, too."

÷

Inside the hangar, Decker, Mabro, Lucy, Jose, and the pilot Carlos stood around the plane wreckage.

Decker began by examining the exterior of the plane. He saw traces of red dust on the fuselage, but no other signs of the fungus. The wings were about two-and-a-half meters off the ground, too high for him to get a close look from floor level. He asked Mabro for a step ladder, which the farm manager retrieved from the rear of the hangar. Decker climbed up to inspect the wing on the starboard side. He wiped the surface with a finger. *There's red, probably fungal spores, in the dust on the leading edge of the wings*, he thought. *It must have gotten there when the plane was already on the ground, after the crash.*

Decker climbed down from the ladder, and he squatted down to inspect the tire on the landing gear below the wing on that side. He walked around the tail of the plane to inspect the tire on the opposite side. Then he moved to the front of the plane to examine the tire on the center strut, which had been bent backward in the crash. *No sign of dry rot or other fungus infecting the tire rubber. These aircraft tires don't have any tiny sipes that could have held spores in them during the flight, and the wide circumferential grooves in the treads are too open to have held them either.* He said aloud, "I don't see anything from the plane's exterior that might have triggered the infestation."

Decker opened up the hatch on the port side of the plane to access the small baggage compartment behind the rear seats, but there was nothing inside and no evidence of fungus.

Decker walked back to the front of the plane. While looking at the damaged engine, he noticed a crack near the center of the windshield above and behind the engine. He brought over the step ladder and climbed up. He reached a hand to feel the surface of the large sheet of tinted acrylic where the spidery crack appeared to have initiated from an impact.

"Eduardo," he asked, "do you know how this crack got here?"

Mabro replied, "I don't know. When the plane crashed, maybe it kicked up a rock from the ground. Or maybe a piece of the propeller hit it when it broke off on impact."

Decker came down from the ladder. He went to the door on the pilot's side, and climbed into the cockpit. He felt the crack in the windshield at its point of impact, then he said, "The surface of the crack is smooth on the outside, but chipped at this spot on the inside. I think something from the interior caused the crack."

Decker looked around the interior of the plane, including under the seats. He was climbing back out when a patch of color caught his eye. Splatters of dried blood on the pilot's side of the instrument panel had turned brownish, but one tiny splotch only a few millimeters across was still bright red.

"Eduardo, please get me a sample bag."

Mabro went to a cabinet in the rear of the hangar and came back with several clear zip top plastic bags and sterile swabs.

Decker swiped up the red substance on the instrument panel and sealed it in a bag, then he climbed out of the plane.

Decker asked, "Eduardo, after the plane crashed, were the men still strapped in their seats?"

"Yes."

"Any idea what could've cracked the windshield from the inside? It must have been something fairly hard and heavy."

"I can't think of anything. When I gathered up all the men's things from inside the plane and sent them to Sede, I didn't see anything that might have done that. The pilot's flight headset wasn't heavy enough to crack the windshield."

"What kinds of things did they have?"

"Both men had small backpacks containing their lunches, their hats, and a few handheld electronic items, like cell phones and a GPS. Those were undamaged. I also found a couple of small water bottles on the floor. Those were made out of very thin plastic that couldn't have cracked the windshield."

"Any experimental equipment?"

Mabro shook his head.

"Were the backpacks in the rear storage area or up front in the seats?"

"After the crash, they were on the floor behind the front seats."

"Did anyone check the men's phones for recent pictures?"

"I looked at the pictures on Miguel's phone. The most recent ones were of his wife and daughter, taken a few days before the crash. The doctor's phone needed a code to be entered, which I didn't have, so I couldn't see what was on his."

Lucy added, "Dr. Mendonça's wife knew the passcode for his phone. When we got it back at Sede, she looked on it but didn't find any pictures."

Decker asked, "Did Dr. Mendonça have a notebook in the plane?" He made scribbling motions with his hands.

Mabro said, "No."

Decker's mind raced through possible scenarios that might fit all the information, but none did. "Ask Jose to describe everything that happened when the plane crashed."

Mabro instructed Jose, who motioned with his hand like a plane coming in for a landing, then he flexed the hand downward.

Lucy translated the lengthy description. "Jose says that the plane came into the field very low, barely above the tree tops. Then the front landing gear clipped a coffee tree, and the plane crashed. Jose sent one of the workers, Aldo, to run to the farmhouse and fetch help, while he and another man, Theo, went to the plane." Jose pointed to his sling. "He says that because he hurt his collarbone jumping off the harvester, he was unable to assist very much." He motioned with his hand at a steep angle. "The plane's front end was stuck into the ground, and the airplane was standing almost straight up, leaning against a couple of the trees. The two men inside were held in their seats by the safety belts. The pilot was bleeding from the side of the head." Jose put his good arm in a position like he was steering, then he moved it straight out in front of himself. "The pilot's hands were still on the steering control. The other man's arms were hanging straight out, like someone *sonambulismo*, sleepwalking. Jose couldn't see below the men's waists because with the plane sticking up, the windows were too high off the ground. Theo climbed onto the wing strut on the left side to try to open the door, but he couldn't get it open. Theo then went over to the right side, where he was able to open the door a minute before help arrived."

Decker motioned to pause. He asked, "Who were the people who came to help?"

Mabro replied, "A few field workers that had been at the farmhouse, as well as myself and *Senhorita* Pima, who does clerical work in my office. She's also a registered nurse, and she takes care of the first aid needs of the field workers. When Aldo came to the farmhouse, I immediately called for an ambulance, then we all climbed into my pickup truck and drove out to the field as fast as we could."

Decker motioned for Jose and Lucy to continue. "Jose says that when the pickup truck got to the crash site, *Senhorita* Pima checked the men inside the airplane. The man on the right was already dead. The workers thought the pilot was dead, too, but when *Senhorita* Pima checked his pulse, she said he was still alive. She told them not to move either of the men until the ambulance arrived. The workers got the door open on the pilot's side of the plane while they waited for the ambulance, which took almost an hour to get here..."

Mabro explained, "The nearest medical facility is far from here."

"...When the ambulance came, the medical technicians put a big brace around the pilot's neck. Then they removed the pilot from the plane, which took a long time because his body was very stiff, and his back was arched. The body was so stiff that when they got him out, they couldn't lay him flat on a stretcher. They had to lay him on his side..." Jose was noticeably uneasy describing the scene to Lucy as she translated. "...They loaded the pilot into the ambulance, and it drove away, but one of the medical men remained behind with another stretcher. The workers helped him remove the dead man's body, which was not so stiff. When they got the body onto the stretcher, they slid it onto the bed of the pickup truck, and the medical technician climbed on back. Jose got into the front of the truck with *Senhorita* Pima and *Senhor* Mabro. They drove the body to the farmhouse, where it stayed until a second ambulance arrived."

Decker asked, "And the other workers?"

Mabro said, "I told them to walk back to the farmhouse. All except Theo. I had him move the harvesting machine to another field."

"Can I talk to Theo?"

Mabro replied, "I don't know where he is, *Senhor* Decker. He was one of the workers that I had to let go because we have no more crops to harvest."

Mabro asked Jose a question in Portuguese. Jose shook his head.

Decker asked, "Do you have a way to locate him? He may have seen whatever it was that cracked the windshield. He might even have it. It's crucial for us to find that item."

Mabro said, "I'll attempt to locate Theo. He doesn't live in this area. He's a migratory worker. I'll ask around among the remaining workers if they know where he went."

"Where was the plane flying from when it crashed?"

"*Doutor* Mendonça and Miguel had dropped off two people at his experimental hectares in the remote forest to the north. After that, they were supposed to be flying to the other experimental plots to the west for *Doutor* Mendonça to conduct more tests himself."

"Is it normal that they would be flying low over this plantation on that route?"

"No, that isn't normal at all. In fact, I wasn't expecting them back here until later in the day."

"Do you know what Dr. Mendonça was planning to test at the other experimental fields where the plane was headed?"

"I'm sorry, *senhor*. I don't know. The doctor didn't explain much about the nature of his experiments, at least not to me."

Decker glanced back at the wrecked airplane. "Did the pilot communicate any problems with the plane while it was up in the air?"

"Not as far as we know, although we wouldn't necessarily know." Mabro pointed toward a workbench in the rear of the hangar. "We have an aviation radio, but it's not normally manned."

Carlos apparently grasped the nature of the conversation, and made a series of comments in Portuguese, which Mabro translated, "Carlos says that the area around Fazenda Fiorva is *espaço aéreo não controlado*, uncontrolled airspace, meaning there's no air traffic controller. Ours is the only airstrip for many kilometers. Planes take off and land here without air to ground communications. Pilots use a designated frequency to broadcast their positions and actions air to air in case other planes are nearby. Even if Miguel did try to radio for help, no other planes might have been in the area to hear it. Not many planes other than our own fly around out here."

Decker asked, "Does this plane have a gadget that records everything in case of an accident?"

Mabro relayed the question to Carlos. "He says no. Small aircraft like this don't have flight data recorders or cockpit voice recorders."

Decker rubbed his chin a few times. "On the day of the crash, had the plane taken off from here?"

Mabro replied, "Yes, the plane picked up *Doutor* Mendonça and a woman at Sede, then came here to get Sergio Moreno, one of my field supervisors."

"You said earlier that the airplane had dropped off two people at a remote field before crash landing here. Presumably that was Sergio and the woman from Sede?"

"Yes. I don't remember the woman's name, but she was tall and thin, with blond hair." He partially closed his hand and made a gesture at the back of his skull. Ponytail.

Lucy said, "Larissa Júnior."

Decker told Lucy, "I'll want to talk to her later." He turned to Mabro. "Can I talk to Sergio?"

"I had him drive to town today to pick up some parts for equipment repairs. I don't expect him back until late in the day."

Decker checked his watch. "We've got to get back to headquarters for our afternoon meeting. Perhaps we'll come back in the next day or two. I'll want to talk to Sergio then. And I'll want to get a look at some of Dr. Mendonça's experimental fields."

They started toward the open end of the hangar.

Before heading out, Carlos the pilot took one last look in the wrecked plane. He reached into the cabin, then called out, "*Senhors.*" He motioned for them to come back in.

Carlos spoke, pointing into the cockpit, then Mabro translated. "Carlos says that he just noticed something unusual inside the plane."

Decker walked around to the co-pilot's side, where Carlos had the plane's handheld microphone between his fingertips. He turned it around to show Decker its rear surface. On it were several tiny brown smudges that were clearly neither blood nor the other red substance. Decker touched one of the smudges, then lightly rubbed it between his fingertips, trying to figure out what it was. He put on his glasses to look at it more closely. Carlos motioned with finger and tongue that Decker should taste it.

Decker didn't dare touch it to his tongue, but he held the finger a few millimeters under his nose and took a deep sniff. The smell was unmistakable, even from such a small speck. With a mixture of glee and bewilderment he declared, "Chocolate?!" He swabbed a sample and sealed it in another plastic bag.

Carlos spoke, then Mabro translated. "Carlos says that Miguel, the pilot of this plane, never ate chocolate. He was allergic to cocoa."

Decker commented, "Most people who think they're allergic to cocoa are actually allergic to other ingredients in the choc... Oh, never mind. If Miguel had consumed chocolate, would it have interfered with his ability to fly the plane? What would have been his symptoms?"

"Carlos says that Miguel would break out in a bad skin rash, but that wouldn't have prevented him from flying the plane. Carlos says he's confused, because a problem with the pilot is the only reason he can think of why the passenger would have used that microphone."

"Were there any signs of a skin rash on Miguel after the crash?"

"I didn't see any," Mabro said, then he translated the question to Jose. "Jose didn't see a skin rash either."

Carlos stuck his head inside the cockpit and moved it very close to the instrument panel on the co-pilot's side. He spoke while Mabro translated, "Another of the brown smudges is on the back of the co-pilot's yoke." Carlos put out his arms as though he was holding the yoke handles. "Carlos thinks that the passenger must have been flying the plane."

Decker asked, "Was Dr. Mendonça a pilot?"

Mabro said, "I don't think so," then he relayed the question to Carlos, who shook his head several times. "No. Definitely not."

"Jose said earlier that the pilot's hands were still on the control yoke on his side after the plane crashed. It doesn't make sense that Dr. Mendonça would have grabbed the yoke on this side if the pilot was still flying the plane."

Lucy postulated, "Maybe Miguel was teaching Dr. Mendonça to fly. Or maybe both men were working together to overcome a mechanical problem with the plane."

Decker rubbed his chin. "Or maybe the pilot was incapacitated, which would also explain why Dr. Mendonça might have used the microphone. Perhaps the doctor was trying to get the plane back to the airstrip here when it crashed in the field. In any case, if Dr. Mendonça was trying to fly the plane, it raises more questions than it answers. Dr. Westphal told me the pilot was in a coma after the crash. Lucy, do you know his current status?"

"I don't know," she responded. "But I do know who will know."

÷ ÷ ÷ ÷ ÷

Werner turned his Beetle off of the two-lane paved road at the discrete sign for Sede de Delcese Agricola and the less discrete sign warning *Propriedade Privada*. He followed the entrance road between the sugarcane fields for half a kilometer until he came to the gate house, where a security guard motioned for him to stop.

"I'm from *Correio Popular*. I have an appointment with *Senhorita* Herrar." Werner handed the guard a business card.

"*Um momento, por favor*." The guard retreated into his hut to make a phone call. A minute later he reemerged. "Park in the visitor's lot there, then wait in the lobby."

÷

"Pleased to meet you, *Senhor* Werner." The perky young woman had styled short hair and wore a white blouse with a pleated gray skirt. "I'm Melissa Herrar, Marketing Communications Manager."

She signed him in at the reception desk. He slapped the *Visitante* sticker onto the side of his canvas briefcase, then she led him to a small conference room with no windows.

Werner set up his laptop computer.

She asked, "Would you care for some coffee?"

He shook his head.

"Well then, what can I do for you today?"

I'll just serve her a lob, he thought, *and see how she hits it back*. "As my editor should have explained on the phone, I'm researching a story about diseases of the coffee plant. I'd like to understand how Delcese, one of the largest coffee growers in the nation, prepares for such things. How do you prevent disease infestation? How do you handle it when an outbreak occurs? What problems and challenges does it cause for the company? Things like that."

"I'd be happy to answer your questions, *Senhor* Werner. Delcese Agricola's efforts begin with an extensively planned and carefully executed horticultural breeding program. Through both conventional selective breeding techniques as well as advanced genetic engineering research, we create and test new variants of coffee trees and sugarcane, subsequently planting and harvesting those which are found to be the most disease-resistant..."

Well scripted, he thought.

"...We also develop and rigorously test various pesticides, including many which are completely organic. In the unlikely event that an outbreak does occur, for example, when an infestation in a competitor's nearby plantation threatens to spread into one of our fields, we may apply judicious quantities of insecticides, herbicides, or other chemical treatments to our fields, reducing the extent to which the competitor's problem might spread into our plants..."

Nice deflection, he thought, *but even I know at a farm like this they apply all that stuff on a regular basis.*

She carried on for a few minutes without imparting any information useful to Werner. When she finally paused, he typed exactly three words into his laptop, "Blah, blah, blah."

He straightened himself up in the chair. "Would it be possible for me to speak to any of the scientists who work on your pest or disease programs, to get more in-depth information? You know, the guys who pour the liquids back and forth in the test tubes, or maybe the women who twiddle the focusing knobs on the microscopes, that kind of thing? Or maybe it's all done these days moving DNA bits and pieces around on computer screens."

"Perhaps I could arrange such an interview for you another time. I can talk to the department manager and see what we can do. I can give you a call the middle of next week."

Skillful stonewall, he thought, *I wonder where she got her Master of Bullshit Administration.* "It was a long drive out here from Campinas, *Senhorita* Herrar. Is there any way I could speak to someone today?"

"I'm sorry. All our scientists are extremely busy. I can't ask them to take time out of their full schedules on such short notice."

"How about a farm supervisor, somebody who works with the plants in the fields, applies the pesticides...?"

"I'm sorry, *Senhor* Werner. Not today."

He took a deep breath. "Is it possible, *Senhorita* Herrar, that all your people are so busy because you have an active disease outbreak in your fields right now?"

"Excuse me?"

"I've heard that just such an outbreak is underway right here. A massive infestation of a new type of coffee leaf rust fungus."

"Delcese company policy is not to comment on rumors, *Senhor* Werner."

"It's not a rumor. It comes from people who saw it for themselves. Are you saying that no such outbreak is underway?"

"I'm not saying anything one way or the other. I'm just saying 'no comment.'" She stood up.

Werner entered exactly two additional letters in his laptop, "NC," then he closed it up.

"Delcese is a public corporation," he stated as they moved out of the conference room. "Don't the shareholders have a right to know whether or not such an outbreak is occurring?"

"We inform our shareholders with quarterly reports and share-holders' meetings, *Senhor* Werner. If you are currently a shareholder or would care to become one, you'd be welcome to attend our next shareholders' meeting in a couple of months. Have a safe trip back to town." She extended a smile and a handshake at the front desk. "And thanks for visiting Delcese Agricola."

÷

Herrar strolled back into the conference room and shut the door. *Foda,* she thought. Fuck.

÷

That was almost a waste of time, Werner thought. *Except her "no comment" was a telling comment. She didn't deny the outbreak. But, the newspaper won't run a story like this without corroboration.*

Werner peeled the Visitor sticker off his briefcase and handed it to the receptionist.

"Where's the toilet, please? I've got a long drive ahead of me."

She pointed him down the hall.

While Werner stood at a urinal, a young man in a blue lab coat pulled up to another fixture. He had a blonde buzz cut and an earring.

Werner threw out, *"Como vai?"* How's it going?

Felix replied, "Oh man. What a tough day."

"How's that?"

"This damn fungus. It's practically brought the whole company to a standstill. The lab boss has got the staff working major overtime, and the *figurões* [bigwigs] are even more anal retentive than usual. And to top it off, now they've got some consultant from the States in here to hold meetings and quote-unquote 'help out.' That's a waste of time and money if you ask me."

They moved to the sinks.

Werner asked, "This fungus, it's coffee leaf rust, right?"

"No. Dealing with that stuff would be *um piquenique* compared to this die-hard bastard we've got now. We don't have a clue how to stop it yet. At the rate it's spreading, it'll wipe out the rest of the coffee crop at this plantation in a few more days. And it kills the trees, so it will take years to recover."

Werner considered the information, then he asked, "Have you got a business card?"

"Sure." The young man reached into his wallet. "Here you go."

Werner glanced at the card. "Nice to meet you, Felix."

"Where are you from?"

"I'm just a visitor. My name's Alexandre Werner. I'm a reporter from *Correio Popular*."

Felix gagged. "A journalist! Shit, you can't use what I just said."

"Doesn't the public have a right to know about something that could impact the nation's coffee crop?"

"Maybe so, but my ass would be thrown out the door if the company knew I told you about the fungus. I need my job. Well, maybe I don't need the job, but I do need the paycheck. I've got bills to pay."

"How about if I don't use your name? I won't describe you in any way that anyone could possibly identify you."

"If you absolutely, positively swear *pela alma da tua mãe*."

"On my mother's soul," Werner replied.

Felix held out a fist. Werner bumped it with his own fist.

"By the way," Werner added, "what do you guys call this fungus?"

"It doesn't have an official name yet, but the nickname we use in the lab is *O Vampiro*." The Vampire.

Werner raised an inquisitive eyebrow.

Felix explained, "Once this fungus infects a coffee plant, it sucks the moisture out of the insides." A second later he added, "And, of course, because it's so red. It looks kinda like blood."

Werner casually strolled out of the men's room.

Before leaving, Felix bent low to check that the stalls were empty.

÷

On the way to the parking lot, Werner said to himself, "Bingo!"

Noticing a tower with cellular antennas behind the main building, he called his editor on his mobile phone to give her the lowdown.

Then, Werner placed another call to a number in the contacts list in his phone. He explained what he had heard.

The man's voice on the other end said, "Thanks for the tip. I owe you another case of Cachaça Anísio Santiago. You have fine taste in liquor, *Senhor* Werner."

÷

Werner drove around the area looking to photograph an infected coffee field, but the only crop he could see from the nearby roads was sugarcane.

Chapter 8

~~~~~

Matthew Cochran, the CEO of Bright Cup Incorporated, sipped coffee from a bright yellow mug while he gazed out his office window. Even from 28 stories high, he could see—or at least he imagined he could see—the blue cups and the red-and-white cups of his two chief competitors in the hands of morning commuters emerging from the San Francisco Ferry Building onto the Embarcadero below. *I'm gonna show those punks up north who's the king of coffee in this country*, he thought. *I'll show them. Soon enough.*

A text message arrived on Cochran's mobile phone from his coffee buyer in Brazil. It said, "*Senhor* Matt, call me. *Urgente.*"

He sat down at his rosewood desk and punched buttons on the speakerphone.

÷

Valmir Pasco was smoking a cigarette on the open plaza Praça Antonio Prado, outside *Bolsa de Mercadorias e Futuros* (Commodities and Futures Exchange, a.k.a. BM&F) in downtown São Paulo.

At 74 years old, Pasco had been smoking for far too long to kick the habit, but when his mobile phone rang, he tossed the cigarette on the ground and snuffed it out with his shoe. He fished around in the pocket of his linen sport coat for the handset he had just dropped into it. "*Olá?*"

"Val, this is Matt Cochran. How's life on the Tropic of Capricorn?"

"Warm as always, and especially interesting today, *Senhor* Matt. The reason for my message is that I received a piece of information that I thought you should hear about right away. It came from a reporter in Campinas, one who feeds me selected news items ahead of schedule, in exchange for valuable consideration..."

When Pasco finished explaining what the reporter had told him, Cochran asked, "This major coffee grower, with all its resources, doesn't know if it can stop this nasty infestation?"

"That's right."

Cochran thought, *Uncertainty is the father of opportunity.* He asked, "If such an infestation became widespread, would it create a coffee supply shortage in Brazil this season?"

"*Senhor* Matt, the Brazilian government is stockpiling about seven million bags of green beans in warehouses in Santos and elsewhere. It's a supply rationing system, like OPEC's, to prop up prices and hedge against the normal range of crop fluctuations."

"What about an abnormal range of crop fluctuation? What if this fungus wipes out most or all of the remaining crop?"

"The forecast for this year's Brazilian crop is fifty-one million bags. If the fungus becomes widespread, stockpiles could be depleted early next year. But right now, nobody at the BM&F knows anything about it."

"Nobody knows? That's perfect. Val, you have a green light to buy. Have our broker on the BM&F buy as many Coffee 'C' futures as he can, as quickly as he can. I mean it. Buy, buy, buy! For the remainder of today and all day tomorrow, don't worry about the price, just have him keep buying every available arabica futures contract in sight."

"The exchange has a maximum allowable daily trading volume from any one account."

"Yeah, and I want our broker to hit the allowable limit today and tomorrow. In the meantime, Val, I want you to go visit the plantation that the reporter told you about, either this afternoon or tomorrow morning, to get a first hand assessment of the fungus situation. And I want you to offer them a huge direct purchase forward contract for delivery over the next year. Then, I want you to work direct deals outside the exchange with other growers to buy even more. Write your own contracts with a crayon on toilet paper if you have to, Val. Buy everything. Don't stop buying until there's nothing left to buy. Is that clear?"

"Yes, *senhor*, very clear. Do you want me to buy options on the exchanges as well?"

"No. Options are for wussies. Go right for futures. And after you visit the plantation, you must call me with an update. I absolutely need to talk to you no later than eight o'clock tomorrow morning my time. You're four hours ahead this time of year, right?"

"Correct, *senhor*."

"Then you've got until, say, quarter of noon tomorrow your time. Got that, Val?"

"Got it, *Senhor* Matt." Pasco stuffed the phone back into his pocket, wondering, *Que é 'wussies'?*

÷

Cochran placed another call on the speakerphone, this time to his coffee broker on the IntercontinentalExchange (ICE) in New York. Since the broker was not a Bright Cup employee, Cochran didn't mention the news tip from Brazil, but he waited to see if she would bring up anything of interest.

Marla Anderman gave him the market lowdown. "...The Coffee 'C' contract volume is a little higher than normal here at the ICE, but prices are stable..."

When he was confident that she wasn't aware of the fungus in Brazil, Cochran said, "Marla, by the end of the day today, I want you to max out our account. Buy Coffee 'C' contracts for September and December delivery, up to the allowable position limit."

"Matt, that's five hundred contracts totaling over eighteen million pounds of beans."

"Do we have sufficient funds in our account?"

"Let me check..." Cochran heard keyboard tapping sounds over the phone. "You have enough to cover initial margin requirements."

"Good, then proceed."

"With that much buying so quickly, you'll be a significant chunk of the entire daily Coffee 'C' volume on the exchange. It's bound to drive up the ask price."

"Acquiring the contracts *today* is very important. Just keep buying at the ask, even when it goes up. Have you got that?"

"I'd advise against it, but I've got it."

÷

Cochran said to his administrative assistant seated at a desk outside his office door, "Julie, get Tom in here right away, please."

A minute later, Thomas "Truck" Macklin, Chief Financial Officer of Bright Cup Incorporated, rolled his wheelchair into the office.

Cochran instructed his assistant, "Julie, have Rami come in here in about ten minutes, please. And ask him to bring along his list of all the attendees signed up for tomorrow's press conference." Then he closed the door, which was an uncharacteristic action.

Macklin rolled his wheelchair up to Cochran's desk. "What's up?"

Cochran took a seat behind his desk, then he leaned back and relayed what Pasco had told him about the coffee fungus.

Macklin responded, "That's bad news, Matt."

"There's an old proverb, Truck: Good news, bad news, who's to say? This is an opportunity."

"You've already got something in mind?"

"I want us to start buying up all the arabica futures contracts we can get our hands on. And I mean *all* the contracts we can get."

"You want to try to corner the market? Or even just short squeeze the market? You can't do that these days, Matt. The exchanges have daily trading limits and contract volume limits specifically to prevent it, although they sometimes allow exemptions for legitimate hedges, which this might constitute."

Cochran shook his head. "We don't have time to worry about getting exemptions. We'll max out our allowable positions for Coffee 'C' contracts on the ICE and BM&F. In addition to the exchanges, we'll draw up our own contracts directly with suppliers. I mean every push-cart and stall that sells arabica coffee beans. If a hobo with a broken down donkey in Guatemala wants to sell arabica coffee futures, I want to buy them."

"If we draw up our own contracts off the exchanges, nobody will trade for them. We'll have to take delivery or pay the sellers to square the contracts against spot prices on the market."

"If this infestation breaks out for real, suppliers won't be able to deliver on their end of the deal, and they'll be forced to square the contracts at a tidy profit to us." Cochran got up and sat on the side of his desk. "I'm not pussyfooting around on this, Truck. We need to move aggressively. And we need to move now. Timing is crucial, especially the next twenty-three hours. We've got to secure our positions as much as possible before tomorrow morning's press conference at eight AM."

"Tomorrow morning?" Macklin looked at his watch. "New York closes its coffee trading at two o'clock Eastern time. São Paulo's open a little later in the afternoon, but still, you're only looking at a few hours of trading time between now and eight AM Pacific tomorrow. For direct contracts, you can keep wheeling and dealing as late as people will stay up and talk to you, but it's impossible to squeeze the market in one day."

"Relax, Truck. We're not trying to squeeze the market. We're just trying to get the biggest piece of it we can get by tomorrow morning."

"How much money do you want to throw at this?"

Cochran said, "I want nine figures."

The CFO of the third largest coffee shop chain in the U.S. needed a moment to parse the number of digits. "A hundred million bucks?" Macklin clutched at his chest. "You tryin' to give me a heart attack? I doubt I can shake loose commitments from the banks for that kind of scratch so quickly. Even if I could, if you go spreading around that much in less than twenty-four hours, you'll be a giant blinking bull's-eye on everyone's profit-seeking radar. It'll run up the contract prices. The BM&F has daily price fluctuation limits on arabica futures, but the ICE doesn't. And direct deals might have to be above exchange prices."

"What I need, Truck, is to have unlimited buying power for one day, from now through tomorrow morning. One friggin' day. Besides, I want to run up the prices."

"You *want* to run up the prices?"

"That will trigger all the swing traders on the exchanges to jump on the bandwagon, pushing prices up even further in the coming days, which will increase the value of any contracts we hold, including the direct contracts. I just don't want the public to know who's running up the prices. Not until our press conference tomorrow."

Macklin responded, "That would violate market manipulation rules, Matt, especially if you talk about it at the press conference."

"I won't be the one to raise the issue at the press conference, and I won't say anything that isn't true. It might not be the whole truth, but every single thing that I do say will be the truth. It will all be based on public information. And the entire press conference will be preceded by the usual SEC legal disclaimer about forward-looking statements. Our actions will be fully justifiable. We will have a perfectly valid and publicly defensible reason for aggressively buying up the futures as a hedge against the fungus. What law would we be breaking?"

"I don't know, but I'm not an expert on futures contract law. And I remind you, futures contracts are *contracts*, they're legally binding."

"I know, but we won't have to cough up the full amounts until the due dates, which won't be until in September and December. We have enough cash in our accounts to cover the initial margins on the deals, so we're OK for now. If futures prices on the exchanges move unfavorably before the contract dates, we'd have to mark-to-market, forcing us to pony up more funds, but my plan will prevent that from happening."

Macklin swiveled his wheelchair in Cochran's direction. "If I didn't know you better, I'd say you've gone nucking futs. And what's this *we* shit? This is entirely *your* idea. If it succeeds, the Commodity Futures Trading Commission will probably fine us for market manipulation. If it fails, our shareholders' lawyers will cry 'gross negligence,' 'corporate malfeasance,' 'failure to do due diligence,' and a host of other '-ences' that will come crawling out of the legal dictionaries. We need to get Maxwell in here to give us his legal opinion."

"We don't have time for that. We've got to start buying right now. The clock is ticking." Cochran failed to mention that he had already set the buying process in motion. "Truck, I respect your input, but I got us here..." He waved a hand toward the view out the window. "...by taking big risks. You know it's in my blood. If shareholders had wanted to invest in a company with a namby-pamby CEO, they wouldn't have bought shares of Bright Cup Inc." He tapped two fingers on the top of the desk. "This unique situation has created two simultaneous windows of opportunity for us—one hedge window and one speculative window—that will only be open for the next day. If this fungus does destroy a sizable chunk of the remaining Brazilian crop, this aggressive buying action on our part will keep our shops pouring coffee when our competitors are faced with a choice between running dry or paying even higher contract prices. And if the fungus conks out, we should still be able to make a tidy profit trading the contracts, at least if things go as I plan in the wake of the press conference tomorrow. The best part is that we're better off in either situation."

"I don't see it that way, Matt. Even if you succeed in locking up that much supply in the short term, you'll have to unload it later without taking a beating on price by dumping the excess back on the open market. As they say in the commodities biz, after you make a killing in the market, you've still got to bury the corpse."

Cochran shook his head. "The worst case scenario, which is highly unlikely, is that we've got a mother-lode of overpriced coffee beans on our hands. But you know what, Truck? Even that wouldn't be a total disaster. Most of the commodities traders out there are pure speculators. It doesn't matter to them whether they're buying and selling coffee beans, precious metals, or pork bellies. They're just shuffling dollars and contracts from over here to over there and back again. That's why they stick to the exchanges, where they can always unload the contracts. But if one of them got stuck with millions of pounds of real coffee beans, they'd be screwed. We, on the other hand, are in the business of *using* millions of pounds of coffee beans. If this fungus turns out not to be a big deal and for some reason we can't sell off the contracts at a profit, we won't have to slash prices to unload the beans on the open markets. For any contracts we can't resell at reasonable prices, we'll absorb the beans into our coffee operations. We won't have to bury the corpse, we'll roast it and grind it."

Macklin restrained himself from smiling at the mental image induced by Cochran's last remark, then he replied, "If this fails, Matt, our shareholders will want to roast and grind your corpse. If I were a normal CFO at a normal company with a normal CEO, it would be my fiduciary responsibility to tell you that this plan represents total fiscal irresponsibility. But since this isn't a normal company, and you're not a normal CEO, I won't waste my breath. I'll get you as much money as I can to cover September and December contracts. I'll let you know later today how much you can throw at this harebrained idea."

"This isn't harebrained, Truck. That Squawkie toy idea of mine, that one was harebrained."

"That phony bird toy has a nice profit margin, and no risk the feds might spank us over it." Macklin swiveled his wheelchair in the direction of the door. "When did you come up with this gem of a concept?"

Cochran pointed to the speakerphone. "When I talked to Pasco."

"You mean to tell me you devised this whole plan in ten minutes?"

"It was more like ten seconds."

Macklin raised a hand to his forehead. "Why do I stick with you?"

Cochran motioned at the wheelchair. "Because who else will let you ride their roller coaster?"

÷

Rami Parananda stepped aside to let Macklin out of the office.

"Close the door, Rami," Cochran instructed.

Bright Cup's VP of Marketing took a seat across from Cochran.

"Rami, I need us to plant a question into the financial analysts and reporters at tomorrow's press conference."

Parananda held up his hands in a T sign. "Timeout, Matt. Give me some context."

Cochran spewed a condensed version of the plan and the discussions he had had with Pasco and Macklin.

"You've got big ones, Matt." Parananda grabbed his crotch like a baseball player adjusting his cup. "Can't we just announce the fungus issue and our aggressive buying?"

"No, for a bunch of reasons. First, it's not exactly in the spirit of the rest of the press event. Second, if we announced it, it'll smack of commodities market manipulation, which is what it is, but we can't tell people that. And third, to have the optimal impact on the attendees, it has to appear as though the guy who asks about it thinks he's blindsiding us. It can't seem like we brought up the topic."

"Then why not let the usual media forces work on their own? If this fungus becomes a real threat to the coffee crop, the worldwide press will be all over it within a couple of days."

"That would give our competition and every speculator in the business a chance to catch on. Our opportunity to jump on this only exists during the brief period when almost nobody knows it exists yet, and even the few people who do know about it don't know if it can be stopped. And to maximize the media triggering effect, I want as much as possible of the American press to find out about this thing at the exact same moment. Our moment. Tomorrow. The press conference attendees will be journalists and stock analysts, not commodities traders. I can't see how any of them would have heard about this story coming out in one little Portuguese language newspaper in Brazil." Cochran then returned to his original meeting objective. "So we need to get one of them to ask, and we need to do it in a way that he or she doesn't know we instigated it."

"You're the boss, Matt." Parananda held up a sheet of paper. "Here's the list of confirmed attendees."

Cochran perused the list. "Damn, Rami. The usual who's who. How do you always get them to come to our shindigs, especially ones so early in the morning?"

"Are you kidding? We serve the most sumptuous food, and they know the coffee is the best they'll get anywhere in town. And we always have plenty of bags of freshly roasted sitting by the door for them on the way out. It still amazes me how even the guys pulling in a couple hundred grand a year can't resist a free twelve dollar bag of our Primo Cup beans. Of course, it doesn't hurt that you always deliver them a press conference to remember."

Cochran smiled broadly. "We need to pick a target." They scanned the list. "Any of them speak Portuguese?"

Parananda pointed to a name. "Tony Goterrez. His parents are from Lisbon."

"I can't put a face to the name."

"Remember a few years ago when we held a briefing for a bunch of journalists, and just for yucks we served them Kopi Luwak?"

Cochran nodded.

Parananda explained, "At the time, Goterrez had just started and didn't know beans about coffee. He's the guy that when I told him how Luwak was processed, he went, 'No shit?' and spilled the cup all over his shirt."

"Stocky guy with the furry moustache and curly black hair?"

"Yep, that's him."

"Any ideas how we do the plant?"

Parananda hunched his eyebrows while he considered possible methods. "We could get someone to email him a link to the article."

"Nah. If it comes from someone he doesn't know, he'll get suspicious. And it couldn't come from anyone at Bright Cup."

"I've got it. The caterer at the hotel has a couple of waiters who are Brazilian. We slip one of them a C-note, and it'll be no problem."

÷

Three hours later, Macklin rolled his wheelchair back into Cochran's office. Without preface, he said, "Forty-two million," then he turned and rolled back out.

Excellent, Cochran thought. *That's more than I'd expected he'd say. Not that it matters.*

Chapter 9

"Some circumstantial evidence is very strong, as when you find a trout in the milk."

Henry David Thoreau, 1850

~~~~~

The Cessna landed on the runway at Sede de Delcese Agricola. Decker and Lucy hopped in a cart and drove to the Administration Building.

At the 2:00PM progress meeting, Decker slid from his pocket the two plastic bags with samples from the wrecked airplane at Fazenda Fiorva. He handed them to Manling. "These are from inside the airplane. I believe the red one will contain the fungus. The other one is chocolate. You might as well test it, too."

"We'll start analyzing them right away," Manling responded.

"The plane's windshield was cracked from the inside. Dr. Mendonça must have had some kind of container with the fungus in the airplane, although Mr. Mabro never saw it. Someone might have taken it before Mabro searched the plane."

Doutor Ribiero said, "But Dr. Westphal and I found no record that he was developing a fungus of his own."

Decker responded, "When I was reading his notebooks last night, I noticed omissions of some things that I would have expected to be there but weren't. I suspect that either he was keeping a lot of things in his head, or he was keeping another notebook or maybe an electronic file where he tracked additional experiments and observations."

Westphal said, "We've gone over everything in his office and every potentially relevant file we could find on his computer. We haven't seen anything like that."

"Have you checked his home?"

Westphal sighed. "No."

"I'd like to go there myself. I'd also like to speak to his wife. And I've got a bunch more trails to follow over the next few days."

Lucy interjected, "*Doutora* Munhoz is already on your agenda, sir. We can try to see her right after this meeting."

Decker stared blankly for a moment, then remembering back to when he had read Mendonça's obituary, he made the connection that Dr. Munhoz was Mendonça's wife (now widow).

Duarte said, "Mr. Decker, please continue your excellent efforts to get to the bottom of the situation. If no one has anything else, that will do it for today's meeting. And remember, dinner at six o'clock this evening in the dining room of the Executive Residence."

÷

When Duarte came out of the conference room, Melissa Herrar approached him and said, "I think we're about to have a problem."

Duarte motioned for her to come with him back into the conference room, then he closed the door. "What is it, Melissa?"

Herrar explained her meeting with Werner. "...This journalist clearly had some inside information," she insisted, "and it was from more than one person. I distinctly recall him saying that it came from *people* who saw it for *themselves*."

"Did he know about Fazenda Fiorva?"

"I don't think so. He was talking about the situation here at Sede."

"It doesn't sound like he knew that much. And you didn't give him much, but even a 'no comment' can be twisted to anyone's purpose. Sooner or later we'll have to disclose the fungus publicly, but I was hoping we would have a solution in hand before we had to announce that we have a problem. Now we'll need to issue a press release about the infestation, but with a soft spin, to take the wind out of the sails of whatever might appear in the news. Have a draft for me to review in half an hour."

÷

While Herrar was composing the press release, the phone on her desk rang. "Hello, this is Melissa."

"*Senhorita* Herrar, my name is Yasmin Pinto. I'm a copy editor at *Correio Popular*. Can you confirm that employees at Delcese refer to the disease outbreak currently among the coffee plants as *O Vampiro*, because of its red color and the way it sucks moisture from the plants?"

"I haven't even confirmed that there *is* a disease outbreak among the coffee plants."

"Then, would you care to do so?"

Herrar replied, "No comment," then she hung up the phone.

÷

Herrar said to Duarte, "When I talked to the reporter, he barely knew anything. He was grasping at straws. He might have talked to someone else after me. *I* didn't even know about The Vampire thing."

"I'll have Mr. Costa look into that. Fortunately, the story is only for a local area newspaper, at least for now." Then, referring to the Rio de Janeiro Stock Exchange, Duarte said, "Let's hope that when *Bolsa do Rio* opens tomorrow morning, not many of our shareholders will have seen the article. Hold off on that press release until we see what's in the news story, otherwise we might make fools of ourselves."

÷÷÷÷

Decker and Lucy walked along the hallway on the second floor of the Employee Services Center. They slowed down approaching the entrance below the sign for *Centro de Saúde* (Health Center). The reception area was empty, but that's where Decker first heard the woman's voice, emanating in Portuguese through the partially open doorway to a treatment room. The voice was an inexplicably catchy, staccato sing-song that was melodious yet not quite mellifluous.

Lucy whispered, "She's telling the patient to change the bandage twice a day for the next week."

The woman's voice ceased, and then a farm worker emerged from the treatment room clutching his forearm on which a gauze bandage was taped. A minute later, Fabiana Munhoz appeared. A huge smile adorned her rosy cheeks, and her shoulder-length frizzy hair jutted out as though her skull was unable to contain her sheer ebullience. Decker was immediately captivated by her, yet simultaneously perplexed. *Not what I expected for a recent widow*, he thought.

Lucy said, "Dr. Fabiana Munhoz, this is Mr. Sam Decker, from the United States."

Decker extended a hand to shake. Instead of responding in kind, she embraced him, pressing her lab coat against his shirt, accompanied by petite kisses on both cheeks in the manner of greeting an old friend.

"It's a pleasure to meet you, Professor Decker," she said when she released him. "My late husband spoke of you with reverence, not only because he was a devout chocolate lover, but also because he admired your ingenious solution to the cacao problem in Côte d'Ivoire. I heard that Mr. Duarte had engaged you as a consultant, and I was hoping I'd have the chance to meet you."

Taken aback, Decker simply responded, "I'm pleased to meet you, doctor. Please call me Sam." He paused, unsure how to broach the subject of his visit.

Lucy jumped in, "Mr. Decker needs to discuss some sensitive matters with you, doctor."

Decker explained, "This morning, Lucy and I visited Fazenda Fiorva..." Munhoz's smile diminished but did not disappear. "...We were there to investigate the start of the fungal outbreak. We also saw the wreckage of the airplane in which, regrettably, your husband died. I have several important questions to ask you, Fabiana."

"Ask away, Sam."

Decker took a deep breath. "I now suspect that the outbreak started from something that was inside the airplane. Had you recently seen Paul with a container that he might have used to hold cultured fungus?"

Munhoz replied, "I had seen him with such a thing once or twice in the lab. It was a stainless steel cylinder with orange biohazard stickers on the sides. I don't know what he had in it. A bunch of those containers are around the lab, so it could have been anything."

"Did your husband have a work area at home, an office or perhaps a lab where he worked sometimes?"

"He had a small office area with a computer in our home, but no lab of any kind."

"If it's not too much trouble, I'd like to examine that area and his computer at your earliest convenience."

"Of course."

"How much did he talk to you about his work?"

"Paul would occasionally tell me of his experiments and findings with great enthusiasm."

"Did he recently mention anything about testing a new fungus, perhaps even a fungus that he had created?"

"The only time that I heard him talk about fungus in the last month or so of his life was in the context of him describing your work."

"I'm sorry to be asking such prying questions, Fabiana. I know this must be difficult for you to discuss, but Paul's work probably holds the key to comprehending this fungus. What did he tell you in that conversation?"

"I remember him talking about *symbiosis*. He used that word several times. Paul said he might have discovered a three-way symbiosis. He mentioned your work with the cacao plants and fungus as an example of a two-way symbiosis. He said he thought he had come up with a three-way version, although he didn't say what the three things were. I asked, but he said he was keeping it a surprise until he was sure it worked."

"Did Paul frequently work late in the lab here at Delcese?"

"We both worked late on many occasions. When I got done for the day, I would go over to the Administration Building and often find him alone in the lab."

"Did you ever see anyone else with him there late? Anyone who might have more details about what he had been working on?"

"Not that I can remember. Maybe from time to time I saw people working elsewhere in the lab, but I don't think I saw anyone else working directly with him."

Decker paused before changing subjects. "I need to ask you about a more sensitive topic, the bodies of your husband and the pilot, Miguel."

"Miguel is still alive. I'd prefer if you not refer to him as a body."

"Forgive me, please." *Chalk up another faux pas*, he thought. "I understand from Lucy that you examined Miguel and your husband shortly after they were brought to the hospital in Piracicaba."

"Yes."

"What was the official cause of death for your husband?"

Munhoz's smile faded away. "*Porretadas*. It's what you call in English 'blunt force trauma,' from the rapid deceleration of his internal organs upon impact."

Decker cringed. "I'm sorry to have brought it up." He held up a hand. "This is going to seem like a bizarre question, but did your husband have traces of chocolate on his fingers when he died?"

Munhoz's smile returned. "Yes, he did, but that was not unusual. I discovered an empty wrapper from a Garoto chocolate bar in a pocket of the pants he was wearing. Paul loved to eat chocolate, at all hours of the day and night. That was one of the reasons he was so enamored with your work. Why do you ask about that?"

Decker took another deep breath. "I have reason to believe that your husband may have been flying the airplane, or attempting to fly it at least, to land it on the airstrip at Fazenda Fiorva when it crashed. There were smudges of chocolate on the microphone and the co-pilot's controls."

"But Paul wasn't a pilot."

"I understand, but the pilot may have been incapacitated."

"Are you suggesting Miguel's injuries occurred before the crash?"

"Possibly."

"The other doctors and I have been working under the assumption that Miguel's coma and physical symptoms were due to his skull fracture, which we think was sustained from a loose object that flew around the cockpit when the plane hit the ground. However, I must admit that his collective symptoms have not been entirely consistent with that thinking."

"If Miguel had developed a problem that prevented him from flying the plane, do you believe Paul would have attempted to fly it?"

"If it was between that and near certain death, yes, I believe he would have."

"At this point, we don't know what happened on the plane. This is just one theory I'm investigating. I'd like to understand more about Miguel's medical condition. Is it possible for me to examine him?"

"If it's important, I can bring you to see him in the hospital in Campinas. It's better equipped than the one in Piracicaba where the ambulance took him, so I had him transferred there. However, the hospital in Campinas is further away. It would consume half a day to go there and back. But what does Miguel's condition have to do with this fungus?"

"I don't always know in advance what will turn out to be important, so it's important for me to pursue every avenue of investigation."

"Then we'll go. I have a busy morning tomorrow. How about if we go tomorrow afternoon? Then afterwards, I can bring you to see Paul's working area at our home outside of Piracicaba."

"Excellent. Thank you so much for your cooperation, Fabiana. I understand how it feels to lose a spouse, and I realize this must be a difficult time for you." Decker extended a hand once again.

This time Munhoz shook his hand. "I'll help you however I can."

÷

After Lucy and Decker had moved well out of earshot from the Health Center, she turned to him and said, "I can only think of one reason, sir, why you think it's important to see Miguel. Only one reason why his condition would be relevant to what's happening with the fungus." She paused.

"Go on, Lucy."

"You believe what happened might not have been an accident. The possible presence of the fungus inside the plane adds an element that's too coincidental."

Decker asked, "Are you coming to Mr. Duarte's dinner tonight?"

"I wasn't invited. Besides, I'd be a fish out of water there. I'll meet you in the cafeteria tomorrow morning."

÷÷÷÷

Costa stood behind Tulio, a hulking dark-skinned security guard, who was seated at a console. The array of three upper and three lower monitors cycled through video feeds from the facility's many security cameras.

Costa pointed to the top center screen. "This one, in the reception area. Werner signed in at ten thirty-seven AM. Roll it back to then."

They both peered at the time code counting down in the lower right corner of the screen. When the numbers approached the target time, the operator slowed down the speed.

"This must be him at the front desk," Tulio said. "Only a journalist would wear a necktie with sneakers."

"Back it up further, so we can see him coming in the front door... OK, play it from there."

The guard mocked a sports play-by-play, "He opens the front door. He walks in. He approaches the desk. He sets down his briefcase. He says something to the receptionist..."

Costa nudged the guard on the shoulder with the back of his hand. "Knock it off, Tulio."

"Here's Herrar coming to meet him. Then it looks like they're going straight to the conference room."

"OK. He signed out at eleven o-nine. Roll it forward."

They both watched the replay of Herrar walking Werner back to the reception desk.

Tulio described the scene, "Werner signs out in the book. Herrar walks away. He hands his Visitor sticker to the receptionist, who points down the hall." Tulio turned toward Costa. "Most visitors ask for the toilet before they leave on their long drive back to wherever. We don't have a camera covering that section of hallway, though."

They watched Werner walk out of the frame. Tulio sped up the replay. At four minutes and nineteen seconds later, Werner returned to the picture, then he walked out the front door.

Tulio commented, "Either he's got the biggest bladder in the State, boss, or he made a substantial deposit to our fertilizer bank."

"Or maybe he stopped to chat with someone in the men's room. Keep it rolling. If we're lucky..." Costa pointed to the monitor when he saw a young man stroll through a corner of the screen.

÷÷÷÷÷

Martina Hasse packed up her gear and walked from the coffee fields back toward the buildings. *A bad day of birding is better than a good day of lab work*, she thought.

÷÷÷÷÷

In the dining room at the Executive Residence, the senior scientists sat around the oblong white tablecloth. Two waiters in black tie served appetizers of butterfly shrimp and smoked trout, followed by *caldo verde* (green soup), then platters of sliced beef and pork with grilled vegetables.

Duarte attempted to engage them in lighthearted banter. But the mood was glum, with the fungus, the imminent bad press, and a likely decline in company stock price, all hanging over the room like the weighty drapery.

Decker didn't eat as much as he had expected he would. Despite being the guest of honor, he was lost in thought, mulling over details of his prior conversation with Munhoz. And one question in particular nagged him: *Why would anyone want to harm Dr. Mendonça and/or Miguel?* Then another thought began to nag: *If Miguel had been incapacitated intentionally to bring down the plane carrying Dr. Mendonça, then someone at this table could have been involved. Of course, that's a mighty big "if," but if it was indeed the case, then I can't trust the people and resources I most need to accomplish my mission of stopping the fungus.*

Decker poked at food on his plate. *I probably can trust Duarte and Westphal, since they brought me into this whole affair. Unless one of them planted evidence that they want me to uncover to implicate someone else, but that seems far-fetched. I probably can trust Fabiana Munhoz. Unless she had a plot to bump off Paul. She seems rather happy for a woman who recently lost her husband. But that wouldn't explain anything about the fungus. I probably can trust Lucy. She's been awfully helpful. Unless she's doing so at someone else's bidding, like Costa's, while they lead me where they want me to go.* He took a bite of food. *This is paralyzing. I won't be able to function if I keep thinking this way. I've just got to keep plugging away to find out whatever I can. I can't trust anyone. At least not yet.*

÷÷÷÷÷

In the JJ Room, pairs of jiu-jitsu practitioners sparred. Normally, sparring partners were matched by approximate weight, but in this room on that evening, an exceedingly large man grappled with a much smaller one.

Tulio firmly held Felix's arm twisted behind his back in a position called a hammerlock. The massive man leaned his mouth close to the much smaller man's earring and whispered, "Mr. Costa wants you to know that he knows."

"He knows what?" Felix squirmed in a fruitless attempt to escape from the hold.

"He knows you talked to the reporter." Before Felix could protest, Tulio added, "Don't try to deny it. We have you on video leaving the restroom just after the reporter." Tulio fibbed, given that they didn't actually have a camera covering the hallway by the restroom.

"Is Mr. Costa gonna have me fired?"

"No. At least not yet. But he wants you to know that he knows. Perhaps an opportunity will arise to redeem yourself."

Felix tapped the mat three times with his free hand, and the big man released his hold.

Chapter 10

~~~~~

AUGUST 7

The headline on the *Correio Popular* story read, "*Fungo Infecta Rapidamente Fazenda de Café*" ("Fungus Rapidly Infects Coffee Farm"). It included a file photo of the plantation at Sede de Delcese Agricola, noting that the company declined to permit the newspaper to view the infected fields.

The story ran below the fold on the front page of the print edition of the newspaper and in mid-level positions on Correio.RAC.com.br and several other Campinas-region websites operated by the paper's parent company, *Rede Anhangüera de Comunicação* (Anhangüera Communication Network). The news organization published only in Portuguese, so on the morning of August 7th, web crawlers had not yet funneled the story into English language news feeds. A handful of Brazilians had noted the story in their blogs and tweets, but that was as far as it had gone. Early that morning, few people inside Brazil, and even fewer outside the country, were aware of the new coffee fungus. The story was still hours shy of its destiny to become worldwide news.

÷÷÷÷÷

At 6:50AM, Roberto Duarte received a phone call at home from Victor Cavila of the *Associação Brasileira de Cultivadores de Café* (Brazilian Coffee Growers Association).

÷÷÷÷÷

Decker and Lucy entered the doorway to Manling's office adjacent to the laboratory. The lab manager was busy working on the computer with his back toward them and did not notice their entrance. Decker knocked on the door frame.

"Ah, Mr. Decker, *bom dia*," Manling said, swiveling around his chair. "I have preliminary results from the testing of your two samples from the airplane. I'll have more detailed findings at the two o'clock meeting. As you surmised, the brown one is dark chocolate, and the red one contains our fungus."

"That's good to know. While I'm here, I'd like to speak to one of your lab staff..." Decker was unable to recall the name.

"Larissa Júnior," Lucy reminded him.

"...yes," Decker continued, "I understand she was at the fields where Dr. Mendonça's plane had taken off shortly before it crashed."

"That's correct," Manling said. "I'll go get her for you."

Through the glass panel in the door, Decker and Lucy watched as Manling walked to the rear of the lab, then through a door into the biosafety area. While they waited, Decker noticed the dome of a security camera on the ceiling inside the lab.

A minute later Manling returned with Júnior, who wore a blue lab coat. She was rearranging her hair into a new ponytail, having just removed it from a protective cap.

"*Senhorita* Júnior," Manling introduced, "Mr. Decker here would like to speak with you."

Decker extended a handshake.

"Of course," Júnior responded in accented English, "I was at your meeting with the lab staff on Monday afternoon."

"I'll be in the lab," Manling said, closing the door on his way out.

Decker pointed to a guest chair. "Please, sit down, Miss Júnior." He sat in Manling's chair, while Lucy remained standing. "Yesterday Lucy and I visited Fazenda Fiorva. Tell me everything you can remember from the day the plane crashed."

"Early that morning, Miguel picked up Dr. Mendonça and me here at Sede, then flew us out to Fiorva, where we picked up Sergio Moreno. Then we all flew out to the remote fields to the north."

Decker indicated for her to stop. "In the airplane on the way to the fields, who sat where?"

"The doctor was in the co-pilot's seat on the right, I was behind him, and Sergio was behind the pilot."

"Was your gear with you in the seats or in the storage area behind the back seat?"

"Most of our gear was in the rear storage area."

"After the plane landed at the remote field, and you and Sergio took your gear, did any gear remain in that storage area?"

"No. At that point, the small packs for the pilot and the doctor went onto the back seat."

"Among the doctor's gear, did you see a container that he might have used to hold cultured fungus? Perhaps like that one?" Decker pointed through the glass door panel to a stainless steel canister with biohazard labels on a shelf inside the lab.

"I didn't see any. I didn't look inside his pack."

"Any idea if his pack was heavy?"

"I wouldn't know. Sergio and the pilot moved the gear around."

"Did you notice anything unusual about the pilot?"

"Like what?"

"His behavior, his appearance."

"I didn't notice anything."

"How about Dr. Mendonça? Anything strange?"

"No."

Decker motioned for her to continue the story.

"We landed at the remote airfield. It's just a tiny dirt strip with a windsock on a pole. It's within walking distance of the hectare plots that Dr. Mendonça set up to conduct his experiments. Or maybe I should call it hiking distance because it's a kilometer along a rugged Jeep track. The doctor and the pilot helped us carry our gear to the first plot."

Decker signaled her to stop again. "What was your assignment?"

"The field where we went was planted a few years ago with genetically modified coffee trees. Sergio and I visit there periodically to check the trees and study the environmental impact. He's the one who had planted the trees, and he helps me examine them for diseases, measure growth, count the number of cherries, and such."

"And the environmental impact?"

"We count the number of insects, birds, small mammals, and weeds in the field. Then we go to a nearby control field planted with our usual Isabela trees, and we do the same to compare the findings."

"What's the nature of the genetic modifications to the trees in the experimental field?"

"The trees in this particular field were engineered to be pest-resistant without the use of pesticides."

"Do you know the specifics of the genetic modifications?"

"Yes. My primary job here at Delcese is to do such modifications in the lab. For these coffee trees, we extracted genes from a tree, *Salix babylonica*. The common name in Portuguese is *salgueiro chorão*. I can't recall the name in English at the moment." She dangled a hand with the fingers down.

Lucy said, "Weeping willow."

"Yes, that's it. The willow tree produces a chemical, salicin, which makes the bark bitter and discourages insects and animals from eating it. We had isolated the gene responsible for the production of salicin, and spliced it into coffee plant cells, creating enough seedlings to stock the field. Dr. Mendonça's theory was that the salicin gene would give the coffee trees inherent resistance to the coffee berry borer beetle,

Hypothenemus hampei. After planting, we had to wait several years for the trees to bear fruit."

Lucy asked, "Does adding the gene for bitter bark make the coffee beans bitter?"

"Yes, but only temporarily. Dr. Mendonça had determined that the salicin undergoes chemical disintegration during the fermentation stage of coffee bean processing. The resulting beans taste fine."

Decker asked, "Do the field trials bear out Dr. Mendonça's theory of pest resistance?"

"Yes. The experimental coffee field has far fewer insects than the control field."

"Any negative side effects?"

Júnior hesitated, then answered, "Some people consider fewer insects to *be* a negative side effect."

"How so?"

"For a variety of reasons, like environmentalism, biodiversity, or even aesthetics."

Decker cocked his head. "Aesthetics?"

Júnior held up both hands with the thumbs intertwined, then she flapped the hands back and forth pivoting around the thumbs. "Butterflies," she said. "Years ago in the United States, a variety of corn was modified with a gene from *Bacillus thuringiensis*, a bacterium which produces a protein toxic to moth larvae. The modification discouraged moth pests from feeding on these corn plants, greatly reducing crop damage. Unfortunately, pollen from the BT corn was blowing onto other plants, in particular the leaves of *erva de leite daninha*, or milkweed in English. This plant is the only host on which the *lagartas*..." She wiggled the fingers of a hand. "...that is the caterpillars, of the species *Danaus plexippus* feed. As a result, the moth-resistant corn unintentionally caused the preterm loss of countless thousands, maybe millions, of Monarch butterflies."

Decker said, "I remember there was a public uproar over that because the Monarch is a marquee species."

Júnior nodded. "The corn industry had to switch to a variety of BT corn that contains little or no toxin in its pollen."

"Did you notice a reduction in the number of butterflies in your experimental field here?"

"Yes and no. We discovered caterpillars on the leaves of the coffee plants in the experimental field. I had never seen caterpillars in our coffee fields before, and they were not present in the control field."

"Then the genetic modifications to the coffee plants led to an increase in the number of butterflies in the experimental field?"

"Unfortunately, no. When the caterpillars went into pupae stage, that is the chrysalis, they all died prior to completing metamorphosis, probably from the effects of consuming salicin. The mature butterflies never appeared. I only determined that the species was the Tropical Leafwing by post-mortem dissection. Sergio said that when he worked in a shade plantation in Costa Rica when he was much younger, he saw larvae of that butterfly species on the coffee plants there."

Decker wrote a note for himself on a yellow sticky pad that was sitting on the desk, then he continued his questioning. "Did experiments in that field include infecting the plants with fungus?"

"No. Not in that field."

"In other fields then?"

"I know Dr. Mendonça tested fungus in some of the other experimental fields, but I wasn't involved in those tests."

"Was anyone else involved in the coffee fungus test sites besides Dr. Mendonça? Perhaps someone similar to yourself?"

"As far as I know, the doctor handled all fungus tests himself. In fact, I think he handled all of the experiments in the fields west of Fiorva himself."

"On the day of the plane crash, did he talk about tests he planned to conduct later that day?"

"No, and I didn't ask. I didn't see it as my place to inquire what the department chief was doing."

"OK, Miss Júnior. Please continue describing what happened on the day of the crash."

"Dr. Mendonça and the pilot Miguel left the field to hike back to the airplane. I heard the plane take off about twenty minutes later. The plane was supposed to come back and pick us up later that day. Sergio and I waited by the airstrip, but the plane never came back, and we had no means of contacting anyone. I had my mobile phone, but there aren't any signal towers out there in the jungle. So Sergio and I waited. We weren't even sure who else knew we were out there. For a while we wondered if we would have to spend the night in the field. Eventually, someone at Fiorva remembered we were there, and they sent the other plane to pick us up. That's when we heard about the plane crash."

"Anything else you can tell me that might be useful? Perhaps even something that you might not think is important?"

She looked as though she was about to speak, but she didn't.

"What is it, Miss Júnior?"

She hesitated a few more seconds, then said, "I heard that the pilot is in a coma since the plane crash."

"Yes."

"You know how some people like to talk about gruesome stuff over lunch? One day in the cafeteria, one of the lab technicians, Felix, the young guy with the earring and the *corte masculino* haircut..." She motioned over the top of her head with a flattened hand. "...he said that when the ambulance guys took the pilot out of the airplane his body was extremely stiff, almost like rigor mortis, even though he was alive. Then, Felix pulled out his mobile phone and showed a photo of Miguel the pilot all cramped up, with his back arched, lying on his side on a stretcher."

"Where'd he get the photo?"

"I wouldn't know. Anyway, when I saw the photo, it reminded me of something. When I was a university student, I took a class in Toxicology. The photo of the pilot's body reminded me of a toxic infection."

Decker asked, "Do I have to guess which one?"

"*Tétano*," Júnior said.

"Is that tetanus? As in lockjaw?"

She nodded. "I'm probably wrong, though, because Miguel didn't show any of those symptoms when I saw him less than an hour before the plane crash. *Tétano* infection develops gradually over a period of days. But when I was a student, I saw a farmer who had contracted the full blown *tétano* disease, and he appeared very much like the pilot in the photo after the plane crash."

"Curious." Decker made another note on the sticky pad.

Júnior looked down at her hands in her lap, then she looked up at Decker. "Maybe I'm just not thinking straight. Since that day I've thought many times about Dr. Mendonça's death, and about how I too could've been killed. The plane that crashed was the very plane I had flown in earlier that day. Such experiences make one question oneself."

÷

When Júnior left the office, she stopped to talk to Manling in the lab. "I'm not feeling well," she told him. "I think I'll go over to the Health Center at lunchtime to see *Doutora* Munhoz."

÷

When Manling came back to his office, Decker told him he wanted to talk to Felix. Manling fetched the technician, then left him in the office with Decker and Lucy.

Felix fidgeted in the chair.

Decker asked, "Should I have Lucy translate?"

"My English is good."

"Larissa told us that you showed her a picture on your mobile phone of the pilot from the plane crash at Fazenda Fiorva, a picture that was taken after he was pulled out of the plane."

Felix reluctantly nodded. "Am I in trouble for having that?"

"No. But you may be able to help us figure out what happened to the pilot. Can I see the picture?"

Felix took the mobile phone out of his pants pocket then pulled up the picture on the screen. He handed the phone to Decker.

Decker put on his glasses to examine the image. "Where'd you get this picture? I need to talk to the person who took it."

"One of the ambulance guys took it. I don't know him myself. I just know somebody who knows him."

"It's very important. It relates to finding the source of the fungus that's infecting the plantations. I don't want to get him in trouble. I just want information."

Felix said, "All right. Give me a couple of minutes."

Decker and Lucy went into the lab, leaving Felix in the office.

÷

Felix dialed a number on his phone and had a brief conversation. A minute after that call, he received a text message containing a phone number which he dialed. Felix told the emergency medical technician, "We both might get fired if you don't talk to this guy, but everything will be cool as long as you tell him what he wants to know."

÷

Felix waved for Decker and Lucy to come back into the office. He handed Decker the phone and said, "He speaks English."

Decker asked the EMT, "Have you ever seen a case of tetanus?"

The voice on the other end replied, "Not in person, only in textbooks. But I understand that the man in the picture might look like he had that disease because all his muscles were so stiff. I practically had to pry his fingers off the control handles to get him out of the airplane. I don't see how tetanus would be possible, though, if he had just been flying the plane. That's a slow-acting disease. The symptoms don't kick in suddenly. My guess is that he had some kind of seizure."

"Would that have been before or after the plane crashed?"

"Hard to say. The patient had a wound on the side of his head, a skull fracture, which appeared to have happened during the crash, and that injury could have caused the seizure. But if the seizure happened before, it could have been the cause of the crash giving him the head injury. *O ovo ou a galinha?* Which came first, the egg or the chicken?"

"Did you see anything inside the plane that could have caused the head injury?"

"The only thing I saw that could've done it was a drink thermos, like people use for hot coffee. This one was bare metal, like it was made of stainless steel."

"That was inside the plane?"

"Yes. It was down by the pilot's feet. I saw it there when we were pulling him out of the plane wreck."

"Did it have bright orange stickers on it? Biohazard labels?"

"I didn't notice any labels on it, but I didn't look closely at it."

"Did you take the thermos out of the airplane, or see anyone else take it out?"

"No. I left it right where it was. In the event of a plane crash, we first responders are trained not to touch anything we don't have to touch. Stuff like that is for the aviation authorities, or police investigators, or, I guess, guys like you, whatever you do."

Decker thanked the EMT and hung up the line. He handed the phone back to Felix.

Decker asked, "You've been doing tests on this fungus, right?"

Felix replied, "That's about the only thing I've been doing lately."

"What would happen if someone consumed the fungus?"

"Nothing, except maybe an upset stomach if they ate a whole lot of it. There's nothing in it that's hazardous to humans." As he stood up to leave, Felix added, "It tastes pretty good."

Decker raised his head. "What?"

"The fungus." Felix pointed to his tongue. "It tastes good."

"You ate some of it?"

"Just a little. One of the other lab techs bet me twenty *reais* that I wouldn't do it."

÷

Decker told Lucy that he had one more question for Larissa. Lucy retrieved her from the lab.

Decker asked, "Did you see a stainless steel drink thermos in the airplane?"

"Yes, I think one was in there," Larissa replied.

"Why didn't you tell me about it a few minutes ago when I asked if you had seen anything that might have contained cultured fungus?"

"You asked if I had seen a biohazard container. That was just a coffee thermos."

"Where in the plane was it?"

"It was in a storage bin on the floor between the two front seats."

"Did you see anyone drink from it?"

"No."

"Did it have any red smudges on its exterior or maybe on its lid? Like it might have contained something red?"

"Not that I saw, but I didn't pay any special attention to it. Sorry."

÷÷÷÷÷

Roberto Duarte walked briskly from the helicopter landing pad on the rooftop of the office building in Rio de Janeiro.

Inside the meeting room, sixteen members of the Associação Brasileira de Cultivadores de Café awaited, seated around a large, U-shaped assemblage of tables made from dark-toned imbuia wood. Duarte scanned the occupants of the room, recognizing all the faces. *At least there aren't any journalists here*, he thought. Then he spotted several copies of the *Correio Popular* newspaper on the tables, as well as two tablets displaying the story from the paper's website.

After allowing Duarte to get settled in a chair, *Secretário-Geral* (Secretary General) Victor Cavila spoke, "Roberto, thank you for joining us today in this emergency session."

Duarte replied, "Victor and my fellow coffee growers, it's both an honor and a responsibility to meet with you today."

Cavila immediately broached the topic of everyone's interest. "Your fellow coffee growers, some of whom are in the room, and many more who could not be present, are deeply concerned about the outbreak of the fungus on Delcese Agricola's plantations." He motioned to the newspapers on the tables. "To begin, please update the assembled members on any new developments."

Duarte cleared his throat. "Delcese Agricola's staff scientists, with the assistance of Professor Decker from the United States, have been investigating the fungus to discover its origins, to stop its spread, and to prevent its reoccurrence in the future. Professor Decker already has uncovered several key pieces of information, and I have every confidence that he and my staff will succeed in stopping this fungus. At this time, however, I must report that the organism continues to spread unabated."

Denis Taves of Fazenda Briole in São Paulo State asked, "And how many of our plantations will become contaminated while your scientists keep scratching their heads?"

Duarte maintained his composure. "*Senhor* Taves, I can't answer your question. We're doing everything we can to address the situation with all the resources we have. While I regret any damage that might befall your plantations, I remind you that Delcese is the company at greatest risk. Therefore, I would gratefully accept assistance that any of you could provide."

João Pacheco of Párano Agricola noted, "Your scientists already have been studying this organism for weeks. At the rate it's spreading, by the time our scientists could get up to speed, our plantations may be consumed."

Duarte responded, "What do you suggest then, *Senhor* Pacheco?"

"We must protect the common good of all our crops. I propose a quarantine of any infected plantations."

"We don't know that a quarantine would stop the spread of the fungus. And we can't know for certain until we have established all its mechanisms of distribution. We already know that the spores can be airborne. A quarantine will not be effective against such a mechanism, unless you propose to quarantine the wind, *Senhor* Pacheco."

The other attendees let out subdued laughs.

Pacheco sipped from a coffee mug. "I understand from one of my staff who has spoken to one of your staff, that incineration destroys this fungus. In fact, it's the only method your cadre of elite scientists has devised that will actually kill the fungus. If you burn down all the plants in your infected fields, it will stop the spread."

Pacheco just suckered me, Duarte thought, then he said, "If the fungus is already outside the infected plantations, such a drastic step will still fail to stop its spread."

Pacheco continued his argument, "Do you agree, *Senhor* Duarte, that destroying your infected crops will lessen the likelihood of further spread?"

"Yes, but..." Murmuring broke out. "...but doing so might destroy data critical to finding a true solution."

The Secretary General commented, "We do not have the luxury of academia here..." A jab at Duarte's importing of Decker. "...Our growers have ripe cherries on our trees. We are harvesting at our maximum rates, but we can't harvest faster than the fungus could spread. Any solution now is preferable to an ideal solution later."

Pacheco added, "If Delcese needs to sacrifice its crops to help the rest of us, that company should be willing to do so. Besides, for all we know, this fungus was created by one of the late *Doutor* Mendonça's genetic tinkerings."

Duarte retorted, "Such an accusation is outrageous!"

"Gentlemen, please," Cavila said, "let's maintain decorum here."

Pacheco held up his hands. "Forgive me, *Senhor* Duarte. I didn't mean to imply that *Doutor* Mendonça intentionally created an organism this destructive. I only meant that he might have created it for some other purpose, without knowing that it would have such destructive consequences."

Taves asked, "Can you say with absolute certainty, Roberto, that this fungus was not created by *Doutor* Mendonça?"

Tag team suckering, Duarte thought. He paused for a long time before answering. "No, I cannot say with certainty that he didn't create it. However, I don't have any evidence that he did."

Another attendee, Stephan de Rosa, owner of three medium sized *fazendas* in the State of Espírito Santo, added ominously, "*Senhor* Duarte, if evidence does come to light that this fungus was created by your Chief Scientist, Delcese will be held financially responsible for any damage that it inflicts on my crops."

Another jumped in, "Delcese has failed to contain its own experiments. If my plantations get infected, I will demand compensation."

"We will all demand compensation!"

Uproar ensued, with attendees shouting and table pounding, and no one putting forth effort in Duarte's defense.

They've turned into a lynch mob, Duarte thought. *I should have brought along Costa for my personal protection.*

÷

On his desolate walk back to the helicopter pad, Duarte dialed on his mobile phone the number of Raul Espindola, Chairman of the Board of Directors of Delcese Agricola.

"Raul, we must urgently convene a meeting of the Board..."

÷÷÷÷

Decker and Lucy approached a door labeled *Segurança*, which unlocked upon detecting her ID. Inside the central Security area, a large black man sat in front of the video monitor array.

"*Oi*, Tulio," Lucy said. "Boss in?"

"*Sim*." The guard nodded and jerked a thumb at the office in back.

Before they went to the office, Decker waved a hand at the video monitors. "Any of these show the lab?"

Lucy spoke in Portuguese to Tulio. He pressed a button on the console to switch feeds. "*Aqui*," he said, pointing to the monitor on the right in the upper row.

Decker asked, "Do these get recorded?"

"Yes," Lucy said.

"Could we go back and look at videos from a few weeks ago, before the plane crash? I'd like to see if Dr. Mendonça was working with anyone in particular in the lab after hours."

"We only store the video recordings for a week, unless we have a reason to archive one. It would take up too much space on our server storing all twenty-four video feeds indefinitely."

Lucy asked Tulio a question. He turned to a computer monitor and called up a directory. He spoke to Lucy, which she relayed. "Nothing is saved from the lab camera several weeks ago."

"That's too bad," Decker said. "Let's go see Mr. Costa." He and Lucy started toward the office door, then he stopped. He pointed back at the man at the console. "How late does this guard work?"

"Tulio's here until five o'clock? Why?"

"I don't need to see stored recordings. If there's a person sitting at that console all the time watching the monitors, I want to talk to the person who's there in the evenings. He or she might have what I want stored up here." He tapped a temple of his own head.

"Alberto is the guy who comes in for the second shift. We can talk to him later."

Decker and Lucy started toward the office door again, then he stopped again. He pointed to his ID card. "Do you keep records of the passing of these badges?"

"Yes." She realized his point. "And we keep those indefinitely. The lab door is unlocked during normal work hours, so no access card is required, but those records could tell us who else was in the lab at about the same times Dr. Mendonça was there after hours."

"Although they wouldn't necessarily tell us who might have been working *with* him. We'll still want to talk to your man Alberto who watches the camera feeds."

÷

Costa looked up from the paperwork on his desk. Decker looked around the office then pointed to an item on a shelf and described what he wanted to do.

Costa protested, "That's a birthday gift for my daughter."

"I'll order you another one."

"As long as it's here within a couple of weeks."

÷

Lucy drove the cart with Decker aboard out to the field of infected coffee trees.

Senhora Hasse put down the binoculars and stood up from her stool when she saw them approaching.

Getting off the cart, Decker asked Hasse, "Any luck?"

"Sorry, nothing yesterday, and so far nothing today," she replied. "No parrots eating coffee cherries. In fact, no parrots at all. Only a couple of bush tanagers way back in the sugarcane and a few wild Muscovy ducks passing overhead."

"Parrots like to congregate with other parrots, don't they?"

"Sure."

Decker reached into the back of the cart and lifted the box containing the Squawkie toy. "Here, take this," he said. "You can set it to make parrot sounds."

"I'll need something to hold it on a tree branch."

Decker turned to Lucy. "Have you got a tool kit in this cart?"

"Under the rear bench seat. It flips up."

Decker dug around in the storage compartment and pulled out a roll of duct tape.

÷÷÷÷

Bright Cup's coffee buyer Valmir Pasco waited impatiently in the lobby at Sede, pacing back and forth, checking his watch. Finally, a man arrived. Pasco had never seen him before, but he immediately knew what the man's job position must be from the coiffed hair style and the tasseled loafers.

"Good morning, *Senhor* Pasco. I'm Silvio Damani, the new Vice President of Sales."

"Nice to meet you." They shook hands and exchanged business cards. "Did *Senhor* Valiente retire?"

"Yes, a few months ago." Damani escorted Pasco into a conference room. "I'm sorry that *Senhor* Duarte isn't available. He apologizes for missing his appointment with you."

"I imagine he's been quite busy today."

"*Senhor* Duarte was attending a meeting of the Brazilian Coffee Growers Association in Rio this morning. Originally, he was due to arrive back here half an hour ago, but now he can't return until late tonight, so he asked me to meet with you instead. I've been in several of your Bright Cup Cafés on my travels in the States. Your company is doing many things very well."

"We like to think so. To get right to the point, *Senhor* Damani, my company's CEO sent me here to get a firsthand look at the fungus. It's critical for our business planning to understand how this fungus might impact Delcese's ability to supply beans. We're changing our purchasing procedures to buy more of our beans directly from growers rather than through the commodities exchanges."

"Very interesting, *Senhor* Pasco." Damani touched a hand to his own hair. "What quantities are you considering?"

"I'd like you to give me quotes for one million, five million, and ten million kilograms. If the price is right, Bright Cup is prepared to commit at the ten million level."

Damani maintained a poker face. "Excellent. I can send you a proposal tomorrow morning."

"If you can draw up contracts while I'm here, I'm empowered to close deals immediately. But with the fungus on your premises, how do I know that you'll be able to deliver?"

"I've barely seen the fungus myself. Would you care to take a look in the fields with me?"

"Lead on."

÷

Damani drove the cart among the stricken coffee trees.

Pasco was taken aback by the extent of damage from the fungus. He thought, *Why is Damani showing me this? He must have known how bad it looked before bringing me out here. He must want me to think there'll be a shortage so he can try to jack up the price.*

"As you can see, *Senhor* Pasco, the fungus has done considerable damage in this plantation. Of course, Delcese has many more plantations which are not affected. If you can commit now, we should have no problem supplying your needs, but if you delay, demand could outstrip supply. For a ten million kilogram contract, I could guarantee you shipment priority ahead of all our other customers."

At the back of the fields, the cart came around a corner between two rows of trees, and Damani had to swerve to avoid hitting a woman sitting on a stool, fiddling with a parrot on her lap.

Damani said to Pasco, "I don't want to know what she's doing out here with that bird."

Pasco craned his neck back at the woman and told Damani, "Hold on a second. That's one of our Squawkies."

"Excuse me?"

"She's got one of Bright Cup's toy birds. Stop the cart, please."

Pasco got off and walked over to the woman. "I'm Valmir Pasco. I work for Bright Cup, the maker of that Squawkie bird. Can I help you with it, *senhora*?"

"I'm trying to get it to do the parrot calls," Hasse explained, "but I can't figure out the instructions." She held up a large sheet of paper with numerous crease marks in it. "I'm not sure if the problem is my poor English or the poor English of the guy somewhere in Asia who wrote the directions."

"Allow me," Pasco said. He took the bird from her and turned it over. "If you hold down these two buttons like this until you hear the beep, it goes into random call mode."

The toy bird emitted two high-pitched notes.

"Thank you, *senhor*."

÷

Watching the cart drive away, Hasse thought, *That sure was nice of the Bright Cup company to send a customer support guy in Brazil all the way out here to help me with this thing. Mr. Decker must have really good connections at the company.*

÷÷÷÷÷

Still before dawn in California, Cochran was at his home on the lower slopes of Mt. Tamalpais, north of the Golden Gate Bridge. He read an email from Pasco containing a link to the morning's story on the *Correio Popular* website, along with a machine-generated English translation. When he finished reading the article, Cochran forwarded the email to Parananda. He thought, *this will be even better than I expected for the press conference.*

Chapter 11

"One man's 'magic' is another man's engineering."

Science fiction writer Robert A. Heinlein (1907–1988)

~~~~~

After signing the coffee supply contract with Valmir Pasco and escorting him back to the receptionist's desk at Sede, Silvio Damani stopped by Melissa Herrar's office. He told her, "I've just closed the biggest single coffee deal in company history."

÷

Pasco handed his Visitor sticker to the receptionist. He was about to ask where the men's room was, but before he had the chance, she pointed and said, "It's down the hall to the right."

Pasco stood at a urinal. *The price I negotiated from Damani is lower than what we paid on the exchange yesterday. Even factoring in the volume discount, either the coffee fungus problem isn't as bad as it looks, or the VP of Sales doesn't know how bad it really is.*

A young man with a blonde buzz cut and an earring walked up to the fixture next to Pasco. Felix said, "Man, I'm surprised I'm not pissing red from all the fungus testing I've been doing."

Pasco asked, "Oh? What do you know about the fungus?"

"You're not a journalist are you?"

"No, just a business guy. Is the fungus as bad as it looks?"

Felix looked out of the corner of his eye to check for anyone else in the room. "This fungus ain't so bad. We just came up with a way to stop it. It'll be history by the end of the week."

"*Cê tá brincando?*" Are you shittin' me?

Felix tipped his head backward. "If I was shittin' you, I'd be in one of the stalls."

÷

After the older man had exited the men's room, Felix thought, *Trouxa!* [Sucker!]

÷÷÷÷

In the Colonial Ballroom of the St. Francis Hotel on San Francisco's Union Square, Matthew Cochran stood on the ornate balcony, wearing a black blazer over a black T-shirt and black pants. Beneath the Tuscan mural on the opposite wall of the ballroom was a 20 x 30 foot black stage platform that had been designed and constructed for the imminent presentation. Cochran looked down at the hundred or so guests milling around the banquet tables on the lower level of the room, fueling themselves on fresh-baked croissants, made-to-order omelets, smoked salmon on buckwheat blini, and fresh local berries. The guests were all sipping selections of Bright Cup's finest gourmet brews from special edition yellow ceramic mugs, poured by wait staff in yellow satin jackets.

Cochran's mobile phone rang. He noted the caller ID. "Hi, Val."

"*Senhor* Matt. I'm at the plantation with the fungus. I was taking a leak in the men's room, and this lab technician kid walked up to the next *pinico*. I was chatting him up, and he told me the fungus, quote, 'will be history by the end of the week.' I didn't trust the sales guy for a second, but this kid had no reason to lie to me. He had no idea who I was or why I was here..."

"Halt buying, Val."

"But, *Senhor* Matt, per your previous instructions, and just before I talked to the kid from the lab, I closed a mammoth deal with the VP of Sales at very favorable pricing. Private forward contracts of this type don't have cancellation provisions. Backing out would be expensive."

"Then we'd better pray the kid is mistaken."

After he hung up, Cochran thought, *I'd better play up the fungus in the press conference so we can still profitably unload the futures before everyone else finds out.*

Rami Parananda approached Cochran on the balcony.

Parananda said, "The waiter confirmed that he passed along the info to Tony G." He pointed into the crowd below. "Tony's at that table, looking at his laptop. Probably reading the story right now."

"Well done," Cochran said. "And I hope you've got plenty of extra bags of Primo Cup beans on hand. When I'm done with these folks, I bet a lot of them will be taking more than one bag."

÷

Ten minutes later, Parananda took hold of a wireless microphone. "Attention ladies and gentlemen," his voice boomed throughout the ballroom, "Please take your seats."

Parananda ascended the steps onto the stage, followed by the lenses of three video cameras stationed around the room. "Welcome, from Bright Cup Incorporated. I'm Rami Parananda, Vice President of Marketing. Portions of this press conference contain forward-looking statements based on management's expectations and projections. Actual results may differ materially from what is discussed here due to a variety of factors, including but not limited to: our CEO's inability to stick to a business model for more than two consecutive quarters;

increasingly fickle customer preferences in pastry fruit filling flavors; a possible shortage of soy-based yellow ink to print our paper cups; labor unrest on the part of our Squawkie bird toys seeking free range status; and my distant cousin from Central America, El Niño. In all seriousness folks, stuff happens, so take everything we say here with a grain of salt substitute. We ask that you hold any questions until the designated Q-and-A period at the end of the presentation. And now, without further ado, please welcome the CEO and Founder of Bright Cup Incorporated, Matthew Cochran."

While the audience applauded, Cochran sprinted from the rear of the ballroom. He leapt up the stage stairs two at a time. Parananda handed him the microphone and stepped off the stage.

Standing on the barren platform, Cochran brushed back his hair with an overhead motion, then he raised the microphone. "The day I announced the formation of Bright Cup Incorporated, nine years ago in this very room, I slipped and fell coming onto the stage like that, breaking my nose. I had to give the rest of my speech with a handkerchief pressed to my face sopping up the blood drips. I still keep that hankie as a memento." He pulled out from his coat pocket a blood-stained handkerchief, which he waved back and forth. "How many of *you* folks were here that day?" About a dozen in the audience raised their hands.

"From that inauspicious beginning, I am here today to announce the greatest series of innovations in our company's history. Since our launch, we at Bright Cup have been on the cutting edge of the retail coffee business." Cochran stretched the handkerchief by two opposing corners between the microphone and his free hand, forming a straight edge along its top. "Innovation is the cornerstone that has enabled us to grow from being just another lowly startup, into a bona fide high flyer." Cochran tossed the handkerchief into the air, and a small red bird flew away from it.

Parananda applauded, and the audience half-heartedly followed.

Cochran continued, "Today ladies and gentlemen, we are unveiling three new innovations that will poise Bright Cup to leap to the top, past our competitors from up north in Pork-land and Chichi-attle. But first, can I have a volunteer?"

Several attendees raised their hands. Cochran pointed to a man seated nearest the back of the room. "Sir, what's your first name?"

"Derek."

"I'd like you to get up, Derek, and pick out one of those bags of coffee we have on that table at the back of the room. Pick any one you like. You're all going to get them on your way out later, by the way."

Derek walked over to the table and picked up a bag.

"Bring it up here to the front."

Derek carried it around the side of the room to the front edge of the stage, where he remained standing on the lower level of the floor.

Cochran instructed, "Please open up the bag and confirm that it contains coffee beans."

The man unfolded the top of the bag, dug his hand deep inside, and pulled out a handful of coffee beans for all to see.

"Now pour the beans back into the bag and close it up again. Then for the next few minutes, please stand right there holding that bag."

Derek nodded.

Cochran raised both hands over his head, then lowered them as a giant projection screen descended behind him. He stepped to the side, and a Bright Cup parrot logo appeared on the screen.

"For starters, we at Bright Cup are about to bring a whole new meaning to the term 'hot coffee.'" The image on the screen faded to video of a worker hand-plucking small reddish-orange fruits from a leafy bush. Accompanied by Mexican instrumental music, the camera zoomed in until it became apparent that the fruits were the wrong size and shape to be coffee cherries. "That's right, folks, chili peppers. And not just any chili peppers. Habaneros. These suckers are not only the hottest but also the most flavorful beasts to ever grace the branches of a pepper bush. In the past, some enterprising coffee brewers have experimented with pepper-flavored coffees, going nearly as far back as the origins of coffee as a beverage. However, those prior offerings were not well received by the drinking public. Now, Bright Cup's master food scientists have developed a proprietary process that extracts not only the heat-inducing capsaicin from Habaneros, but also flavor-enhancing compounds that are at their peak during a specific stage of pepper ripeness. Our test marketing has revealed a surprisingly potent market for a specialty coffee spiced with just the right amount of this Habanero extract, as demonstrated in these actual consumer reaction videos from recent taste testing sessions."

The video image faded to a scene of a man drinking from a yellow cup. When he lowered the cup, he shook his head wildly, flapping his lips like a cartoon character. Then he yelled, "Wow, that's good!"

The audience laughed.

In the next video scene, a woman took a sip from a full cup, then she savored it on her tongue. The video faded to her draining the last few drops from the bottom of the cup. "Oooo... It leaves me feeling all tingly." She lowered her voice to a whisper. "Don't tell my husband, but this is better than you-know-what."

The women in the audience laughed.

A woman outdoors bundled up in a winter coat drank from a steaming cup. Text superimposed on the screen indicated the locale as St. Paul, Minnesota. "That's the best warm-me-up drink I've ever had. It's got me glowing from the inside. And I bet in a pinch I could use it as anti-freeze in the SUV."

This time the men laughed.

Another woman chugged down a whole cup in under five seconds, then she held it out for a refill. "Talk about a wake up call! A cup or two of this stuff in the morning, and I'll be done with a whole day's work before lunch."

The video image faded back to the Bright Cup logo.

Cochran continued, "We call this new specialty drink Hot Stuff, and just to deflect any prospective class action lawsuits, no, we don't recommend its use as an automotive anti-freeze. In Phase One of the product rollout, starting next week, we'll begin offering Hot Stuff in our shops in the southwestern States. We're also finalizing an agreement with a major chain of Mexican restaurants in that region to offer Hot Stuff in all its outlets. In Phase Two, starting in November, we'll introduce Hot Stuff in the northern States. And in Phase Three, by next February, it will be in all our Bright Cup Cafés nationwide. The launch will be supported by a multi-million-dollar ad campaign with interactive television spots and mobile promotions in major markets. Soon, all of America will be burning with desire for our Hot Stuff."

The audience applauded politely.

Cochran walked over to the front of the stage and squatted down to where the man stood with the bag of coffee beans.

"Derek, please hold up the bag toward me. I'm not going to touch it, but I need to work my mojo on it." Cochran put the palm of his hand about a foot away from the bag, then rapidly thrust the hand forward a few inches, as though he was smacking something away. "Now, Derek, gently shake the bag to transform the beans." The man began doing so. "You may feel the bag getting lighter." After a few more seconds, Cochran said, "Go ahead, open up the bag, and dump out its entire contents onto the stage."

Out from the bag came a pile of Habanero peppers, and no coffee beans. Nearly every face in the audience, especially Derek's, bore a look of surprise, and a smattering of applause broke out.

"Thank you, Derek." Cochran clapped for Derek and the audience followed along. "You may return to your seat."

Cochran paused to set down the microphone at the edge of the stage and take a sip of water from a glass. While he did so, two workers carried to the center of the stage a table with chrome legs and a plate steel top. Another pair of workers carried an empty glass fish tank and set it on the table. The tank was about three feet long and two by two feet on the sides. Cochran then stood up and walked all around the table, occasionally poking an arm in the tank or underneath the table to demonstrate that the spaces were indeed empty.

Cochran motioned to a man in the front row of banquet tables to come up and check the table and tank. The man hopped up on stage and looked all around the tank and table, then finished by crawling completely under the table on his hands and knees. Cochran gave him a mock kick in the butt to dismiss him from the stage.

Parananda tossed to Cochran a hefty sheet of black velvet cloth. Cochran flamboyantly swept the giant cloth back and forth high up in the air as though he was an undersized matador, to show that the cloth wasn't concealing anything. He then draped it over the tank and table such that the edges of the cloth extended about a foot below the surface of the table but well above the floor, so anything coming up from below would have been visible.

Cochran took a step away from the table, then he silently waved his arms in abracadabra fashion at the glass tank under the cloth. When nothing happened, he thrust his hands to his hips in pretend frustration. He took another step further away from the table, towards the front of the stage, and repeated the attempt with the same result. Next, he pointed a finger into the air in a moment of realization, and he turned to the audience. He made funny faces at people in the front row of tables, then he pointed to a woman and motioned for her to stand up. She did so only after encouragement from the woman seated next to her. He pantomimed for her to perform the abracadabra movements along with him. She waved her arms in a wimpy manner, and the audience laughed. Cochran rolled his eyes. He motioned for her to partake more vigorously. When she finally got into it, he circled a finger beside his head, implying that she was cuckoo. She stopped and glared at him.

Cochran picked up the microphone from the stage floor. "Thank you, ma'am. I couldn't have done it without you." He ran to the table and yanked off the black cloth, revealing a stainless steel machine that now occupied nearly the entire glass tank. The machine had polished chrome trim, an oval door, and two pushbuttons on the front.

"This, ladies and gentlemen, is our second major innovation, the Roastronic, a fully automated coffee roaster for installation in our cafés." Murmurs from the crowd. "Experts know that the best tasting coffee is achieved by grinding and brewing beans within a day or so of roasting. Most specialty coffee shops grind their own beans, but except in rare cases, those beans are provided by separate facilities that have roasted them days, weeks or even months in advance of consumption. What's the result? A loss in coffee flavor.

"For the last nine years, we at Bright Cup have operated our own regional roasting plants around the country. All our beans are delivered fresh to our cafés within two days of roasting, through a special agreement with FedEx." Cochran lowered his voice in a stage whisper. "We give all the FedEx drivers free coffee."

The crowd laughed.

Cochran walked up to the front of the stage. "A small number of independent coffee shops around the country roast their own beans on site, and they can produce excellent coffee by doing so. But the process is cumbersome and finicky, not to mention demanding a large investment in equipment. The process is also inherently inconsistent due to variables such as bean variety, size, age, and moisture content, which make it less than ideal to use time-based or temperature-based methods for automatically detecting when the beans are at their optimum roast. And, more importantly, it has been futile to attempt to take large numbers of baristas and train them to roast beans consistently from batch to batch and store to store. Due to such factors, no major coffee retailer has ever introduced on-site roasting to its entire nationwide chain. It simply wasn't feasible. That is, until now. Ladies and gentlemen, with the Roastronic, Bright Cup is taking the next step forward in coffee freshness, and the next step ahead of our competition."

Cochran walked back to the table and rapped on the top of the machine with his knuckle.

"The Roastronic can be fueled via hookup to propane or natural gas, and we'll have an all-electric version soon. It features automatic chaff removal to prevent any tainting of the flavor, as well smoke and vapor recovery through a miniature catalytic oxidizer, for suitability in virtually any retail establishment with no emissions of volatile organic compounds or other hazardous substances. But the Roastronic's greatest feature is its patented roasting system. For those of you who have never witnessed the process, when coffee beans are roasted, they crack audibly during the process. And, if roasting continues long enough, they'll crack a second time. With the Roastronic, through the use of electronic audio sensors in the roasting chamber..." Cochran pointed to the front of the unit. "...and sophisticated digital audio processing, this machine listens for the cracking sounds, and just like an expert roastmaster, it distinguishes the subtle cracking from the louder noise of agitating the beans.

"The exact roasting process varies with the bean variety and the desired level of roast. In the case of our House Blend, the Roastronic automatically shuts off the heat when it hears that the beans have begun cracking a second time, producing the perfect roast for the tastes of Bright Cup's customers in the North American market. All the operator does is pour a load of beans into the chamber, then wave a barcode past this scanner on the front identifying the variety of beans. The Roastronic takes care of the rest. With the patented Roastronic system, beans are perfectly roasted every time. And it's a Bright Cup exclusive. Starting next week, we'll begin installing these Roastronics in dozens of our retail outlets, and by next year, every Bright Cup Café in the country will be roasting beans on site."

The audience applauded enthusiastically.

Cochran picked up the black cloth from the floor, shook it out, then laid it back over the glass tank and table. "And now, for our last major announcement."

The video image on the screen displayed a series of statistical charts and graphs correlating household income, age, education level, and coffee consumption rates.

"Bright Cup's retail coffee business has been successful at attracting American adults to our shops by offering a broad selection of foods and beverages in comfortable environments. But our nation's teenagers prefer to hang out and spend their money at mall food courts drinking soda pop."

The video screen showed a red soda can with computer-generated devil horns and tail.

"To foster the next generation of America's coffee drinking consumers, to help them acquire a taste for our black gold, and of course to inculcate them with Bright Cup brand loyalty, we announce the launch of a new chain of teen-oriented beverage shops called Bright Teen Cafés, to be located in select shopping malls across the country beginning in October."

The video image dissolved to a stylized Bright Teen logo. The crowd mumbled in curiosity.

"These shops will feature fruit juices, energy drinks, carbonated beverages, and specialty coffees, with comfortable, moveable seating and of course blazing fast wireless Internet connections to foster social networking both in person and online. In addition, over the next year, we'll be introducing in those Bright Teen Cafés a range of teen-targeted drinks and snacks, including coffee-cola combination sodas in regular and decaf, freshly baked espresso-bean-and-chocolate-chip cookies, and a host of additional products."

Cochran paused for effect. The audience waited in rapt attention.

"And a critical component of the Bright Teen Café business will be our marketing strategy to reach those teens, to hold their interest, to bring them into our shops, to encourage them to consume there, and to entice them to keep coming back for more."

Cochran strolled over to the table with the glass box still covered by the black cloth.

"To that end, Bright Cup announces a four-year endorsement contract with teen singing sensation and performer of three top ten pop hits including 'Drink Up My Love,' the one and only Miss Jennifer Halstead!"

Pop beat music began to blare over the loudspeakers, and colored stage lights flashed along. Cochran grabbed a corner of the black cloth and yanked it off in one swift motion.

Where the Roastronic device last had been seen in the glass tank, this time crouched inside was a small person in bright yellow attire. The audience let out a collective gasp of astonishment. The young woman rose to a standing position in the tank. With arms pointed upward, she revealed her flowing blond hair and her petite physique squeezed into a sequined one-piece body suit with a gaping hole in the midriff. The audience broke into spontaneous applause.

Cochran held out a hand to help Halstead climb out of the tank and down from the table, then he stepped to the side of the stage.

Halstead rhythmically danced to the beat of the music, then she came to a stop and broke into song, "You've got my heart/You know what I'm made of/You've got me flowing/Now drink up my love..." After several minutes of alternately singing and dancing with increasing intensity, the music reached its crescendo. Her acrobatic dance finale concluded with her on the stage floor in a full leg split with arms outstretched.

"Ladies and gentlemen," Cochran raised his voice to a fever pitch, "Let's hear it for Jennifer Halstead!" Profuse cheers and applause.

Cochran offered Halstead a hand up from the floor. Standing side by side, he was a full head taller than the singer. He paused to allow her to catch her breath, then he spoke into the microphone. "Jennifer, we at Bright Cup are thrilled that you've agreed to endorse our Bright Teen Cafés and our new line of Bright Teen drinks and snacks."

In her girlish speaking voice, which contrasted markedly from her full-throated singing voice, she responded, "Mister Cochran, I'm soooo excited to represent your company. I look forward to four years of actively promoting Bright Cup and Bright Teen, and I thank you for this precious opportunity to bring your products to my generation. I just loooove your Java Jive blend." She pointed a hand out toward the audience. "And I hope to see all of you..." She looked back and forth at the faces. "...well, maybe all of your kids..." Audience laughs. "...or maybe even your grandkids..." More laughs. "...during my upcoming concert tour, to be sponsored by Bright Cup Incorporated."

The audience applauded while Cochran helped Halstead climb back onto the table and into the glass tank. She crouched down inside the clear box. He picked up the black cloth from the stage and again draped it over the tank and table.

Cochran turned to the audience. "Everybody help me out with the abracadabra."

Most of the attendees flailed their arms in the direction of the box beneath the cloth.

After about 10 seconds, during which Cochran marveled to himself at the easily manipulated crowd, he counted down, "Three, two, one..." He grabbed a corner of the black cloth and yanked it away, exposing the now-empty glass tank.

The audience broke into another round of applause.

Cochran took a dramatic bow. "And now, ladies and gentlemen, I'd be happy to entertain your questions."

÷

Sitting at a banquet table near the rear of the ballroom, Hank Ridley of *Businessweek* tapped away at the Bluetooth keyboard for his iPad, feverishly attempting to capture his notes before they slipped his mind, "...wild ideas from Cochran. Impressive showmanship. Remains to be seen if the resulting business will be equally impressive..."

÷

Cochran pointed to a man with his hand raised on the left side of the room. An attendant jogged over with a microphone.

"Bob Mackenstein, from *San Francisco Chronicle*. I think what we'd all like to know, Matt, is how you got Jennifer Halstead to appear like that."

Cochran let out a wry smile. "How'd I get Jennifer Halstead to appear? I paid her a lot of money."

"What I meant was..."

"I know what you meant, Bob. The answer is: It was *magic*. And it was just as easy to do with the living, breathing Miss Halstead as it was with the inanimate Roastronic machine. But if I told you folks how it was done, it wouldn't be a secret anymore, would it? However, if you'd like to see the trick again, Miss Halstead will be appearing, and disappearing, at the grand opening of our first Bright Teen Café in The Mall Of America on October seventeenth."

He pointed to a woman on the right.

"Shameeka Johnson, from *The Wall Street Journal*. How much capital equipment expenditure will it take to outfit your shops with the Roastronics, Mr. Cochran? And how much savings do you anticipate in operating expenses at your regional roasting facilities as a result of installing these units at retail?"

He answered these and a dozen more questions regarding the announcements, but he avoided pointing in the direction of Tony Goterrez, who repeatedly raised his hand. Then Cochran began to close, "If that's all the questions for today, I'd like to thank..."

"Mister Cochran," an unamplified voice shouted from the back.

"Do we have another question?" Cochran waved in the direction of the voice, and an attendant brought over a microphone.

"Mister Cochran. Tony Goterrez of *Coffee Retailer News*."

"Ah, yes, Tony. It's always a pleasure to have your moustache grace our coffee cups."

"I hate to put a damper on your festivities, sir, but I just read this news story from Brazil, the world's largest coffee-producing nation." Goterrez pointed to his laptop. "The story, in this morning's edition of the Portuguese language newspaper *Correio Popular*, is about a previously unknown plant fungus that has already devastated one major coffee plantation and is spreading rapidly. This disease spoils the beans and kills the trees." Murmurs progressed through the crowd. "Scientists haven't found any means of stopping it yet. If it becomes widespread, it could ruin the nation's coffee trees for years to come."

As if they had been prompted by a conductor from the San Francisco Symphony, in unison, all the attendees glanced at their iPhones to check their Twitter streams. Seeing no mention yet of a new coffee fungus infestation in Brazil, they simultaneously began composing tweets about it. Over the next few minutes, their messages would go collectively to tens of thousands of their Twitter followers. Those messages would be retweeted again and again to millions, launching a wavefront of news, like sympathetic vibrations from an underwater earthquake reinforcing each other to generate a powerful tsunami that radiated in all directions. Later that day, *Correio Popular*'s web server would crash from traffic more than 20 times higher than its prior historical peak.

Cochran asked, "Do you have a specific question, Tony?"

"Are you aware of this development, Mr. Cochran? And if so, what will you do to ensure the supply of beans to your Bright Cup Cafés? A shortage of beans could leave you without product to sell."

Loud murmurs swept across the crowd.

Perfect, thought Cochran. *Absolutely perfect.* He motioned with his hands for people to simmer down, then he calmly said, "To answer Tony's first question, yes, we became aware of the situation in Brazil yesterday. And earlier today, I spoke by phone with our coffee buyer there for an update. He was on site at the very plantation described in that news article. He told me that the entire coffee plantation was now engulfed with the fungus, and the Vice President of Sales for the coffee grower told him, quote, 'demand could outstrip supply.'"

Murmuring increased further, then settled down as the audience waited for Cochran to continue.

"To answer Tony's second question, I'll note that Bright Cup stockpiles a sixty day supply of green beans in the warehouses at our roasting plants. Beyond that, we at Bright Cup cannot directly affect the production, or lack thereof, of coffee beans in Brazil, so we took the only practical action that we could. As soon as I heard of this threat to our supply, I instructed our staff to aggressively buy up additional arabica futures on the exchanges and to sign direct forward purchase contracts with multiple growers in Brazil and other nations.

"Bright Cup cannot do anything to stop such a destructive organism, but we have protected our supply interests to the fullest degree possible for as long as beans remain available. I guarantee you folks, and our loyal customers, that if a coffee bean shortage does occur, Bright Cup will be the *last* national chain of coffee specialty shops to run out of beans."

A flurry of hands shot up among the attendees. Cochran spent the next 15 minutes answering questions about the implications of the story. Goterrez chimed in at a few points, translating aloud portions of the newspaper article.

Finally, Cochran called a halt to the barrage. "Folks, I just got a signal from the hotel management that we're way over our allotted time. We've got to clear out of the room for another group coming in." He didn't mention that the next group consisted only of workers whose task was to disassemble the special stage. "But on behalf of myself and the entire staff of Bright Cup, thank you all for coming. And don't forget to pick up your bags of freshly roasted Primo Cup beans on the tables by the exits."

÷

Attendees gathered up their gear, then headed toward the doors.

Hank Ridley sidled up to Goterrez. "Hey, Tony. Got a second?"

"Sure, Hank."

Ridley pulled Goterrez out of the flow of moving people. "How'd you find out about that story? Do you check the websites of Brazilian newspapers on a daily basis, or do you get an RSS feed from some-where, or did someone forward you a link?"

Goterrez replied. "I occasionally check major Brazilian websites for coffee-related news, but I'd never seen anything from this *Correio Popular* before today."

"Then how'd you come across the article?"

"Before the press conference started, I was coming out of the men's room, and these two waiters were standing in the hallway, talk-ing in Portuguese about a new and nasty coffee plant disease in Brazil. I asked them about it in Portuguese. One of them told me I could find the news story on RAC-dot-com-dot-BR."

"Which waiter was that?"

Goterrez scanned the room, then pointed to a man coming out of the kitchen from behind an embroidered red curtain. "That one there. The tall guy with the eyeglasses."

"Thanks, Tony. See you around."

÷

Ridley spoke into his iPhone, "Find the coffee fungus article on RAC-dot-com-dot-BR."

The phone beeped twice, and the computerized Siri voice replied, "One moment please...," then a few seconds later, "I cannot find the article in English, but I have translated the Portuguese."

When Ridley finished reading the story on his iPhone, he headed straight for the waiter. "Excuse me," he said to the tall man.

"What can I get for you, sir?" the waiter asked with an accent that Ridley would not have identified had he not just had his prior conver-sation with Goterrez.

"Are you the waiter who told Mr. Goterrez..." Ridley placed a finger horizontally above his upper lip. "...about the coffee fungus story in Brazil?"

"Yes, sir."

"How did you find out about it?"

The waiter stiffened up and was slow to respond, then he said, "I was born in Brazil. I like to check the hometown news now and then."

"Really? It seems rather coincidental that you would mention a story in a minor newspaper about a coffee plant disease at a farm in Brazil in front of a guy who was probably the only Portuguese-speaking journalist here, right before a press conference where a CEO told the attendees that his company just invested in loads of coffee beans because of that same disease, one which nobody else in the roomful of industry professionals had heard about yet." Ridley reached into a pocket, then discreetly showed the waiter half a dozen $20 bills. "Or would you prefer that I ask your supervisor about the matter?" *Carrot and stick*, Ridley thought.

The waiter made a subtle motion with his hand. Ridley folded the bills and pressed them into the man's palm.

The waiter leaned in close and spoke in a low voice, "The man on stage at the beginning of the show, the one with the Indian name, he told me about the story. He said he wanted the man with the big moustache to see it because he knew the guy speaks Portuguese." Then the waiter dashed behind the red curtain back into the kitchen.

Ridley pondered why Parananda might have wanted Goterrez to see the story, leading him to surmise, *Something's fishy here in San Francisco Bay*. A moment later another concern dawned on him. *How the heck can I expense the money I just forked out to that waiter? I can't tell my editors I paid for information. I'll have to fish around for unused restaurant meal stubs and taxi receipts*. A moment later, yet another concern dawned on him. *What if the Brazilian coffee trees do get wiped out?*

On his way out of the ballroom, Ridley glanced around, then he grabbed two bags of coffee beans from the table. In the hallway, he opened them both to make sure they didn't contain Habanero peppers.

÷÷÷÷÷

Delcese Agricola issued a press release acknowledging the fungus in a portion of its coffee crops, stating that the company was "pursuing every available means of investigating and treating the infestation." It noted that Delcese had procured the services of Distinguished Professor Samuel Decker from Tufts University in the United States, and quoted Delcese CEO, Roberto Duarte, "I have every expectation that Professor Decker, working in conjunction with our highly skilled staff scientists, can quickly find a cure."

÷÷÷÷÷

Cochran was exiting the hotel when his mobile phone rang. The caller ID was from his coffee broker in New York. "Hi, Marla."

"Matt, all of a sudden, there's a lot of action on Coffee 'C' futures at the ICE, and the ask price has risen even higher than your heavy buying yesterday pushed it. I just heard it has something to do with a new and nasty coffee fungus in Brazil. You already knew about that yesterday, didn't you?"

He replied, "That's why I pay myself the big bucks."

Chapter 12

"Evil enters like a needle and spreads like an oak tree."

Ethiopian proverb

~~~~~

Larissa Júnior sat across the desk from *Doutora* Munhoz.

"I'm sorry your husband died, doctor. He was always very nice when I worked with him."

"Thank you, Larissa."

"Normally, I'd go to my own physician, but I decided to come and see you because I've been feeling ill on the job. I'm concerned that it might be something from the fungus that's being handled all over the lab now. I've been nauseous the last couple of days. I've been pretty tired. And I'm peeing an awful lot. Maybe I've just got myself a case of the flu, but it doesn't feel like any flu I've had before."

"Could be a few other things, too." Munhoz held up a specimen cup. "Can you give me a urine sample, please?"

When Larissa returned from the toilet, she handed Munhoz the container.

"Excuse me while I test this," Munhoz said, taking the sample into an adjacent room.

While she waited, Larissa stared at the farm safety informational posters on the walls. Feeling queasy, she closed her eyes.

Munhoz returned several minutes later, holding up a test strip. "Larissa, this is a test for HCG, human chorionic gonadotropin..."

Júnior, holder of a Master's degree in biochemisty, shook her head. "But that's not possible."

"Of course, this is preliminary," the doctor added. "You'll need to confirm it with a blood test. I suggest you make an appointment with your own physician. But it looks like you are *grávida*."

Júnior was speechless for a full 10 seconds. Then she said, "I have polycystic ovary syndrome. I found out I had it when I was a teenager. That's why I exercise like crazy, to fight off the tendency for obesity."

"Did you have sexual intercourse two to three weeks ago?"

The patient nodded. "But the PCOS makes me infertile. I can't be pregnant."

The doctor said, "Perhaps your view of your own fertility is in need of review."

÷÷÷÷

At the 2:00PM meeting of the senior scientists, Manling began, "We have confirmed that the sample Mr. Decker obtained from inside the wrecked airplane contains the new coffee fungus. And it's in an agar-based growth medium."

Decker said, "Paul may or may not have created the fungus, but the presence of the growth medium indicates he at least cultured it."

Manling added, "The other sample, by the way, contains dark chocolate with no apparent contaminants. I understand from Fabiana that Garoto *semiamargo* was one of Paul's favorites."

Next, *Doutora* Horton, the biochemist spoke up. "I believe I've made an important discovery." Everyone else looked up from taking notes or fiddling with their mobile phones. "After the meeting the other day when *Senhora* Hasse said she saw the parrot eating coffee cherries, something kept bugging me, but I couldn't put my finger on it." She held up a finger. "Then it finally dawned on me lying in bed at four o'clock this morning." She snapped her fingers. "The reason most parrots don't eat coffee cherries is because the caffeine is poisonous to them. When I got here this morning, I decided to run some quick tests on a few parts of infected plants: leaves, cherries, and beans, and sure enough, they've got very little caffeine remaining. I haven't determined the exact mechanism, but I believe that the fungus is metabolizing the caffeine from coffee plants."

Decker smacked himself in the forehead for the first time that day. "Of course! That's why Dr. Mendonça wanted to test this fungus, to produce a natural decaf. I should have thought of that sooner. It parallels the model I used to remove toxins from cacao, which explains why he was referencing some of my work. And cacao is also poisonous to parrots. It seems obvious now." He looked around the room. "Anyone else got anything interesting?"

Dr. Nestor said, "Since this morning's news, two more plantations have reported outbreaks of the fungus, one in São Paulo and one in Paraná. Neither of them are Delcese's. I think the phrase you Americans use is, the shit is hitting the fan."

Decker inquired, "This morning's news?"

Westphal responded, "You probably haven't seen this." She pulled out from her briefcase a *Correio Popular* newspaper and tossed it on the conference table. She gave Decker a two sentence summary.

Decker commented, "This story will become a distraction for all of us. I guess the news was bound to get out sooner or later. At least the expansion of fungal infestation will generate lots more data, some of which might prove useful. In the meantime..." He turned to Lucy.

"Tomorrow morning I want us to take an excursion in the small plane. We fly up to Fiorva to pick up Mr. Mabro. Then we go get an aerial look at the experimental fields where Dr. Mendonça was headed when the plane crashed. If anything looks interesting, we land at the airstrip out there and hike to the field to check it out up close. Then we head back to Fiorva, drop off Mabro, and talk to the worker Sergio. Then we fly back here."

Lucy replied, "And what'll we do with the rest of the morning?"

÷÷÷÷÷

Decker walked into the Centro de Saúde and sat in the waiting room while Munhoz finished with a patient.

After the patient left, Munhoz took off her lab coat and asked, "Where's your sidekick, Sam?"

"Lucy? I gave her a well-deserved break from me for the rest of the day. Your English is good enough that I think we can manage."

÷÷÷÷÷

Lucy sat at a computer terminal in the security office. She opened the database file containing ID card access records, and she entered search criteria to see all the entries into the lab between 5:00PM and midnight from May through the present. Almost all the technicians had at least one late access in the month before the plane crash. Six staff people had entered the lab after-hours several times each week. Only two, Felix Mina and Martina Hasse, had no late accesses during that period.

÷÷÷÷÷

Munhoz drove her Mercedes on the journey with Decker. They passed through the resort town of Águas de São Pedro, where Decker could smell the sulfur of the natural mineral springs that attracted both tourists and chemical engineers. They continued through the city of Piracicaba and onward to Campinas.

They parked in a lot outside *Hospital das Clinicas* (Clinics Hospital) on the premises of *Universidade Estadual de Campinas* (State University of Campinas), commonly known as UNICAMP.

÷

Miguel Silva lay on a bed with a feeding tube up his nose and a bandage on the right side of his head.

Even through the top sheet, Decker could see that the pilot's body was contorted as though he had been flash-frozen in the midst of a dance step. Decker had never seen a person in a coma before, and he was intrigued by the half-open eyes.

Munhoz checked Miguel's written chart, then noted his pulse and temperature on the electronic monitor. "He's stable," she said, "and at least he's off the respirator. But he doesn't appear to have progressed much otherwise since the last time I visited."

Decker removed the entire covering sheet from the patient, leaving Miguel in just a hospital gown. Picking up a hand and attempting to flex the arm, Decker noted that the arm muscles were still stiff. He put on his reading glasses to inspect Miguel's bare feet, after which he covered the man back up with the sheet.

"When you first examined Miguel after the plane crash, Fabiana, other than the obvious head trauma did you notice any cuts or gashes in the skin? Maybe ones that Miguel had incurred prior to the crash, perhaps days earlier? Any scabs or necrotic tissue?"

"No," she replied. "What are you thinking?"

"It's a long shot, based on something one of the lab scientists told me. Isn't extreme muscle stiffness like Miguel's a primary symptom of tetanus infection?"

"Yes."

"Have you tested him for it?"

"I considered the possibility of that infection at the outset of his treatment, but tetanus couldn't have come on as quickly as Miguel's symptoms. And I believe lab tests done by the hospital were negative for it. We can check with Dr. Barada. He's in charge of Miguel's care here. I was planning to speak with him next."

÷

Through an archway to the *Departamento de Ciências Neuro-lógicas* (Department of Neurological Sciences), Decker and Munoz proceeded to an office marked with a name plaque, "Barada, Nicholas Tomás, MD."

The elderly doctor was seated at a desk, with half-glasses perched on his nose, reviewing patient records. He pushed himself up from the chair for introductions, then he remained standing.

Munhoz asked Barada to explain Miguel's status and prognosis.

Barada responded in fluent but accented English, "*Senhor* Silva's progress has been limited. His skull fracture and related external wounds seem to be healing well. Superficially, he should be back to normal in a few more weeks. Regarding his comatose state, however, I've seen little progress."

Decker asked, "Could anything other than the apparent concussion, like a seizure of some sort, put Miguel into his state?"

"A massive stroke possibly could have produced the spasticity—that is, the muscle stiffness—evident in *Senhor* Silva. But we did a brain MRI, and it did not reveal damage consistent with a stroke. On the contrary, we found no brain damage at all. And on an EEG, his brain functioning appears normal for a sleeping person. His brain responds to stimuli, but his body does not. Such contradictions are not uncommon with comas, which medical science doesn't understand very well."

"Dr. Munhoz told me that Miguel was tested for tetanus."

"Yes, with his evident spasticity, we took an anaerobic culture from his skull wound, and ran the standard test for *Clostridium tetani* bacteria. That test came back negative. We also performed the ELISA immunoassay for tetanus antibodies. That test was positive, which is normal for anyone with an up-to-date vaccination. And records from his personal physician indicate he received a tetanus vaccination only three years ago. So I had ruled out that disease."

Decker said, "Please bear with me, doctor. How does tetanus cause muscle contractions?"

Barada gestured with his eyeglasses in his hand as he replied, "Technically, tetanus doesn't cause muscles to contract, it prevents them from relaxing. The disease usually starts with dormant spores introduced through a wound. Inside the blood stream, the spores germinate into live *C. tetani* bacteria which produce tetanospasmin, a neurotoxin which blocks the release of the normal inhibitory neurotransmitter gamma-Aminobutyric acid in the spinal cord and muscle nerve endings."

"And how would you treat someone with tetanus infection?"

"We can kill the bacteria with antibiotics, and we can remove the freely circulating toxin in the blood stream with tetanus immunoglobulin. But once the toxin affects a given nerve synapse, it cannot be induced to relent."

"The effects of tetanus are permanent?"

"No. Several weeks after infection, assuming the patient lives that long, the nerves regenerate sufficient presynaptic compounds to re-enable neurotransmission, and the patient begins to recover." Barada paused and ran a hand across the top of his balding scalp. "I admit that aspects of *Senhor* Silva's symptoms do strongly resemble the disease. He did have a high fever when he was admitted. And his muscles had little response to an injection of Baclofen, a powerful muscle relaxant we use for treating multiple sclerosis."

"Did you test Miguel for the presence of the tetanus toxin itself?"

Barada shook his head. "None of the hospitals where I've worked have a standard lab test for the toxin, just tests for the bacteria and antibodies. But *Senhor* Silva tested negative for the bacteria and positive for the vaccine antibodies." Barada raised his hands and shrugged. "I don't see how tetanus could be possible."

Decker continued to press the point. "Theoretically speaking, Dr. Barada, would it be possible to..." He carefully considered the choice of his next word. "...*acquire* the toxin by another means, such as injection or ingestion?"

"I suppose it could be injected in a serum, and it would only take a tiny amount, maybe just a pin prick. The pure toxin is quite toxic. I think the fatal dose is only a couple hundred nanograms. But ingestion, not likely."

"Why's that?"

"The scientific literature indicates that tetanospasmin does not pass through the mucous membrane of the digestive system. Besides, I don't know where someone would acquire the toxin. It's not kept anywhere other than at a few labs researching the disease."

"What if someone wanted to make the toxin?"

"To culture anaerobic bacteria *in vitro* would require a well-equipped biological laboratory. Tetanus disease itself isn't contagious, and the bacteria die if exposed to air, so a Biosafety Level Two lab probably would suffice."

Decker's eyebrows rose. "If someone were injected with the toxin, doctor, how long would it take for spasticity to appear?"

"That would depend on the magnitude of the dose. Normally, the bacteria take a week or more to produce enough toxin for symptoms to appear. If the toxin was injected, symptoms might appear in minutes. But I don't know of any cases of tetanus disease happening that way." Barada stopped, then he added as an afterthought, "...except for a couple of isolated cases mentioned in the literature of experimental lab workers handling the toxin and accidentally sticking themselves with hypodermic needles. In all my decades as a physician, I've never seen such a case myself. And I understand that *Senhor* Silva was a pilot, not a biology lab technician."

"Correct. Thank you for all your help, Dr. Barada. This has been most informative."

"And thank you for your continuing care of Miguel," Munhoz added.

÷

After they left Barada's office, walking down the main corridor of the hospital, Munhoz turned to Decker and asked, "Do you believe that Miguel was injected with tetanus toxin?"

"I think it's possible, Fabiana, and at this point I must stress that it's only a possibility."

Munhoz halted walking. "Then my husband's death might have been murder?"

÷

In the hospital lobby, Decker took out his mobile phone. "I need to call Mr. Manling. What's his number? Do I have to start with a one or a zero?"

"Allow me." Munhoz pulled the phone from her purse and dialed. When the line began ringing, she handed the phone to Decker.

"Delcese Agricola. *Como posso direcionar sua chamada?* How may I direct your call?"

"Tomás Manling, please."

After several rings, Manling's voice mail picked up. *I can't leave this on a recorded message*, Decker thought. Then another possibility occurred to him. *What if Manling is involved?* He hung up the line. *But if Miguel was infected deliberately, and if Dr. Barada is right about how long it would take for injected tetanus toxin to kick in, then it must've been one of two people: either the farmhand Sergio, or the lab scientist Larissa. Hmmm, which of them would be more likely to procure an unusual biological poison and inject a man with it? Not too hard to figure out. Besides, if the farm worker had wanted to bring down the airplane, he could have just sabotaged the plane. But if Larissa had done it, why would she have told me that Miguel looked like he had tetanus? Something doesn't make sense.*

÷÷÷÷÷

Lucy's last task before leaving work for the day was to stop and talk to Alberto, the second shift security guard at the video console. She asked him if he had seen anyone in particular working with Dr. Mendonça after hours.

He closed his hand and made a gesture at the back of his skull. He said, "*Rabo-de-cavalo.*" Ponytail.

÷÷÷÷÷

Dr. Barada's last task before leaving the hospital for the day was to find the head nurse on duty.

"Giselle, draw a vial of blood from Miguel Silva," he instructed, "and send it overnight to *Doutor* Neto at The Snake Farm, along with this sample and note." He handed her a covered glass petri dish and a sealed envelope.

÷÷÷÷÷

Getting back in the car, Munhoz suggested to Decker, "Do you want to stop for a drink? I need something to get my mind off that disturbing thought about what might have happened to Paul."

"OK," he replied. "I wouldn't mind if we grabbed a bite as well. I haven't eaten since breakfast."

÷

The small upscale restaurant, named *A Cidade Irmã*, contained a mix of university professors, high tech entrepreneurs, and agricultural executives. *From the appearance of the pastel artsy decor*, Decker thought, *this place could be in southern California.*

"The name means 'The Sister City,'" Munhoz explained once they were seated. "Campinas and San Diego are *as irmãs*."

Decker gave a nod of understanding.

"Perhaps if you're still here over the weekend, Sam, I can take you to someplace more sandy. No that's not the right word, more..." She ground her teeth together. "...more gritty... to give you a taste of the real Brazil."

Decker perused the drink list. "How's the beer in this country?"

"We have many German immigrants in Brazil. We even have our own Oktoberfest. Our *cerveja* is better than you might expect."

The waiter arrived to take their drink order. Munhoz suggested Decker try Antarctica Original as a typical Brazilian brew. She ordered a *caipirinha* for herself.

After the waiter left, Decker asked Munhoz, "What's the drink?"

"It's *um aperitivo* that's sticky sweet. It's based on *cachaça*, which is a liquor distilled from the juice of sugarcane. Then you add more sugar and a lime, and you've got a little peasant girl."

"Huh?"

"*Caipirinha*. The word means 'little peasant girl.'"

After the waiter brought the drinks, the pair raised their glasses, and Munhoz said, "*Saúde*."

"Which means...?"

"To your health."

"Of course." Decker smacked his forehead for the second time that day. "That word is above the doorway of your clinic."

They clinked glasses and sipped, then Fabiana licked from her fingertips the liquid that had sloshed over the rim of her drink.

Decker's mind drifted off. *If I wanted to poison someone, injection would be tricky to pull off without the person knowing something happened. Ingestion would be so much easier.*

Chapter 13

~~~~~

Including Duarte, who was a member of the Board, nine of the 12 Directors of Delcese Agricola were in the conference room, housed in the São Paulo offices of Raul Espindola's transportation firm.

Duarte began by summarizing the events of the past few weeks, including Decker's recent discovery in the wrecked airplane, and the uproar at that morning's meeting with the Associação Brasileira de Cultivadores de Café.

"...In light of these events," Duarte explained, "I asked *Senhor* Espindola to convene this extraordinary meeting of the Board. I'm concerned that Delcese Agricola may be on the cusp of financial catastrophe. I've led this company to fourteen consecutive years of growth. I've built it into a formidable force in Brazil's economy and in the worldwide coffee industry. It would pain me deeply for it all to collapse now due to factors out of our control." Duarte fought back tears.

One of the Directors, Hector Barnsião, stood up and went to the whiteboard on the wall. "Ladies and gentlemen, with all due respect to *Senhor* Duarte's many accomplishments, rather than respond to our situation emotionally, we must examine it logically. Let's consider two variables as a matrix."

Barnsião picked up a marker. He drew on the whiteboard a vertical rectangle, then one line through it vertically and two horizontally, forming six sections.

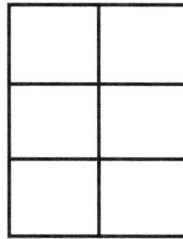

"First, either *Doutor* Mendonça did create this fungus, or he did not." Above the rectangle Barnsião wrote the words *nossa criação* (our creation), then *não* (no), and *sim* (yes). "Second, this fungus could stop soon, or it could continue to destroy all of Delcese's *fazendas*, or it could continue even further to destroy many others' *fazendas* as well." To the left of the rectangle he wrote the word, *destruição* (destruction), then the three words *parar* (stop), *nossas* (ours), and *delas* (theirs).

nossa criação

não   **sim**

parar

destruição

nossas

delas

"Let's consider each of these possibilities," Barnsião continued. "First, we will assume that *Doutor* Mendonça did not create the fungus. If it stops soon, our problems are still significant given the existing destruction, but they are limited. We will still have adequate crops to sell this year from our other *fazendas*. We will carry on and rebuild with only a modest drop in revenues and competitive position over the next several years while we wait for new trees to bear cherries at the infected plantations. Let's consider that our baseline situation." In the upper left section of the rectangle, he drew a dash. "If the fungus continues to destroy Delcese's other *fazendas*, we will be wiped out for several years. We could secure commercial loans to help replant our fields and rebuild our business, but by the time the crops return, our competitors will have displaced us in the market." In the appropriate segment, he drew two down arrows. "If the fungus continues to destroy everyone's *fazendas*, we will be in a financially difficult situation for several years, but so will all of our competitors. The Brazilian government would probably step in to help us all out." He drew one down arrow, then he stood back to examine the diagram.

"Now, let's consider the possibility that *Doutor* Mendonça *did* create the fungus. If the fungus stops soon, from the financial and competitive perspectives, the situation is no different than in the prior case where he did not create the fungus. If he did create it, that might increase chances of stopping it sooner, because the doctor could have left behind notes or records that haven't been discovered yet. But we can't count on that." Barnsião drew a dash in the upper right section. "However, if the fungus continues to destroy all of Delcese's *fazendas*, we will be even worse off than in the prior case, because we will have difficulty obtaining loans to rebuild the company. And we would probably face legal action from some of our own shareholders. We might be forced to seek acquisition." He drew three down arrows. "And if the fungus destroys everyone's crops, that will be the worst case scenario for us. We would lose our revenue stream and our customers. The government likely would step in to help our competitors, but not us. We would face lawsuits not only from our own shareholders, but from our competitors as well. And no reasonable company would want to acquire us." He drew four down arrows, then he stepped back to view the completed diagram.

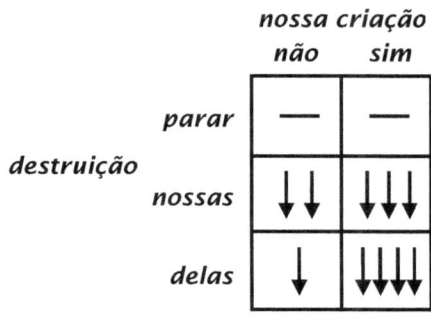

"In this case," Barnsião concluded, pointing to the lower right, "in all likelihood, the company would be forced into bankruptcy."

Espindola spoke, "Thank you, *Senhor* Barnsião, for your enlightening analysis." He motioned to the diagram on the white board. "This makes clear two aspects of our situation. First, we probably will end up worse off if *Doutor* Mendonça did create the fungus than if he did not. And second, if he did create it, we will end up worse off if our competitors' *fazendas* do succumb." He pointed to the lower right segment. "Ladies and gentlemen, we cannot allow that scenario to occur. Therefore, we must do everything in our power to prevent further spread of the fungus into our competitors' fields. I motion that, as suggested by the Associação de Cultivadores, we incinerate the infected crops in our *fazendas* at the earliest opportunity. We must actively try to prevent the fungus from further spreading. Then, if it does continue to spread to our competitors, we can truthfully say that we did everything we could. We even took this drastic step demanded by the Associação de Cultivadores. It will be a defensible position."

And, Barnsião thought, *it will help destroy the evidence.*

Duarte sat aghast as heads nodded around the room.

Barnsião then announced, "And I further motion that *Senhor* Duarte immediately suspend investigations on the part of his consultant Professor Decker. If *Doutor* Mendonça did create this fungus, we don't want to know. What we don't know can't hurt us."

Espindola added, "In an effort to make certain that no such evidence comes to light in the future, *Senhor* Duarte should destroy all of *Doutor* Mendonça's records. What no one can know can't hurt us."

Heads nodded again.

Another Director, *Senhora* Ana Bortos, sat quietly. *The obvious flaw in Barnsião's analysis*, she thought, *is that it fails to account for the differing probabilities that any of the given combinations would occur. But I'm not willing to risk my company shares that he's wrong.*

÷

After the meeting, Duarte knelt in a stall in the restroom, heaving up the contents of his stomach into the toilet bowl.

÷ ÷ ÷ ÷

Martina Hasse sat at the kitchen table in her apartment on the fifth floor of a high-rise in Piracicaba. The Formica surface of the table was covered with unfolded pages of newspaper. She placed the toy bird on top of the paper. She flipped open the metal lid of her art painting box, and took out several tubes of brightly colored acrylic paints. Using synthetic bristle brushes, she painted the Squawkie to resemble her memory of the parrot she had seen in the field weeks earlier.

"...Some blue over here... A little red over there..." When she was finished, she called out, "Gunter, come look."

Her husband padded into the kitchen in his slippers. "That's lovely, dear. You should submit it to the Carmen Miranda Museum in Rio." He jocularly jabbed her with an elbow.

"Say something into it, honey."

Gunter leaned toward the table and in an imitation Miranda voice said, "Bananas is my business."

Martina pressed a button, and the toy squawked back the phrase.

They both laughed so hard that their cheeks turned beet red, like those of the plastic bird.

÷ ÷ ÷ ÷

Tastefully furnished, Decker thought when he entered the living room of the townhouse condominium in the suburban neighborhood. *And a condo makes sense for a couple of busy doctors with no kids.*

Munhoz showed him to the room on the second floor that was set up as a combination home office/den/spare bedroom. The bed was strewn with books, papers, clothing, and assorted household detritus. "Please pardon the mess in here, Sam," she said. "I haven't been quite as tidy since Paul..." Her voice trailed off, then she continued. "Feel free to look around at anything here. In the meantime, would you care for a cup of coffee?"

"I'd love one," he replied, "especially if you have any of those handpicked beans from Delcese's shady little mountain farm. Lucy made a pot of that stuff on my first day here. Best coffee I've ever had."

"Sorry, I don't have any of those beans, but I do have some others that you might like to try."

Decker sat down in the swivel chair at the desk and turned on the computer. No log-in window appeared prior to the desktop screen, so he commenced looking through the files.

Fabiana soon returned with a cup of coffee in one hand and a silver foil bag in the other hand.

After he took a sip, Decker said, "This coffee is *muito bom.*"

"Your 'very good' is very good," she said.

"I've been studying my Portuguese phrases. I've got an Android app on my phone that pops up a new one every few hours." He took another sip. "In fact, I like this coffee even better than the stuff Lucy made the other day." A few more sips. "It's definitely a new winner for the best coffee I've ever had. What is it?"

Fabiana grinned. "It's from the wild plant known as *Coffea gracinha.*" She showed him the foil bag with the letter "G" handwritten in black marker on the outside.

"Gracinha? Of course!" Decker smacked himself in the head for the third time that day. "I should have guessed. Mr. Duarte told me about it. It's the one Paul named in your honor."

"Yes, and it's the only coffee Paul would drink since we discovered it several years ago. He hadn't consumed much recently though. He was conserving the supply. He was down to a few kilograms of the beans. The only known mature plants are in the small patch we found in the remote mountains. Last year Paul and I even hiked back to the spot he had marked in his GPS, and we retrieved more cherries. He was growing new plants in one of his experimental plots, but they're not yet mature."

"I consider myself honored to be served it."

Fabiana's smile faded. "It just occurred to me that the *Coffea gracinha* plants in Paul's experimental plot might be infected with the fungus."

"Do you know where the plot is located?"

"I think it's west of Fazenda Fiorva."

"That's the area I'm slated to check out tomorrow. But even Mr. Mabro at Fiorva didn't know what was in Paul's test fields. Maybe a couple of the lab technicians can identify some of the fields. Fabiana, do you know if Paul kept a map or a chart identifying what he was testing in the experimental fields?"

"Yes. In fact, it was a picture from above, from an airplane. I know I saw him with it somewhere." She gazed askance for a moment, then she realized where it was. "It was on this computer screen."

Decker put on his reading glasses, and within two minutes he had located a file called ExperimentalPlotMapWest.jpg.

He opened the file and issued the print command before he looked at the contents. Examining the output from the printer, it was an aerial photograph of the hectare plots, with notations of a few words typed on top of each field indicating plant variants and experiment names. He located a similar file ExperimentalPlotMapNorth.jpg and printed it as well. Then he located a file PlotExperiments.doc, which described the variables being tested at each field.

"These are exactly what I need," Decker said, looking over the prints. "But I don't see anything about a new fungus in his descriptions of the experiments." He folded the papers and slid them into his shirt pocket. "Paul must have been carrying the fungus in the plane to test it on one of the experimental fields. But which field? And why?" Decker smacked himself in the forehead for the fourth time that day. "At the status meeting this afternoon, Dr. Horton said she discovered the fungus was metabolizing caffeine." He pulled the papers back out of his pocket. "Maybe Paul was going to test it on all of them to see which variety would yield the lowest caffeine beans. And the lab technician Felix said the fungus itself tasted good. Maybe Paul was trying to use the fungus to alter the flavor of the beans." Decker took a sip from his coffee cup. "But wouldn't Paul have known that the fungus would destroy the plants? Something doesn't make sense."

"You can keep looking. I'll be reading a book on the couch in the living room downstairs if you need anything."

An hour later, he still had not located any files on the computer mentioning the new fungus. His mind wandering, he scanned the titles of the books on a shelf to the right of the desk. Amid the collection of scientific and medical reference books, old paperback novels, and travel books about South America, a tiny colorful picture on a book spine caught his eye. He tilted the volume out of the shelf.

He trotted down the stairs. "Fabiana, was Paul a birdwatcher?"

She looked up from the couch. "No. He liked nature, but he wasn't specifically a birdwatcher."

Decker showed her the book, *Os Papagaios do Mundo* (*The Parrots of the World*). She shrugged, not having seen it before.

He said, "Paul may have seen a parrot in the coffee fields, perhaps the same species spotted by *Senhora* Hasse, one of the lab scientists." Then Decker noticed two tiny slivers of silver foil stuck between the pages at the top of the book, apparently as bookmarks. He picked through the paper edges and opened to the first marked page. It had a picture of an olive green bird with orange coloration on its head and wings. Decker scratched his head. "This doesn't look at all like what *Senhora* Hasse described."

He held out the page to Fabiana. She translated the description for the bird, "The Jardine's Parrot, *Poicephalus gulielmi*, of central Africa. Habitat includes mountain forests and coffee plantations..." He pointed to the second mark, and she flipped to the page. The picture showed a smaller, bright green bird. "The Monk Parakeet, *Myiopsitta monachus*, only known species of parrot to build stick nests in trees rather than chambered earthen mounds..."

Decker spun around and ran back up the stairs. He immersed himself looking through the computer files again, but he found no reference to parrots. He searched the papers on the desk, a hodge-podge of scribbled notes, receipts, and photocopies of journal articles.

The next thing Decker remembered was waking up with his head resting on the computer keyboard.

Fabiana was tapping him on the shoulder. "Sam, it's getting late. I should take you back to Sede."

He straightened out his glasses and rubbed the side of his face where the keyboard had left an impression. "If you don't mind, I'd like to keep looking. If there's anything here about the fungus or the parrot, I'd really like to find it before I go to the experimental fields tomorrow. There's got to be something here somewhere." He waved his hands around the room.

"Then it will be too late for me to drive you back tonight. You'll have to spend the night here." She looked at the piles of stuff on the guest bed in the room. "I'll leave bedding for you on the couch in the living room. Goodnight." She started to walk away.

"*Boa noite*," he replied, then he added, "...and thank you, Fabiana. Thank you for all your help. With everything."

She walked back to him and put her hand on his. "Sam, if anyone in the world can figure out what happened to Paul, it's you. I'm sure I'll be thanking you one day soon."

After another half hour searching the desk, Decker's attention wandered, and his consciousness began to fade. He stretched his arms out and turned sideways in a yawn, and that's when he saw the scrap of paper. On the wall about two meters to the left of the desk, a cork bulletin board was crowded with papers held by pushpins. Among them was a torn-edged piece no larger than three centimeters a side. He got up from the chair to look at it closely. Three words were scrawled on the scrap, arranged in a triangle, with arrows pointing from each word to the other two. He pulled the pushpin from the cork and held up the paper, looking at the three words: *Café, Fungo, Ave.* Coffee, Fungus, Bird.

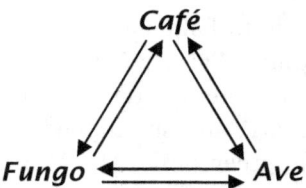

"Of course!" Decker narrowly missed poking himself in the forehead with the pointy end of the pushpin when he smacked himself for the fifth time that day. "The three-way symbiosis that Fabiana had mentioned." He mulled over the effects that the three might have on each other. "But I guess Paul misjudged the impact that the fungus would have on the coffee plants."

He slipped the piece of paper into his pocket and headed downstairs to the couch to get a well-deserved night of sleep.

Sprawled on the couch, staring at the shadows cast by the street-lights onto the ceiling, another thought prevented Decker from lapsing into slumber. *Why would anyone want to kill Paul over this?*

÷÷÷÷÷

Larissa Júnior lay on the couch in the living room of her apartment on the second floor of a brick home in Águas de São Pedro. A single woman such as herself would have been better off socially if she had resided in a more urban environment like Piracicaba rather than in the small town, but she never had been a social butterfly. Besides, she abhorred long commutes to work.

Leaning her head into the decorative pillow against the armrest, she stared at the ceiling fan rotating around and around.

This wasn't exactly in the plan, she thought. *What am I going to do? No matter what I decide, it will have a major impact on my life.* She rolled sideways and propped herself up on an elbow. *How will I tell him that I'm pregnant? And how will he react?* She sat upright. *First things first. I've got to get confirmation.*

÷÷÷÷÷

At Kraton Kupu Kupu, Zeger poked his head into the small office. "Brother Pyrrhus, any message from Sister Cleobaea?"

"No, Brother Goliath," Pukartra replied. "Nothing for two days."

Zeger kicked the side of the desk hard enough to leave a dent in the sheet metal.

Chapter 14

"Thieves take men's money, not their lives."

From *King Vikram And The Vampire*, a Hindu legend originally in Sanskrit, recorded and translated by Richard R. Burton, 1870

~~~~~

AUGUST 8

The largest news gathering organization and highest circulation newspaper in Brazil was *Folha de S.Paulo*. The word *Folha* (pronounced "Fol-ya") means "Sheet" or "Leaf," in this case referring to the newspaper's broadsheet size. Some in Brazil jokingly referred to the newspaper as *Falha*, meaning "Flaw." On this day, however, the paper might have been called *Olho*, or "Eye," as in Eye-In-The-Sky.

Folha had picked up news of the fungus from the previous morning's *Correio Popular* and the later press release from Delcese, then had devoted substantial resources to the story, including an investigative reporter, a financial reporter, a photographer, and the services of a small airplane.

Folha's article ran on the front page of its August 8th *Mercado* (Markets) section, headlined *"Novo Fungo Ameaça Safra Cafeeira"* ("New Fungus Threatens Coffee Crop"). It began with an aerial photograph of the plantation at Sede de Delcese Agricola, showing an eerie luminous red hue on row after row of coffee trees. The photo's caption noted that the picture was taken with a special infrared-sensitive camera to enhance the visibility of the fungus.

The *Folha* article stated that several additional plantations had become infected with the swiftly spreading microorganism. The article also included an analysis of the potential financial damage to Brazil's economy should the fungus not only wipe out the remainder of that year's crop but also kill off the trees, threatening the entire nation's coffee industry for years.

Folha published the complete article in Portuguese in its printed newspaper and in its *edição digital* for tablet and mobile download, as well as a condensed version of the story in Portuguese, Spanish, and English on the Folha.com website.

Within Brazil, many readers considered the *Folha* article to be sensationalized for the sake of selling papers and racking up online eyeballs. Outside of Brazil, reaction to the article was bordering on panic, especially among viewers who saw the supernatural red color of the fungus in the picture but not the caption describing its capture with a special camera. The aerial photo was seen by many worldwide as evidence of impending destruction of the coffee crop. The image was viewed and linked so many times that it soon became the top ranked result on Google when searching on the phrase "coffee fungus."

÷÷÷÷÷

Shortly after the dawn sky yielded to daylight, Martina Hasse again assembled her photo equipment in the coffee field. When the gear was ready, she pulled the wax paper wrapping off the painted toy bird. She chose a solid branch about one and a half meters off the ground and 10 meters away from her tripod, then she affixed the toy to the limb with duct tape around the feet. When she was satisfied that it would not come crashing to the ground, she pushed the buttons on its backside to set it into calling mode. She returned to her camera and focused the telephoto lens on the bird's position. She picked up the binoculars and began scanning the trees. Every 20 to 30 seconds the toy bird let out a synthesized squawk.

÷÷÷÷÷

Emerging from the minor traffic delay in a construction zone on the road out of Piracicaba, Munhoz drove the car faster than usual.

Decker said, "The plane is scheduled to leave at eight o'clock." He rubbed the beard stubble on his face and looked down at the clothes he had worn the entire previous day and slept in the previous night. "I was hoping to get in a quick shower and shave and a change of clothes before heading out for a day in the airplane."

Munhoz checked the clock on the dashboard. "If we're lucky, we'll still get you there in time for that."

But she hadn't anticipated the old man driving the decrepit old Cadillac in Águas de São Pedro. Without so much as a glance in her direction, he pulled out from a driveway directly into her path.

"*Idiota*," she grumbled as she blared the horn and slammed on the brakes.

Unfortunately, the other driver's reaction was also to step on the brakes. Munhoz's right front bumper contacted his left rear bumper. Fortunately, the Mercedes had decelerated enough and the impact was light enough that the airbags did not deploy.

They all got out to inspect the cars. No apparent damage had been done to her vehicle, but the old man's sustained an insignificant mark out of which he insisted on making a significant issue.

"As if it matters on that rusty piece of oversized junk you're driving," Munhoz said.

"*Senhora*, I've been behind the wheel of this fine automobile for nearly all of its kilometers, and I've never before had an accident. If you hadn't been speeding, that would still be the case."

"If you looked where you were going, that would still be the case."

Decker put a hand on Munhoz's shoulder. She took a deep breath then smiled at the old man.

The drivers exchanged pertinent information, and by the time they were back on the road, another 20 minutes had passed.

÷

Munhoz flashed her ID badge at the guard in the shack at the Sede entrance. When the Mercedes came screeching into the parking lot, Lucy was standing on the sidewalk in front of the Administration Building. Munhoz pulled the car up to the curb in front of her, and Decker jumped out.

"Sorry I'm late, Lucy. We got delayed playing bumper cars this morning." He motioned to the car as it pulled away, headed to a vacant parking space on the other side of the lot.

Lucy said, "Sam, I tried to get ahold of you earlier to tell you. I knocked on your door over an hour ago, but you weren't in. I asked at the desk in the Visitor's Residence, but their records showed you didn't access your room door last night..."

"That's because I spent the night at Dr. Munhoz's home."

"You spent the night with Dr. Munhoz?" Lucy's jaw fell open wide enough that an oral surgeon could have extracted her molars without prodding.

"No, no, I was on her couch. Well, she was on her couch first, while I was in the spare bedroom, then she was in her bed, and I was on her couch. I mean... Oh, never mind. What was it that you needed to tell me?"

The front door to the Administration Building opened, and Costa emerged. Lucy and Decker both turned his way.

"Come with me please, *Senhor* Decker," Costa stated in a manner that did not allow objection. "*Senhor* Duarte would like to speak with you. Now."

Lucy stayed on the sidewalk while Decker followed Costa inside.

÷

"Have a seat, Sam." Duarte motioned to the leather-clad guest chair opposite his desk. Costa closed the door on his way out.

"What's happening, Mr. Duarte?"

"Sam, I must deliver some bad news. Your consulting contract is terminated forthwith. You must immediately cease your investigations into this fungus and the death of Dr. Mendonça."

Decker was dumbfounded. "What? Why?" He stared down at the desk. "Does this have anything to do with me spending last night at Dr. Munhoz's home?"

Duarte raised one eyebrow but didn't say anything.

"I mean I just slept on her couch... Oh, never mind."

"Sam, last night the Board of Directors of Delcese Agricola held a meeting. Your investigation has already uncovered information that, if the fungus continues to spread, could make our corporation liable for hundreds of millions, perhaps billions of *reais*."

"That's all the more reason to continue my work, Mr. Duarte, to prevent further spread of the fungus."

Duarte shook his head. "If Paul engineered this fungus, or even if he only cultured it, Delcese could be held responsible for damage to other growers' coffee crops."

"Then you just want to cover up the truth?"

"I would describe it more as though the Board has decided that we do not want to discover the truth."

"You want to play ostrich?"

"I can assure you, Sam, that I would prefer not to be *um avestruz*. However, the Board has made this decision for me. My hands are tied."

"But, Roberto, the situation is more complicated than any of you know. It's probably even more complicated than I know. For starters, I believe that Miguel the pilot might have been poisoned, which might have been done to kill Paul in the plane crash. And someone might be growing tetanus bacteria in your lab to produce a dangerous toxin. You've got to warn Mr. Manling. He's got to search the lab."

"Do you have evidence of this, pointing to who might have done these things and why?"

"I don't have evidence yet." Decker smacked the top of Duarte's desk with his hand. "But I'm so close, I can smell it. All I need is a day or two more to blow this whole thing wide open."

"I'm sorry, Sam, but I can't allow you to continue. Mr. Costa can investigate whether any criminal wrongdoings may have occurred, and he'll call in the authorities if necessary. You may retain the balance of the payment we've already made for your services, and I remind you that your confidentiality agreement remains in effect."

"What about the fungus? How are you going to stop it?"

"We're going to incinerate all the infected fields."

"But if the fungus transmits via air, that might not stop it. Some of the dormant spores could survive the burn and get blown around. You can't just suck all the air back into your plantations. You've got to find a scientific solution to the fungus problem."

Duarte stood up. "This is no longer a scientific problem, Sam. It is a business problem."

Duarte's remark got Decker pissed off for the first time that day.

÷

Costa escorted Decker out the front doors of the building toward Lucy, who was standing next to a cart with his luggage loaded aboard.

"I need your ID card, please," Costa said.

Decker handed it over, then Costa turned back into the building.

Lucy patted Decker's bag. "I think I packed everything you had. The helicopter is waiting to take you to São Paulo. Here's your flight reservation back to the States." She handed him an envelope.

"Lucy, I think I've figured out what happened. Remember what Larissa Júnior said yesterday about tetanus? I think Miguel the pilot was poisoned with it. I think the poison was made in the lab here. And it may still be around. I need to talk to Dr. Westphal, and I need to talk to Mr. Manling about it. And I need to talk to Dr. Munhoz before I go."

"Sam, I've got orders to take you straight to the helicopter. And I don't think I'll be able to help. Mr. Costa already assigned me to other duties." She looked away. "We'd better get going."

After he climbed into the helicopter, the last thing Decker said to her was, "Lucy, if I'm right, people could die. If you find anything, talk to Dr. Munhoz. I trust her."

Lucy looked up at him. "I'll see what I can do." She closed the helicopter door and turned back toward the Administration Building.

÷÷÷÷

Instituto Butantan is a serious—some might say deadly serious— biological science institute on an 80 hectare parcel of a former colonial era *fazenda*, adjacent to what is now *Universidade de São Paulo*. It's operated by the State government to research infectious diseases and produce medicines for public health. Among its other distinctions, Instituto Butantan is one of the world's major suppliers of anti-venoms for treatment of snakebites, such as those of *Crotalus durissus* (rattle-snake) and *Bothrops atrox* (fer-de-lance).

The production of anti-venom involves injection of small amounts of the venom into a host animal, typically a horse, then subsequent extraction of antibodies produced in the bloodstream in response to the toxin. In order to produce snake anti-venom, one must have snake venom, and to have snake venom, one must have snakes.

To enable industrial scale production of anti-venom, Instituto Butantan includes facilities for breeding and housing thousands of snakes. It also features several museums, a huge outdoor *serpentário* (snake pit), and numerous other displays viewable by the public. These enticements have made the hard-core scientific institute paradoxically also one of the most popular tourist attractions in the city of São Paulo, and bestowed upon it a nickname: The Snake Farm.

÷

Doutor Fábio Neto, head of the *Laboratório de Bioquímica e Biofísica* (Biochemistry and Biophysics Laboratory), entered his office in a research building at Instituto Butantan. Neto, who was approaching his planned retirement, had sported for four decades a naturally bald scalp accompanied by a goatee beard, and as such found amusing the more recent fad for similar hair styling among younger men.

Before he had a chance to get seated at his desk, an assistant carried in a small cardboard box with red stickers on its exterior noting *Sangue Humano* (Human Blood).

"This courier package arrived for you this morning, *Doutor* Neto."

"*Obrigado*," Neto replied, taking the box he had been expecting.

He sliced open the sealing tape and removed the glass vial and petri dish that were packed in bubble wrapping. He read the letter in the enclosed envelope, reiterating what *Doutor* Barada at UNICAMP had told him over the phone. He set down the letter on his desk, and he carried the box with the samples out the door. He walked to an adjacent building, to the office of *Doutora* Helen Strath, in *Seção de Vacinas Anaeróbicas* (Anaerobic Vaccines Section).

The 36-year-old Strath was exceptionally tall at 190 centimeters (about 6 feet, 3 inches). At that height, with her long wavy red hair and freckled pale skin, she literally stood out among women in Brazil. Combined with the almost unheard-of Australian accent to her spoken Portuguese, she looked and sounded so foreign that small children peeked at her from behind their mothers' legs when she went among the public areas at The Snake Farm.

Strath was typing on her computer when *Doutor* Neto appeared in her doorway.

Neto liked to practice his English when he talked to her. "Good morning, Helen. I have an unusual request."

After eight years in Brazil, Strath didn't get to use her own English often enough. "Good morning, doc. What's your request?"

Neto held up the box. "I'd like to have these two human blood samples tested for both *Clostridium tetani* bacteria and tetanospasmin toxin." He set down the box on her desk.

"That request isn't so unusual."

"It might become unusual if the results are what my colleague at UNICAMP hospital speculates they could be. The samples are from a live patient."

Strath didn't press for details. "I'll assign a lab tech to it *o mais rápido possível.*" ASAP.

Two minutes later, Strath stood up to take the box to the lab. Before she left her office, she popped several bubbles in the wrapping material.

÷÷÷÷÷

"You did *what* to Decker?" Westphal screamed at Duarte in his hastily arranged meeting with the senior scientists.

"I had no choice. The Board of Directors dictated this course of action. Incineration must commence *o mais rápido possível....*"

÷÷÷÷÷

Larissa Júnior stepped out of the doctor's office building in downtown Piracicaba. Her *ginecoligista* had been almost as surprised as the patient had been the previous day. *At least I know for certain,* Larissa thought. *Now what am I going to do?*

Instead of returning to her car, she sat down on a bus stop bench, watching the *mendigos* (beggars) and businesspeople pass by, listening to the sounds of traffic swirl in her consciousness. Tires screeched and fenders bent in the intersection directly in front of her. Numerous horns honked as impatient drivers became delayed by the accident. *Do I really want to raise another human being in this mess? I need time and a place to think.*

She got up and walked two blocks to the branch office of Banco Santander Brasil on Rua 15 de Novembro. She went inside the bank to a live teller—something she hadn't done in years—because she wanted to withdraw more cash than the ATM outside would allow.

On the sidewalk alongside her car, she placed a call on her mobile phone. After she heard the voice mail recording, she left a message, "Mr. Manling, this is Larissa. I need to take some vacation time, starting immediately. I'm not sure exactly when I'll be back. I apologize for the extremely short notice, but I have a personal medical emergency." She hung up the line, then she powered off the mobile phone.

÷÷÷÷÷

When the helicopter landed at Guarulhos Airport at 10:30AM, ground crew led Decker into the general aviation terminal. On the shuttle ride to the main terminal, Decker opened the envelope containing his plane reservation, then he got pissed off for the second time that day. He didn't mind that the seat was in Economy class, although that added a touch of insult to injury. What irked him was that his flight back to the U.S. didn't depart until 11:00PM that evening, a wait of more than 12 hours.

÷÷÷÷÷

Delcese workers at Sede, Fazenda Fiorva, and Fazenda Madrigal all began uprooting and clearing away coffee trees from the perimeters of the fields. They used bulldozers, dump trucks, and other pieces of harvesting and construction equipment to create buffer zones to prevent the planned fires from spreading beyond the desired incineration areas. At Sede, extra care was needed to make sure the fires wouldn't reach the highly flammable sugarcane.

÷

Martina Hasse heard the rumble of equipment long before she saw it. *Damn*, she thought, *no bird will show up now with that racket going on.*

A backhoe approached from the far end of the row, its driver waving at Hasse to get out of the way. She stood up, but did not otherwise move. The vehicle halted, and the operator shouted something at her. She cupped a hand behind her ear. He shut off the engine.

"*Senhora*," the operator yelled down from his seat, "you must move. I'm under orders to clear away these coffee trees."

Hasse protested, "I'm here with direct authorization from *Senhor* Duarte."

"You can move over a few rows, and you'll be out of the way."

"I need to be right here." She pointed to her camera tripod. "I'm waiting to take pictures of a parrot in that tree." She pointed to the branch on which the Squawkie bird toy was perched.

The operator gave her a look as though she was insane.

"It's a long story," she attempted to explain, "You see, there's this parrot that may be carrying around the fungus, so I have this decoy set up here to attract the other parrot..." As if on cue, the toy bird let out a synthetic squawk.

"*Senhora*, I've been working this field for years, and I've never seen a parrot here..."

Just as the words were escaping his lips, a large blue parrot with red trim came flying into the field and alighted on the tree branch, next to the plastic creature. Both Hasse and the machine operator gawked in disbelief. Hasse came to her senses after a second, and she grabbed the remote shutter release cord for her camera. She pushed its button and continued to hold it down, the camera's motor drive rapidly clicking. The bird pecked at a coffee cherry, then a few seconds later, it fluttered its wings and flew away. Another second later, the camera's motor stopped, having exposed the last frame on the roll of film.

"*Senhora*, I'll come back for these trees in an hour, after I've cleared away the other side of the field."

÷÷÷÷

Melissa Herrar spent the better part of her morning returning phone calls to journalists she had been avoiding the previous two days.

"Delcese will incinerate the infected coffee fields," she boasted into the telephone. "We're inviting the press to come and observe our company's extraordinary willingness to sacrifice our own crops for the good of the national coffee industry. The fires will begin promptly at ten AM tomorrow..."

÷÷÷÷÷

At the terminal doorway for United Airlines, Decker was carrying in his bags, and a woman in front of him dropped a passport. When he stopped to pick it up for her, someone bumped into his backside. He glanced behind at a boy 10 or 12 years old, although he didn't give the occurrence any thought. He handed the passport back to the woman and proceeded into the terminal.

At the check-in counter, Decker showed his printed itinerary to the agent and explained that he wanted to see if any earlier flight was available.

The agent looked at his final destination, and without entering a single keystroke on her computer, she said, "I can get you out of São Paulo sooner, sir, but you won't arrive in Boston any earlier. You're ticketed on the non-stop to Newark. All the non-stops to the United States are evening flights. I could route you through Rio on the eight-fifty PM to Houston, but with the long layover there, you'd still end up in Boston an hour and forty-three minutes later than your existing itinerary."

Decker shook his head. "How do you know all that without looking on your thingamajig?"

"Perhaps after hundreds of people had asked you the same question, sir, you'd know the answer off the top of your head, too."

"Can I at least check one of my bags?"

"I'm sorry, sir. I can't do that until three hours before your flight. Security regulations."

"OK. Thanks then. I'll be back later." He reached for the itinerary.

"I can check you in, though, sir, to lock in your seat assignment. Aisle or window?" Her fingers blurred across the keyboard.

"Aisle seat from here to Newark, then a window to Boston."

"Aren't we picky? May I see your passport, please?"

Decker reached into his right rear pocket, but it was empty. *That's funny*, he thought, *I could have sworn I put my passport and wallet in that pock...* "Shit," he blurted out.

"Is there a problem, sir?"

"Uh, I uh, think I..."

"*Um carteirista?* A pickpocket, sir?"

Decker got pissed off for the third time that day.

÷÷÷÷÷

Sitting on the bed in her apartment, Larissa Júnior considered her impromptu vacation plans. *Where do I want to go for a getaway?* she thought. *I could go to Rio. No, too many people... I could rent a cabin up in the mountains. No, too remote, and what if I need any medical attention?* She patted her belly. *I've got it. It's perfect. It will be totally relaxing. I've snuck into the place enough times before, but I've never stayed there as a paying customer. It might cost me a little more than I should spend, but I've been saving plenty of money for years, and it won't cost me anything at all to get there. Why not?*

She filled a duffel bag with clothes, and placed her laptop computer and several books in a small backpack. She put on the backpack, picked up the duffel bag, then went down the stairs and out the door. Instead of stopping to load the gear into the trunk of her car, she kept on walking.

÷÷÷÷÷

Decker sat in a security office in the airport terminal explaining to the uniformed officer what he believed had happened, including a description of the boy, noting the red color of his sneakers.

The officer eyed Decker with a degree of skepticism. With his wrinkled clothes and unshaven face, the would-be passenger looked like he might have been a vagrant who had just woken up from sleeping on a bench, perhaps a pickpocket himself, although he was more well-spoken than the average homeless person.

"We get many victims of pickpockets here, *senhor*. I'll file *um boletim de ocorrencia*, an official report. However, the culprit is probably far away by now. It's very unlikely that we'll be able to recover your wallet and passport."

Decker got the feeling that the man had no intention of expending any effort in that direction.

The officer asked, "Do you know your passport number, *senhor*?" "We could contact the American Consulate here to see about providing you with temporary paperwork to reenter the United States."

Decker thought for a moment, then dug through this briefcase and pulled out a sheet of paper.

The officer read the paper multiple times, then said, "Please wait here, *senhor*."

The officer left the room. He returned a few minutes later with another officer whose uniform bore the word *Imigração* on a patch on the sleeve.

The two officers spoke back and forth in Portuguese. It seemed to Decker as though they were debating what to do. Finally, the first officer left the room.

The *Imigração* man turned to Decker and said, "*Senhor* Decker, I'm Officer Vieras. I see from this paper that you are here at the invitation of the Brazilian Ambassador to the United States. I can assure you that we will pursue every means of recovering your stolen items. We would be profoundly embarrassed to have a distinguished guest such as yourself return to his home country without his possessions and with horror stories about our fine nation."

And the Ambassador would probably ream a few people new anal orifices, Decker thought.

Within two minutes, the first officer returned, yanking the young perpetrator by the ear. Vieras spoke sharply to the boy, and the youth reached into his pocket to retrieve the wallet and passport. The immigration officer grabbed the items from the boy, then graciously handed them to Decker.

Vieras asked, "Do you want that we should punish this criminal offender, *Senhor* Decker? If we let him go, he'll be right back on the sidewalks prowling for more unsuspecting travelers. We could detain him and attempt to locate his parents."

Decker said, "Ask the boy his name, please."

To Decker's surprise, the child answered directly in English. "My name is Benito, mister."

Decker looked up at the wall clock, which showed a quarter to noon. He said to the boy, "I have an idea for suitable punishment. I propose that you serve a sentence of giving this visitor a tour of São Paulo city this afternoon."

Benito responded enthusiastically, "Yes, mister. I'll take you for a tour of our city. I know many fun and interesting places."

"That is unwise, *senhor*," Vieras said. "He'll just take you for a ride to rob you again."

"No. I will watch out for you, mister. I will make sure the other pickpockets give you no problem. I will protect you." From under the straggly blond hair, Benito beamed a glorious smile.

"We have a deal, Benito. My name is Sam." Decker reached out and shook the boy's hand. "But first I need to make a few phone calls."

Vieras offered him the use of the phone on the desk and storage of his bags in the office, then left the room. The first officer waited outside the door with the boy.

Decker called his daughter Evelyn, and he left a message ending with, "...I'll be back tomorrow."

Then he called Munhoz's office, leaving a message, "Fabiana, I've been summarily dismissed by *Senhor* Duarte. Apparently evidence I discovered that Paul cultivated this fungus could cause massive financial problems for the company. I'm not sure what you can do about the possible tetanus situation, but the only two people there that I trust besides yourself are Lucy and Westphal. I'll try to call you back later."

Then he called Westphal, who caught him off guard by answering her office phone.

"Sam, I found out what happened. The whole situation is horrible. Duarte is having all the fields burned down."

"Wendy, listen carefully. I believe that Miguel the pilot may have been deliberately infected with tetanus or some similar disease."

"What?"

He went on to elaborate what information he had.

"What would you like me to do, Sam?"

"If I had more evidence, the most logical approach would be to have Mr. Manling search the lab. Unless, of course, he's involved. How well do you know him?"

"Very well." She paused. "We've been sleeping together."

Decker thought, *What if they're both involved? But, if that was the case, she wouldn't have told me what she just did.* "For now, you and Manling should keep your eyes open for suspicious behavior or unidentified substances around the lab."

÷ ÷ ÷ ÷ ÷

Only two kilometers from her home, Larissa Júnior spun through the revolving door under the authentic 1940s art deco sign for "Grande Hotel," into the busy grand foyer at the foot of the grand staircase.

The young man at the reception desk asked, "Do you have *uma reserva, senhora?*"

Because he had used the term for Mrs. rather than Miss, it took Larissa a moment to realize that he was speaking to her rather than to another woman standing nearby. *I guess they don't have too many single women checking in by themselves here,* she thought, *and I'm not exactly a young chick anymore.* "No, I don't have a reservation," she said, "but I'd like your least expensive room for a week or more."

The clerk ran his finger up and down the computer screen, then he offered her a package rate.

She gulped. "That's your least expensive?"

"Afraid so, but it's inclusive of all meals."

After entering her requisite information in the computer, he asked, "Would you like me to summon *um carregador* to assist with your baggage, *senhora?*"

"No thanks. I'm self-sufficient. And it's *senhorita*."

Larissa hoisted her bags and ventured into her temporary new home away from home.

When she entered her room, she started to take her laptop out of the backpack, but then she stopped. *No. I'm here to get away from everything. I should have left the laptop at home.*

She unpacked the duffel bag, then went out for a jog.

Chapter 15

"No Comment"

Title of an art exhibit in New York City inspired by the Occupy Wall Street protest movement, 2011

~~~~~

The August 8th print and online editions of major U.S. news organizations, including *The New York Times*, *The Wall Street Journal*, and CNN.com, prominently featured articles on the front of their Business sections about the coffee fungus in Brazil and the rise in coffee futures contract prices. Several articles included the quote from Matthew Cochran that Bright Cup would be the last national chain of coffee specialty shops to run out of beans. A few mentioned that Professor Samuel Decker was involved in investigating the fungus, a tidbit gleaned from the Delcese press release (unaware that Decker had been axed from the project).

The *WSJ* also ran a commentary by Shameeka Johnson about the potential impact of a coffee shortage in Brazil on the U.S. economy. Her article included the statement, "...a significant supply shortfall would grind to a halt the productivity gains of the past year and be devastating to the positive economic momentum rebounding from the recession of recent years."

While not the top headlines of the morning, the articles were sufficient to entice television and radio news programs to mention the stories, which then jump-started response by the American public.

By noon Eastern time, 9:00AM Pacific, the public response had already fueled the leading edge of the next iterative news cycle.

÷

Matthew Cochran switched on the TV panel on the office wall.

"...This is Karen Fellows, Channel Four News. I'm outside a Bright Cup Café in Phoenix. Excuse me, ma'am..." She waved to a woman emerging from the shop with a large bag under her arm.

"Have you heard about the possible shortage of coffee?"

"Yes I have."

"And what's your reaction?"

The woman opened the bag she was carrying and tilted it toward the camera. "I just bought ten pounds of beans. I'm gonna make sure we don't run out in *my* household."

Cochran pressed a button on the TV remote to change channels.

"This is Kelly Small, CNN Financial News, in New York. Coffee futures prices continue to rise today on the IntercontinentalExchange. Contracts for September and December delivery are up twelve percent and fifteen percent respectively since yesterday's close..."

Next channel.

"...I'm here with grocery store manager, Gabe Preston. I understand Mr. Preston, that you've instituted a limit of five pounds of coffee per customer in your store..."

Truck Macklin rolled into the office. Cochran shut off the TV.

Macklin held up a laptop computer. "I've been looking at numbers from this week's futures contract purchases and your direct deals, Matt. These buys add up to a hundred thirty-two million dollars. I only gave you clearance for forty-two million."

"I leveraged us further. I told you I wanted nine figures."

"But we don't have bank backing to cover a hundred thirty-two million in new contracts."

"You worry too much, Truck. We won't have to cover them. Take a look." Cochran swiveled the LCD panel around on his desk and pointed to the screen. "At BM&F our contracts are already up sixteen percent, and on the ICE, they're up twenty percent."

"Jee-zus, Matt. Let's sell to take the profits."

"Prices have hit daily maximum fluctuations at the BM&F, and they're still rising at the ICE. We'll wait until tomorrow, to let them kick up again. Then, we'll start selling. We'll dump the exchange contracts, including a portion of the ones we already had. Plus, some of the growers have called me looking to buy themselves out of the direct contracts because our competitors are now offering them even higher prices. At the rate things are going, we'll clear a profit of at least thirty million. That's thirty mil net, straight to the bottom line. If we could do that every week, we'd be earning a billion and a half bucks a year, putting us squarely on the list of the most profitable corporations in America." Cochran clicked the mouse. "And Bright Cup's own share price is up seven percent today. When we present our quarterly results in a couple of months, the stock will shoot up again."

"I've got to hand it to you, Matt. It looks like you've pulled off another magic trick."

"I bet you didn't think I could fit a bull up here." Cochran held up his arms in the magician's nothing-up-my-sleeves display.

Macklin started to spin his chair around, then stopped. "But what if the shortage is real? If we sell off the contracts, we could get caught short on beans in a few months."

"Pasco's source at the plantation in Brazil said the fungus will be history in a matter of days."

"You're willing to bet our business on the word of a kid Pasco ran into in the men's room while taking a leak?"

"I've bet it on slimmer evidence in the past. Besides, I talked to Pasco a little while ago. He says that the growers are going to burn all the infected fields tomorrow."

"If the fungus is destroyed, won't that dry up futures demand?"

"When pictures of flaming coffee fields hit TV news, the public will panic even more, taking it as a sign that a shortage is imminent. That's why we have to sell everything we can tomorrow, when demand peaks, before everyone realizes that the fungus is toast."

Rami Parananda entered just as the CFO was leaving. The VP of Marketing closed the door then remained standing. "Matt, we've got a serious problem."

"What is it?"

"A phone message from a journalist." Parananda went to the speakerphone on Cochran's desk and punched in a lengthy sequence of buttons to access the voice mail for his own extension.

"Please try again," the automated voice on the speaker said. Parananda punched the buttons again. "Please try ag..."

Parananda grunted, "Goddamned phone system." He tried a third time, which finally succeeded and enabled him to replay the message.

"Hello, Mr. Parananda. This is Hank Ridley of *Businessweek*. I was at your little magic show yesterday. I have a couple of questions. Among other things, I talked to the waiter who told Tony Goterrez about the coffee fungus news story in Brazil. I was wondering if you'd care to comment..."

Parananda pushed a button on the phone to hang up the voice mail. "Matt, we're fucked."

"Rami, you don't know how much or how little he knows."

"He's already talked to the waiter. What do you want me to do? Should I just give him a 'no comment'?"

"That would be like pleading the Fifth Amendment on the witness stand. It's like waving a flag that says, 'I'm guilty, but you can't prove it.' No, you can't give him a 'no comment.' You just have to not give him a comment. Don't return his call."

"But aren't we better off putting our own spin on it?"

"Not until we know what cards Ridley is holding."

Parananda rubbed his chin. "I could talk to him to feel him out."

"That may be riskier than chancing it on what he already knows."

"Since when are you risk-averse, Matt?"

"Good point." Cochran smirked. "Maybe I should talk to Ridley."

Parananda crossed his hands back and forth. "Then he'd know for sure something was wrong."

"All right, Rami. You talk to him. But tiptoe around his questions. Your mission is to get him to tip his hand, not to tips ours. And whatever you do..."

"...Yeah, I know. Don't give him a 'no comment.'"

÷÷÷÷÷

Decker and Benito rode an airport shuttle bus on the 20 kilometer journey from Guarulhos into São Paulo city.

"How old are you, Benito?"

"Twelve."

"Shouldn't you be in school right now, or are you out on summer vacation, or rather, winter vacation?"

"This is the last week of winter break before school starts again. I don't learn much in school anyway. I learn more on the streets. The teachers in school are stupid."

"Oh?"

"For example, the math teacher. He asked the class a question, 'If the exchange rate was two *reais* to the U.S. dollar, and you had ten U.S. dollars, how many *reais* could you get?' I said fifteen *reais*. He said I was wrong, you could get twenty *reais*. How can I learn anything from him?"

"Benito, two times ten equals twenty."

"Of course, but you have to subtract the five *reais* it costs to get it exchanged at *o câmbio de moeda*. Nobody changes money for free."

Now there's a kid, Decker thought, *who truly understands money. I should get him to manage my stock portfolio.* "The school teachers seem to have done a good job teaching you English."

"I already knew English before they tried to teach it to me."

"Don't tell me you learned to speak this level of English on the streets of São Paulo."

"No, I learned it watching pirated American TV shows."

Decker thought, *How is that possible? His English is better than most of what's on TV.*

The bus pulled into the Centro terminal. When they stepped off, Decker asked, "Where to first, Benito?"

"Do you like creepy creatures, Mister Sam?"

"Yes. In my regular job, I deal with administrators every day."

"Good, then I know the perfect place to go."

Benito led Decker to a municipal bus for the destination Butantã.

÷÷÷÷÷

"Hello, Ridley here."

"Hi, Hank. This is Rami Parananda from Bright Cup."

"Hi, Rami. Thanks for returning my call. Your press event was great yesterday. Best food, coffee, and live entertainment in town, as is always the case with Bright Cup."

"We aim to please the press, Hank."

"Speaking of press, something was bugging me right after the event. I was wondering how Tony Goterrez heard about the coffee fungus story in a minor newspaper in Brazil. When I asked him, he said one of the waiters at the hotel told him about it. And when I asked the waiter, he said you told him about it."

If I deny it, Parananda thought, *that would be calling the waiter a liar. And what reason would the waiter have to lie?* "That's right. I told him about it."

"Why?"

"I knew the caterer had a couple of Brazilian waiters, and I heard one speaking Portuguese, so I thought he'd like to know about it."

"The waiter told me that you instructed him to tell Tony Goterrez about the story. Is that true?"

"I merely suggested he might pass it along to Tony because I knew Tony speaks Portuguese, too."

Ridley continued, "I've been pondering why Bright Cup's VP of Marketing might have wanted Goterrez to find out about the story then and there. The only reason I can think of would be to get him to ask about it at the event. And the only reason I can think of that you'd want that to happen would be to give Mr. Cochran the opportunity to talk about the fungus and the possible coffee shortage."

"I think your imagination is getting the better of you, Hank. It was our own press conference. If we'd wanted to talk about something, we would have just talked about it. That's what press conferences are for."

"I considered that possibility. But then I got ahold of a broker on the IntercontinentalExchange in New York, who talked to me on condition of anonymity. He told me that the day before the press conference, Bright Cup's broker purchased for your company's account the maximum limit of Coffee 'C' contracts on the ICE. And, I'm guessing your broker in Brazil did the same on the exchange down there. With all the news coverage today about the coffee fungus in Brazil and a possible shortage of beans, including juicy quotes from your CEO, those contracts are all way up in value since you bought them. Plus, one of your competitors told me he can't place orders for arabica beans directly from the major growers in Brazil right now because you guys have locked up the previously uncommitted direct supply."

"Matt told everyone at the press conference that we were aggressively buying up contracts and closing deals. And none of the suppliers were complaining when we offered them prices above the market rate at the time. What's your point, Hank?"

"You guys have amassed an awful lot of coffee futures in a very short time. If you had raised the issue of the fungus at the press event yourselves, it would have been commodities market manipulation. By getting a press person to ask about it, it became fair game to discuss in front of the room full of press, who obviously were going to make it into very public knowledge."

"Nobody told Goterrez to ask anything."

"If I'm right in my estimation of how much credit you guys could get on short notice, Bright Cup's newly purchased contracts already have appreciated in value ten or fifteen million dollars."

His estimate is low, Parananda thought, *but that's better for us than if he knew the real amount.*

Ridley continued, "What would you say if I told you I'm going to write in my *Businessweek* column for tomorrow that I believe this was deliberate market manipulation on the part of Bright Cup?"

"I would say that your editors or their lawyers will shy away from publishing it."

"It's only libel if it's not true."

"Do you have evidence that it's true, Hank?"

"Like I said before, I talked to the waiter who told Tony about the coffee fungus. What do you believe the waiter would say in court if he was compelled to testify under oath?"

"You'd have to ask him."

"If your lawyers were to file libel charges against me and my publisher, you'd be fair game to be called to the witness stand. What would you say, Rami, if you were under oath?"

"You'll find out when I testify."

Parananda heard Ridley sigh over the phone, evidently frustrated that Parananda hadn't taken his bait.

"By the way," Ridley said, "that guy Derek at the press conference, the one who held the bag when Cochran did the magic trick with the Habaneros. I'd never seen him around the industry before. So, I took a screen capture of his face from the event video, and I had a buddy of mine who's a computer scientist at UC Berkeley run a facial recognition search on the web. The face came up as a Derek Zhang. He's not a journalist or analyst. His Facebook page says he's a barista at a Bright Cup Café in Los Angeles and a part time professional actor. The magic trick was a setup. I'm gonna put that in my story, too."

"Did you think it was real magic, Hank?"

Ridley replied, "No comment."

÷÷÷÷÷

Doutora Helen Strath walked into *Doutor* Neto's office at Instituto Butantan. She said, "I've got the results of those blood tests that you wanted. They're quite interesting. What were those samples?"

Neto explained, "The petri dish was from a swab of a head wound, taken about three weeks ago, shortly after the patient was injured. He's in a coma, with severe spasticity, possibly due to tetanus. The blood in the vial was drawn from the same patient yesterday."

"That doesn't make much sense. From what you just said, I would have expected to find *C. tetani* bacteria in the first, and maybe some in the second, depending on how the patient had been treated. And I would have expected to find tetanospasmin in the second, but not in the first. Neither of those samples contained *C. tetani* bacteria, dead or alive, and they both tested positive for tetanospasmin. No way bacteria introduced at that wound could have produced this much toxin so quickly. And the first sample had plenty of IgG antibodies specific to the anti-tetano vaccine. The patient must have been up to date on his vaccination. He shouldn't have been susceptible unless it was a dose high enough to overwhelm the antibodies."

"Any theories how this might have happened?"

"Maybe a lab worker accidentally sticking himself with a needle of the toxin. Does the patient work in a biology lab?"

"According to *Doutor* Barada at UNICAMP, the patient is a pilot."

"If you don't mind, *Doutor* Neto, I'd like to run some additional tests on these samples."

"By all means."

Strath left the room, and Neto immediately picked up the phone to call *Doutor* Barada. After that conversation, Barada immediately dialed Munhoz at Delcese. After that conversation, Munhoz immediately called Westphal. After that conversation, Westphal immediately walked into the lab and spoke to Manling.

÷÷÷÷÷

Elsewhere at Instituto Butantan, the boy insisted he and Decker begin at the *serpentário*. On the walkway to the outdoor snake pit, Decker stopped to tie a shoelace. When he stood up, he inadvertently bumped into a woman passing by.

"Excuse me," he said.

The woman was surprised that the man in the disheveled clothes spoke to her in English, but walking away, she nevertheless checked her purse to make sure that her wallet had not been lifted.

Decker and Benito approached the snake pit, the size and shape of which reminded Decker of a hockey rink, only with an earthen surface several meters below ground level. They spotted about two dozen snakes, including rattlesnakes and jararacas, amid the vegetation, rocks, and artificial mounds. But Decker was underwhelmed, having expected to see the pit filled wall to wall with seething serpents, along the lines of the underground tomb scene from the *Raiders of the Lost Ark* movie.

Decker was more impressed with the Museu, the institute's main biological museum, where numerous glass enclosures housed snakes, venomous spiders, scorpions, and frogs in a variety of natural habitats such as woodlands, marshes, and savannahs. Decker stared at a three-meter-long *Boa constrictor amarali*, a stunning tan creature with brown saddle patterns. He was about to tap on the glass to see if the snake would move, but Benito tugged on his sleeve and pointed to the sign reading in English, "Don't tap on the glass!" In another room, they watched a staff person demonstrate venom extraction from a Chinese cobra (*Naja atra*), piercing the snake's fangs through a latex sheet stretched across a glass beaker to milk out a few drops of the dangerous but precious fluid.

When they were ready to leave the Museu, Decker stopped to use the toilet. He entered through a restroom doorway before he had a chance to see that Benito was pointing in a different direction.

That's funny, Decker thought. *Either that man has really long hair, or I'm in the ladies'...*

A woman behind him screamed. Decker turned to get out of the restroom as quickly as possible, but the woman kept screaming. As he emerged from the door, he bumped into a security guard on the way to investigate the noise. The woman came out behind Decker, pointing at him and yelling.

The guard grabbed Decker and pushed him against a wall.

Decker tried to explain, "I'm sorry. It was an accident. I didn't realize I went into the ladies' room."

Another woman told the guard in Portuguese, "That bum was the same one who tried to steal my wallet out by the snake pit."

When the guard reached for his handcuffs, Decker got pissed off for the fourth time that day.

Then Benito stepped in. He said to the guard in Portuguese, "Please excuse my grandfather. He's senile. He doesn't always know what he's doing. He doesn't mean anyone any harm. And he wasn't trying to steal her wallet. He's far too clumsy for anything like that. He looks like he might be getting ill again. I'd better take him home to get him his medication before he has another one of his seizures." Benito grabbed Decker's hand and pulled.

The guard released his grip.

"Thanks, Benito," Decker said when they got outside, "whatever you told the guard in there."

"I told him you were an important visiting dignitary. And I think you owe me an ice cream, grandpa."

÷

At a refreshment pushcart, Benito ordered a vanilla cone with chocolate sprinkles. Decker ordered a lemon gelato in a cup.

Watching the merchant roll the white ice cream in the tiny brown bits for Benito, Decker asked, "OK. Where to next?"

"Do you like painting, Mister Sam?"

"Interior or exterior?"

Benito thought for a second. "Interior."

÷÷÷÷

Westphal, Manling, and Munhoz sat in a conference room, discussing the implications of the call from *Doutor* Barada.

"If Sam was right," Munhoz said, "then somebody is cooking up *C. tetani* bacteria in the lab here and producing the toxin."

Manling responded, "*Clostridium tetani* has distinct morphology. The bacteria shouldn't be too hard to identify."

"*Doutor* Barada's associate at The Snake Farm will email us procedures to test for the toxin."

Westphal said, "We've got to shut down the lab to search for it. But, we've got to do it in a way that the lab staff doesn't even know we're looking."

Munhoz asked, "How do you propose to do that?"

Manling smiled. "That will be simple. Leave it to me."

Westphal said, "We won't be able to keep our searching and testing secret from the rest of the senior scientists. Either we've got to trust them, or we've got to keep them away from the lab. And what do we tell *Senhor* Duarte?"

Manling replied, "*Senhor* Duarte instructed me to destroy all the fungus specimens in the lab. As far as he and the other scientists are concerned, the lab will be closed tomorrow while Wendy and I carry out Duarte's wishes. If we find anything, then we'll decide what to do."

Munhoz asked pointedly, "We're going to mislead our own CEO?"

The three of them stared at each other in silence.

÷÷÷÷

From a bus heading toward the city center, Decker and Benito got off at Avenida Paulista, then they walked two blocks along the busy urban street. Decker stopped in his tracks when he first saw their destination. It was a striking example of modern architecture: a giant shoebox of glass, steel, and concrete, suspended from above by two massive red U-shaped trusses, like steroidal staples resting their tips on the ground.

Inside the *Museu de Arte de São Paulo*, widely known as MASP, a security guard suspiciously eyed the unshaven man and the boy as Decker paid their admission fees.

Benito whispered, "You'd better behave yourself in here, Mister Sam."

Just what I needed, Decker thought, *a 12-year-old pickpocket telling me to behave.*

Decker's first mission was to find the restroom, not having gone amid the fiasco at Instituto Butantan. This time, he triple-checked the symbol on the door before entering.

They strolled the museum's galleries, Decker stopping to admire the large number of paintings by major European artists, including Van Gogh, Monet, Picasso, Renoir, and Botticelli. For a long time, he studied a piece called *O Lavrador de Café* (*The Coffee Worker*), painted in 1939 by Brazilian artist Candido Portinari. The image was of a dark-skinned man with oversized hands and feet, holding a hoe while staring into the distance in front of a vast field of coffee plants. The descriptive placard noted that the painting had been stolen from the museum in December 2007 and recovered the following month. *Displaced coffee workers can quickly return*, Decker thought.

After an hour, Decker had turned into a listless museum zombie, and they exited onto the sidewalk beneath the suspended building.

Benito asked, "What do you want to do next?"

"I think it's time to take you home. It's been a taxing day, and I'm getting tired."

The boy frowned. "I was having fun with you, Mister Sam. But now I'll take you to the bus station to go back to the airport."

"No, Benito, I want to go with you to your home. I feel obligated to make sure you get there safely."

Benito started laughing.

Decker asked, "What's so funny?"

"You're worried about me getting home safely? I only have ten kilometers to get home. You must have ten thousand. But you'll be less safe if you come home with me."

"Why's that, Benito?"

"It's in a not nice part of the city."

"I want to see a not nice part of the city."

"I won't take you there."

"I insist."

"No!" Benito started to cry.

Decker put his arm on the boy's shoulder. "What's wrong?"

Benito wiped his cheeks. "I live in a *favela*, what you'd call a slum. I don't want you to see it. It's overcrowded and filthy and smelly. Drug dealers and thieves are everywhere. I wouldn't be able to protect you. I won't take you there. A *gringo* like you would get hurt or even killed. I don't want you to die, Mister Sam."

Benito grabbed Decker's hand and threw it off his shoulder, then the boy ran away down the sidewalk. Decker briefly pursued, but Benito was out of sight within seconds.

When Decker stopped running, he got pissed off for the fifth time that day.

Chapter 16

~~~~~

In the training room at Sede, Manling stood in front facing the lab staff. He said, "You already may be aware the company plans to burn the infected coffee fields tomorrow. That will alleviate the urgency of lab work investigating the fungus. In recognition of the long hours and outstanding efforts everyone has put in over the last few weeks, the lab will be closed tomorrow. You all have Friday off. Starting right now, enjoy your three day weekend. I'll see you Monday morning."

÷÷÷÷÷

Decker rode the airport bus back out to Guarulhos. Along the way, the bus halted in traffic, and he found himself gazing out the window at a road resurfacing project on a street adjacent to the highway. A green tanker truck was spraying oily liquid on a freshly laid stretch of gravel, and Decker could smell the stench inside the bus.

When Decker arrived back at the airport terminal, he retrieved his bags from the security office. In a VIP lounge, he showered, shaved, and changed into fresh clothes for the long flight north, the start of which was still several hours away. He took a seat in the lounge and booted up his laptop. His email inbox had dozens of messages from journalists seeking comment about the impending shortage of coffee beans from Brazil. He checked his voice mail and discovered that his home and office mailboxes were full of inquiries from journalists. He wondered, *What the heck is going on?* He went to a section of the lounge where a television was tuned to CNN in English.

The TV news anchor said, "...the Dow Jones Industrial Average was off two point three percent today, on fears of a possible coffee shortage stemming from disease infestation in the farm fields of Brazil. Here's another angle on the story from CNN's Judith Garnett."

The video switched to a three-quarter length shot of the woman standing across the street from a grocery store. "Major coffee retailers and supermarkets are reporting runs on coffee in all forms: beans, ground, and even instant." The video switched to a shot of an empty shelf in a grocery store. "Consumer hoarding behavior appears to have kicked in with gusto." Video returned to the woman outside. "I've also heard reports of a few stores severely price gouging, charging as much as two to three times the regular prices for packaged ground coffee. I just hope my husband had a chance to pick up some earlier today. In Chicago, this is Judith Garnett reporting."

The video switched back to the studio anchor. "Coffee 'C' futures contracts for arabica beans at the IntercontinentalExchange in New York today reached three dollars and sixty cents a pound on volume of sixty-three thousand contracts, the highest in both price and volume ever recorded on the ICE." Video cut to piles of burlap coffee sacks. "At thirty-seven thousand five hundred pounds per contract, that trading volume exceeds a staggering two billion pounds." Back to the talking head. "And stocks of the major coffee-related companies were down today, with the notable exception of Bright Cup Inc..." A Bright Cup logo appeared, superimposed in the upper left corner of the screen. "...That company's shares rose nine percent on the statement yesterday by CEO Matthew Cochran that he had been aggressively buying up coffee futures since he learned of the fungus earlier in the week, beating the competition to the punch..."

Decker scratched his head. *Not a single bean has failed to show up for delivery yet,* he thought, *and this is how the markets react? I guess I would have failed as an economist.*

÷÷÷÷÷

Martina Hasse entered her apartment in Piracicaba carrying the pack on her back. She beamed at her husband, "Gunter, honey, I saw the new parrot species today at the plantation. And this time, I got it on film."

"You must be the last person in Brazil still taking pictures on film. Why don't you switch to digital?"

"I like my film cameras just fine." She took off her pack and set it on the kitchen table. "Besides, when the electric power grid collapses, all my pictures will still be viewable with sunlight or even candlelight."

"You're being apocalyptic, dear."

Ignoring his remark, she said, "Delcese is burning the infected fields tomorrow. *Senhor* Manling gave the whole lab staff the day off. I think I'll go into São Paulo a day early this weekend. I'll get the film processed so I can show the pictures to my birding club on Saturday."

÷÷÷÷÷

At her home in Piracicaba, Fabiana Munhoz slammed the door, leaving the man standing outside. *They've got some nerve*, she fumed.

÷÷÷÷÷

After taking a shuttle bus from the gate out to the plane on the tarmac, Decker's last act before turning off his mobile phone was to call Munhoz's home phone number.

She picked up. "*Olá?*"

"Fabiana, this is Sam."

"Where are you?"

"I'm at Guarulhos. I'm on a plane, about to fly home."

"It's awful what Mr. Duarte did to you."

"Yes, but how are you holding up?"

"Things are horrible, Sam. Where do I start? I got a call from Dr. Barada. After we were there yesterday, he decided to send blood samples from the pilot Miguel to a colleague at Instituto Butantan..."

"The Snake Farm?"

"Yes, how do you know of that place?"

"I was there today. It's a long story. Go on, please."

"The blood samples tested positive for high levels of tetanospasmin, but no sign of the bacteria, even in the first sample taken right after Miguel was admitted. You were right, Sam. It looks like Miguel was directly infected with the toxin. I talked to Manling and Westphal. Manling has shut down the lab for tomorrow, and the two of them are going to search it for signs of the tetanus bacteria or toxin. I hope they can find it. I mean, I hope they don't find anything because I hope it's not there. But if it is there, I hope they find it. Then I found out that Delcese is destroying Paul's records."

"I still have two of his notebooks in my briefcase."

"Good. Hang on to those. Then, a little while ago, Mr. Costa came to my home, demanding to see Paul's computer and his papers here. I wouldn't let him in. I told him, *vai se foder*, to go fuck himself."

"Good for you, Fabiana. I don't like Costa either. But I think you can trust Lucy."

When he hung up at the end of the conversation, Decker was pissed off for the sixth and final time that day.

÷÷÷÷÷

Amid the marble floors and walls of the Hall of Baths, behind one of the numerous sets of frosted glass doors, Larissa Júnior lay in an oval tub in a *sala de banhos*. Soaking in the therapeutic hot waters from the nearby sulfur springs, wisps of steam rose around her. She thought, *A vida é boa*. Life is good.

÷÷÷÷÷

Matthew Cochran sat in a leather Eames chair in his study at home, sipping a glass of cognac. He flipped open a cedar box on a side table and removed a cigar. The Montague Corona No. 2 Maduro had been hand rolled in Pandaan, on the island of Java, from Indonesian binder leaf, Indonesian and Brazilian filler tobaccos, and a Brazilian broadleaf wrapper. He picked up the lighter, a silver sphere etched like a globe with the continents of the world. He glanced at the sphere, first locating South America, then the amorphous blob representing the numerous islands of Indonesia. He depressed the lighter button. He raised the flame to the end of the cigar and began puffing until a glowing ember was established.

Cochran drew a puff from the cigar and rolled around the lighter in his palm. *Tomorrow,* he thought, *the profits will come rolling in when we start selling off the futures contracts and letting suppliers buy themselves out of our deals. Or maybe we'll sell the supplier deals ourselves. We'll trade the contracts people said I wouldn't be able to trade. Maybe I'll even start my own commodities exchange.* He exhaled the smoke upward in a set of three well-formed smoke rings. *And Bright Cup's share price will keep going up, up, up.*

AUGUST 9

In the coffee fields at Sede, some of the trees uprooted from the perimeters were now piled in the centers of the fields. Other trees were laid perpendicular to the rows of still-standing trees to act as bridges for the soon-to-be-lit fires to jump from row to row.

The operations manager of the Sede plantation, Javier Pedra, had rigged a remote control to trigger the fires by electronically igniting plastic barrels of bio-diesel fuel placed near the upwind corner of each field. Four fire trucks from Piracicaba stood by in the parking lot in case things didn't go as planned.

A news helicopter hovered overhead, and a row of journalists and photographers lined the edge of the closest coffee field, about half a kilometer from the building complex. Television news crews had set up a cluster of microphones, assuming the Delcese CEO would deliver a statement prior to ignition.

At 10:05AM, with Duarte conspicuously absent, Melissa Herrar stepped up to the microphones. "Good morning," she said. "Today, we at Delcese Agricola are doing our part to eradicate this fungus, as will our competitors whose fields are infected. Our company is sparing no effort or expense to benefit the entire coffee industry of Brazil..." She continued for two minutes, concluding, "...Now, Delcese Agricola CEO,

Senhor Roberto Duarte, will commence the incineration." She stepped back from the microphones and checked her watch.

The assembled journalists looked around at each other. Alexandre Werner whispered to a man next to him, "Did we miss something?"

After 15 seconds, another helicopter approached. It maneuvered to a position 10 meters above the ground and 30 meters in front of the line of people. Duarte was visible in the front passenger seat, holding a black box with a stubby antenna sticking out of it.

Javier Pedra raised his arm, signaling that all was ready.

÷

Inside the helicopter, Duarte put his finger on the button of the black box. He closed his eyes, then he pressed the button.

÷

The bio-diesel fuel ignited, not in violent explosions, but in oozing waves of liquid flames as the plastic barrels melted, and the burning fuel spilled across adjacent trees. Within minutes, plumes of dark smoke billowed skyward.

Similar fires were due to be lit at Delcese's other infected plantations later in the day, albeit in less dramatic, less public fashion.

÷÷÷÷

Hank Ridley's story, "Bright Cup: Real Magic, or Just Smoke and Mirrors?" appeared early that morning on Businessweek.com, and the story's URL was linked in numerous financial news feeds.

The first trade of the day for shares of Bright Cup Inc. on the NASDAQ exchange was a gap opening 2.5 points lower than the previous day's close of 41.675, a six percent drop. As the day would progress, the shares fell further.

When the President of the IntercontinentalExchange in New York read Ridley's story, he ordered a halt in trading of coffee futures in Bright Cup's account, pending an investigation. He then called to inform Bright Cup's broker.

"The exchange does not take lightly deliberate attempts at market manipulation, Ms. Anderman."

Her reaction was to cover the telephone's mouthpiece with her hand and mutter two words, "Fucking Matt."

When Tony Goterrez read Ridley's article, he composed an email in Portuguese, linking to the article. The recipient list consisted of six people at the Bolsa de Mercadorias e Futuros. Goterrez hit the Send button, thinking, *That'll teach Matt Cochran to play me for a fool.*

Bright Cup's broker on the trading floor at the BM&F had been selling heavily, until a *parar* (halt) command from the exchange's *Diretor-Geral* (Director General) put an end to it.

In an office at Sede, Silvio Damani read the article. The Delcese VP of Sales had landed the biggest deal in company history. He wasn't looking to let it go in favor of smaller potential deals from other buyers, even if those deals might be at slightly higher prices. He looked out the window at the plumes of smoke above the fields, thinking, *Mais vale um pássaro na mão que dois na cafeeiro ardente.* A bird in the hand is worth two in the burning coffee bush.

÷÷÷÷÷

At 7:15AM Pacific time Truck Macklin was out for his daily exercise spin in the racing wheelchair. When he rolled back in the driveway dripping sweat, his wife and 5-year-old daughter were in the garden tending to the flowers.

His daughter told him, "Matt called. He said to tell you, 'Our fuchsias are frozen,' but I don't see how it could be that cold, even where he lives up by that mountain in Marin county."

÷÷÷÷÷

Westphal and Manling began their systematic search in the main lab area. They wore lab coats, safety goggles, and gloves. Westphal went through each storage cabinet, reading off the labels on every container, jar, bag, and dish. For each item, Manling checked on his tablet computer that it was something recorded in his log, and they assessed whether the contents looked like a match for the label.

In the two hours it took them to search the cabinets, they had flagged three questionable items: an unlabeled brown glass jar containing a white powder; a capped test tube containing a milky liquid; and a zip-type plastic bag with an oily substance inside;

Next, they went to the specimen refrigerator, a tall upright box with glass doors on the front, which superficially looked like a model used to chill drinks in the nearby BR Mania convenience store.

Westphal pulled out items from the refrigerator shelves. She held up an unlabeled plastic jar containing a yellowish-brown paste. "This looks like the mustard jar from my fridge at home."

Manling took it from her and unscrewed the lid. He quickly waved the mouth of the jar several inches below his nose without inhaling, a technique he had learned the hard way over years of working in labs. "I'm gonna kick someone's ass," he said.

"Why? What is it?"

"It's mustard. Hemmer's Extra Forte, I believe."

They both laughed knowing his prohibition against personal food items in the lab.

They returned to checking the refrigerator and found three petri dish samples with numerical code labels that didn't match anything in

Manling's log. The petri dishes appeared to contain the fungus, which they assumed were Paul's work.

The only other questionable item in the refrigerator was a small jar containing a clear liquid, about as viscous as water. The only label on it was a round yellow smiley face sticker on the lid.

"Somebody's got a sense of humor," Westphal said. She swished it around. "Maybe it's *cachaça*." She faked like she was going to drink it.

Manling took the jar from her hand and held it up to the light. "Put it back in the cooler for now. We'll test it later."

When Westphal and Manling opened the door into the separate bio-containment lab area, a momentary rush of inward breeze accompanied them into the reduced air pressure, which helped prevent stray particles or microorganisms from escaping. They searched the biological safety cabinet (BSC), the anaerobic chamber, and the centrifuges. In the cabinet below the tabletop Bioscreen machine, they looked through stacks of honeycomb plates for holding growth cultures. The plates in that cabinet all should have been clean and unused, but several of them appeared to contain fungus. And in one of the incubation ovens, they found a covered plate for the Bioscreen.

Westphal asked, "Why was this incubating in here and not in the Bioscreen itself?"

"What's the number on it?"

When she read it off, Manling responded, "That's an outdated number for a mold that would have been kept refrigerated."

She looked closely at it. "The cover is sealed with silicone around the edge."

He said, "Most of the anaerobes we deal with here are facultative. They can tolerate some air. Silicone sealant around the cover is only needed for obligatory anaerobes."

Westphal handed him the plate. "Such as *C. tetani*."

Manling loaded the plate and some supplies through the outer door of the airlock on the Bactron anaerobic chamber. He started up the chamber's pump, which removed the oxygen-containing air and replaced it with inert AMG (anaerobic mixed gas) consisting of nitrogen, hydrogen, and carbon dioxide. When the machine's "auto cycle" light indicated the proper anaerobic pressure, Manling inserted his arms into the cuffs and stepped on a pedal to suck the remaining air from the arm sleeves. He opened the arm port doors, reached into the chamber, and opened the airlock from inside. Through the latex gloves he still wore, Manling laboriously picked away the silicone sealing the specimen cover. When he removed the cover, he swabbed a sample from the honeycomb and smeared it onto a glass slide. He placed the slide into the airlock and shut the door, automatically triggering the exchange of gas. He removed his arms from the cuffs.

He took the glass slide from the airlock. "If there are anaerobes on this," he said, "they're dead ones now."

He lit up a Bunsen burner and waved the slide through the flame a few times to heat fix the sample's cells. Using an eyedropper, he applied crystal violet stain onto the slide to cover the specimen. He let the stain sit for a minute, then he rinsed the slide with Gram iodine reagent. After another minute, he rinsed the slide with acetone-alcohol decolorizer until no more of the purple stain color appeared in the rinse, then he washed off the slide in water. Next, he applied Fuchsin counterstain to the surface of the slide, after which he again rinsed the slide in water. He held the slide at an angle to allow the last few drops of water to drain off, then he set down the slide on bibulous paper to let the specimen surface air dry. He pulled off his latex gloves and threw them in the disposal bin.

"Let's take a look at the morphology info," he said to Westphal.

She handed him the tablet computer. He swiped through the half dozen micrograph images on its screen.

When the glass slide was dry, Manling put on a new pair of latex gloves and carried the slide to an Olympus microscope. He rotated the lens turret to place the 40X objective into position, which combined with the 10X eyepiece produced 400X magnification. He checked that the illumination was set for brightfield, then he inserted the slide. He looked into the microscope's binocular eyepiece, adjusting the focus. "We've got some nice little purple Gram-positive tennis rackets," he said, noting the coloration and the shape of the organisms. He looked back at the images on the tablet. "I'd say we have a ninety percent likelihood of a match for *C. tetani* here." He motioned for Westphal to take a look.

When she lifted her head up from the microscope, she said, "I concur. Now what?"

He pointed out into the main lab area. "On to our smiley-faced friend. We'd better be really careful handling that."

They proceeded to test the liquid from the jar using the lab's Raman spectroscope.

÷÷÷÷÷

Standing beside the burning coffee fields at Fazenda Fiorva, field supervisor Jose asked plantation manager Mabro, "And what about the remote experimental fields, *senhor*? Should we burn those, too?"

Mabro had been so busy directing preparations to torch the plantation fields that he hadn't previously considered that question. *We don't even know if the fungus is out there,* he thought. *Our planned trip to look at those fields yesterday got cancelled, and nobody's been out to any of them since the day of the plane crash.* "No, at least not yet," Mabro replied to Jose. "The risk of fires spreading into the wild would be too great. We must leave them for the time being."

᛭᛭᛭᛭᛭

Martina Hasse accepted the envelope from the clerk behind the counter at the Labtec professional photo lab, one of the few facilities in São Paulo that still processed slide film on the premises. She opened the packet and spread out the slides on a light table in front of the counter. Using a magnifying loupe tethered to the table, she lowered her head and meticulously examined each image. When she finished, she thought of a uniquely American expression which she said out loud, "Gotcha!" She returned to the counter to have several slides scanned and printed.

᛭᛭᛭᛭᛭

Fabiana Munhoz entered the lab soon after Westphal and Manling had finished testing the contents of the jar.

Munhoz asked, "You guys find anything noteworthy?"

Manling deadpanned, "Other than a plate of *C. tetani* bacteria and a jar of tetanus toxin, not much."

"Please tell me you're joking."

"If I was joking, your husband might still be alive."

Westphal slapped him hard on the arm. "Don't say something like that, you idiot."

"It's all right, Wendy," Munhoz said. "Please elaborate on what you found."

᛭᛭᛭᛭᛭

Lucy was passing by the video console in the security area when something caught her eye on one of the screens. She paused to look over Tulio's shoulder. *What is she doing in there,* she thought, *with them?* Without saying a word, she went out the door.

᛭᛭᛭᛭᛭

"...and analysis of the jar contents," Manling explained, "found a tetanospasmin-like compound diluted in a saline solution."

Westphal added, "Presumably the straight toxin would have been way more potent than needed for practical purposes."

Manling said, "The question now, is: Who?" Then, he noticed out of the corner of his eye Lucy entering the lab.

Lucy and Munhoz looked at each other, both thinking the same thought, *Sam said he trusted her.*

Lucy said, "I think I know who."

÷÷÷÷

Costa was passing by the video console in the security area when something caught his eye on one of the screens. He paused to look over Tulio's shoulder. *What is she doing in there,* he thought, *with them?* The two men watched the monitor as Lucy raised a hand to the back of her head and made the sign of the ponytail.

÷÷÷÷÷

Westphal said, "If Miguel was injected with the toxin..." She pointed to the smiley face jar. "...it must have been someone who had contact with him very shortly before the crash. Assuming Paul didn't do it, only two other people qualify: Larissa Júnior, or a farmhand from Fazenda Fiorva. Larissa had full access to the lab, and she had the know-how to cook up something like that."

Manling added, "Larissa wasn't at work yesterday. She called in and left a message that she had to take leave for a medical emergency, and she didn't know when she'd be back."

Lucy said, "Maybe she suspected that she was about to be discovered, and she flew the coop."

Munhoz considered whether she should divulge all she knew, but she decided that doctor-patient confidentiality took precedence, even when it came to the possibility that the patient in question might have been responsible for her husband's death. *And I wonder, who's the father? Does he work here at Delcese? And if so, is he involved, too?*

"But if Larissa is the one," Westphal wondered, "why did she tell Sam about tetanus?"

Munhoz suggested, "Perhaps she was feeling guilty."

Lucy added, "She did sound dejected about Dr. Mendonça's death when Sam and I talked to her."

Manling and Westphal were uncertain about the plausibility of that explanation.

Manling asked, "Now what do we do?"

The answer walked in the lab door, in the form of Duarte accompanied by Costa.

After everyone was finished uncomfortably explaining everything, Costa said, "We must inform the police." The others agreed.

"The question now," Manling stated, "is: Why?"

÷÷÷÷

A CNN talking head spoke, "...Fears of a possible coffee shortage eased today, due to two factors. First, a *Businessweek* article exposed an apparent plot on the part of coffee retailer Bright Cup Inc. to incite consumer panic in an attempt to drive up the price of coffee futures contracts in which the company had invested heavily earlier in the week. Securities regulators vowed to launch an investigation. Bright Cup's share price plummeted twenty-one percent today, and coffee futures contract prices fell eight percent." Video cut to an aerial shot of the burning fields at Sede. "And in Brazil, fungus-infected coffee plantations burned, as growers incinerated their fields in the only known method of destroying the pathogen. This extreme measure may seem like throwing out the baby with the bath water, but coffee growers expressed confidence that a potential crisis has now been averted, and that the remaining unaffected fields are now safe from further contagion. Brazil's Bovespa stock index was up two point three percent on the news today."

÷÷÷÷÷

In a corner of an experimental crop field north of Fazenda Fiorva, in the dark of night with virtually no moon, a man pulled a tarpaulin over the payload in the rear of a pickup truck. With the vehicle's headlights remaining off, he drove away down a bumpy dirt road.

Part II:
Javanese Dark Roast

Chapter 17

"In their most primitive form, the communicative powers of ritual give even the simplest creatures the ability to send and receive messages that allow important interactions to occur. Consider, for example, the mating ritual of the butterfly known as the silver-washed fritillary... Neurobiologically, the butterflies are 'vibrating' in harmony, like a pair of tuning forks. This sense of closeness and common purpose allows them to transcend the normal self-protective instincts that would usually compel them to avoid interaction with others and reap survival benefits they could not have managed on their own."

From *Why God Won't Go Away: Brain Science and the Biology of Belief*, by Andrew Newberg, Eugene D'Aquili, and Vince Rause, 2001

~~~~~

AUGUST 10

With no Daylight Savings Time employed in Indonesia, and DST not active during the winter season in Brazil, the time zone difference put the island of Java 10 hours ahead of the São Paulo region. On this Saturday in mid-August, sunrise near Yogyakarta was less than two hours after it had set the previous evening in southern Brazil.

÷÷÷÷

Sixty kilometers southeast of Yogyakarta, 12 people in hooded puce-colored robes stood in the pre-dawn light on the crest of a now verdant promontory of coral that had been geologically uplifted from beneath the Indian Ocean. The elevation of this hill jutting out next to Baron Beach was sufficient to afford them a clear view of the imminent sunrise, with the appearance that the sun would be emerging out of the ocean on the horizon.

Ten of the people held hands, forming a circle enclosing the other two, who faced each other in the center. The diffuse light silhouetted them all against the sky.

Eddy Zeger, one of the men in the center, pushed back the hood from his head, then commenced speaking, "We, the Curators Of The Earth, have gathered here by the light of this dawn to welcome a new member. Those of us present in body, and those of us far afield in body but present in spirit, are united in our celebration of the burgeoning of our swarm."

The circle of people released hands and clapped one time.

Zeger rotated as he continued, "We, the Curators Of The Earth, dedicate ourselves to preservation of The Earth and all its creatures.

We dedicate ourselves to mending mankind's spiraling destruction of The Earth and its natural resources. And we pledge our efforts and our lives to enhancing The Earth by our presence."

Another clap. The top of the sun broke the ocean horizon, its orange rays creeping down the hillside toward the beach below.

Zeger went on, "Each of us displays a unique mark of a delicate Lepidoptera, a butterfly, as our emblem of fellowship and as our symbol of the fragility of the creatures of The Earth."

Zeger grasped his robe and pulled it open. He slid the robe off his shoulders and let it drop to the ground, revealing his naked body. In the light of the rising sun, he turned and displayed for everyone the immense life-size tattoo of the Goliath Birdwing butterfly emblazoned across his upper back.

One by one, the members of the circle disrobed, then turned so that all could see their marks: a woman with a broad Zebra Longwing (*Heliconius charithonia*) across the small of her back; Jarma Pukartra with a Tailed Emperor (*Polyura pyrrhus*) on the rear of his right calf; a woman with a tiny Western Pygmy Blue (*Brephidium exilis*) between her breasts; a man with a Mariposa Copper (*Lycaena mariposa*) on the side of his left shoulder muscle; and so on.

When the outer circle all stood naked, Zeger turned to the man with him in the center. "By virtue of these similar emblems, we indelibly mark ourselves as members of a unified tribe. And by virtue of our personal choices of species and location of these markings, we signify our individuality within that unified tribe. Join us now and forever as one individual within our unified tribe, by revealing your mark."

The man lowered his robe. He turned toward the sun and stepped forward his right leg, displaying the Red Admiral (*Vanessa atalanta*) ornamenting the front of his thigh.

Zeger proclaimed, "Welcome, Brother Atalanta."

Zeger extended his right hand toward the newest member of his personal coterie. When the other man reached out his right hand to shake, Zeger grabbed that hand with his left hand and guided it into a particular position. The resulting configuration consisted of their two right hands still open, but hooked together by the thumbs. Zeger began flapping his hand back and forth, pivoting around their thumbs. The man followed along, creating a sympathetic motion resembling the movement of a butterfly. Then everyone in the circle applauded.

÷÷÷÷

Still the prior evening in Brazil, Ramon Costa stood alongside *Primeiro Tenente* (First Lieutenant) Oscar Azevedo of the *Departamento de Polícia Federal* (DPF).

Eight years earlier, Costa had been a *Capitão* (Captain) in the DPF station in Campinas, and Azevedo a rookie fresh from the academy. Thus, the dynamic between the two men was quite different than might normally be the case in an abnormal case such as this.

They were at the door of Larissa Júnior's second floor apartment in Águas de São Pedro. Their first few knocks were gentle, but when no one answered, the next set of knocks resembled pounding.

A woman who lived on the first floor opened her door and yelled, "What do you want up there?"

The two men tromped down the stairs

"We're looking for *Senhorita* Júnior," the policeman in the dark blue uniform said. "Do you know her whereabouts?"

The young woman stood inside in her nightgown. "I haven't seen her since yesterday morning. Her car is here, but maybe she took the bus out of town. Maybe she went rock climbing. Or maybe she went to Rio to have a boob job. I don't know, and as long as she pays her rent on time, I don't care. What's she done?"

"We just need to speak with her," Azevedo said. "Do you know the names of any of her friends that she might have gone to see? It's very important." He rotated his torso to highlight his gold and red Polícia Federal badge in the light emanating from the woman's doorway.

"The only friend of Larissa's that I know is Luiza Rosela, an old schoolmate of hers who lives across town."

"We need to look in *Senhorita* Júnior's apartment."

The landlady replied, "Don't you need a search warrant for that?"

The officer reached into a pocket and pulled out a warrant.

"Very well," she said. "I'll get the key."

Azevedo told the landlady to wait outside while he and Costa looked inside Larissa's apartment, being careful not to disturb the position of anything, at least not during this preliminary inspection.

Azevedo checked the refrigerator for any suspicious bottles or jars, prepared to call in a HAZMAT team if necessary, but he found nothing out of the ordinary. "The fridge has plenty of food," he said to Costa. "Either she plans to come back soon, or she left unexpectedly."

In the bedroom, noting the open dresser drawers with piles of clothes missing, Costa said, "Looks like she has indeed gone on a little trip." He examined trails in the dust in front of empty spaces on the bookshelf. "Looks like she took some things from here. Perhaps she needs them with her for whatever she's planning to do."

"Or she didn't want them left behind as incriminating evidence."

"No computer here," Costa observed. "She probably has a laptop or tablet with her. And, no landline phone."

"The DPF is checking her mobile phone records for calls, cellular locations, and data accesses."

On their way out, Azevedo said to the landlady, "*Senhorita*, if you see *Senhorita* Júnior, please don't mention that we were here. But do give me a call. *Obrigado*." The policeman handed her a business card.

"Yeah, right," she mumbled.

÷

"I haven't talked to her in over a week," Luiza Rosela told the men at the door of her apartment. "She didn't say anything about going out of town. Does this have anything to do with the time she got arrested at the logging protest in the Amazon way back when?"

"No. But, if you do see *Senhorita* Júnior, don't mention that we were here. *Obrigado*."

As soon as the two men had gone, Rosela picked up her phone and dialed. When the messaging system beeped, she said, "Lari, it's Luiza. Two policemen were just here looking for you. The one in the uniform was a hunk, tall and muscular with deep blue eyes. He was a federal guy, not one of the locals. I don't know what you've done to deserve such attention, but I hope it was fun."

÷÷÷÷÷

Eddy Zeger sat at a desktop computer in his office on the second floor of Kraton Kupu Kupu, scanning news stories from the United States. *Look at how these American fools react*, he thought, *as though coffee was the staff of life. What happened? A few measly coffee fields got infected, and the people panicked. And when the people panicked, their economy cramped... Dear Mother Earth! Why didn't I think of this before? Imagine how they would react if a widespread coffee shortage really happened. Without their precious coffee, American workers' productivity would plummet, and otherwise sane people would be at each other's throats. This is even better than what we had been planning. And we won't have to kill anyone ourselves, although they might start killing each other. If only I can get my hands on enough of that fungus.*

Zeger got up and walked to the back office.

Jarma Pukartra looked up from the computer. "Still no word from Sister Cleobaea."

Zeger said, "Brother Pyrrhus, I urgently need to talk to her. Or to Brother Aidea. I must speak to one of them as soon as possible."

"Brother Aidea doesn't have a scheduled contact standby, but we have another way to reach him in an emergency." Pukartra opened a file on his computer, then he tapped the front of the monitor. "Sister Cleobaea's regular contact standby is Sunday morning, Brazil time. I could email a Brother in Brussels or a Sister in Helsinki with a signal to make the call."

Zeger said, "The matter I need to discuss with Cleobaea is too important to risk ambiguity in the communication. Our faithful Brother Mariposa is headed back to Hong Kong later today. I'll personally instruct him to place the call from his city tomorrow evening. Let's hope Cleobaea sticks to her standby schedule. If not, then we'll contact Aidea. And Brother Pyrrhus, immediately post a homing flag on the website. All members in Indonesia and surrounding areas must come to an important meeting at the beach on Monday at sunrise. And post a call-to-arms standby notice for all our Brothers and Sisters further abroad. I plan to mobilize them soon, although I must communicate with Cleobaea or Aidea before deciding when that will happen."

÷÷÷÷÷

Early Saturday morning in Brazil, Martina Hasse met up with friends from *Clube de Observadores de Aves de São Paulo* (Birdwatchers' Club of São Paulo) who were about to leave on an outing.

"I think I discovered a new species of parrot," she excitedly told them. "Have any of you seen this one before?" She showed two photo prints that the group passed around. Everyone shook their heads.

"How'd you find it?"

"Where was it?"

"Where'd you get that decoy?"

"You should take these photos to *Homem Velho* [Old Man] Arpão. He'll know whether or not it's a new species."

÷÷÷÷÷

A man stood in a shopping center parking lot with a mobile phone pressed tightly to one ear and a hand over the other ear to ward off the incessant street noise.

He listened to the outgoing message from the other end of the connection, "This is Larissa. I'm swimming laps in the bathtub, so I can't take your call. Leave a message, and I'll call you back..."

After the beep, the man left his message, "Larissa, what's going on? And where are you? Word is that you're in some kind of major trouble. Let me know what I can do to help. I miss you." He lowered the phone from his ear to hang up, but before he pressed the button he stuck it back up to his ear and added, "I love you, baby."

÷÷÷÷÷

Sitting on the couch in his living room, Old Man Arpão examined Hasse's photo prints through a handheld magnifying glass. "It most closely resembles the common Scarlet Macaw, *Ara macao*, but it's definitely distinct. Perhaps it's a hybrid with *Ara couloni*, the Blue-headed Macaw, which is itself quite rare. It's clearly genus *Ara*, but I don't recognize it. Congratulations, Martina, I believe you've discovered a new species of parrot."

Hasse's face lit up as though she had just won a lottery jackpot.

÷÷÷÷÷

Decker spent most of the day in two pursuits: sorting through the massive influx of emails; and fending off attempts by journalists to get the inside scoop on the situation in Brazil. Two of the news hounds had knocked on the front door of his home. His standard reply to them was that his non-disclosure agreement with Delcese prevented him for commenting about the fungus.

They don't know diddly about the tetanus, he thought, *and the last thing I'm going to do is tell them. The world doesn't need another panic, especially when nobody knows what was going on in the lab at Delcese... What am I talking about? I'm no longer on that job. I've got to focus my attention elsewhere. I've got to gear up for classes only a few weeks away. I've got to start preparing some new lesson plans. The coffee fungus would be a great topic, except with that NDA, I can't talk about it for a couple of years.* He dug through his briefcase and found the scrap of paper with the three Portuguese words in a triangular formation. *If only I could have figured out where Paul went wrong with the fungus. But I'll probably never get that chance.*

AUGUST 11

Sunday morning, Martina Hasse rose even earlier than she had the day before, and she tiptoed out of the apartment so as not to wake her host. She took a local bus to Rodoviária Tietê, the main bus station in São Paulo, arriving in time for the first departure to Campinas.

An hour and a half later, the bus pulled into Estação Rodoviária Dr. Barbosa de Barros, the central bus station in Campinas. Inside the terminal, she sat on one of the orange plastic seats in the waiting area. She checked her watch, then she lowered her head and closed her eyes.

÷÷÷÷÷

That morning, Larissa Júnior swam 60 laps in one of the Grande Hotel's outdoor pools, ignoring the feelings of nausea, periodically changing strokes and occasionally dodging another occupant who wandered into her imaginary lane. To be there legitimately felt odd to a woman who, merely by exuding unflinching confidence, had passed herself off as a hotel guest at the pool nearly every week.

When she climbed out of the water, she grabbed a fluffy white towel and wiped herself with it. She laid out the towel on a poolside lounge chair. She reclined on the chair, then she put on her sunglasses.

Unlike many of her fellow countrywomen, Larissa wore a one-piece swimsuit rather than a bikini, partly because its sleek fit was better for swimming laps, and partly because it covered the mark on the skin of her abdomen about which she was more self-conscious than she ought to have been. Her exposed skin was well tanned, and she knew that despite her advancing years, her body still looked good. As an unaccompanied woman, she wasn't too surprised when the first man approached her, although she was taken aback by the audacity of his opening line.

With her eyes closed, she heard the man's voice say, "Would you care to wrap your legs around a muscular torso, *senhorita*?"

She opened her eyes behind the sunglasses and looked over at the man sitting on the edge of the adjacent chair. He had a gold chain around his neck, graying chest hairs, and a dark tan on the pot belly drooping over his skimpy Speedo swimsuit. She suspected that the hair covering his scalp had been surgically assisted.

She said, "That couldn't be your torso you were talking about."

"I'm insulted, *senhorita*." He feigned a frown. "I was planning to go for a horseback ride this afternoon. It's a nice day for fresh air in the great outdoors. Would you like to come along for a ride?"

Making a reasonable assumption, she replied, "What about your wife? Will she be coming along, too?"

"No, she's uncomfortable in the saddle. She will remain behind." He patted himself in the butt. "How about it?"

"Can I lead the way?"

"You like to be in control, do you, *senhorita*? I like a woman who likes to be in control."

"I was going to leave you behind..." She patted herself on the butt. "...and go with my boyfriend."

She leaned back and closed her eyes again.

÷÷÷÷÷

Within the luxurious bar and restaurant The Felix on the 28th floor of the Peninsula Hotel in Tsim Sha Tsui, Gabriel Bonnington was peeing into the freestanding conical granite urinal directly in front of the plate glass windows facing out over the evening lights of Kowloon. *Too bad these windows don't look out on the Hong Kong side of the hotel*, he thought. *I guess the best views are reserved for customers while they're consuming the drinks.*

He stopped at the mirror to adjust his tie. *Just another anonymous Western businessman*, he thought. Exiting the men's room, he checked the time on his mobile phone, then headed down the elevator to the lobby. At a payphone there, he took from his wallet a phone card and a slip of paper with a phone number on it. He dialed the lengthy sequence of digits. He flipped over the paper to look at a sentence written out phonetically in Portuguese in case he needed to use it.

"*Alô*," the voice answered on the other end of the line.

"Hello, I need to page someone. It's a medical emergency."

"What's the name to page, *senhor*?"

"*Senhora* Cleobaea."

÷ ÷ ÷ ÷ ÷

Cleobaea's eyes jolted open when she heard the name over the loudspeaker. She had been coming to this designated location at the appointed time every week since the last random safety shuffle, but this was the first time she had been contacted here. She got up and walked to the *balcão de informações* (information desk), where she identified herself. The attendant handed her a telephone receiver.

She guessed that the caller would speak English. "Hello?"

"Hello, Cleobaea, this is your Brother Mariposa. Our Big Brother has an urgent message. Goliath wants you to procure a substantial quantity of the tiny red vegetable that has been appearing recently in your vicinity. He has plans for a new business proposition that will overshadow even your current small animal project. He wishes for the unintended consequence to become intended, on a worldwide basis, as soon as possible."

Cleobaea maintained her composure. "I'm sorry to hear that your brother had the accident," she replied, cognizant that the attendant might overhear her half of the call. "I'll see if the medical supplies necessary to treat him are readily available. Unfortunately, the storage facility suffered a severe fire last week due to arson. If the supplies are not on hand, it might take weeks or even months to produce sufficient quantities. I'll investigate the situation as soon as I can and reply by email, although I may not be able to find out until tomorrow morning when I return to work."

"Brother Goliath requires you to respond today, no later than midnight his time. He has called a gathering of the swarm at sunrise tomorrow, at which time he will announce the new mission."

She glanced at her watch. "That's only a few hours from now. I'll go into my workplace immediately."

Cleobaea hung up the phone thinking, *A fungus isn't a vegetable, and a bacterium isn't an animal.*

÷

Bonnington exited the Peninsula Hotel onto Nathan Road and walked a few blocks to the Holiday Inn. There, he used a public Internet terminal in the lobby to send an encoded contact confirmation to an email address that was monitored by Pukartra at Kraton Kupu Kupu. Then he headed to the Star Ferry terminal for a ride across Victoria Harbour, returning to his apartment in the Englishtown section of Hong Kong.

÷÷÷÷÷

"...I was watching you swim laps earlier, *senhorita*," the next man said. "Your butterfly stroke is graceful for such an awkward means of propulsion. I was wondering if you'd give me pointers on my stroke."

"Jump in the pool, and let me see," Larissa replied in a chipper voice, rolling her eyes behind the dark glasses.

The man dove in and swam a lap back and forth freestyle. He dripped down onto the chair next to hers. "What do you think? Would you care to see my breast stroke? Or perhaps you'd give me close personal instruction on rhythmic hip thrust techniques?"

"I suspect, *senhor*, that you already stroke yourself just fine." She leaned back and closed her eyes again. *The perils of vacation*, she thought.

÷÷÷÷÷

Martina Hasse boarded the next bus departing for Piracicaba, a coach adorned with the stylized logo "Cristália." She smirked as she noted how the bus company's name resembled the Portuguese word *crisálida* (chrysalis).

When she returned to her apartment, her husband wasn't home. She dropped off her overnight bag and picked up the car keys.

Hasse couldn't remember the last time she had been to Sede de Delcese Agricola on a Sunday, but she was surprised at how many cars were in the parking lot, along with two fire trucks and a police car. *I guess a lot of clean up work remains*, she thought, looking out at the traces of smoke still rising from the ashes of the coffee fields.

She walked to the edge of the sugarcane fields, where operations manager Javier Pedra was instructing some of the workers.

When Pedra became available, she asked him, "Are all the coffee fields destroyed?"

"Yes, *Senhora*," he replied with both pride and sadness. "All gone. No more fungus."

"How about at our other plantations?"

"Everywhere the fungus had been detected has now been burned."

Damn, she thought, *if I have to culture a huge amount of this fungus from scratch in a hurry, it will be difficult if not impossible to do it without being detected.* Then another possibility dawned on her. *I can do it in one of Dr. Mendonça's remote experimental fields. And nobody will notice if I go there.* Then yet another possibility dawned on her. *Maybe the fungus already has infected those fields and is ripe for the plucking. The company couldn't have burned the fields way out in the boondocks.* She smiled to herself momentarily, then she relaxed her expression. *But I can't count on the fungus being there. I need a backup plan.*

Hasse entered the Administration Building using her ID card. Without encountering anyone in the hallways, she headed upstairs toward the lab, where she intended to find some samples of spores or active fungus to seed her new project if needed. When she got to the lab, she was surprised to find the door open. She stopped short when she saw Manling and two police officers inside. The small jar with the yellow smiley face label was sitting on the counter in front of them.

Hasse started to retreat, but the squeak of her sneakers on the vinyl flooring caused the men in the lab to look up.

Manling asked, "*Senhora* Hasse, what are you doing here?"

"I work here. Remember, Mr. Manling?"

"Of course, but why are you here today? It's Sunday. You don't need to be back to work until tomorrow. Did you lose track of the days with the extra day off?"

"No, Mr. Manling. I needed to pick up a few personal things. My husband's brother has suddenly taken very ill, and I'm going to need to take next week off to help out his wife with the children. But I'm glad I found you here, so I could tell you in person. Sorry for the short notice, but illness always seems to happen at the most inopportune times."

"That's all right, *Senhora* Hasse. I don't think much work will get done here next week." He tilted his head toward the policemen.

Hasse asked, "What's going on? Did somebody steal something?"

"It wouldn't be appropriate to discuss the details at the moment. Permission granted for the vacation. I hope your husband's brother gets well. See you in another week."

"Thank you, sir." She turned away.

When she was almost to the doorway, one of the policemen called out, "*Senhora!*"

She stopped and turned around. "Yes?"

"Do you know anything about this?" He pointed to the jar.

She shook her head. "No."

"Have you seen anyone in the lab handling it before?"

Hasse hesitated before responding. "Let me take a look." *Do I want to just fade into the background,* she thought, *or do I want to misdirect everyone?* She walked up to the counter.

"Don't touch the jar, please, *senhora*," the policeman warned. "But do you recall seeing anyone with it?"

She shifted the position of her bifocals, then bent over to take a closer look at the jar. *If I just skip town and don't come back, they'll know it was me. If I finger someone else, eventually that will end up pointing the finger back at me. I can just keep showing up for work after another week to allay suspicions. But what if they discover some other evidence in the interim that points to me? I will have missed my chance for a getaway. I must consult with Goliath before deciding how to proceed.*

"I haven't seen it before." She shook her head. "What is it?"

"We don't wish to disclose that information just yet."

She was about to turn away when the other policeman spoke up. "*Senhora*, do you by chance know the whereabouts of Larissa Júnior? Did you hear her say anything recently about going away somewhere?"

They already suspect someone else? Hasse thought. *How fortunate.* She shook her head. "Sorry, but Larissa didn't talk to me much. I don't think she liked me."

"Thank you, *senhora*. You may go now."

She was almost to the door when Manling called out, "Martina!"

She stopped and turned again.

He asked, "Aren't you forgetting something?"

"Huh? Oh, yes. I need to get my things."

Hasse walked back into the lab and retrieved a few personal items from a drawer before heading out the door.

When she was gone, Manling turned to the policemen. "As I was saying, officers. You probably won't find any fingerprints on that, since everyone in the lab wears latex gloves..."

÷

Exiting the Delcese access road, Hasse pounded a fist against the steering wheel. *My usefulness here to the swarm is blown now,* she thought. *I won't be able to culture anything in the lab. I won't be able to proceed with the tetanus project. And I wasn't even able to get my hands on the coffee fungus.*

She glanced at the clock on the dashboard. *Shoot. I have to hurry to send a message to Brother Goliath in less than an hour. He won't be pleased with me. He'll probably decide that I've failed the swarm. The last person that happened to ended up as shark food in the Indian Ocean. I can't send him this bad news. Maybe I'm better off not sending any message at all. I could go to the police and spill the beans. Yeah, and then I'd spend the rest of my life in jail. Maybe I should flee. But where would I go? Who could I trust? I can't go to Brother Aidea. That would just tip off Goliath. And what about my husband? Poor clueless Gunter. Do I just abandon him after all these years?*

I suppose I simply could forget about the Curators Of The Earth, and keep living the life I have been, going to work in the lab and hanging out with the birding buddies on the weekends. But if I do that, Goliath will soon figure out that I've deserted him. And he'll send someone after me, probably Aidea. I've got to run for it. I'll have to pick up some things at home first.

She pounded the steering wheel again. *Why couldn't I have just gone on living the nice quiet life preparing a deadly new bacterial strain to wipe out a sizable chunk of the world's human population?*

÷÷÷÷÷

At half past midnight in Yogyakarta, Zeger pounded his fist on the desk, rattling the computer keyboard and monitor. He said to Pukartra, "Sister Cleobaea has let us down, Brother Pyrrhus. This does not bode well for my planned announcement at dawn."

÷÷÷÷÷

The doorbell rang at the Hasses' apartment in Piracicaba. Gunter came in from the tiny balcony overlooking the city. He opened the door and was surprised to see the tall, burly man with curly graying hair and leathery skin. "Hey, Sergio. *Quanto tempo.*" Long time no see.

"It's good to see you again, *Senhor* Hasse." They shook hands.

"Come in, please." Gunter closed the door behind the guest. "I've only seen you a couple of times since the Amazon River trip when you fixed the broken down *gaiola* in Santarém. Martina tells me she sees you occasionally at work." They sat down in the living room. "Can I get you anything? How about a cup of coffee? Heh, heh. I bet you hear that one all the time."

Sergio Moreno shook his head. "No thank you, *senhor.*"

"How've you been?"

"I've been busy tending the fields, but I don't know what'll happen to my job now that most of the fields have been burned."

"One heck of a bonfire you folks had. I saw it on the TV news."

"That was at Sede. I work at one of the other plantations, Fiorva. No news people there, but even bigger fire."

"How's your cousin Gilberta?"

"She's good."

At the lull in the conversation, Gunter asked, "So, what brings you here today?"

"I was hoping to speak to *Senhora* Hasse. It's a work matter."

"I don't know where she is at the moment. Her bag is here, and her car is gone. She must have come back from her weekend jaunt to São Paulo and gone out again. I'm not sure when she'll be home. Do you want me to give her a message for you?"

"It's very important. If you don't mind, I'll wait here for her."

"That's fine. Are you sure you wouldn't like something to..."

They both turned when they heard the front door open.

Gunter called out, "Honey, look who's here. Our old pal, Sergio."

Oh, shit! Martina thought, straining not to pee in her panties. *Brother Aidea. I'm dead meat.*

After exchanging pleasantries, Sergio said, "I must speak with you, *senhora*, regarding the coffee fields."

Gunter headed back toward the balcony. "I'll leave you two to chat about work."

When her husband was outside, Martina said, "Why have you come to my home, *Irmão* Aidea? You know it's a breach of protocol."

Sergio replied, "I have something important for you. I couldn't risk driving around in my truck, so I hitchhiked all the way here." His voice was somber and gravelly. He reached into his pocket.

Martina cringed, expecting the deed to be done by knife. *Brother Goliath must have gotten a message to him after I failed to respond. God, please let it be quick and painless.*

Sergio opened his hand to reveal several coffee cherries covered with red fungus. "I took a bunch of these from the experimental crop fields north of Fiorva. I thought that the fungus should be preserved. I thought that *Irmão* Goliath might find it useful."

Martina's eyes grew wide, but when she didn't speak, Sergio misinterpreted how the ranking Sister was reacting to the initiative he had taken without explicit orders.

He said, "I'm sorry, *Irmã* Cleobaea. I should've asked permission first, but I was concerned that Delcese might burn the experimental fields soon. Perhaps I made a mistake."

When Martina finally took a breath, she asked, "How much do you have?"

"After we burned the plantation fields at Fiorva on Friday, instead of going home, I drove out to the experimental coffee fields. At the first field where I saw fungus, I pulled over and started handpicking as fast as I could. I stayed there into the middle of the night, picking cherries non-stop until the bed of my pickup truck was full. Then I drove to an isolated garage in Campo do Coxo. My cousin, who is *Irmã* Harmonia's brother, owns the place. He's away for a week visiting his mother up in Manaus. I slept on the garage floor yesterday. My pickup truck is still there holding the load. I think I collected a couple hundred kilograms. My arms are sore from all the picking."

The farm worker was quite startled when his sister-in-arms took him into her arms with a hug.

When she released him, she said, "You've done well *Irmão* Aidea. I must examine the haul to assess the effort required to prepare it for use." She called out to her husband, "Gunter, I have to go out again to deal with an urgent matter at work. I'll be back late. Don't wait up."

÷

Starting up her car with Sergio in the passenger seat, Hasse said. "I need to make a detour on the way. I must get word of your good work to *Irmão* Goliath at once. And I must find out how he wants us to proceed on this new project."

She drove northwest out of town, then instead of taking the right turn toward Campo do Coxo, she continued straight ahead. Shortly, she pulled into a parking lot.

"Wait in the car," she said to Sergio as she got out.

Inside the Grande Hotel, Hasse casually strolled past the reception desk and down the hallway to the business center room. She had never been there before on a Sunday, and it hadn't occurred to her that the door might be locked. *Shit*, she thought, *I can't ask anyone to open up the room for me. Where else can I find email access that's totally untraceable to me and available right now? I don't have time to go searching all over town if I want a prayer of Goliath seeing the message before dawn there. I might have to risk a direct phone call or a text message, but either of those could piss him off even more.*

She looked through the door glass at the computers so near and yet so far. She pounded her fist against the door frame.

÷

Larissa Júnior was walking in her swimsuit with a towel wrapped around her waist, headed from the pool back to her room. After she passed through the lobby and into a hallway, she nearly bumped into a woman standing outside a door.

The two women, both startled to see a familiar face and embarrassed to be discovered at the hotel, said the same thing at the same time. "What are you doing here?"

After a moment of silence, Hasse said, "I left something inside the business center. I came back to get it."

Larissa asked, "Are you staying here?"

Hasse shook her head, avoiding direct eye contact.

Larissa smiled and held up her room key card. She slid it into the card reader, unlocking the door. "Have fun, Martina," she said, and she walked on.

"Thank you, Larissa."

A moment later, both women were thinking the same thought. *I should have told her not to tell anyone she saw me here.*

÷

Hasse scrunched her lips while she composed her message:

> goliath, sorry for late response. good news i discovered new species this week named a. deckerii. i was so busy with that i did not have time to communicate back earlier. now bad news, lab manager discovered jar, and suits are involved. i have not been linked, but i wont be able to continue my work there. must seek new lab job. now second good news, brother aidea procured couple hundred kilograms fruit with tiny red vegetable you desire. need a few days to separate it. will know more when I examine. how do you intend consequence to be distributed. we await your instructions. cleobaea

Then she encoded it with the standard scheme, which took more than 30 minutes for the relatively long message. When she clicked the Send button, she mumbled, "I just hope someone checks the messages before dawn over there."

Hasse's message had been more explicit than usual, but she needed to make sure critical information was communicated correctly. As always, she was concerned about the potential to be implicated if the message fell into wrong hands. *At least I'll have an easier time finding other anonymous Internet access points while I'm not working during the day.* Then she thought of something that further increased her concern. *Larissa saw me here. If this communication becomes compromised, to prevent her from implicating me, I may need to make her extinct.* She scrunched her lips again while she considered how she might perform the task, but she decided, *I'll worry about that later, after the fungus project.*

÷÷÷÷

Larissa was standing at the entrance to the hotel's dining room when she felt a tap on her shoulder. She turned and faced a woman, about 50 years old with permed hair and wide-rimmed eyeglasses.

Larissa gave her a quizzical look but didn't say anything.

"I saw you at the swimming pool earlier, fending off the lechers," the woman said. "And I noticed you eating dinner alone last night. You must be here by yourself. My name is Cicera."

"I'm Larissa."

"Would you like to join me and my lady friends for dinner?"

"I... uh,..."

"Good," the woman said, not waiting for a reply. She took Larissa by the arm and led her to a table where two other women, apparently identical twins, sat.

"My name is Esta," the first twin said.

"Mine is Oesta," the second added.

Larissa had to chuckle at the twins' names, roughly the feminized equivalents of the words for "east" and "west."

"Our parents had an odd sense of humor," Esta said with a shrug.

Cicera explained, "We all come here without our husbands for our annual *semana das meninas* [girls' week]. We're always looking for a fourth to play cards."

Esta asked, "What games do you know?"

Larissa replied, "I used to play Sueca when I was in school, and a little Truco, but I haven't touched a deck of cards in years."

"Ever play King?" Despite the conversation taking place in Portuguese, Esta used the English word for male monarch.

Larissa shook her head.

"Then we'll teach you," Oesta said. "You'll be playing with the best of them in no time."

Cicera asked, "Where are you from, dear?"

Larissa replied, "I live here."

"You live at the Grande Hotel?"

"No. I mean I live here in town, in Águas de São Pedro."

"Coming to this hotel isn't exactly getting away," Esta noted.

Oesta said, "She must be hiding out from the law."

÷÷÷÷

In Campo do Coxo, Hasse's car bounced along the lengthy dirt driveway, at the end of which sat a weathered single-story cinderblock garage with three bay doors. When they got out of the car, Sergio manually lifted the door on the right, exposing his pickup truck parked inside. He flipped on the lights in the bay and pulled back the tarpaulin on the rear of the vehicle.

Hasse dug her hands into the load of fungus-covered coffee cherries, lifting them up and letting them tumble through her fingers as though they were piles of money.

"We must devise a way to separate the fungus from the cherries," she said.

Sergio switched on the lights in the other two bays, revealing an assortment of light-duty construction equipment.

Walking between the pieces of machinery, Hasse asked, "What does your cousin do for work?"

"He builds swimming pools."

Hasse pointed to a particular machine. "That will do it."

Chapter 18

"**The mark of your ignorance is the depth of your belief in injustice and tragedy. What the caterpillar calls the end of the world, the master calls a butterfly.**"

From "The Messiah's Handbook," in the novel *Illusions: The Adventures of a Reluctant Messiah*, by Richard Bach, 1977

~ ~ ~ ~ ~

AUGUST 12

In the dawn light on the hill at Baron Beach, 21 people in hooded robes stood in a line facing another hooded man.

Eddy Zeger hung his head, contemplating how to proceed. *The mission will be far more difficult without Sister Cleobaea*, he thought, *but it's still feasible.* He decided to begin by reinforcing the necessity of communications for the survival of any society. He brushed back his hood, lifted his head, and began orating, "Brothers and Sisters, I have called you together..."

Before Zeger completed the first sentence, Pukartra came running up the hill yelling, "Brother Goliath! Brother Goliath!" His voice grew louder as he approached. When he reached the group, Pukartra bent over with hands on his knees to catch his breath.

Zeger asked, "What is it, Brother Pyrrhus?"

Pukartra gasped for air. "I have word from Sister Cleobaea."

The two men conversed in hushed voices for a minute, then Zeger patted Pukartra on the back and turned away beaming.

"Brothers and Sisters," Zeger began again, "I have called you together to celebrate the dawning of a new era." He waved an arm at the rising sun. "A new era, not only for the Curators Of The Earth, but a new era for The Earth itself." He waved an arm toward the assembled people. "For years our members here and abroad have been working quietly in the shadows, hiding from view while we have been preparing to initiate The Apocalypse. Soon we will emerge from our cocoon, and our presence will become widely known. World leaders will tremble at our actions. Yes, some innocent people will suffer in the process, but it will be for the greater good of The Earth." He paced back and forth. "This time of action has come about sooner than I had anticipated, because our plans have changed for the better. Our prior plan, Operation Sweet Surprise, is a good one, and it will proceed in due course.

But first, we will implement a revolutionary new plan, called Operation Intended Consequence. This new plan focuses our efforts not on destroying the people, but on destroying their social structures and their leadership. Brothers and Sisters, we will bring the world's largest economies to their knees." He pointed straight down with both hands. "We will achieve this monumental goal by virtue of a new weapon now in our possession. This new weapon is not a weapon of mass destruction, but a weapon of economic destruction. And with it, my friends, we will bring new meaning to the term 'eco-terrorism.'" He carried on for five minutes without once mentioning coffee or fungus.

When the speech concluded and robed people were wandering off the hillside, Zeger thought, *I still must punish Sister Cleobaea for her lab work being discovered by the law.* He started down the hill. *But not until after she has completed her new task.*

÷

Standing alone in front of a world map on the wall of his office at Kraton Kupu Kupu, Zeger contemplated the logistics of the operation. His first major decision was where to deploy the fungus. Using published coffee production statistics, he stuck colored pins on the map into the 20 largest coffee-growing nations, those that had produced a million or more 60 kilogram bags the previous year.

Countries that primarily produced arabica beans were marked with red pins:

- Brazil
- Colombia
- Costa Rica
- El Salvador
- Ethiopia
- Guatemala
- Honduras
- India
- Kenya
- Mexico
- Nicaragua
- Papua New Guinea
- Peru
- Venezuela

Countries that primarily produced robusta beans were marked with yellow pins:

- Cameroon
- Côte d'Ivoire

- Indonesia
- Thailand
- Vietnam
- Uganda

Collectively, those nations accounted for approximately 95 percent of worldwide coffee bean production. Zeger was aware that so far the fungus had only struck in arabica fields, but he didn't know whether that was due to resistance on the part of robusta plants or to lack of opportunity in robusta fields. Out of scientific curiosity, he planned to do the world a favor in finding out, although he was only willing to devote a small portion of his limited resources to the robusta fields.

The next decision was his most critical: how to distribute the fungus to the coffee fields.

Zeger realized that timing of the distribution was critical to the success of the project, for three reasons. First, spores had to be spread to target plantations worldwide in one or two days, before preventative measures could be instituted to block entry into the coffee-producing countries once the outbreak began. Second, simultaneous infection worldwide would generate a critical mass of mass media attention, maximizing fear of an impending shortage. And third, simultaneous infection worldwide would make it evident the infection was intentional, just as airplanes crashing into the two towers of the World Trade Center within minutes of each other could not have been coincidental.

He came up with a number of basic scenarios for consideration:

a. Ship fungus from Brazil directly to unsuspecting individuals working at the coffee growers in each country, hoping that they would carry it in on their clothing or possessions, or that it would simply spread through the air once unleashed locally.

b. Ship fungus from Brazil to his own members around the world, who would then similarly forward the packages to unwitting carriers.

c. Ship the entire lot of fungus to a single location outside Brazil, then have each of his members pick up some and personally travel to the coffee fields to spread it.

d. Have his members travel to Brazil to carry fungus onward to coffee fields from there.

e. Ship fungus from Brazil to his own members individually, each of whom would then travel to the coffee fields.

Zeger quickly eliminated the first two scenarios because the risk was too great that transmission to the coffee fields would fail. The recipients undoubtedly would be wary of packages spewing red powder when opened, particularly once the outbreak began and media reports

emerged, as he had learned from his attempts years earlier to dissemi-
nate anthrax spores and later ricin through the U.S. Postal Service. (On
those projects, he was of mixed opinion about whether or not spawn-
ing of copycats was beneficial to his objectives.) The decision meant he
would need to use his own people to spread the fungus to the coffee
plantations.

Zeger ruled out shipping the entire lot of fungus to a single location because the risk to the mission was too high if the package got lost
in transit or was delayed in customs. He considered the possibility of
using Colombian drug runners to move the entire lot out of Brazil for
him, but he decided smugglers from that nation in particular might be
problematic if they were to discover what it was they were carrying on
his behalf.

Zeger's decision narrowed down to whether or not he wanted his
members all to travel to Brazil to obtain the fungus. He concluded that
it would be too risky to bring them to Brazil, as a sizable chunk of his
group could be wiped out in one fell swoop if they were caught red-
handed. So by process of elimination, he elected to have packages of
the fungus sent from Brazil to various members who would then carry
the fungus to coffee fields of the world and spread it themselves.

Of the 53 current members of his organization, Zeger was willing
to deploy up to half of them to distribute the fungus. Sitting at his desk
with a pencil in one hand and a printout of coffee production statistics
in the other, he looked back and forth between the world map and the
statistics. He tallied the number of people that would be assigned to
each country based on a combination of that country's coffee production capacity, geographic size, proximity to other coffee-producing
regions, and arabica to robusta ratio (favoring arabica). He repeatedly
scratched out and rewrote numbers until he came up with a suitable
list totaling 26 people:

    - six for Brazil
    - three for Colombia
    - three for Indonesia
        (one of whom would also cover Papua New Guinea)
    - three for Mexico
    - two for India
    - two for Vietnam (one of whom would also cover Thailand)
    - one for Ethiopia
    - one for Peru
    - one for Venezuela
    - one for El Salvador, Guatemala, and Honduras

COFFEE CRASH

- one for Nicaragua and Costa Rica
- one for Kenya and Uganda
- one for Côte d'Ivoire and Cameroon.

Next, he examined his available assets: who was already located where; of which countries were they citizens; and who already had visas or exemptions for which countries. The group's members included citizens of 19 countries, many of whom were frequent travelers.

In the years following the September 11th attacks, most countries' passports had been enhanced with security features such as embedded electronic chips, holograms, and ultraviolet inks. In addition, border entry was now more closely scrutinized. Zeger weighed the risks of exposing his members' true identities versus the chances that they might get stopped at the borders using fake passports. He decided that completing the mission took precedence, so international travel would have to use the members' real passports. (Fake local ID cards still were easy to obtain and relatively low risk to use.)

The computer file in which Zeger maintained pertinent information about his members identified each by his or her species code name, covert email address, countries of citizenship and residency, among a host of other details, but excluded their real names and street addresses. Some individual members knew or even were related to each other, such as cousins Sister Harmonia and Brother Aidea. However, for their mutual protection, Zeger's head was the only place the real names of all his members collectively resided.

To spread the fungus in Brazil, Zeger planned to have pairs of members share driving duties to cover the large geographic area containing coffee plantations in the limited time that would be allotted. He wanted three pairs, but he only had four members already inside the borders. Checking his lists, he chose to add a Canadian man whose wife was Brazilian-born, giving the man a permanent visa by right of marriage. For the sixth person, Zeger selected his only member from Iceland, one of the countries whose citizens were not required to have visas for tourist travel to Brazil.

A disadvantage of the fungus distribution scenario Zeger devised would be the need to get numerous packages out of Brazil into the recipients' countries. If he had chosen to have the participants fly to Brazil, they could have hand-carried the fungus out in their luggage. International package shipments entailed the risk of delays clearing customs, not to mention the paper trails they left behind.

Zeger decided the packages would be sent from multiple locations across Brazil using over-the-counter outlets of the major international package delivery services DHL, FedEx, and UPS. No two packages would be sent from the same location or to the same location. No two packages would bear the same sender's information.

The package recipients would use fake local identities to check in at business-oriented hotels in their home countries, where they could collect a delivery to themselves as a guest. The recipients would then hand-carry the fungus to the target countries, travelling under their real identities. In that way, no trail would connect the package shipments from Brazil to the fungal infestations that would occur in the target counties.

For customs declaration, Zeger had to decide what the packages of red powder would purportedly contain. When he came up with an idea, he laughed at the connotation of removing filth from The Earth.

For timing of the project, Zeger estimated: five days for Sister Cleobaea and Brother Aidea to separate the fungus from the coffee cherries and load it into laundry detergent boxes; one day to pack and label the shipping boxes; four more days for a team to drop off the packages at shipping locations around Brazil; three days for worldwide express shipping; plus two extra days to allow for customs delays or other unforeseen circumstances.

He tallied the numbers and concluded that the distribution of the fungus into the coffee fields could begin as soon as 15 days. The actual sprinkling of the fungus into the fields would need to occur worldwide within a coordinated window of two days (effectively two and a half days factoring in the span of time zones at coffee-producing nations around the globe). He would need Cleobaea to confirm how long from then until overt signs appeared in the coffee fields, but he estimated that starting with spores that had gone into exogenous dormancy while stored in the boxes, it would take two days for initial germination. That made a grand total of 19 days.

Zeger flipped the page of his desk calendar to September. He considered the possibility of the 11th as a nod to history, but he decided the date would only cast him in someone else's shadow. He considered the autumnal equinox on the 22nd, which had the appeal of astronomical forces at work, but his objective of inciting panic would be better served by leaving no doubt that the new fungal outbreak was manmade. Then he spotted a notation in one of the boxes on the calendar, and he immediately knew the target date for the project, exactly 21 days away. *What better day to commence economic collapse,* he thought, *than a national holiday celebrating capitalist workers? On Labor Day in the U.S., the butterfly will flap its wings. And when the financial markets open the following day, the tornado will strike.*

To coordinate everything for this project, Zeger and Pukartra would have to manage a larger number of simultaneous messages and more detailed messages than the group had ever before attempted. For communications security, Pukartra had configured his and Zeger's computers to use both a virtual private network (VPN) and the Tor anonymity network. But they considered that solution unworkable for their distant members, who needed the ability to communicate using public Internet terminals anywhere in the world, without necessarily having their own laptops, tablets, or even USB flash drives loaded with applications.

The group's rules prohibited use of mobile phones or other cellular network devices for group-related activities because the devices' usage and movements were too easily tracked. (Members were free to use such devices for personal or business purposes not related to the group.) From a practical standpoint, the group's text-heavy communication method made it cumbersome to use mobile phones to encode messages anyway.

Zeger and Pukartra deemed email via standard Secure Sockets Layer (SSL) encryption to be adequate protection for text messages that were already encoded by another method that members could perform without special software or memorized encryption keys. The greater potential risk lay in prying eyes seeing decoded messages on one end or the other.

Their strategy was to embed their actual messages into innocuous passages of text. The encoding method which Pukartra had devised for this was a combination of simple concealment techniques including elements of a null cipher and a space code. All their emails appeared as text cut and pasted from online news articles, mated to appropriate subject lines such as, "Football World Championships!" and, "Politics As Usual?" The base news article could be in any language using the Roman alphabet. The subject matter of the body text was irrelevant. The message to be transmitted was contained in subtle additions to the text. The sender would compose a desired message, preferably in English, then go through the text from the base article and just add an extra space character before each letter of the message at the beginning of a word along the way. No more than one extra space would be added to any paragraph of text. Space characters within the desired message (between the words) were merely implied. Punctuation was kept to a minimum, although where essential, a line break could be added after a corresponding mark in the base text.

The example below illustrates how the word *goliath* might be encoded.

This passage:

> Bus·drivers·have·gone·on·strike·over·health·care·issues,
> ·causing·many·commuters·to·endure·lengthy·trudges·to·work
> ·on·foot.·Independent·limousine·and·taxi·drivers·happily
> ·experienced·a·surge·in·fares.

becomes this:

> Bus·drivers·have··gone··on·strike·over·health·care·issues,
> ·causing·many·commuters·to·endure··lengthy·trudges·to·work
> ·on·foot.··Independent·limousine··and··taxi·drivers··happily
> ·experienced·a·surge·in·fares.

(In practice, extra spaces were interspersed less frequently and over much longer passages of text.) The theory was that if a casual observer, such as a spouse or coworker, noticed anything unusual at all, he or she would assume the extra spaces were unintentional due to sloppy typing, not suspecting that the extra spaces *were* the message. The problem that the sender often faced was finding a base document long enough that a even a brief message could be encoded by interspersing the extra spaces infrequently enough that they wouldn't be noticed at all. Casual observers never noticed anyway, as the untrained human mind paid no attention to excess nothingness.

The intended recipient usually could identify the extra spaces by eye, but if necessary, he or she could electronically search for multiple consecutive space characters. The entire process was quite simple for both sender and receiver, although the sender needed to ensure that the base text did not already possess any double spaces. A few letters—Q, X, and Z—could be hard to find as leading letters in base text, at least in English language documents, and, if needed, spaces could be added in the middle of words. Those were more difficult for the recipient to find through electronic search, but easier to spot by eye, which made them riskier. As a last resort, the sender could add a word or two into the text to fabricate base words for letters. To reduce the chances of raising suspicion, most senders stuck to using articles with themes related to their own personal interests such as sports or hobbies, and they never added any spaces in the first few paragraphs of an article.

A skilled code breaker—or even an unskilled one—easily could have figured out the system, but the objective was to employ a practical method that never would be brought to the attention of a professional code breaker. The system, rather than hiding messages in unbreakable form, was hiding the fact that messages were being hidden, and doing so from people who weren't looking for hidden messages.

As a security measure, each valid email message needed to have an exclamation point or a question mark at the end of its subject line.

In addition, the presence of three consecutive exclamation points (!!!) or question marks (???) at the end of the subject line would signal that, respectively, the sender's or the receiver's identity had been compromised. At the time, neither "compromised" signal had ever been used.

÷÷÷÷÷

Early Monday morning, Sergio Moreno phoned *Senhor* Mabro at Fazenda Fiorva, urgently requesting a week's vacation due to an illness in the family. Considering the lack of viable plants at his plantation, Mabro had no problem granting the request, although if he had consulted with Manling in the lab at Sede, the two of them might have wondered if an epidemic was breaking out in the region.

Hasse left home at the usual hour, never telling her husband that she wouldn't be going into work that day, or that week.

÷

At the garage in Campo do Coxo, Sergio pulled the pickup truck out of the bay. He turned it around and backed it up so the tailgate was just inside the bay doorway. With a shovel and a broom, he pushed the payload out onto the cement floor, then he parked the pickup truck out of the way. He moved aside several pieces of equipment in the garage and rolled the portable cement mixer outside. The portable unit, with only half a cubic meter capacity, proved adequate albeit time consuming for the task at hand. (A large cement mixer truck, which his cousin only hired by the load, would have been overkill for the amount of material Sergio had to process.)

Sergio ran a heavy duty extension cord out to the mixer and plugged it in. As a test, he shoveled coffee cherries in through the mouth of the upward tilted drum until it was about half full. He flipped on the power switch and moved a manual lever. The drum began to spin. He sat down on a stool to wait. After a few minutes, he stopped the mixer to inspect its contents. He realized that the cherries' surfaces were too smooth to scrape the fungus off of each other. He walked around the exterior of the garage looking for material to enhance the friction. He came back with a shovelful of gravel that he dumped into the mixer. He restarted the motor and sat down again.

Soon, Hasse's car came up the driveway. From the trunk of the car, they unloaded three hefty cardboard cartons. Sergio opened one of the cartons to reveal small boxes of powdered laundry detergent, 0.75 kilograms each. Hasse pulled out one of the boxes, which were blue with yellow lettering for the brand name Dirt-Away. Using a lock blade knife, Sergio surgically separated the glue holding the bottom flap, then he dumped the white powdered contents of the box into a wheelbarrow. He set aside the empty box.

They went to check the load in the cement mixer. Sergio stopped the mixer, dug his hand to the bottom, and came out with a handful of mixed pieces of coffee cherry husks, pulp, beans, chaff, and a small amount of fine red powder from the fungus and spores.

Hasse asked, "How long has this run?"

"About half an hour."

"Let it run another fifteen minutes. Then we'll sift it."

Sergio looked through the tools and equipment in the garage. He came back out with a coarse metal mesh mounted in a wooden frame about one meter a side. "It's for sifting rocks out of dirt."

Hasse said, "We can use it for a first pass to weed out the major debris, but the gaps are too big for the mesh to separate the fungus from the rest of the material."

Sergio returned to the garage and after much searching came back with a mosquito head net. He scooped a handful of the mixture into the net and shook it back and forth for a few seconds, but only a tiny amount of red material fell through.

"The net is too fine," Hasse said. "I'll look for something in town."

Hasse got back in her car and headed down the driveway. Sergio started up the mixer again, then pulled out another box of laundry detergent and opened the bottom flap.

When Hasse returned two hours later, she had a meter-wide roll of window screening material, which had been a challenge to find since few homes in the region had window screens.

Sergio got up from his seat in front of the wheelbarrow now full of detergent powder. He shut off the mixer. He cut a piece of the window screen and laid it on top of the mesh frame. He scooped some contents from the mixer onto the screen, and he jiggled the frame over another wheelbarrow. Hasse inspected the particles below. She smiled. About 80 percent of what had come through was red.

Sergio sifted for 20 minutes to produce enough powder to fill a detergent box, scooping it in with a trowel. Using a hot melt glue gun, he resealed the bottom of the box.

Hasse checked over the completed box. "One down," she said, "fifty or sixty more to go."

÷÷÷÷÷

Costa and Lieutenant Azevedo entered the Security office in the Administration Building at Sede de Delcese Agricola. Costa took a seat behind the desk. Azevedo closed the door and remained standing.

The policeman spoke, "My superior, *Capitão* Ratiba, discussed the situation with his superiors, who brought it to the attention of the *Diretor-Geral*. They all agree that we should keep this affair under wraps for now. We don't want to cause public panic, especially when we don't know what *Senhorita* Júnior planned to do with the tetanus bacteria and toxin."

Costa asked, "Any luck locating her?"

Azevedo replied, "We've checked all the hospitals in the region on the chance that Júnior really had a medical emergency as she claimed in her phone message for Manling. No sign of her, though. She hasn't used her credit or debit cards since she disappeared, but she withdrew a substantial amount of cash from her bank account. We're checking all the calls to and from her mobile phone over the last month, as well as her data accesses and text messages. But her phone hasn't even been turned on since Thursday, so we haven't been able to get a fix on her current location."

"I heard that mobile service companies could track a phone's location even when it's turned off, as long as the battery is still in place."

"That's just a myth spread by the FBI up in the States to keep the crooks paranoid. If we'd known in advance that we wanted to track her, we might have been able to remotely install software on her phone to trick her into thinking she powered it off when she actually hadn't. But if the phone is already off, we can't access it." Azevedo set down a sheet of paper on the desk. "The last call Júnior made before turning off her phone was from downtown Piracicaba to this number here." He pointed to a line on the paper.

Costa scanned the employee list. "That's Manling's line. Must have been when she left him the message."

"In addition, two voice mail messages have been left for her. One was from her girlfriend in Águas, the one that we visited Friday night. The other was from a man. According to the cellular records, that call was placed from a number assigned to a prepaid mobile phone. We don't know the owner's identity yet, but we should have it from the mobile service provider by the end of the day."

"Can I hear the messages they left?"

Azevedo took out his mobile phone. He navigated to the audio files, then pressed the Play button.

When Costa heard the woman's recorded message, he smirked at Azevedo. "You've got an admirer." When the man's message started, Costa's eyes bugged out.

Azevedo said, "You recognize the voice?"

"He works here." Costa wrote down a name on a note pad, then he opened a computer file to retrieve and add the employee's telephone number and home address to the paper. He peeled it off the pad and handed it over.

Azevedo looked at the telephone number on the note. "His number matches the one that left the message on Júnior's phone. We must question him."

Costa shook his head. "It's clear from the message that he doesn't know where Júnior is, and neither of them knows that we know they're involved with each other. If we want to find her, I suggest keeping him under surveillance. That'll be easy to do while he's at work." Costa motioned to the central console, visible through the glass panel in the office door, where Tulio sat in front of the bank of video monitors.

Azevedo said, "Then we'll stake out his house and have a detail keep an eye on him wherever he goes. We'll tap his phone, too. Sooner or later she's bound to contact him."

÷÷÷÷÷

The four women sat around a table in the hotel's *sala de carteado* (card room), with Cicera across from Larissa and, naturally, Esta and Oesta across from each other. On the green felt surface, Cicera spread out the cards, a Copag da Amazônia #139 *naipe grande* (large print) deck manufactured in the city of Manaus, Brazil.

While Cicera shuffled, Esta explained to Larissa the rules of King.

When Esta finished, Larissa said, "You want to lose tricks most of the time? And the rules change for each of the ten contracts?"

Esta nodded.

"That's more complicated than Bridge."

"We make it even more complicated, honey," Oesta added. "For the hands with negative contracts, we play Turkish style. The cards are dealt out and played counter-clockwise."

Larissa rolled her eyes.

÷÷÷÷÷

With the view overlooking San Francisco Bay, Truck Macklin and Matthew Cochran stared at each other across Cochran's desk.

The CFO spoke to the CEO, "Matt, our stock is down twenty-two percent since Friday's opening. With the futures price drops on Friday and today, this little project of yours is now underwater, or should I say below the ice. With our ability to trade in a deep freeze, the values of the futures have dropped by millions, and the losses will only pile up further as the prices keep falling. We've already received a margin call from the ICE. And if our trading is still frozen when the contracts come due, we'll be forced to take delivery and pay for all those beans. But since you bought triple what I OK'd, we don't have the cash on hand or the financial backing to pay for them all. After Ridley's article, no banker in her right mind will pony up more funds for us. We'll be lucky if our bankers follow through on what they already agreed to loan us. In short, we're screwed."

"Relax, Truck. The first contracts aren't due until late September. A lot can happen between now and then. I wouldn't mind if the fungus made a comeback. Hell, I'd spread it around myself if I could. It would scare the shit out of everyone and bump up the market again."

Macklin rolled out of the office just as Parananda was coming in.

"You wanted to see me, Matt?"

Cochran got up and closed the door. He walked back and stood next to his VP of Marketing. "I've been thinking, Rami, with all the bad press we've been getting, we've got to change our image."

"I can bring in a new ad agency. We can test out some alternative branding ideas in focus groups."

"That's not what I had in mind." Cochran put a hand on Parananda's shoulder. "I was thinking at a higher level. The financial analysts and our shareholders will be looking for a more meaningful change. Something to clearly indicate that Bright Cup is cleaning up its act. Or perhaps I should say shaking up its senior management."

Parananda stared at the CEO for a few seconds before he grasped the underlying message. "I hope you're not thinking what I think you're thinking."

"Rami, the way I figure it, Ridley's article points to you and me as the brains behind the project last week." Cochran went to the desk and retrieved some papers. "I've drafted a letter of resignation for you. You've decided to spend more time with your family, pursue other interests, yada yada. I've generously agreed to give you severance of two years' salary. Of course the confidentiality clause of your employment contract remains in effect."

Chapter 19

"A quoi sert un enfant nouveau-né?"
["What use is a newborn baby?"]

Benjamin Franklin, 1783

~~~~~

AUGUST 13

At 9:00AM, *Doutora* Strath stood in the doorway of *Doutor* Neto's office at Instituto Butantan.

Strath said, "Remember those blood samples from *Doutor* Barada at UNICAMP last week?"

Neto replied, "You wanted to run some more tests on them."

"Exactly. I've now isolated and analyzed the toxin using affinity peptide mapping. Some of the histidine residues differ from conventional tetanospasmin. This toxin is a variant we haven't seen before. It must be from a new strain of *C. tetani*."

"Interesting."

"It gets more interesting, *Doutor* Neto. Normally, tetanospasmin antibodies offer a good deal of protection from the toxin, but in the case of this new toxin, the standard antibodies offer no protection at all. The new kid on the block is a very bad boy."

"Hopefully he's confined to one block."

Strath sat down in the chair across from Neto's desk. "I'd like to run some additional tests. Can I get more of the blood, or better yet, a sample of the live bacteria?"

"After I called *Doutor* Barada to report your findings last week, he administered tetanus immunoglobulin to the patient. There might not be any more of the toxin in his blood. And the source of the bacteria is unknown."

"Where did the patient come from?"

Neto picked up from his desk the envelope that had been included with the blood samples. He unfolded the letter and skimmed it. "It says the patient lives in Piracicaba and works for Delcese Agricola."

"The coffee grower? The one that's been in the news lately with the red fungus killing the crop?"

"Yes, that's the company."

"That's quite a coincidence, a new fungus and a new bacterial strain both appearing at the same company around the same time."

Neto asked, "Are you thinking that the new tetanus bacteria might not have been naturally occurring? Maybe the result of some genetic engineering?"

Strath replied, "I don't know, but I'd like to find out. And I'd like to come up with a vaccine for it. For that I need the bacteria. I can't synthesize the toxin in the lab. As far as I know, nobody has produced tetanospasmin apart from using the bacteria. All the toxins of this sort are extremely complex molecules."

"If it had been easy to synthesize toxins, we wouldn't be known as The Snake Farm. I'll see if I can get you the name of someone to talk to up at Delcese."

"That'd be great."

÷

When Strath returned to her office, the message light on her phone was blinking.

The recording said, "This is Captain Ratiba of the Departamento de Polícia Federal. Please call me immediately..."

When she returned the man's call, he told her, "We have suspected samples of tetanus bacteria and toxin that we'd like you to confirm for us. This is a confidential matter of national security."

÷

Early that afternoon, Lieutenant Azevedo and another man from the DPF appeared in the doorway of Strath's office. When the doctor stood up for introductions, she and the tall lieutenant were eye-to-eye in height. The other man was shorter with a wiry build, and he wore street clothes rather than a uniform. His name was Emílio Melan, a forensic chemist with the title of *Perito Criminal* (Criminal Expert).

Melan carried a stainless steel case with biohazard labels on its sides. The men followed Strath to a lab. Melan put on latex gloves and opened the latches on the case. He handed Strath a honeycomb plate and a small vial of clear liquid.

Melan said, "My tests found *Clostridium tetani* on the plate but were inconclusive on the liquid."

Azevedo asked Strath, "How long do you need to test these?"

She checked her watch. "Give me a couple of hours."

÷

When the men returned to Strath's office later that day, Melan asked, "*Doutora*, have you confirmed the presence of *C. tetani* bacteria and its toxin in the samples?"

"Yes and no," she said. "They're tetanus bacteria and toxin, but they're not garden variety tetanus. Would you gentlemen care to tell me where these samples came from?"

Azevedo answered, "We're not at liberty to disclose the source of the samples at this time."

Strath said, "OK. Then I'll tell *you* where they came from: Delcese Agricola."

AUGUST 14

Shortly after sunrise, a farm worker at a small plantation in the Paraná region discovered traces of red fungus in coffee trees. Without fanfare, the field was burning by noon.

÷÷÷÷÷

That afternoon, a monkey in a cage at Instituto Butantan died of suffocation, unable to move its diaphragm to breathe. After an autopsy and examination of tissue specimens, its remains were cremated.

AUGUST 15

At 10:00AM, Helen Strath, Lieutenant Azevedo, Captain Ratiba, and Criminal Expert Melan walked into the second floor conference room at Sede de Delcese Agricola, where the waiting group consisted of Costa, Duarte, Manling, Munhoz, and Westphal.

After introductions, *Doutora* Strath stood at the head of the table and spoke. "When I tested the samples from the patient at UNICAMP last week, I was perplexed. A man with an up-to-date vaccination had succumbed to tetanus toxin without the presence of the bacteria in his blood. The most plausible explanation would have been a needle stick, but that seemed unlikely in the case of a pilot rather than a lab worker. The unusual nature of the infection led me to run additional tests, one of which was to isolate the toxin. I discovered that the toxin in his blood was different than normal tetanospasmin. Let's call this new toxin tetanospasmin-D. After I tested the plate sample and the liquid that the policemen brought on Tuesday, I wondered why someone would want to cultivate the bacteria and collect the toxin."

Ratiba asked rhetorically, "Isn't it obvious? For bio-terrorism."

Strath responded, "That wouldn't be obvious. *Clostridium tetani* is anaerobic, even this new strain of it. You can't spread it through the air. You'd have to get the spores or the bacteria into the bloodstream for infection. The toxin can handle oxygen, but you'd also have to get it into the bloodstream."

Duarte asked, "Then why do you believe this *C. tetani* was being cultivated, *Doutora* Strath? And why here?"

Strath continued, "Those questions are what led me to yesterday's test on a laboratory monkey. Using the diluted toxin solution provided to me by *Perito* Melan, and estimating the amount of toxin to achieve a lethal concentration in the monkey's blood, I mixed the solution into the monkey's food. I used twice the requisite amount, to accelerate any reaction."

Munhoz raised her hand. "When Sam... Professor Decker and I spoke to *Doutor* Barada at UNICAMP, he told us that tetanospasmin does not pass through the mucous membrane of the digestive system."

"Ordinarily, that would be correct. But what we're dealing with is not ordinary tetanospasmin. Twenty-two minutes after ingesting the toxin-laced food, the monkey began showing signs of muscle spasms and difficulty breathing. Twelve minutes later, it was dead. The monkey had been vaccinated against tetanus. I don't know how, but this new toxin passes through the digestive membrane, and conventional tetanus antibodies don't protect against it."

Everyone in the room was silent, until Duarte spoke, "So our lab was being used to cultivate pernicious new bacteria to produce an ingestible toxin, and our pilot, Miguel, was poisoned with this toxin?"

Strath said, "I believe that's correct."

Azevedo called out, "Attempted murder of the pilot, and murder of *Doutor* Mendonça!"

Strath continued, "Probably, but that would be a lot of work just to bring down a small plane. I think something else was afoot."

Duarte asked, "Like what?"

Strath strolled over toward the conference room window, and she gazed out at the remnants of the coffee fields in the distance. "If dormant spores of this bacteria are ingested, a portion of them could end up in anaerobic pockets within the digestive system. There, they could germinate into active bacteria that produce the toxin, which could then pass into the blood stream." She turned back to face the others in the room. "Spores of *C. tetani* are extremely durable. They can withstand boiling water." She stopped and waited.

Duarte was the first to catch on. "The coffee beans," he said matter-of-factly. "Sprinkle around these new tetanus spores on the processed beans, and you've got a means of spreading disease around the world. What better place to do it than at one of the world's largest coffee suppliers?"

Westphal asked, "Can these spores survive the roasting process? Roasting doesn't happen until the beans reach their destination country. It wouldn't do much good to apply the spores to the beans here only to have them killed off later."

Strath asked in response, "What's the roasting temperature?"

Manling answered, "It varies. Typically, coffee roasting is at about two hundred fifty degrees C. And the roasting process could last from five minutes to twenty-five, depending on the beans and the desired level of roast."

"How hot do the beans get?"

"Again it varies. For our Isabela beans, the stuff that used to grow out there..." Manling motioned toward the window. "...the first crack of the beans happens at a little over two hundred degrees C, and the second crack at about two twenty-five to two thirty."

Strath said, "That will be borderline for destroying the spores in the time frame you mentioned."

"We need to test this experimentally," Westphal said, standing up. "To the lab."

The rest of them stood up, except for Munhoz, who asked, "What about the sugarcane?"

They all sat down again.

Strath asked, "How is sugarcane processed into crystal sugar?"

Westphal explained the basic steps.

Strath gave her assessment. "The concentration of calcium oxide added to the cane juice probably would destroy the spores, and even if it didn't, the centrifugation to separate the crystals from the molasses would separate out the spores as well. To be effective, the spores would have to be added after the sugar has gone through the mill."

Westphal said, "Since we don't process any sugarcane on site, that crop wouldn't be a suitable target for someone developing the toxin here. It must be the coffee."

Manling stood up. "I'll go fire up a roaster in the lab."

÷

Manling moved a small electric roaster into the bio-containment room, where the scientists extracted tetanus spores and applied them directly onto coffee beans. After a slew of tests, the group reconvened in the conference room.

Westphal described the test results. "The new tetanus spores were viable after the beans' first crack, and remained so for less than one minute after the second crack."

Duarte observed, "Then coffee beans would be most useful for distributing these spores to regions where consumers tend to prefer lighter roasts."

Westphal and Manling both said, "The United States!"

After a pause during which everyone contemplated the potential magnitude of the plot, Munhoz asked, "What, if anything, does this have to do with the coffee fungus?"

Everyone else looked at her, looked around at each other, then looked back at her and shrugged.

÷

Costa and Azevedo retreated to Costa's office. They were discussing the criminal implications of the new tetanus bacteria and toxin when they heard a knock on the door. Tulio stood outside holding a large cardboard box. Costa waved for him to come in.

"This just arrived for you, sir," Tulio said. He handed over the box then closed the door on his way out.

The two other men stared at the package.

Costa wondered, "What the heck is it?"

The international air waybill on the exterior ambiguously listed the contents as "Promotional Item." The return address was from a generically named company, Distribution Fulfillment Warehouse Inc., at an industrial park address in Trenton, New Jersey.

Costa noted, "Way back when the U.S. had that anthrax scare through the postal service after the September Eleventh attacks, some of the postmarks were from Trenton, New Jersey." Not that either of the men knew the precise location of Trenton.

"Do you suppose our employee friend knows we're on to him?" Azevedo pointed a thumb toward the door glass, beyond which Tulio sat at the video monitoring console.

Costa said, "We'd better not take any chances."

Azevedo gingerly carried the package out of the office, following Costa upstairs, then into the lab.

When Manling saw them, he asked, "What can I do for you men?"

Azevedo responded, "We suspect this package could contain bio-terror substances such as anthrax."

Manling said, "Allow me." He put on a fresh pair of latex gloves. He fetched a respiratory filtering mask and stretched it over his head. He garbled through the mask, "Wait out here."

Manling carried the package into the bio-containment room, where he set it down in the biological safety cabinet. A crowd of lab workers surrounded Costa and Azevedo, watching through the window to the inner room. Manling switched on the BSC's airflow to capture any escaping particulate matter. He meticulously examined the box seams for traces of powdery substances, but saw nothing other than the usual dust from routine handling and transportation. He sliced the packing tape with a scalpel, then he nudged open the top flaps of the outer carton. A sheet of paper sat atop the contents.

Manling emerged from the bio-containment room. Pulling off the mask, he said, "You, *Senhor* Costa, are the proud recipient of..." He read from the packing list. "...one Bright Cup Squawkie Bird Toy, courtesy of Mr. Samuel Decker."

AUGUST 16

At the garage in Campo do Coxo, Sergio ran out of coffee beans to process after he had filled the 53rd detergent box with powdered fungus and other fine residue from the sifting.

AUGUST 17

Hasse brought to the garage a load of small cardboard shipping boxes, a package scale, and stacks of shipping forms from the three major international express shipping companies.

Hasse and Sergio spent the day preparing packages and filling out customs paperwork for shipments to 20 recipients around the world. Each package contained two of the detergent boxes. The balance of the detergent boxes would remain in Brazil for domestic distribution.

Hasse had received detailed shipping instructions via a lengthy series of encoded emails that she had picked up at an Internet café in Campinas, avoiding any further use of the Grande Hotel. Each package would have a different "ship from" name and address, all real, unwitting people at real businesses in Brazil, one of which, coincidentally, sold cleaning supplies including laundry detergent. The shipments would be charged to the actual shipper's accounts of those businesses. This information came from a German man who had been a passenger on a *gaiola* boat which had departed years earlier on the Amazon River from the city of Manaus. The man now worked as a computer database analyst at a freight forwarding service that handled shipments through the airport at Frankfurt, providing him access to detailed information for tens of thousands of active shipping accounts.

Hasse and Sergio marked each package with the date on which it needed to be shipped, all during a four day span the following week. When all 20 packages were ready, Sergio loaded them into the back of his pickup truck and covered them with a tarpaulin. He transferred the pile of loose laundry detergent powder from a wheelbarrow into plastic garbage bags, which he also put in the back of the truck. With a garden hose, he washed off the cement mixer, the wheelbarrows, and the garage floor, making sure no visible trace of either detergent or fungus remained. Then he rearranged the contents of the garage to resemble the way they had been before he arrived a week earlier.

After Sergio was finished, Hasse told him, "*Irmão* Calanus from *Canadá* and *Irmã* Cardui from *Islândia* will arrive Monday in Brazil. *Irmã* Harmonia will pick up the packages from you Tuesday morning and meet them at the Ibis Hotel in Piracicaba. *Irmão* Calanus will have a rental vehicle that the three of them will use to drop off the packages for shipping."

Sergio asked, "Have you ever been to *Islândia?*"

"No," Hasse replied, then she added, "I heard that Iceland is so isolated it has no native butterflies."

Driving home, Sergio pondered the previously unimaginable concept of a nation without butterflies. At home, he transferred the cargo from the pickup truck into a tumbledown storage shed in the backyard, where it sat untouched for several days.

AUGUST 18

On Sunday morning, Larissa was jogging on the pathway through the hotel's masterfully landscaped *área verde* (green space). The path curved around the trunk of a massive Blue Jacaranda tree. On the other side of the tree, on the lush lawn to the side of the path, a man was lifting a small boy into the air. Larissa slowed to a walk, observing the pair. The boy, about three years old, laughed hysterically when the man grabbed him around the chest, turned him upside down then right side up again. Next, the man grabbed the boy's arms and started spinning around. As the spinning speed increased, the boy's legs rose from the ground, as though he was on an amusement park ride.

When the man put down the boy, the youngster cried out, "*De novo, Papai!*" Do it again, Daddy! The man picked him up again, this time spinning him by an arm and a leg.

Larissa recommenced jogging. As she approached the hotel door, she sat down on a bench. She was thinking about the man and the boy when she heard a woman's voice.

"How was your jog, Larissa?" Cicera sat down next to her.

Distracted, Larissa replied, "Oh, it was fine."

Cicera studied the younger woman's face. "Tell me, dear, what's a nice woman like you doing in a place like this all by yourself?"

"I'm on vacation."

Cicera maintained a steady gaze. "I've been around long enough to know when something's up with someone. And when that someone is a young woman, the something that's up usually involves a man."

"If you must know," Larissa said, "I just found out I'm pregnant."

"That's wonderful. I just became a grandmother myself last year. My daughter had a beautiful little boy."

"But I'm not married. The father doesn't even know yet."

"So you came here to get some time to yourself, to think things over, to decide what to do?"

Larissa nodded.

"And have you decided?"

"I think I just did."

÷

Larissa returned to her room. She picked up the receiver from the hotel's telephone on the desk, but before she started dialing she set it down again. *They must charge an arm and a leg to make calls on that thing*, she thought. She located her backpack, then dug around in it until she came up with her mobile phone. She was about to press the power button, but she stopped. *If I'm going to surprise him with this news, I might as well surprise him in person.*

She quickly packed her bags and checked out of the hotel. On the way out the front door, she took the receipt the desk clerk had given her and threw it in the trash. *I'll just drop off this dirty laundry at home, pick up my car, and drive over to his house.*

÷

Two plainclothes DPF officers sat in an unmarked car half a block away from Júnior's apartment house. They were sipping coffee and chatting about prospects for various countries' *futebol* teams in the upcoming 2014 *Copa do Mundo* (World Cup) tournament throughout Brazil and in the 2016 Olympics in Rio. They didn't pay attention to the woman walking along the sidewalk with a backpack and a duffel bag, until one of them noticed that she went up the steps to the building under surveillance, then he gagged on a mouthful of coffee.

÷

Larissa tossed her bags on the bed and picked up her car keys. When she reopened the front door of her apartment, two men were on the landing at the top of the stairs.

One of the men quickly displayed his DPF badge and asked, "Are you Larissa Júnior?"

"Yes. What's going on?"

"We have a warrant for your arrest."

"What?"

"Keep your hands where we can see them, *senhorita*," the policeman said, reaching for his handcuffs. "You're under arrest."

"Under arrest? For what?"

"We have orders not to discuss the case until you're in custody and back at the station."

Larissa suddenly felt intense nausea. She said, "I think I'm going to be sick." She sank to her knees, banging her forehead against the door frame, then she collapsed on the floor.

÷

Lieutenant Azevedo entered a holding room at the Departamento de Polícia Federal station in Campinas. The prisoner was seated at a table, glaring at him.

Azevedo looked at the bandage on her forehead and asked the uniformed officer in the room, "Did she resist arrest?"

"Not exactly, sir. The arresting agents say she hit her head when she fainted."

"That's what they say," Larissa spoke up. "I say your *valentões* [bullies] hit me. I want to talk to a lawyer."

Azevedo said, "I'll allow that shortly. But first, I'd like to ask you a few simple questions, *senhorita*." He motioned for the other officer to leave, then he sat down across the table from her. "I'm Lieutenant Azevedo, the detective in charge of this case. Would you mind telling me where you've been for the past week?"

"In charge of this case? What case? And where I've been is a personal matter. It's none of your business."

"On the contrary. If you've been conspiring with cohorts, it's very much my business."

"Conspiring? Cohorts? What the hell are your talking about?"

"Do I really need to spell it out for you, *Senhorita* Júnior?"

"I don't have a clue what this is about."

"Very well. It involves a substance discovered in the laboratory of your employer, Delcese Agricola."

"Substance? What kind of substance?"

"A certain jar in the lab refrigerator."

Larissa put her elbows up on the table and dropped her head into her hands. "Is that what all this fuss is about?" She picked up her head. "All right, I confess."

That was easy, Azevedo thought. He rhythmically thumped his fingers on the table.

Larissa continued, "I can't believe that Manling would make a federal case out of that. I know he has strict rules about items prohibited in the lab, and I know I broke one of the rules. But it was only a jar of *mostarda*, for God's sake. I promise I won't do it again."

"*Mostarda*? What are you talking about, *senhorita*?"

"I'm talking about the jar of mustard I kept in the lab refrigerator. I used it on my sandwiches for lunch. It's the whole grain brown kind, much better than that bright yellow crud they serve in the cafeteria. What are *you* talking about, lieutenant?"

"I'm talking about the ingestible toxin from the new strain of tetanus bacteria."

"Ingestible toxin? New strain of tetanus bacteria? I don't know anything about anything like that. You've got the wrong person."

"That's what every prisoner here claims."

÷÷÷÷

That evening, Decker received a phone call at home from Fabiana Munhoz.

"...You were mostly right, Sam," she said. "Miguel was deliberately infected, but not by injection. We found a new strain of tetanus bacteria that was being cultivated in the lab. Its toxin can pass into the bloodstream when ingested. Larissa Júnior has been arrested."

He asked, "What about the coffee fungus?"

"The scientists think it's under control."

"If I'm right about Paul's research, you haven't seen the last of it."

AUGUST 19

On Monday morning, Hasse and Sergio both returned to work and went about their jobs as though nothing improper had happened.

The lab at Sede was abuzz with word of Larissa's apprehension.

÷÷÷÷÷

Also that morning, a HAZMAT team from the DPF, led by Emílio Melan, entered Larissa's apartment in full protective gear to search for traces of the new tetanus bacteria, spores, or toxin. When the team emerged two hours later, Melan spoke to Azevedo, who was waiting outside with Costa for clearance to go in.

"Nothing obvious," Melan said when he removed his head gear, "but we've taken a few pieces of her clothing to analyze for traces of spores. I've already got soil samples from the shoes she was wearing when she was arrested to see if we can identify where she's been. We've also got her laptop computer. I gave it a quick look, but didn't see anything of interest. We'll do a more thorough examination of its contents back at our crime lab."

Azevedo turned to Costa. "Let's see if *we* can find anything that tells us where our prisoner has been."

The two men entered the apartment, which was in disarray from the prior search. They quickly discovered the items in the bedroom that had been dumped out of her baggage for examination, mostly dirty laundry.

"She likes to work up a sweat," Azevedo commented, daintily holding out a used sports bra.

Costa picked up a damp swimsuit. "And she's been swimming." He sniffed the suit. "In a pool."

Then Costa spotted a purple nylon toiletries kit that was unzipped from having been searched for toxins. He parted the opening with a hand, and he smiled when he saw the miniature bar of soap in a wrapper adorned with the hotel's name.

÷÷÷÷÷

That afternoon, Larissa's lawyer, Rodolfo Dumont, stood by her side at the arraignment.

"...Your honor," Dumont said, "the police have absolutely no evidence linking my client to the hazardous materials discovered in the lab at Delcese Agricola. And they used excessive force arresting her."

The judge replied, "I will grant your request for bail, counselor. However, given the immense gravity of the potential crimes that could have been committed with the substances in question, I'm setting the bail at one million *reais*." He banged his gavel.

÷

When they were back in a holding cell, Larissa said to Dumont, "A million *reais*? I don't have that kind of money."

"You only need ten percent plus collateral to have a bail bondsman put up the rest. Can you raise a hundred thousand? Do you have collateral of value?"

"Not that much value." She wrote down a name and mobile phone number. "Maybe he can help."

÷

When the Delcese employee received the call from Dumont, he was overcome with panic. He immediately left work without telling anyone where he was going or why. He got in his car and drove from Sede straight to Campinas.

÷÷÷÷÷

Azevedo flashed his badge to the clerk at the front desk in the Grande Hotel. Costa showed his mobile phone with the picture of a woman on its display.

"*Senhorita* Júnior," the clerk said.

Azevedo was surprised that she had registered under her own name. "How long did she stay here?"

The clerk typed on the keyboard, then ran his finger down the computer screen. "She arrived a week ago Thursday, and she checked out yesterday."

"We need to search the room where she stayed."

The clerk looked at the computer screen. "That room is now occupied by another guest."

"We don't mind," Costa said, "And if the new guest does, then offer him a few free drinks."

"I'll need to speak to the manager."

"You can do that in a moment," the lieutenant said. "But first, do you have any idea what *Senhorita* Júnior did while she was here?"

"I saw her out at the swimming pool a few times. And I think she played some cards."

Costa commented, "Cards? I take it she wasn't playing *solitária*."

"A group of three ladies comes here for a week every year," the clerk explained. "They find other guests to play cards with them."

"Are they still here?"

The clerk queried the computer. "They checked out yesterday."

"We'll need their names and addresses," Azevedo said.

"I'll need to speak to the manager."

÷

A few minutes later, the clerk was thankful that his knocks on the guest room door went unanswered. He slid in the master key card and opened the door. He stood outside while Costa and Azevedo looked in the room.

When they came back out shaking their heads, Azevedo asked the clerk, "Can we talk to the chambermaid who serviced this room over the last week?"

"The maids all went off duty an hour ago." The clerk mindlessly tapped the key card in his hand. "Anything else I can do for you?"

The lieutenant began saying, "I guess that's it...," but he stopped when Costa tapped him on the shoulder.

Costa pointed to the card in the clerk's hand and described what he wanted.

The clerk replied, "I'll need to speak to the manager."

÷

On a couch in the hotel lobby, Azevedo and Costa scrutinized two pages of printouts of electronic lock accesses made by Júnior's key card on the days of her stay.

Azevedo ran his finger down a column on the paper. "It looks like she was fairly regular in the times entering her room each day."

"Her card was used to access a few other locks," Costa noted. He carried the papers to the front desk.

The clerk said, "That code number is for the fitness center." He consulted a reference sheet for another one. "And that one is for the business center, where we have computers, printers, and fax machines for guest use."

When Costa described what he wanted, the clerk replied, "For that, you'll need to speak to TI Guy."

A minute later, they stood at the doorway of a tiny windowless office. The hotel's *Gerente de Tecnologia da Informação* (Information Technology Manager) sat between three computers arrayed around an L-shaped desk. He was chomping on a sandwich.

"...I can get you what you're asking for," TI Guy uttered between bites, "but it might not be what you want."

Azevedo asked, "What do you mean?"

"I can provide a list of all the outgoing telephone numbers dialed from the fax machines in the business center. That'll be a short list, but the transmission content is untraceable because it's analog. Tracking emails is more complicated. Your suspect could have connected her own laptop to our network via WiFi from anywhere on the premises. If she did that, there'd be a record of her logging into our system with her guest room info. Let me check." He typed commands on a keyboard, then ran his finger down the list of data that appeared on the screen. "Looks like she did not connect to our WiFi at all during her stay. If she used one of the open access computers in the business center, we wouldn't have any record of the messages on the computer itself. Even if she wasn't smart enough to clear the computer's cache manually, we clear them automatically every Sunday night. I'd have to give you a packet-level data dump from the storage drive for our network analyzer. Any messages she might have sent or received using web-based email won't be segregated like employee emails sent or received using our internal email servers."

"Then there's no way to retrieve an email that a guest might have sent from the business center?"

"I didn't say it's impossible, but distinguishing a web-based email page hit from other web page hits isn't necessarily easy. Somebody will have to do it the hard way, searching for URLs and strings of HTML code likely to be used by any of the thousands of web-based email services worldwide. Fortunately, overall web traffic here would have been light at the time of day on a Sunday when the business center was accessed. However, if the web email service used secure mode with SSL encryption at the one-twenty-eight bit level, even if you find the page traffic you want, you won't be able to make heads or tails out of the message contents. As far as I know, nobody anywhere has ever cracked one-twenty-eight bit encryption. Cracking even a single message would take lifetimes. And if it was encrypted with two-fifty-six bit, you can forget about it ever being cracked before the entire universe fizzles out."

Azevedo said, "*Caramba.*" Dammit.

TI Guy continued, "It gets worse. You might need to look at a lot more data than you think."

"What do you mean?"

TI Guy picked a piece of food from between his teeth using the fingernail of his pinkie. "The business center is unlocked from six AM to ten PM Monday through Friday. Your suspect could have used it numerous times besides the entry on Sunday with her key card."

"Then get us all the web activity from the business center during her entire stay."

"That would be one gigantic load of data, even if I exclude all the video traffic. Of course, there might not be anything there to find. She could have used her own laptop computer with old-fashioned dialup modem access. I wouldn't have any way to distinguish that phone call from any other phone call except by the phone number dialed. That would be an incredibly slow connection, but quite shrewd on her part, because there wouldn't be any record of the digital data flow." TI Guy took another bite of sandwich.

Costa asked, "Did she make any phone calls from her room?"

Still chewing, he turned to the computer on his right. A minute later he shook his head. "Not a single call incoming or outgoing during her stay. She must have been using her mobile for calls. And of course, she could have been sending and receiving text messages and emails through the mobile, which wouldn't go through our systems at all."

"We've already checked her mobile phone records," Azevedo said. "Assemble all the data you can, and I'll have our computer guru at DPF main headquarters in Brasília comb through it."

"How soon do you need it?"

"Yesterday. This is a matter of vital national security." Azevedo wrote a name and phone number on one of his business cards. "Call this guy when you've got it ready."

÷

Before leaving the hotel, Costa and Azevedo stopped at the reception desk.

Costa asked the clerk, "Had *Senhorita* Júnior ever stayed here prior to her recent visit?"

The clerk typed on the computer keyboard. "No record of her staying here before, at least not under that name."

"Had you ever seen her before she checked in? She lives right here in town."

The clerk shook his head.

(If Costa and Azevedo had asked the same simple question to the clerk who worked the Grande Hotel front desk on Sundays, they would have gotten a very different response.)

÷÷÷÷

When the man from Delcese entered the Departamento de Polícia Federal station in Campinas, he identified himself to the desk clerk and named the prisoner he was there to see. After waiting 20 minutes, he was called into an empty visiting room, where he sat down on a metal folding chair. When Larissa entered a minute later, he jumped up, sending the chair screeching across the polished floor behind him. Unable to put her cuffed arms around his torso, she lifted them over his head to his neck. He bent down to embrace her.

When they separated, Larissa was crying. "I hope you believe me that I didn't do it."

"Of course I believe you, baby." He wiped the tears from her cheeks. "I'll try to get you bailed out."

"Thank you so much." She looked him in the eyes. "I have something else to tell you."

"What's that?"

Larissa lifted the base of her prison blouse, exposing the skin of her abdomen. She took his hand and placed it on her belly, directly atop the large dark birthmark adjacent to her navel.

When he left the visiting room, Tulio wiped a tear from his own cheek.

Chapter 20

"A mathematician is a machine for turning coffee into theorems."

Hungarian mathematician Paul Erdös (1913–1996)

~~~~~

The Director General of the DPF told Captain Ratiba that with the suspected perpetrator in custody, the release of information would be in the public interest. Ratiba knew the Director's unspoken objective was to bolster the department's image both domestically and abroad.

÷

Midway through the morning's news report, the CNN anchor shifted to international news. "In Brazil, a potential bio-terrorist plot involving a new strain of tetanus bacteria has been thwarted. An official of that country's Federal Police Department said the new bacteria produce a vaccine-resistant toxin that, unlike conventional tetanus, can induce the disease after being consumed in food or drink. Scientists involved in uncovering the plot, according to the official, believe that spores of the bacteria would have been applied to coffee beans for export and distribution into the U.S. population..."

Watching the report from a television at home in Yogyakarta, Eddy Zeger began laughing.

"...Police suspect that toxin from the bacteria had been used to poison the pilot of a small plane, leading to the crash last month in which the chief scientist of Delcese Agricola, Dr. Paul Mendonça, was killed. Larissa Júnior, a bioengineer working in Delcese's laboratory, has been arrested in connection with the plot..."

Zeger laughed so hard he lost his breath.

"...The announcement sparked speculation that the recent outbreak of a new coffee fungus in Brazil, which began in the plantations of Delcese Agricola, also may have been part of the terrorist plot."

Zeger stopped laughing.

÷÷÷÷÷

"You should take some time off from work, Tulio." Costa's suggestion was more of a command. "Lieutenant Azevedo will want to question you. Come back next Monday, and we'll discuss your job status, pending police investigations."

÷÷÷÷÷

In the waiting area of the lobby at the Ibis Piracicaba Hotel sat a diminutive woman with close-cropped brown and gray hair. She wore a yellow tank top and blue jeans. Per the instructions from Goliath, Sister Harmonia had taken the entire week off from work at her job as a bookkeeper at the nearby sugar mill. She had told her boss she was still tending to her mother who was recovering from surgery, which she actually had been doing the previous week. She had never met Brother Calanus or Sister Cardui, although they would have no trouble identifying her by the tattoo visible on the back of her left shoulder, the orange, tan, and black Harmonia Tigerwing (*Tithorea harmonia*).

Her mark was especially appropriate, she had reasoned when choosing for her initiation. Not only was the Harmonia Tigerwing a common variety of butterfly in Brazil, but Harmonia was also the name of a mythological Greek sea nymph who mothered the race of females known as the Amazons. Few Brazilians were aware that the Greek term for which their vast jungle and river were named, *a mazos*, literally meant "without breast," as these warrior women voluntarily cut off one of their mammary glands to improve their skills in archery and javelin. Sister Harmonia never intended to follow the Amazon women in that regard. *Besides*, she had thought, *mine aren't big enough to get in the way of anything*.

"*Irmã* Harmonia," the man's voice said.

"*Sim*," she replied. Harmonia had studied in advance how the visitors' marks would look. The man in his late 20s bore the Banded Hairstreak (*Satyrium calanus*) on his right bicep. She extended a hand, to which he interlocked thumbs, and they made the flapping sign of the butterfly. She said, "Pleased to meet you, *Irmão* Calanus."

"And you, as well," he replied.

A minute later, a young woman approached them. She had milky skin, a pierced eyebrow, and shoulder-length blond hair so straight it could have passed for uncooked angel hair pasta. She wore sandals, the gaps between the straps revealing the mark of the orange and black Painted Lady (*Vanessa cardui*) on the top of her foot.

Barely out of her teens, Sister Harmonia thought. "Is it true," the older woman asked, "that *Islândia* has no *borboletas*?"

The Portuguese word for butterflies was close enough in pronunciation to the Spanish word which the young woman had heard several times. Sister Cardui replied, "Yes, it's true, at least no native ones."

Harmonia asked, "Then how did you pick your mark?"

Cardui explained, "When I was a little girl walking along the rocky coastline one day, I came across a dead Painted Lady." She pointed to her foot. "I brought it home and asked my father where it came from.

He told me, 'It must have been blown from across the seas by the winds of the world.'"

Harmonia replied, *"Como será o objeto de nossa missão."*

Brother Calanus translated for Sister Cardui, "As will be the object of our mission."

÷

Earlier that morning at Sergio's home, he had loaded the 20 packages into the trunk of Harmonia's car, which was just large enough to hold them with the rear seat folded down. She had joked to him that the biggest risk to the entire mission was that her aged Ford Escort, with more than 200,000 kilometers on the odometer, would break down en route to Piracicaba.

At the Ibis Hotel, the threesome of Calanus, Cardui, and Harmonia transferred the packages from Harmonia's car into Calanus's rental vehicle, an Opel Zafira minivan with less than 2,000 kilometers on the odometer.

The previous day, Harmonia had plotted their course for the next four days and entered the waypoints into her GPS navigation device. Each day, they would ship out four to six of the packages, each one from a different over-the-counter outlet of the designated international carriers. Initially, they were concerned about Sister Cardui doing this, since her lack of Portuguese language skills could have been problematic if a counter clerk asked her questions. In practice, however, the transaction consisted of simply handing the prepared package and paperwork to a clerk, and saying, *"Obrigada"* or *"Obrigado."*

They spent the afternoon releasing the first set of packages out of the shippers' facilities in Campinas, then they drove south to spend the night near São Paulo.

÷÷÷÷÷

Departing early that same morning, Azevedo flew from Campinas to Belo Horizonte, capital of the neighboring State of Minas Gerais. He was met there by Lieutenant Nazaré from the local DPF office. The two men drove to a suburban district north of the city, where they rang the doorbell of a stately home along the shore of the manmade lake, Lagoa da Pampulha.

A young woman answered the door. "Yes, officers?"

"We're here to speak with *Senhora* Cicera Benjor," Nazaré said.

"Come in, please." She beckoned them into the foyer, then turned and shouted, "Mother, the police want to talk to you."

When Cicera descended the staircase, she said to her daughter, "You can go back to the baby, dear." She eyed the men's uniforms and badges. "How may I help the Federal Police?"

Azevedo took out his mobile phone and showed her a photograph on it. "Do you know this woman?"

"That's Larissa Júnior. My friends and I played cards with her when we stayed at the Grande Hotel in Águas de São Pedro. Did something happen to her?"

Azevedo shook his head.

"Is she in some kind of trouble, then?"

"I'm afraid so, *senhora*."

"Darn. She was such a nice woman. I knew she was having a hard time deciding whether or not to go through with it."

Azevedo asked, "What did she tell you about her plan?"

"Only that she decided to go ahead with it."

"Did she mention anyone else involved?"

"The man who got her into the situation, of course."

"What man? Who is he? Was the plan his idea?"

"She never told me his name. But isn't a man always involved? And isn't the sex usually his idea?"

Nazaré asked, "*Senhora*, what are you talking about?"

"The baby, of course."

Both policemen blurted out, "The baby?"

"Didn't you know? Larissa is pregnant. What plan have you men been talking about?"

Azevedo said, "The bio-terrorist plot to poison Brazilian coffee beans."

The statement took a moment to sink into Cicera's mind before she responded. "You think Larissa is a terrorist?"

"Yes, *senhora*."

"I find that hard to believe."

"Why?"

"Larissa said she was hoping people would be able to get along better with each other, so her baby would get to see all the wonderful things in the world without fear or intolerance. Does that sound like something a terrorist would say?"

After they left Cicera's home, Azevedo said to Nazaré, "Perhaps I have underestimated *Senhorita* Júnior. She's more shrewd than I had imagined. She appears to have fooled everyone."

Nazaré responded, "Or, maybe she really isn't a terrorist, and she really is pregnant."

"Even terrorists have babies. Maybe, this woman Cicera is covering for her. Maybe Cicera is involved in the plot, too. Maybe she is even *o cérebro*." The mastermind.

÷÷÷÷÷

Tulio and the attorney Dumont sat across the table from Larissa.

"I can't raise enough money to post a bond of million *reais*," Tulio said. "My entire house is worth less than two hundred thousand, and I don't have enough equity to draw a hundred thousand."

Dumont said, "The judge refuses to reduce bail."

÷÷÷÷÷

Martina Hasse sat alone at a table in the cafeteria at Sede, eating a sandwich for lunch. *If Larissa fingers me as being at that hotel,* she thought, *the police might not take too long to figure out what happened. I've got to get rid of her before she talks. But how can I get to her while she's in jail? Maybe Brother Aidea can do it.*

÷÷÷÷÷

In the main offices of the Departamento de Polícia Federal in the nation's capital of Brasília, Vinícius Búzia stared at his computer screen. He had just downloaded from TI Guy's server over 400 gigabytes of Internet traffic data from the computers in the Grande Hotel's business center during Larissa's stay.

The phone on his desk rang. "*Oi*, Búzia here."

"Viní, it's Oscar Azevedo."

"I just got the data from the hotel, lieutenant. Where do I begin?"

"The most important slice of time is just after Júnior accessed the business center on that Sunday. Look for web-based email activity. I'm still in Belo Horizonte, but I'm flying to Brasília tonight. I'll check in with you in person tomorrow morning."

AUGUST 21

The mobile butterfly contingent spent the day dropping off packages at the shipping depots of the major carriers in the posh Alphaville district west of São Paulo city.

÷÷÷÷÷

Azevedo stood looking over Búzia's shoulder.

"Show me what you've got, Viní."

"In the hour following Júnior's access into the hotel business center a week ago Sunday, there were no calls in or out on the fax machine there. The computers in the business center use static IP addresses, so I could isolate activity on each of the machines individually. During that time frame, only two of the computers in the business center were used for any Internet activity. One of them had a bunch of hits on Yahoo! followed by a series of hits to an anonymous IP address. That user was signed in to Yahoo! in Standard mode, meaning the traffic was not encrypted. Turns out he—must have been a he—was checking a bunch of emails, all in Portuguese, one of which contained a link to an offshore porn site." Viní reached for the computer mouse. "You want to see the site?"

"Not at the moment. Any outgoing emails from that user?"

"One, sent to three recipients, about setting up a golf game the following week. And that's all from that computer."

"What about the other computer?"

"This one must be your lady. First, she went to a few websites full of articles about forest conservation and endangered species. Is she some kind of *ativista ecológico*?"

"Yeah. She's a tree hugger. She got busted once at a logging protest up in Amazonas."

Búzia pointed to his computer screen. "Then things get interesting. The user logged on to a web-based email account. Guess where the account is."

"I have no idea, Viní."

"Come on, Oscar, guess. If you wanted to hide *anything* from prying eyes, in what country would you open an account?"

"Switzerland?"

"*Correto!* Your lady logged in to SwissMail-dot-ORG. Unfortunately, once she hits the log-in page, all the traffic back and forth with that site is encrypted at a hundred-twenty-eight bit SSL. Unlike most web-based email services, SwissMail encrypts the session in a way that we can't even sniff out the 'To' and 'From' fields of a message."

"You're telling me it's a dead end, Viní?"

"Not entirely. First, SwissMail is not a free site. You might want to check your suspect's credit card and banks records to see if she's paid for anything in Switzerland in the last year, although she could've paid via an anonymous method like Bitcoin. Second, while I can't read the contents of the traffic, the size of each piece of traffic is indicative."

"Indicative of what?"

"For any given web page hit, a whole bunch of crap comes from the server to the computer, but in the other direction, not much flows from the computer to the server. If a string of data sent from the computer to the server is short, it probably just represents clicking a link or some cookie data being transferred. But if the string of data is much longer, it's got content of its own. That is, it might be an outgoing email message. And about half an hour after your suspect entered the business center, one outgoing chunk was much larger than any of the others. She must have sent a message with a whole lot of text or an attachment."

Azevedo said, "But if I understand the encryption thing, there's no way for us to crack the code and read the message."

"That's correct. At least we can't crack it here at DPF. We're not crypto specialists. As far as the public knows, no one in the world has a computer fast enough to crack one-twenty-eight bit encryption. But, I've heard a rumor that the National Security Agency up in the United States has a classified computer system that can possibly do it. I don't have a contact up there, though."

"Neither do I," the lieutenant said, "but I know someone who knows someone who does. Good work, Viní. I'll get back to you on how to proceed."

÷

From an office down the hall, Azevedo phoned Costa. After their conversation, Costa placed a call to the United States, using the direct number for the Brazilian Ambassador, *Senhor* Evandro Aguiar. After that conversation, Aguiar called his contact at the U.S. Department of State, who subsequently called the National Security Agency.

The sentence that Aguiar used which generated the desired degree of attention throughout the chain of communication was this: "The encrypted message in question pertains to the terrorist plot to spread a new strain of deadly tetanus through the supply of coffee beans."

Each person hearing that same sentence was aroused to action by a different two-word phrase, none of which was "deadly tetanus." To the man at the Department of State, "terrorist plot" got his attention. To the Deputy Director of the NSA, "encrypted message" was adequate stimulation. And to Louis Martelli, a mathematician and NSA's Senior Cryptanalyst assigned to handle the decryption task, the magic catch-phrase was "coffee beans."

÷

Viní Búzia was napping with his head down on his desk when he was awakened by the telephone ringing.

"*Oi*, Búzia," he said groggily.

"Hello, Mr. Búzia, this is Louis Martelli calling from the United States. I'm with the National Security Agency. I understand you have an encrypted message for us to crack."

Wow, Viní thought, noting the response time of less than two hours, *somebody's got connections all right*. "That's correct. Hang on a minute, please. I'll go fetch the detective in charge of the case."

He ran down the hall to find Azevedo. When they returned, Viní switched the phone to speaker mode. "I'm back now with Lieutenant Azevedo."

Martelli asked, "What can you tell me about the message?"

Viní responded, "It's about two hundred kilobytes, encrypted with Thawte SSL at one-twenty-eight bit."

"That'll be a combination of symmetric and asymmetric. If we have the public key from the asymmetric handshake, we can use it to reverse engineer the private key, with which we could determine the symmetric session keys used to encode the actual message. The technique we've developed at the NSA for doing that involves an inverse adaptation of the Chinese Remainder Theorem. That's more efficient than using pure brute force on the one-twenty-eight bit data. Plus, we can exploit the fact that the seeds for most keys aren't truly random, they're only pseudorandom, and we at the NSA know exactly how they differ from truly random. Do you have the public key, Mr. Búzia?"

"Yes. I captured it from the certificate in the handshake data."

"Excellent. I must warn you, though, that when we try to decrypt these messages, usually we can't do it in the timeframe people need it done. Most of the time, we're SOL."

Unfamiliar with the Americanism, Viní asked, "SOL?"

"Shit Outta Luck. But once in a while we get lucky. Go ahead and send me your data, and I'll feed it into Nowell to attempt decryption."

"Noel?"

"It's 'No-well.' That's the code name for our secret supercomputing system. Most people who know about supercomputers think the fastest system in the U.S. is at Oak Ridge National Lab in Tennessee. Nowell can run an order of magnitude faster, although it costs us about half a million dollars an hour to run her."

Viní abruptly coughed at hearing the price tag. "What platform is this Nowell built on?"

"That's classified information. I could tell you, Mr. Búzia, but I'd have to kill you, or at least I'd have to have somebody take away your coffee. If you guys down there at the DPF are anything like our guys up here at the NSA, that would amount to about the same thing. We'd be raving lunatics without our extra-strength cerebral energy drink."

"I know what you mean," Viní said. "I went through three pots of coffee working on this straight through last night."

"Of course," Martelli added, "there's another approach that would be a lot easier than this massive decryption effort."

"What's that?"

"You could find the person's username and password, then just log into the email account and see what's in there. You'd be amazed at how many covert operatives don't delete everything. But don't tell anybody that. Massive decryption efforts are my job security."

When the call ended, Azevedo asked Búzia, "Do the URLs which Júnior used show up anywhere else in the data from the hotel? She might have used the business center at other times."

Búzia shook his head. "I've already checked. None of them appear at any other time during her entire stay. Looks like a one shot deal, but I'm systematically going through all the other traffic on the business center computers to see if anything else is of interest."

"Keep me posted. I'm headed back to Campinas shortly."

After Búzia had sent the data for decryption to Martelli, he ran a Google search on the name Nowell, and he poked through dozens of the listings returned. One of the links he clicked led him to a web page in Denmark. It described the Nowell Codex, which combined with the Southwick Codex constituted the earliest known manuscript containing the epic Old English poem, *Beowulf*.

÷

From his desk at Fort Meade, Maryland, Louis Martelli phoned a man 50 miles away in Dulles, Virginia, at the headquarters of one of the world's largest Internet content providers.

"This is Frank Yin," answered the Chief Technology Officer of America Logged On, widely known by the acronym ALO.

Martelli said, "We need to activate Nowell."

"How long do you need it?"

"Might be a few days or more. We need to decrypt a one-twenty-eight bit message that is of vital national and international interest. Can you accommodate us, Frank?"

"America is our first name here at ALO. That must be one hell of an important message. Who's paying the bill this time?"

"The State Department," Martelli said, "but you can charge it to my American Express card. I could use all those frequent flyer miles."

When their conversation finished, Yin went to a glassed-in control room at ALO. He whispered to a man at a terminal, and with a few keystrokes, the world's most massively distributed computing system came to life.

Nowell performed parallel processing on an unprecedented scale by utilizing idle computing resources from tens of millions of personal computers around the world. It was based on a system architecture for clustering multiple off-the-shelf personal computers to achieve super-computer performance, a concept first developed in 1993 and dubbed by its creators, Donald Becker and Thomas Sterling, as the Beowulf Project.

Whenever an ALO user's computer was logged on to his or her account, which was often 24/7, if the computer was otherwise idle, unbeknownst to the user a portion of its CPU cycles was available to Nowell over untraceable Internet pathways. The size of that portion varied dynamically, based on how long the computer had gone since any keystrokes, cursor movements, or screen touches. For a computer that had been unattended for hours, up to 80 percent of its CPU cycles could be diverted to Nowell.

This secret distributed computing system was enabled thanks to a special module of program code built into all recent versions of the world's most popular computer operating system, Doorways, from the software giant Macroprog. Only a handful of insiders at Macroprog, ALO, and the NSA were aware of the true function or even the real name of this disguised module: Backdoorway. To other technology gurus who poked around such things, the running process labeled Malblock appeared to be an anti-malware protection feature of the operating system, and it did indeed serve that function whenever the Nowell system was inactive.

Backdoorway was provided by Macroprog at the behest of the NSA as part of a settlement of the federal government's antitrust case against the software company. ALO also agreed to drop its own lawsuit against Macroprog (regarding Internet browser intellectual property) in exchange for the lucrative Nowell fees it would collect in the three-way deal. For the parties involved, it was a win-win-win, although the computing public might have disagreed.

Nowell's distributed computing process required a true super-computer to act as a server managing distribution of the tasks to the huge numbers of client machines that could be active at any given time. Nowell's supercomputer server was connected to a fiber optic bundle in the NSA's headquarters at Fort Meade. That machine, code-named Southwick, would have ranked in the top five of the world's fastest supercomputers on its own merits had its existence been public information.

AUGUST 22

In the morning, Cardui, Calanus, and Harmonia worked their way through package drop-off counters in downtown São Paulo, then they drove predominantly east for more than 400 kilometers. For the last night all three would be together, they stayed at a utilitarian roadside hotel on the outskirts of Rio de Janeiro.

AUGUST 23

The Brother and two Sisters completed their package drop-offs in and around the overwhelming conurbation of Rio. They finished with the intended four boxes of laundry detergent still in the back of their vehicle. Then they drove toward nearby Baía de Guanabara, to Santos Dumont Airport, the facility servicing most domestic flights out of Rio.

Harmonia stood at the curbside near the departure terminal, preparing for a brief flight back to Campinas, to be followed by a bus ride to Piracicaba to pick up her car.

"Butterfly. It's such an odd word," the young Sister Cardui said. "Do you know its origin?"

"No idea," Brother Calanus replied.

Surprisingly, Sister Harmonia from Brazil did know the origin of that particular English word. "It comes from folklore," she explained, "about witches who fly into peoples' homes to steal their milk and butter." Harmonia slung her bag over a shoulder. "*Adeus borboletas companheiros.*" Goodbye fellow butterflies.

Brother Calanus watched the older woman walk away, then he turned to Sister Cardui and said, "A hundred years from now, when our group's deeds have become folklore, perhaps the word will become *coffeefly.*"

Chapter 21

"Evil always carries the seeds of its own destruction... Against folly we have no defense."

Lutheran theologian Dietrich Bonhoeffer, in *Letters and Papers from Prison* [*Widerstand und Ergebung*], written 1943 to 1945, prior to his execution by hanging in the Nazi concentration camp at Flossenbürg [original in German]

~~~~~

Over the following week, 19 guests at business-oriented hotels around the world received packages of "laundry detergent sales samples." The one package that didn't make it through had been held up at customs in South Africa, intended for the Curators Of The Earth member who was to cover Cameroon and Côte d'Ivoire.

After receipt of the packages, the members completely burned the outer cardboard packaging materials and labels. Then they traveled onward to be in their destination countries by August 29th, the Thursday before the Labor Day weekend.

÷÷÷÷÷

Sister Cardui and Brother Calanus spent the weekend of August 24th and 25th in Rio de Janeiro, then they continued driving up the coast toward their destination, the State of Espírito Santo, another of Brazil's major coffee growing regions. They parked themselves for the week at a bed and breakfast in the city of Vila Velha, near the state capital, Vitória. The inn's proprietor had assumed the two were married and assigned them a room with just one queen-size bed. Brother Calanus, being married to another woman, was less comfortable with the arrangement than Sister Cardui, although they managed to cohabit without incident until the last day before they were to begin spreading the spores to the coffee fields.

AUGUST 29

Looking out the window of their B&B in Vila Velha, Sister Cardui and Brother Calanus could see several kilometers away the gargantuan yellow and red logo on the side of the Garoto chocolate company factory building.

That day, the pair went on a guided tour of the chocolate factory, where they watched with fascination the high volume, high speed production and packaging processes. Of course, they sampled numerous tasty morsels at the designated stops along the tour. On their way out, they purchased more than a dozen varieties from the gift shop.

After dinner that evening, they sat up in their room at the inn, savoring the luscious flavors and textures.

Sister Cardui bit into a cream-filled bonbon called *Serenata de Amor* (Serenade of Love). "Have you heard of a dessert called Death by Chocolate?" She licked a spot of the filling from her lip.

"Yes," Brother Calanus replied, "but I've never tried it."

"Me neither. But when I have to die, that's how I want to go."

Later, as they lay next to each other in the bed wearing only their underwear, the wind blew in through the open window, fluttering the lace curtains as though they were giant butterfly wings. Sister Cardui reached across the bed and placed a hand on Brother Calanus's abdomen. His muscles tensed up, but he did not express objection. After a minute, his muscles began to relax. She inched the hand down inside the elastic of his jockey shorts.

"In Iceland," Sister Cardui said, stroking him, "we have an entire museum devoted to the penis."

"I find that hard to believe."

"It's true." She tugged the underwear off his hips and slid it down his legs. "It's called the Phallological Museum. It displays male organs from species of all kinds, including man." She bent over, lowering her mouth to lubriciously christen her fellow member's fellow's member. With her moistened tongue, she circumscribed his circumcision, then she paused for circumspection. "Do you want me to stop?"

"No," Calanus replied, "we shall consider this practice for our mission: dissemination."

August 30

Spreading of the fungus spores commenced at dawn on Friday in Papua New Guinea, the eastern half of the island of New Guinea. Outside the small city of Mount Hagen, Sister Charithonia stood on a dirt road upwind of Gumanch, the largest coffee plantation in the Southern Hemisphere. She tore open a Dirt-Away detergent box, and she tossed handfuls of the red powder high into the breeze, continuing until the box was empty. Due to its size, Gumanch was one of only a handful of plantations in the world to receive an entire box to itself. When she was finished, Sister Charithonia burned the cardboard box until nothing remained but ashes, which she pulverized and scattered to the wind.

On the Indonesian island of Sumatra, in the southern province of Lampung, at the edge of Bukit Barisan Selatan National Park, with two large plantations in view and several more in the vicinity, Brother Blumei cast red dust up in the air.

In the State of Karnataka in India, Brother Agathon threw red powder in the direction of Chikmagalur, the second largest cluster of coffee plantations in the world.

And on it went as the sun rose around the globe.

÷

Besides the one member who was still waiting for his package delivery, the only other hitch in the distribution plan occurred in Ethiopia, where a member from France had been assigned. Brother Virgaureae experienced cold feet. Instead of throwing his powder at the large Teppi and Bebeka plantations in Ethiopia's southwest and at the many small farms of the Fair Trade Coffee Cooperative in the Oromia region, he flushed the contents of his two boxes down the toilet in a public restroom at his hotel in Addis Ababa. (Such action might have been problematic for the hotel's plumbing had the boxes actually contained laundry detergent.)

÷

In Brazil, three teams worked to distribute the fungus in various regions: Brother Calanus and Sister Cardui in Espírito Santo and eastern Minas Gerais; Brother Aidea and Sister Cleobaea in eastern São Paulo and western Minas Gerais; and Sister Harmonia and Brother Dido (a coworker of Harmonia's at the sugar mill) covering Paraná and western São Paulo.

Each team in Brazil had four boxes of powder to spread over two days. The 53rd and final box of powder remained as a reserve in the shed behind Brother Aidea's home.

No one distributed fungus to any Delcese plantations, since that company's largest fields already had been infected and burned.

AUGUST 31

The fungus distributors all moved to new spots for Saturday's release of their remaining boxes of powder, in most cases only using portions of the boxes at multiple locations throughout the day.

÷

When Brother Calanus and Sister Cardui completed their assignment, they decided to celebrate by spreading more personal seed. As the evening sky grew dark, Calanus drove the minivan down deserted dirt tracks in the vast forest near Caratinga.

They slid the middle row of car seats forward and folded down the rear row flush to the floor, then they commenced copulation on the spacious flat cargo area.

A few minutes into the act, Brother Calanus said, "I bet they don't advertise this feature in the sales brochures for this vehicle."

Sister Cardui put a finger up to her lips. She whispered, "Shhh. What's that sound?"

Brother Calanus listened for a moment, then he laughed.

She poked him in the ribs. "What's so funny?"

"That sound. It's the monkeys mimicking us."

When they were sated and subsequently clothed, they climbed back into the front seats. Brother Calanus turned the key in the ignition switch, but the vehicle gave no response, not even clicking of the starter, much less cranking of the engine. He repeated the key twist several times with the same result.

"I bet they don't advertise this feature in the sales brochures for this vehicle, either," Sister Cardui said.

Using his mobile phone as a flashlight, Brother Calanus jiggled wires under the hood while Sister Cardui turned the key, all to no avail.

Calanus slammed the hood. "I think the starter solenoid is shot."

They checked their phones, but neither picked up a signal.

The couple left the vehicle, walking together toward the road to seek assistance. When they reached the road, no lights or other signs of civilization were visible in either direction.

She wanted to go south. He wanted to go north.

He said, *"Rocha, Papel, Tesoura."*

"Huh?"

"Rock, Paper, Scissors."

She threw *papel,* and he threw *tesoura.* If either of them had thrown *rocha,* world history might have unfolded differently. But that was not meant to be.

After walking half a kilometer up the road toward the north, Brother Calanus and Sister Cardui heard a truck approaching from behind. By the time they turned to flag it down, their fate was already sealed. The tractor-trailer, traveling around a bend at high speed, swerved sharply to avoid a monkey that was crossing the road. The driver lost control, and the two butterflies were splattered across the front grill of the big rig. Calanus and Cardui would have been pleased to know that the monkey, an adolescent of the critically endangered Muriqui species (*Brachyteles hypoxanthus*), would grow up to sire eight offspring in his later years.

The two bodies and their personal effects were sent to the state morgue in Belo Horizonte, pending notifications of next of kin. Since the cause of the deaths was readily apparent, the coroner, *Doutora Humberta Filete,* deemed full autopsies unnecessary.

When Filete superficially examined the bodies, she noted traces of red dust on their clothing, the similar tattoos on their skin, and the presence of semen on their genital areas. Given the straightforward nature of their demise, however, nothing aroused suspicion. *The only hanky-panky here,* Filete thought, *was between these two lovers, who ended up in the wrong place at the wrong time, ex post sexo.*

Chapter 22

~~~~~

On the morning of that same Saturday (August 31st), the weekend crew working the Gumanch coffee estate in Papua New Guinea noticed the first splotches of red fungus in a few trees. By that afternoon, the urgency of the situation became apparent when nearly a hectare of the plantation was engulfed in red.

Likewise it went at dozens of coffee plantations around the globe that weekend.

SEPTEMBER 1

The first public report of the fungus occurred Sunday morning, after a farm worker tipped off a BBC Radio journalist in India to the presence of the fungus at Chikmagalur.

SEPTEMBER 2

Monday morning, numerous accounts of additional infestations came from plantations in tropical regions far and wide.

The first person in the world to realize that the reports came exclusively from arabica-producing plantations was Eddy Zeger, as he poked colored pins into his world map.

÷÷÷÷÷

At Sede de Delcese Agricola, Duarte saw early news reports of the fungus at plantations throughout the Brazilian States of São Paulo, Paraná, Minas Gerais, and Espírito Santo.

On a conference call with operations staff at all of Delcese's plantations, Duarte asked, "Any new signs of the fungus?"

"*Não,*" was the response all around.

÷÷÷÷÷

On Labor Day in the United States, much of the population first heard about the reappearance of the coffee fungus via news feeds on their mobile phones or on radio reports while driving home from their family excursions on the holiday weekend.

Beginning that afternoon and throughout the evening, any store that was open on the holiday and selling packaged coffee was inundated with customers attempting to buy it by the cartload. Most stores quickly instituted limits of a few pounds per customer. However, wily families would send in each member for a separate purchase, resulting in bizarre scenes of three or four children in a row at the checkout counters, each with a basketful of coffee and a fistful of cash.

÷÷÷÷÷

That evening, a woman practically pounced on Samuel Decker as he pulled his car into the driveway at his home.

As soon as he cracked open the car door, she said, "Professor Decker, I'm Susan Pittman, an assistant producer for CNN. We'd like to interview you for a story about the coffee fungus."

"I'm under non-disclosure on that."

"I don't think your non-disclosure still applies."

"What do you mean?"

"Professor Decker, haven't you heard the news?"

"I'm just getting home from a weekend in the Berkshires, where I was blissfully oblivious to the news, thanks to the blues channel on satellite radio. What's happening?"

Pittman took a minute to summarize for him the known facts of the situation. "You're the closest thing to an expert in that fungus."

"All right," he said. "When?"

"We were hoping to do it, like, *now*."

He grabbed his travel bag from the trunk of the car. "Give me ten minutes to get ready."

She made a call on her mobile phone while he changed into a presentable shirt, tie, and sport coat.

Pittman drove them west on the Mass Pike, then south on Route 128, which was still clogged with homeward bound holiday traffic. They crawled at a stop-and-go pace for a few miles, until they exited in the town of Needham.

Inside the studios of WCVB-TV, Decker told Pittman, "Let me see every shred of information you have on this."

She walked him into a glass-walled room, where half a dozen people sat at computer terminals, every one of them with a nearby coffee mug decorated with the stylized "5" logo of the TV station's broadcast channel number.

"Elliot," Pittman said to a young man, "show Professor Decker the full load on the coffee story."

Decker spent the next 45 minutes with the research assistant, reviewing source reports and story details.

Decker explained to Elliot how he wanted to present an animated world map sequence showing the progression of countries and plantations in which the fungus had been reported. Decker asked, "Can you guys do that?"

"Of course, we do something very much like that everyday. You won't be able to sit at the anchor desk, though. You'll have to stand over there." Elliot pointed to a studio wall that was covered in fabric of a bright color known as Chroma Key Green.

"Will I have to work a handheld gizmo?"

"We'll have someone control it for you."

"How will I know what the heck I'm pointing at?"

"You'll be able to see yourself in the monitors on the sides of the camera. It's like looking in the mirror, only it's not backwards. We'll let you practice before you go on the air." Elliot took a swig from his coffee mug. "I hope you can stop this fungus, Professor Decker. We'd be a bunch of blathering idiots around here without our journalist juice."

Decker replied, "I'm not involved in the investigation anymore."

Pittman came to retrieve Decker, and she ushered him to a prep area, where a makeup artist applied powder to his face and noxious hairspray to his cowlick.

When Pittman led him onto the studio set, Decker said, "I've never been on live TV before. I've got a case of the butterflies."

÷÷÷÷÷

On the island of Java, Zeger was awake at home in the wee hours of the night, monitoring reports of his group's handiwork as they rolled in from around the world on both his TV set and his laptop screen. Up to that point, all the stories had concerned *what* was happening, rather than *why*. Until a particular segment came on the air.

"...For more on this breaking story," the news anchorman said, "CNN has exclusive live analysis from Professor Samuel Decker of Tufts University. Professor Decker investigated an outbreak of this coffee fungus last month in Brazil. Thanks for joining us, Professor."

Video cut to Decker, standing like a TV weatherman in front of an electronically projected world map. "I'm pleased to be here," he said.

"From the information available at this time, what have you been able to deduce about the worldwide outbreak of this coffee fungus?"

The map behind Decker highlighted various countries in red, with animated stars showing the locations of infected plantations. He began his comments, "This projection shows the progression of reports of the fungus appearing around the world. First, we notice that the reports progress from east to west." He waved his hands only slightly out of sync with the accompanying video image. "This could be for several possible reasons. One is that the fungus is being discovered by farm workers as the sun rises progressively over each portion of the globe. However, about half of the plantations that have reported the fungus first discovered it in the afternoon. Another possibility is that the fungus is naturally progressing in that direction. We know from the prior outbreak in Brazil that wind facilitates distribution of the fungal spores." White arrows appeared superimposed over the map. "These arrows represent wind direction and force over the last two days. As you can see, wind directions have been predominantly west to east during this period, making it highly unlikely that winds have carried the spores in the opposite direction."

The video cut away from Decker and switched to a series of close-up images of the fungus on leaves and cherries of infected coffee trees at plantations around the world.

Zeger leaned in closer to his TV screen, fascinated by the effect of his own group's efforts. Prior to this, the only images of the fungus that he had seen were from a distance, such as the aerial photo published by *Folha* and TV video of fields burning at Sede de Delcese Agricola.

Decker's voice continued over the images, "Active spores of this fungus germinate within hours of coming into contact with coffee trees. However, the spores that caused the latest outbreak likely went dormant while being conveyed such long distances around the world, so their germination times would have been longer. I estimate that the spores first came into contact with coffee trees in all these plantations one or two days ago, that is, within a day or so of each other."

Decker and the world map reappeared on the screen, and he continued, "Irrespective of wind direction, wind speeds at ground level or even winds aloft at high altitude could not possibly have carried fungal spores around the globe fast enough to account for the speed with which this outbreak has manifested itself worldwide. The only explanation that I can deduce which meets the available information is that spores of this fungus were deliberately released in a highly coordinated, precisely timed, worldwide effort. If that's the case, the east to west progression of the discoveries would indicate that the spores were *released* in an east to west progression, which probably corresponded to sunrise across the globe a day or two before the reported sightings."

Decker paused while the map behind him shifted to highlight specific countries. "We also see here, that the reports of the fungus all occur in countries which predominantly produce arabica coffees, such as Brazil, Colombia, Mexico, and Kenya." He pointed to the different countries around the map. "In fact, the only major arabica-producing nation which has not yet reported the fungus is Ethiopia..."

Zeger nearly dropped his TV remote control. *Shit, I hadn't even noticed Ethiopia,* he thought. *But Brother Virgaureae reported that he successfully spread the powder. Something to check into, along with why we never got confirmation from one of the teams in Brazil.*

Decker continued, "...This could be, perhaps, because the coffee trees growing in Ethiopia are somehow immune, or it could be because the organization behind this coordinated effort was unable to spread the spores there. The fungus has not appeared, at least not yet, in the countries which predominantly produce robusta coffee beans, such as Cameroon, Ivory Coast, and Vietnam. In areas which produce both types of coffee, such as the island of Sumatra in Indonesia, so far the fungus has appeared only in the arabica plantations. If it's confirmed that robusta coffee plants are immune, then even in the worst case scenario—complete destruction of all arabica crops worldwide—about one third of the worldwide coffee supply would remain viable."

Yeah, the worst tasting third, Zeger thought. *But I love that he's touting the worst case scenario. I couldn't have asked for a better way of inciting panic.*

The anchorman asked, "If this was a deliberate effort, where would the group responsible have obtained the fungus to spread?"

Decker made a hand motion to someone off screen, and the map behind him zoomed in to South America. "The most likely answer is Brazil. Possibly, the culprits had cultured the fungus in a laboratory environment from samples taken during the prior outbreak in that country, or possibly, they simply absconded with a substantial quantity of the fungus from previously infected plantations."

Too bad he didn't suggest we were responsible for the original outbreak, Zeger thought. *Nothing like getting undeserved credit.*

The anchorman asked, "Professor Decker, after the prior outbreak in Brazil, some experts theorized that the fungus had been deliberately released there, and perhaps it even had been created through genetic engineering. Any comments?"

"I can't discuss details, but based on my investigation in Brazil at the time, I don't believe the earlier outbreak in that country was due to a deliberate release."

"Any theories, Professor Decker, on who's behind this worldwide outbreak now? And to what end?"

"I'm not a terrorism expert..." Decker paused, realizing that was the first time he had heard anyone, including himself, utter the T-word in connection with these most recent events. He resumed, "...but if I had to make a guess, I can think of three types of groups. The first would be a group targeting the coffee growers. Perhaps they hold a grudge from mistreatment of workers on coffee plantations. Or maybe they object to environmental harm from the agricultural production methods used on larger plantations: loss of wildlife habitat, pollution from fertilizer runoff, and the like. The second would be a group that holds extremely negative views on coffee consumption, for instance, that caffeine is harmful. Members of such a group truly would believe they're doing consumers a favor by taking away their coffee. The third would be a group that wishes to deprive the world of coffee to achieve some other objective."

"Like what, Professor Decker?"

"Since coffee is heavily consumed in major industrialized nations, a shortage of it could have all manner of repercussions, such as direct economic fallout from loss of coffee wholesale and retail business, and indirect effects from loss of worker productivity in the broader economy, particularly in the high tech sectors. Morally motivated terrorists might never make any demands. Rather than demanding change, they might only seek to cause it themselves."

"Thank you, Professor Decker. Now on to business news. Markets in the U.S. were closed today for the Labor Day holiday, but elsewhere around the world, markets were down..."

That Decker guy is thinking too small, Zeger thought. *I want nothing short of the complete collapse of civilization as we know it.*

÷÷÷÷÷

When Decker stepped off the set, Pittman ran up to him with both thumbs up. "That was great. Excellent ideas, clearly explained. And you're a natural in front of the camera."

He replied, "Got any openings for a weatherman?"

SEPTEMBER 3

As the sun rose over the Eastern Hemisphere on Tuesday, reports of infestations flooded in from numerous additional coffee plantations. A handful of those reports were later determined to have been due to other fungi such as common coffee leaf rust, but that was insignificant in the grand scheme of events. By Tuesday morning, 82 coffee plantations worldwide had reported outbreaks of a red fungus. Although the plantations hit included most of the largest in the world, coffee growing was distributed into about a thousand major plantations, hundreds of thousands of modestly sized farms, and millions of tiny plots. Collectively, the entire annual bean production from the plantations stricken up to that point accounted for less than one percent of the worldwide coffee supply. But none of the popular media outlets had thought to make such a calculation.

On Tuesday, the major stock exchanges in Hong Kong, Shanghai, and Tokyo all fell several percentage points within minutes of opening, followed later by London and the other European exchanges. Brazil's Bovespa dropped six percent soon after its opening.

That was all before Wall Street's bell got rung.

When the stock exchanges in the U.S. opened at 9:30AM Eastern Time on the first trading day after the Labor Day holiday, the bottom fell out of the market in a record session of trading.

The first use of the popular descriptive term for the day came on Twitter. "This isn't another Black Tuesday," tweeted Shameeka Johnson of *The Wall Street Journal*, "This is Red Tuesday." Besides the obvious reference to the hue of the fungus, labeling a dismal day on the stock markets with the color red rather than black was more logical given the traditional accounting implications of the two colors.

Red Tuesday combined with additional incremental drops on the following days that week constituted what is now known in U.S. stock market history as the Coffee Crash of 2013.

~~~~~

When the New York Stock Exchange had collapsed back in October 1929 initiating the Great Depression, on the worst single day of that crash, October 29th (Black Tuesday), the market lost 12 percent of its value.

In 1987, when the U.S. stock markets (by then several) again collapsed, on the worst day of that crash, October 19th (Black Monday), the markets lost 22 percent of their value.

In the wake of the 1987 crash, to reduce the potential for dramatic single-day market declines, the exchanges instituted "circuit breaker" rules to halt all trading temporarily if specific trigger-level declines were to occur. During the years that those original market-wide circuit breakers were in effect, they had been triggered on only one day, October 27, 1997, when the Dow Jones Industrial Average fell 7.2 percent. Some financial analysts considered closure of the markets that day to be premature, because the triggers were set too tightly, with a temporary trading halt occurring after a drop of only 4.5 percent. At that time, the circuit breakers were based on a fixed numbers of points of fluctuation in the DJIA, which had become increasingly lower percentages as the index had grown higher over the years. The 1997 event led the Securities and Exchange Commission in 1998 to loosen the triggers and adjust their point values quarterly based on calculated percentages of the index.

In the economic recession that commenced in late 2008, the U.S. stock markets lost a total of 22 percent of their value over eight consecutive trading days in October. During that period, however, no single day of trading reached the DJIA circuit breaker triggers, and the markets remained open. Some analysts considered the triggers to be set too loosely.

In April 2013, the SEC again instituted revisions to its market-wide circuit breaker rules: shifting the reference index to the broader Standard & Poor's 500; partially retightening the trigger percentages; recalculating the point values of the triggers daily; and shortening the halt periods, except for the final trigger which would close the markets for the remainder of the day if the index dropped 20 percent.

Until Red Tuesday, market-wide circuit breakers based on the 1998 or 2013 rules had never been triggered.

~~~~~

On Red Tuesday, even before the markets opened, tens of millions of individual investors logged on to their online brokerage accounts and clicked the Sell button. Once the markets opened, the immediate dip from the huge backlog of sell orders set off additional programmed selling by large institutional investors seeking to clear their positions before the markets dropped further. The S&P 500 hit its seven percent decline trigger at 9:59AM EDT, less than half an hour after the markets opened. In accordance with circuit breaker rules, all trading was halted for 15 minutes. When trading resumed, the trend continued. The S&P 500 hit its 13 percent decline trigger at 10:50AM, initiating another 15 minute halt. And the S&P 500 reached its 20 percent decline trigger at 11:58AM, when all trading was halted for the day.

As Shameeka Johnson soon put it in a blog post for WSJ.com, "When everyone in a crowded theater smells smoke, temporarily locking the exit doors does not diminish the desire to escape the building, whether or not it's actually on fire."

The tech-heavy NASDAQ composite index was most clobbered that day, losing 24 percent before trading ended. Remarkably, shares on the NASDAQ exchange in one particular company rose on Red Tuesday, a bright spot on the otherwise dark financial markets.

÷÷÷÷÷

At 7:30AM in California on the morning of Red Tuesday, Truck Macklin was just rolling his racing wheelchair back in the door when his wife handed him the telephone. She said, "It's Matt."

He wiped his face on his T-shirt. "What's up?"

"Truck, the stock market is tanking. Investors have freaked out over the coffee fungus."

"Yeah, I heard some of the market numbers on the radio earlier this morning. How bad is it for us?"

Macklin heard Cochran laughing on the other end of the line. "It's amazing, Truck. Bright Cup shares are up three percent."

"What?"

"Our company shares are up. Not only that, coffee futures prices on the BM&F exchange hit the daily maximum increases just minutes after opening. I've already gotten a bunch of calls from our competitors wanting to buy into some of our private forward contracts at a premium over face value. Getting stuck with all those contracts has turned out to be a blessing in disguise."

Chapter 23

"Reports that say that something hasn't happened are always interesting to me, because as we know, there are known knowns; there are things we know we know. We also know there are known unknowns; that is to say we know there are some things we do not know. But there are also unknown unknowns—the ones we don't know we don't know."

U.S. Secretary of Defense Donald Rumsfeld, 2002

~~~~~

SEPTEMBER 4

Wednesday morning, Costa sat behind the desk in his office at Sede. Lieutenant Azevedo paced the floor.

Costa said, "When Júnior stayed at the Grande Hotel, she must have been meeting with others from her international terrorist ring to plot the distribution of the coffee fungus."

Azevedo nodded agreement. "I've checked into that lady Cicera from Pampulha. She hardly seems like the terrorist type. Her husband is a big shot philanthropist, contributing to all manner of politically correct causes."

"You can't judge a crook by her cover."

"True. But, if Cicera wasn't involved, then Júnior must've been meeting with other people at the hotel." Azevedo held up a sheet of paper. "This is derived from a complete list of all the guests who stayed at the Grande Hotel during the time Júnior was there. The full list totaled nine hundred seventy-nine individuals. This list narrows it down to sixty-two that the DPF identified as having prior arrests or other records of interest. One guest was a sheik from Saudi Arabia. He and his entourage of six were at the hotel for five days, purportedly meeting with business interests in the minerals and mining industries in the area."

"What if Júnior was meeting with hotel staff members?"

Azevedo held up another sheet of paper. "DPF has done background checks on the entire staff. One is a Spanish immigrant with prior ties to ETA, the Basque separatist movement."

Costa remarked, "That group has never had any motivation for an attack outside Spain. And, it publicly renounced terrorism years ago."

Azevedo looked back to the paper. "One of the hotel's assistant managers was a pimp in Rio more than twenty years ago. Not much else of interest. The Americans think the Saudi is the top suspect. Their

CIA is investigating him. And their NSA is still attempting to decode Júnior's email. Our guys have had no luck finding the username and password for her email account, and they can't brute force it because of timeouts after failed log-in attempts. We've turned her apartment upside down and thoroughly searched her laptop. Melan hasn't found any tetanus bacteria or the coffee fungus in Júnior's apartment. We've been tailing Tulio since we arrested Júnior, but he's been clean as a whistle."

Costa said, "Maybe Júnior was also working with someone else at Delcese. She had a field project out near Fazenda Fiorva." He picked up the phone and dialed three digits.

A minute later Lucy stood in the office recalling, "...When Mr. Decker and I talked to Larissa, she said one of the workers from Fiorva helped out on her field research. We never got to talk to him, though."

Azevedo asked, "Why not?"

"Mr. Decker got canned by *Senhor* Duarte on the day we were planning to go back out to Fiorva."

"Do you know the name of the worker at Fiorva?"

"It was Sergio Moreno. He was the fourth person in the airplane earlier on the day it crashed."

Costa said, "The three of us should pay a visit to Sergio to find out what he knows."

A minute later, Mabro's voice was on the speakerphone, "...Yes, Sergio is here at Fazenda Fiorva today."

÷÷÷÷

The day after Red Tuesday was the first day Decker was scheduled to teach a class in the new academic year at the Tufts University campus in Medford, Massachusetts. He was slated for a 9:00AM seminar entitled Endocytosis & Exocytosis, for which 14 graduate students were registered.

The Tufts Biology Department was located in Barnum Hall, named for P.T., the circus impresario who had funded its construction in 1884 as a museum of natural history. The structure had housed, among its other treasures, the taxidermied hide of the famed circus elephant Jumbo, until a 1975 fire destroyed the building. Although Barnum Hall had been rebuilt, all that remained of the original giant pachyderm were a fragment of its tail in the university's archives and a clump of ashes kept in a peanut butter jar in guarded possession of the university's athletic director.

When Decker entered Barnum Hall on his way to the classroom, the hallway was packed elbow to elbow with students chatting away in collective cacophony. Decker started to work his way through the crowd to get to the classroom, inadvertently banging his briefcase into numerous innocent bystanders. Twenty feet in, the hallway became impassable.

He asked a young woman against whom he was wedged, "What's all the commotion about?"

She snapped a bubble of chewing gum, then replied, "We're all waiting to hear Professor Decker talk about the coffee shortage."

Decker groaned. *Shortage? What shortage? There's no shortage, at least not yet. And so much for today's Endo & Exo lecture.* He raised both of his index fingers to his mouth and placed the tips of the fingers onto the tip of his tongue. He took a deep breath, then he let out an ear-piercing whistle that reverberated down the corridor.

The throng instantly became silent, except for one male student who got caught in that embarrassing occurrence of loudly finishing a sentence against an unexpectedly silent backdrop, "...and then she licked my nuts... Oh, shit."

When the raucous laughter simmered down, Decker raised a hand over his head and pointed to the exit. "Everybody, outside."

÷

In the courtyard outside Barnum Hall stood Jumbo II, a concrete and *papier-mâché* elephant statue that had been salvaged from a defunct wild animal attraction and donated to the school by a group of alumni. Jumbo II was right at home in the circus-like atmosphere of the 200 or so people assembled in the courtyard.

Decker stood next to the statue as the crowd settled in.

One student kicked off the questions, shouting out, "Professor Decker, do you know how to stop the coffee fungus?"

"I don't know."

Another shouted, "Does anyone know?"

"The last I knew several weeks ago, no one knew how to stop it. I don't know if anyone now knows."

"Do you know who's behind the spread of the fungus?"

"I don't know who's responsible for this week's release of the fungus, nor do I know if anyone else knows."

"What other destructive biological organisms might such a terrorist group possess?"

"That's unknown."

"Do you expect the terrorists to claim responsibility?"

"They might prefer that we know who they are. Or they might prefer that we not know. We just don't know."

And on it went for several minutes until one student asked, "How do the fungal hyphae sporulate so quickly?"

Decker paused. *What? A biology question?* He explained the known details of the fungus's microbiology and reproduction, and most of the crowd wandered away.

÷÷÷÷÷

On the TV news, the CNN talking head said, "The Dow Jones Industrial Average is down another three percent today, and the NASDAQ is down four percent, in the continuing slide in the wake of the worldwide coffee fungus epidemic. As of noon today, one hundred and thirty-eight coffee plantations worldwide have reported the red fungus in their fields..." A large red LED panel mounted above the world map behind the newsman switched numbers. "...Make that one hundred and thirty-nine..."

÷÷÷÷÷

Carlos flew the plane with Azevedo in the co-pilot's seat, and Costa and Lucy in back. When the plane taxied up to the hangar at Fazenda Fiorva, Mabro was waiting for them. Carlos stayed at the hangar while Mabro walked the others over to the maintenance garage, where Sergio Moreno was repairing a tractor engine. Sergio wiped his hands on a clean rag, then politely shook hands with the visitors.

Azevedo began the questioning, "You worked with Larissa Júnior in one of the experimental coffee fields?"

"*Sim*," Sergio replied. "I planted the test crops there a few years ago, then I helped Larissa collect data on the progress of the plants."

"Did the red fungus ever appear in that test field?"

"*Não*, at least not when I was there."

"When was the last time you were there?"

"On the day the small plane crashed a couple of months ago. When the scientist died."

"And you were there with Larissa Júnior that day?"

"*Sim*. We were stranded out there for hours waiting for the plane to return."

"What did you talk about while you waited?"

"We talked about the test plants and the test results."

"Did the topic of coffee fungus ever come up in the discussion?"

"*Não*, that was before all the red fungus appeared at the plantation here. The coffee plants in the test field were an experiment for natural pest resistance, keeping away insects without using insecticide. Nothing to do with fungus."

"Did Júnior mention anything about the human disease tetanus?"

"*Não*."

Azevedo shifted topics. "When you flew in the plane to get to the field, did you see the pilot, Miguel, eat or drink anything?"

"*Não.*"

Azevedo shifted again. "*Senhor* Mabro tells us that you took a week off from work two weeks ago. Is that correct?"

"*Sim.*"

"Where were you during that week?"

"I was up in Amazonas visiting my old aunt who was recovering from surgery."

"Where in Amazonas?"

"She lives in Manaus."

"Would you mind providing us specific contact information for your aunt? We just need to corroborate your story."

Sergio gave out the woman's name and address, which Azevedo wrote down. The policeman ran out of questions, and he motioned to Costa, who shook his head.

Climbing back into the airplane, Costa told the pilot he wanted to fly over the experimental test field where Júnior and Moreno had worked, to find out whether the fungus was there.

While Carlos set switches on the instrument panel, Azevedo said to the others, "Sergio has been so close to this. He works at the plantation where the fungus started, and he was in the plane on the day it crashed. I'll have a man up in Manaus see if his story checks out." He added as an afterthought, "I've never been up to Manaus myself."

Costa shook his head. "Me either."

"I've been to Manaus," Lucy said. Carlos started up the engine, and she raised her voice over the noise to finish her statement. "I went on a tour of the big Copag playing card factory there."

Costa and Azevedo looked at each other, then they both signaled for Carlos to cut the engine.

A minute later, they were facing Sergio again.

"One more question," Azevedo said. "Have you ever been to the Grande Hotel in Águas de São Pedro?"

Sergio asked, "You mean the fancy resort place?"

"That's the one."

"I've driven by it, but I've never been inside."

÷

The plane flew over the experimental fields to the north, where Larissa and Sergio had worked. All the fields appeared to be infected with the fungus. Lucy yelled out the suggestion that they also fly over the experimental fields to the west of the plantation, to see if the fungus was there. Costa nodded. Twenty minutes later, the plane flew over the fields in that area. All but one of them were visibly infected with red growth.

Lucy said, "The scientists will want samples from the field that's not infected."

Costa motioned to Carlos to land at the dirt airstrip.

Lucy jogged to the unaffected field. She broke off several small branches and plucked a pocketful of coffee cherries, then she jogged back to the plane.

÷

Two hours after the plane returned to Sede, Costa and Azevedo reconvened in Costa's office.

The lieutenant said, "Sergio's story checks out so far. DPF up in Manaus confirms from a neighbor of Sergio's aunt that a man matching his description stayed there a couple of weeks ago. And I had an agent run the photo of Sergio down to the Grande Hotel. He showed it to some employees, and none of them had ever seen him before."

÷

The senior scientists entered the conference room, followed by Munhoz and Duarte.

When they were seated, Westphal said, "The branch and cherry samples Lucy brought back from the unaffected field are the low-caffeine variant based on the Bourbon cultivar."

Horton added, "That's in line with our earlier findings that the fungus metabolizes caffeine. The question is whether we can use that characteristic to stop it."

Santini suggested, "Perhaps we could identify and extract the gene responsible for low caffeine in the Bourbon cultivar then implant it into the fungus to create a newer version of fungus that might block the current fungus. The fungal DNA might not take the coffee plant gene, though."

Westphal said, "In any case, that would take months to develop."

"The world can't wait that long," Duarte responded.

After another five minutes of suggestions and countering, Westphal said, "Let's face it. We don't have a clue how to stop the fungus quickly."

Munhoz, who had been silent until then, muttered out loud, "I wish Sam was here."

Everyone else stopped talking, then they all looked at Duarte.

÷÷÷÷÷

Driving home from Fazenda Fiorva after work that day, Sergio Moreno was listening to the radio in his pickup truck. It was tuned to the same AM station out of Piracicaba he always listened to in the truck, not that he had much choice, as it was one of only two stations he could receive out in the hinterlands with the truck's lousy antenna.

After the *esportes* report the radio announcer continued, "...And now, today's anniversary and birthday messages. To *Senhora* Carla Resende, happy fiftieth anniversary from your husband Fernando. To *Senhor* Sergio Aidea, happy eightieth birthday from your brothers and sisters overseas..."

In the nine years he had lived in that region of Brazil, never before had Sergio received an emergency contact radio message. He had forgotten long ago the specific meaning of each of the milestone birthday years, but he calmly continued driving down the road.

When he arrived home, he went to the bedroom closet, where he removed a small, aging notebook from a shoebox on the top shelf. He flipped through the pages to locate the birthday milestones, then he copied the entry for 80th birthday onto a piece of paper. It consisted of a sentence spelled out phonetically in English, along with a member name and a telephone number.

Sergio immediately drove all the way to Campinas, where he purchased an international phone card at a gas station. He drove the truck around for several minutes until he located a public payphone, known in Brazil as an *orelhão* (literally, "big ear," so-called because of the rounded shape of its fiberglass shroud).

He read several times the dialing instructions on the phone card, not having placed an international call in many years. He had no idea that a number beginning with the country code 852 would ring to a line in Hong Kong.

When a voice responded on the line, Sergio read the sentence from his piece of paper, "Ai wu'd li-ka tu pay-ge a pah-sen-jor, Mi-stair Mar-i-po-sa. It is en i-mair-gen-ci."

÷

Gabriel Bonnington checked his watch when he heard the page inside the ferry terminal. *Three hours response time*, he thought. *Not bad for an unscheduled radio hail.*

"This is Mister Mariposa," Bonnington said into the telephone where the announcement directed him. The background noise was loud enough and the flow of people constant enough that he didn't need to worry about anyone overhearing the conversation.

The voice on the other end asked, "*Fala português?*"

"No," Bonnington replied. "Do you speak English?"

"*Não, eu não falo inglês*," Sergio said, then he shifted languages for another try. "*¿Habla español?*"

"*Sí*," Bonnington said, and the rest of their conversation took place in Spanish. "Goliath has assigned you an important new task, *Hermano* Aidea."

"I'm ready to serve the swarm," Sergio responded. "But first I must tell you that I was questioned by the police today at work. I work at the coffee plantation where the fungus first appeared in July."

"Do the police suspect you are involved?"

"I don't think so, but I can't be certain."

"Thank you for informing me, *Hermano* Aidea. By the way, do you have any idea why *Hermana* Cardui and *Hermano* Calanus have not checked in? We know their distribution was successful because their assigned plantations have reported infections."

"I don't know. I never met them. I never even talked to them on the phone."

"On to the task at hand then, the reason for the emergency contact. Now that the fungus has been deployed successfully, Goliath wants you to extinguish *Hermana* Cleobaea."

Sergio resisted the urge to confirm whether he had heard correctly. "May I ask why?"

"She has been compromised by the recent events in the laboratory at Delcese headquarters involving the new tetanus bacteria. It's only a matter of time before the authorities discover that they've arrested the wrong woman for that. We must provide them with a scapegoat. You should try to pin the fungus outbreak on Cleobaea as well. The police and the scientists will believe they've finally found the right culprit, neatly linking both investigations. With luck, they won't have any further leads to follow."

"I will carry out Goliath's wishes."

"*Hermano* Aidea," Bonnington reassured him, "you must realize that if the police take Cleobaea alive, she will implicate you and your cousin."

Chapter 24

~~~~~

Walter Bates, the world's wealthiest man, forever changed U.S. politics with his presence in the 2012 Presidential election. Despite decades as a social liberal, rather than run for the top spot on the Democratic ticket, he founded his own political party. He had desired, with his tongue planted firmly in cheek, to call it the Green Party, but the name was already taken, and the owners refused to sell its rights to him. Bates chose instead the name Sovereign Party, publicly touting one of the word's meanings—independence—and conveniently ignoring another—that of a supreme ruler.

The Democrats found themselves alongside the Republicans on the downside of their own campaign finance reform measures when pitted against the limitless ad spending of the Bates campaign, funded entirely from his personal wealth. (The Sovereign Party did not accept donations from either the electorate or special interest groups.)

Bates ran on a centrist political platform with a moderate conservative Southern female running mate for Vice President. Strategically, their greatest campaign challenge was how to handle the polarizing issue of abortion. The Sovereign Party adopted a rhetorical position, called Pro-Life-Choice, summarized in the slogan, "Women are free to choose to *have* their babies." To that end, Bates proposed a quasi-governmental non-profit child care program to support single-parent and dual-parent households alike. Bates offered to jump start it with one billion dollars of seed money from his own pocket, with ongoing funding from a voluntary national lottery, supplemented by charitable contributions from, as Bates put it, "citizens of means who are willing to put their money where their mouths are when they talk about 'family values.'"

At first, both Democratic and Republican candidates attempted to become more centrist in order to hold voters away from the moderate Sovereign positions on numerous issues. Those efforts backfired by supporting the very messages that Bates was touting. Then both major party candidates reacted and became more extremist to retain their core constituents, but polls showed that those efforts drove away even more of their parties' less extreme members.

In the end, it was no contest. Bates won the 2012 election by outright majority in both the Electoral College and the popular vote, ushering in the 21st century era of third-party American politics. Voter participation was the highest ever that year.

Now, with a full-fledged crisis at hand, the public was demanding action, and naturally the President obliged.

~~~~~

The President tasked the U.S. Department of Homeland Security with coordinating the efforts of federal agencies involved in investigating the spread of the coffee fungus. He did so citing three of the DHS's many roles: to identify vulnerabilities to the nation's economic security; to protect against biological threats; and to help secure the global supply chain. The creators of the DHS hadn't anticipated those roles to meld in a single event quite as they had in the Coffee Crash: a vulnerability to the nation's economic security due to a biological threat to the global supply chain.

÷÷÷÷÷

The President also took the matter into his own hands.

Early Wednesday evening, Roland Fiske, Secretary of Homeland Security, entered the Oval Office.

President Bates was talking into a speakerphone on the Resolute Desk, "...Thank you, Mr. Prime Minister. I knew the American people could count on your support." Bates pushed a button to hang up.

Fiske said, "Good evening, Mr. President."

"Good evening, Roland. I bet you're here to find out the total."

"Correct, sir." (Occasionally, Fiske said "sire," but not this time.)

Bates tallied up his notepad. "We just hit a hundred little ones." In the President's personal vernacular, "big ones" would have signified billions.

÷÷÷÷÷

When Decker came home that evening, the voice mail light on his landline phone was blinking.

The message said, "Mr. Decker, this is Felipe Buarque. I'm an attaché with the Brazilian Embassy to the United States. The Ambassador, His Excellency Evandro Aguiar, requests to meet with you during your upcoming trip to Washington D.C."

Upon hearing the message, Decker thought, *I wasn't aware that I had an upcoming trip to Washington D.C.* He hung up the phone line. *Then again, Decker's Theory of Political Relativity: Normal rules of the space-time continuum don't apply in Washington D.C.*

Less than 10 minutes later, his doorbell rang. The man on the doorstep wore a dark blue suit. Decker might have mistaken him for a businessman except for the badge he held out. It had an eagle's crest in the center of a five pointed star, surrounded by a circle engraved with the words "United States Marshal."

The Marshal asked, "Are you Samuel Decker, sir?"

"I am."

The Marshal handed him an envelope.

Decker asked, "What is it?"

"It's a summons for you to appear Friday morning in Washington D.C., to testify before the United States Senate Committee on Coffee Contamination."

÷÷÷÷÷

At 9:00PM EDT, the Presidential Seal appeared on more than 100 million television sets and Internet streams in the U.S. and tens of millions more worldwide. The off-screen announcer said, "And now, the President of the United States, Walter H. Bates, Jr."

The video faded to Bates, seated behind the desk in the Oval Office. He calmly spoke, "Good evening, my fellow Americans. I come to you today to address the issue foremost in many of your minds, the microorganism which is decimating farms around the world and threatening to deprive you of one of life's simplest pleasures: a good cup of coffee. I can assure you that the full attentions and efforts of America's law enforcement agencies are directed at identifying the organization behind the spread of the coffee fungus and bringing the responsible criminals to justice."

The President had instructed the speechwriter to avoid using the word *terrorists*, since the mere mention of the word fostered terror among the public, giving the terrorists more of what they wanted. Instead, Bates preferred to liken the culprits to small time crooks, only bigger time. "Besides," he had told the speechwriter, "nobody ever died from not having a cup of coffee."

Bates continued his speech, "To help root out the miscreants responsible for spreading the coffee fungus, we have assembled an international coalition to offer a reward for providing information leading to the identification and capture of the criminal group and its leader. With fifty million dollars from the United States government, twenty-five million dollars from our friends in the European Union, twenty million dollars pledged by the government of Brazil, and five million dollars from a consortium of American businesses in the coffee industry, a total reward of one hundred million dollars is available." He motioned toward the camera. "Citizens of the world, you can claim a share of this reward by turning in the people behind this misguided plot to ruin the worldwide economy." He waved a hand down low. "Simply call the phone number appearing now on the bottom of your screen." Then he pointed a finger directly at the camera lens. "And to whoever is responsible, I say that we will find you, and we will bring you to justice. You can bank on it." Bates folded his hands on the desk. "Good night."

÷÷÷÷÷

On the far side of the planet, Eddy Zeger mumbled to his television set, "Typical American capitalist, thinking that money can fix everything." Zeger turned off the TV. "Even if they find me now, it will be too late for them to stop the destruction."

SEPTEMBER 5

Early Thursday morning, in his small apartment in the Russian Hill neighborhood of San Francisco, Tony Goterrez absentmindedly fingered his moustache as he looked through printouts of numerous press releases, news articles, and maps piled on his dining room table.

"Holy Shit!" he cried out to himself, "I know who it is." He jumped out of his chair and nervously stomped around the room. "What do I do now?" He searched for the scrap of paper on which he had written the telephone number shown on TV during the President's speech the previous night. He dialed the number.

"Thank you for calling the Department of Homeland Security. If you're calling to report that your neighbor is a spy, please hang up and dial the CIA. If you're calling to report that your neighbor is a drug dealer, please hang up and dial the DEA. If you're calling to report that your neighbor was featured on *America's Most Wanted*, please hang up and dial the FBI. To speak to a Department of Homeland Security agent, please press one."

Goterrez pressed 1 on his phone.

"All of our agents are currently busy. Please stay on the line to wait for the next available agent..."

÷

Shortly after noon, two Homeland Security agents arrived at Goterrez's apartment. He offered them coffee, and they both readily accepted mugs of Bright Cup's Primo Cup. Goterrez then handed the agents a series of documents. He painstakingly explained the logic behind his identification of the head terrorist responsible for disseminating the coffee fungus.

Later that day, three more people were subpoenaed to appear Friday before the Senate Committee on Coffee Contamination.

✢✢✢✢✢

In his cubicle in the main offices of the Departamento de Polícia Federal in Brasília, Vinícius Búzia received a phone call.

"Mr. Búzia, this is Louis Martelli from the National Security Agency in the United States. I have good news and bad news on that email message we've been cracking for you."

"What's the good news?"

"The good news is that we got lucky. We've successfully decrypted the message."

"*Fantástico*. What's the bad news?"

"The bad news is that the entire decrypted message consists of nothing more than a lengthy article about truffle harvesting in continental Europe. The sender's username was 'birdladyofbrazil,' and the recipient's name was 'NaturEd.' Our analysts have read and reread the article, studied it every which way they can, but they cannot produce any interpretation that relates to the current coffee fungus situation. They've attempted to decipher it further for hidden messages, but they've come up empty. It appears that you guys down there at DPF have wasted tens of millions of U.S. taxpayer dollars to have Nowell decrypt nothing more than an article that some nature lover forwarded to another."

Viní groaned. "Can you send me the decrypted message anyway?"

"Check your Inbox. It should be arriving now."

"Thank you, Mr. Martelli."

"You guys owe us, big time." The line went dead.

Viní opened the email from Martelli. Staring at the text of the article, he thought, *If Azevedo has the right woman in jail, this message must have a hidden meaning.*

✢✢✢✢✢

That evening, Sergio and his female cousin Gilberta drove down to Piracicaba. He stopped the pickup truck at a natural foods store. She ran in and purchased a 250 milliliter bottle of cold pressed *castanha* oil, produced from the nut of the *Bertholletia excelsa* tree, known to foreigners as the Brazil nut. The oil is rich in emollients and is sometimes used as an ingredient in skin moisturizers, but such was not the intention in this case. The unrefined *castanha* oil retained solids from the nut meat, and it provided Brother Aidea and Sister Harmonia an opportunity to use it as a consumable with a nasty side effect for a particular person.

When Sergio first met Martina and Gunter Hasse years earlier in Santarém, he had offered them some of the nuts, which grow wild in that region. Shortly after Martina had eaten just one *castanha*, she got extremely sick, and she had trouble breathing. Gunter had to inject her with medicine from a slender plastic tube with a yellow label on it. She later told Sergio that she'd never been allergic to any other nuts, only to bee stings, and she was lucky that she had the medicine with her or else she might have died in a matter of minutes.

On the sidewalk a block away from the apartment building where the Hasses lived, Sergio telephoned them from an *orelhão*.

"Hello, Gunter. This is Sergio. My cousin Gilberta and I are in the city. We'd like to invite you and *senhora* to have dinner with us. We can meet you at a restaurant near your home."

"I'll check with Martina. Hang on a moment." When Gunter came back on the line, he said, "Yes, she says she has something she needs to discuss with you..."

÷

Sergio and Gilberta waited in his pickup truck near the Hasses' apartment. He spied the building entrance through binoculars which Martina had given to him years earlier when she had bought a better pair for herself. After Sergio saw the Hasses leave the building and drive away, he tossed a small backpack over his shoulder and went inside. Gilberta waited in the truck to run out and intercept the Hasses should they return prematurely for any reason.

Sergio knocked on the door of the Hasses' apartment to make sure no one else was inside. He slipped off his backpack and took out a small tool pouch that contained a lock picking set which Gilberta had ordered for him from a company in the United States. However, before he removed the tools from the pouch, he tried the doorknob and discovered that it was unlocked. He slipped inside, then he crept down the hall to the bathroom. In the medicine chest behind the mirror, he found two of the injectors that he had seen Gunter use on Martina. He checked that the name on the labels matched the words that Gilberta had written down for him on a scrap of paper: "EpiPen Epinephrine Autoinjector." He left the injectors on the shelf and closed the cabinet.

In the hallway, he opened the door of the small linen closet. He took from his backpack the last remaining specially prepared box of Dirt-Away laundry detergent powder, and he placed it behind the stack of towels next to another box of detergent, taking care that it would not be visible even if several towels were to be removed. *Gunter won't find it*, Sergio thought, *but the police will.*

÷

The restaurant was a dimly lit hole-in-the-wall called *A Cavidade* (The Cave). When Sergio and Gilberta entered, Martina and Gunter were already seated on one side of a booth. The new arrivals joined them at the booth, then they all chatted about Amazonas while they sipped a round of drinks. The waitress came to take their meal order. Martina ordered *feijoada* (bean stew), then Gilberta ordered the same dish. Both men ordered *badejo* (sea bass). About 10 minutes later, Gunter excused himself to use the toilet.

When Gunter was out of sight, Martina leaned in close and whispered, "I need you two to make someone extinct."

Sergio and Gilberta glanced at each other, then Sergio suggested to Martina, "Let's step outside to discuss this." Sergio and Martina got up, and he nodded to Gilberta when he saw that Martina had left her purse at the booth.

While Gilberta was temporarily alone at the table, she clumsily dropped her napkin to the floor. She bent under the booth to retrieve it. Under the table, she reached across the booth and pulled the other woman's purse from the bench. She opened the clasp and reached her hand in, feeling around in the near darkness. When she located the EpiPen, she slid it up her pants leg and tucked it into her sock, then she closed the purse and placed it back on the bench. She nonchalantly sat upright.

A minute later, the waitress delivered the meals. After the waitress moved away, Gilberta used her body to shield her activities from the other patrons. She took out from her own purse the small bottle of *castanha* oil, and she dumped about half the bottle into her own large bowl of *feijoada*, hastily stirring in the extra ingredient. She scanned the room, and when no one else was looking, she swiftly swapped dishes with the one in front of Martina's place at the table.

Gunter returned from the toilet. He said, "It was occupied, so I had to wait."

Gilberta replied, "We women are used to that."

÷

On the sidewalk outside, Martina and Sergio strolled away from the restaurant.

When they were half a block away, Sergio asked, "Who is it?"

"Larissa."

Sergio halted walking. "Larissa Júnior?"

Martina nodded. "That day we went to the Grande Hotel in Águas de São Pedro, she saw me there, at the room where I sent the email to *Irmão* Goliath. She is the only person outside the swarm who could connect us to any involvement with Goliath."

Sergio nodded his understanding, but noted, "Larissa is in jail at the DPF. I can't get to her there."

"Maybe you could sneak in and poison her food."

Sergio was about to comment on the absurdity of the suggestion, but they heard Gunter's voice call out from behind, "Come on in, guys. Your food'll get cold."

Back in the booth, Martina tasted a spoonful of bean stew. She wrinkled her nose.

Gilberta picked up a small bowl of *molho apimentado,* a hot sauce garnish, and spooned some into her own bowl of *feijoada.* Then she held it out to Martina. "Try some of this. It's tasty, and it goes great with the stew."

Martina added some hot sauce to her stew then gave it another taste. "That's better."

About five minutes later, Martina started to wheeze. She set down the spoon and raised her chin. Sergio asked Gunter a question to distract him for as long as possible. By the time Gunter noticed that Martina was having a problem, the tendons in her neck were standing out as she strained to breath.

As soon as Gilberta saw that Gunter had noticed, she asked, "Martina, what's wrong?"

Martina gasped for air between words. "I think... I must be... allergic to... something... in the... stew."

Gunter asked, "How bad is it?"

"Very bad... I can't... breeeeeath..."

"Do you have an EpiPen?"

Martina pointed to her purse. Gunter grabbed the purse off the bench. He looked inside, but not finding the medicine, he stood up and dumped the purse contents onto the bench.

"It's not here. Are you sure you had one?"

Martina barely moved.

The waitress came over at the commotion. "Is there a problem here, folks?"

"My wife is having an allergic reaction to the food. If she doesn't get her medication within a few minutes, she could die."

The waitress shrieked. Gunter knocked around the items from the purse, searching in vain.

A voice from the kitchen yelled, "What's going on out there?"

The waitress yelled back, *"Alergia."*

A man came running from a table at the rear of the dining room. He said, "I'm a doctor." He looked at Martina. "She's in anaphylactic shock."

Gunter yelled, "I know! She needs epinephrine!"

The doctor responded, "I've got an EpiPen in my car." He faced Martina directly and added, "Hang on, lady. You're going to be OK."

He turned to the waitress. "Call an ambulance." Then he ran out the front door of the restaurant.

Gunter swept the purse contents from the bench onto the floor to clear room for Martina to lie down. He was generating enough adrenaline of his own to have saved her, had there been a ready means of transfusing it.

Sergio and Gilberta looked at each other, then they slid out of the booth and stood out of the way.

Less than a minute later, the doctor came running back in the door. He popped the cap off an EpiPen. He swung his arm up, then lowered it to bang the tip of the device onto Martina's thigh, instantly releasing the spring-loaded needle and automatically injecting the life-saving medication right through her pants.

In the midst of the diversion now engulfing the entire restaurant, Gilberta sat down in an adjacent booth. Underneath the table, she slid the EpiPen out of her sock and kicked it below the bench where other items from Martina's purse had rolled.

Chapter 25

"It's a travesty of a mockery of a sham of a mockery of a travesty of two
mockeries of a sham."

Woody Allen, on trial as the character Fielding Mellish, in his 1971
film, *Bananas*

~~~~~

SEPTEMBER 6

On Friday morning in Washington, D.C., crowds gathered in the
Caucus Room of the Russell Senate Office Building just north of the
Capitol. The Caucus Room was a vast and elegant space lined with
Corinthian columns and pilasters sculpted from Vermont marble. It
had a high, ornately gilded ceiling from which hung three massive
crystal chandeliers, the largest of which, had it fallen that day, would
have taken out half the Congressional press corps.

All the major television networks were covering the event live.
Veteran ABC commentator Howard Carson noted that the same room
had been the site of numerous historic national hearings, including
those of the Iran-Contra affair in 1987, the Watergate break-in in 1973,
the Army-McCarthy inquiry in 1954, and, most interestingly from a
nominal perspective, the Teapot Dome scandal in 1923. Teapot Dome
had not been related to the beverage of tea, but rather a different
precious dark liquid—oil—as Carson himself pointed out on air. Nevertheless, it was Carson who coined the phrase "Coffeepot Rot," by which
the hearings about to begin would become popularly known.

Behind a long table at the front of the Caucus Room sat the nine
Senators of the Committee on Coffee Contamination, formed only two
days earlier, with chairwoman, Senator Rhonda Caliente (Republican,
New Mexico) at the center. After introductory remarks from the chairwoman, the first witness to be sworn in and occupy the hot seat before
the committee was Rami Parananda.

Caliente commenced the questioning. "Mr. Parananda, prior to
your recent resignation from Bright Cup Incorporated, did you at any
time conspire with that company's Chief Executive Officer, Matthew
Cochran, to manipulate the domestic and/or international commodities markets for coffee beans?"

Parananda leaned forward to speak into the microphone on the
table. "No comment," he replied.

Caliente struck the gavel. "Mr. Parananda, you're out of order. Your testimony isn't optional."

Parananda's attorney tapped him on the shoulder, and whispered into the witness's ear. Then Parananda said into the microphone, "I respectfully decline to answer under the rights provided me by the Fifth Amendment of the United States Constitution, on the grounds that I might incriminate myself. In other words, no comment."

"Very well," the chairwoman said. "Mr. Parananda, prior to your recent resignation from Bright Cup Incorporated, did you at any time conspire with that company's Chief Executive Officer, Matthew Cochran, to incite panic among the populace regarding the outbreak of the coffee fungus in Brazil?"

"I respectfully decline..."

And so it went with another half dozen questions for Parananda.

The next witness called was Matthew Cochran, who took the seat with his personal attorney, Frank Farnsworth, at his side.

Caliente again commenced the questioning. "Mr. Cochran, as Chief Executive Officer of Bright Cup Incorporated, did you at any time conspire with others, including that company's former Vice President of Marketing, Rami Parananda, to manipulate the domestic and/or international commodities markets for coffee beans?"

Everyone in the room assumed that Cochran would respond in a manner similar to Parananda's, but Cochran was never one to follow anyone else's lead.

Cochran cleared his throat and responded, "Madam Chairwoman, I'd respectfully like to point out that the term 'conspire' most often connotes the intent to commit criminal activity. Commodities market manipulation is not inherently illegal. Although it might violate the internal rules of commodities exchanges, it doesn't necessarily violate any laws enacted by the United States Congress. My understanding is that such manipulation might only be deemed illegal if it involved dissemination of untruthful information or if the Commodities Futures Trading Commission had issued a cease and desist order, after which the manipulation in question continued, neither of which applies to my actions. Therefore, would you care to rephrase the question?"

Loud murmurs spread among the audience.

Caliente leaned over to Senator Arthur Pini (Democrat, California) seated next to her. They whispered back and forth, then the chairwoman announced, "While the Committee disagrees with the legal interpretation you described, Mr. Cochran, we will humor you for now. As Chief Executive Officer of Bright Cup Incorporated, did you at any time *plan* with others, including that company's former Vice President of Marketing, Rami Parananda, to manipulate the domestic and/or international commodities markets for coffee beans?"

"Yes, but I did so based entirely on public information. Every statement I made in the process was truthful, and I did not defraud anyone. My understanding, Madam Chairwoman, is that through market manipulation in the oil and natural gas industries, your paternal grandfather, Horatio Pamino, earned the family fortune to which you yourself were an heiress, and upon which you relied for funding of your first Senatorial campaign."

The audience remained dead silent. Caliente banged the gavel. "You're out of order, Mr. Cochran. Confine your responses to the questions asked from the committee members on the topic of the crisis in the coffee market."

Attorney Farnsworth tapped Cochran on the shoulder, then covered the microphone with a hand and whispered, "Matt, are you *trying* to piss off the committee?"

Cochran whispered back, "I'm not playing to the studio audience." He tilted his head in the direction of the TV cameras. "I'm playing to the home audience."

Caliente continued, "Mr. Cochran, did you at any time plan with others, including Mr. Parananda, to incite panic among the populace regarding the outbreak of coffee fungus in Brazil?"

"No. I did, however, inform members of the media about the coffee fungus. They, of their own accord, may have conspired to incite panic among the populace. You would have to ask them about that." Loud murmurings from the audience, followed by another bang of the gavel, but Cochran continued speaking. "I would also like to point out, Madam Chairwoman, that my efforts to inform the public of the fungus in its early stages should have tipped off federal authorities to the potential danger such a biological threat posed to the United States economy, and that agencies of the United States Government failed to act upon such warnings to prevent the global spread of the fungus and the concomitant impact on the U.S. economy. The Government's own negligence caused severe harm in that regard."

Caliente turned to Senator Pini, who then spoke. "Now that you've had your fun at our expense, Mr. Cochran, I will proceed to more substantive questions." Pini glanced at papers on the table through his reading glasses, then picked up a sheet. "This is a press release in the Portuguese language, issued on August seventh by Delcese Agricola corporation of Brazil, in which that company announced it had closed its largest single sales deal ever with Bright Cup Incorporated, for the delivery of ten million kilograms of coffee beans over the period of a year. Did you, Mr. Cochran, direct your employee in Brazil, Mr. Valmir Pasco, to enter into such a deal on behalf of your company?"

The witness nodded, then replied to the Senator, "Yes, sir. With the potential threat of a coffee supply shortage, I wanted my company to have the most secure supply position possible."

Pini held up a newspaper clipping. "This is an article from the Portuguese language newspaper *Folha* [Pini pronounced it 'Fol-ha,' as though it was an English word] of São Paulo, Brazil, dated August fifteenth. This article describes the discovery by Delcese Agricola's senior scientists that another scientist in their laboratory had been developing a new strain of toxic bacteria. As distinct from the fungus affecting the coffee crops, this bacterial strain has been shown to be directly hazardous to human health."

Pini set down that newspaper clipping and picked up another one, continuing, "This is another article from the *Folha* newspaper in the Portuguese language, dated August twenty-first, which quotes the Acting Chief Scientist of Delcese Agricola, Dr. Wendy Westphal, as saying that when spores of the new toxic bacteria were applied to the main type of coffee bean supplied by that company, a cultivated variety known as Isabela, the bacterial spores survived the roasting process for at least thirty seconds after the beans, quote, 'crack a second time,' unquote, and that after appropriately terminated roasting, the bacterial spores also survive the coffee grinding and brewing process. The article goes on to state that when such bacterial spores are ingested, some portion of them may become active bacteria producing a deadly toxin which is capable of being absorbed into the body through the mucous membranes of the digestive system."

Pini set down that newspaper clipping and picked up a sheet of paper, continuing, "And, this is a press release, issued by Bright Cup Incorporated on August seventh, in which, among other items, your company touts the fact that every month, eight percent of American adults consume coffee from your Bright Cup Cafés. The press release also touts the introduction of a new coffee roasting device named Roastronic, which your company plans to install in all of your coffee shops nationwide. You, Mr. Cochran, are quoted in the press release describing how the Roastronic automatically halts the roasting of coffee beans as soon as they begin their, quote, 'second crack.'"

Pini set down the press release. "Taken collectively, these pieces of evidence could lead one to believe that you, Mr. Cochran, are the mastermind behind a sophisticated plot to corner the supply of coffee beans from Delcese Agricola, to which you planned to have deadly bacterial spores applied. Those contaminated beans, when roasted in your Roastronic machines and brewed in your coffee shops, would poison a substantial number of Americans."

Uproar briefly ensued in the audience until Caliente picked up the gavel, but everyone quieted down before she struck it.

Pini continued, "Furthermore, evidence exists that the fungus currently infecting the world's major coffee plantations was deliberately created in the laboratories of Delcese Agricola, perhaps even by the same scientist who created the toxic bacteria. This suggests that your master plan, Mr. Cochran, included disseminating the fungus worldwide to wipe out other sources of coffee beans to force an even larger portion of the population to imbibe the toxin contaminated coffee that you intended to supply. How do you respond, Mr. Cochran, to such evidence?"

Farnsworth whispered into Cochran's ear, "You don't have to answer that question, Matt."

Cochran shook his head, then stated aloud, "The specific pieces of information which you have presented might all be valid, Senator Pini, but your conclusion is preposterous. Besides the obvious problem that what you suggest would kill off my own customers, which wouldn't be too good for business..." The audience laughed. "...I will note that Bright Cup Incorporated is a member of the consortium of American coffee companies which have pledged money toward the reward for capture of the terrorist mastermind. Even I wouldn't be stupid enough to put up money to help capture myself."

Pini thought, *No, but you might be smart enough to do that.*

"I would also like to point out a logical error in your reasoning, Senator Pini."

"Go ahead, Mr. Cochran."

"The plantations of Delcese Agricola were the first ones stricken by this coffee fungus more than a month ago. That goes against the entire concept of a plot such as you described in which I purportedly sought to wipe out other sources of coffee beans in favor of beans I would get from Delcese. The Isabela beans that you mentioned were in fact the ones most threatened by this fungus."

Pini shuffled through items on the table, then picked up a large board displaying a world map. He held it vertically on the table toward the cameras. "The numerous marks on this map show the coffee plantations that have reported outbreaks of this fungus since last Sunday." He set down the world map and picked up another one of just Brazil. "And the marks on this one show Brazilian coffee plantations reporting the fungus since last Sunday. Of the twenty largest coffee suppliers in Brazil, only Delcese Agricola has *not* reported a new outbreak of the fungus. Since the preponderance of evidence suggests that the current fungus outbreak was deliberately instigated, one must assume that Delcese Agricola was deliberately spared from further infestation for a reason. Now, Mr. Cochran, how do you respond to all this evidence?"

"No comment."

The audience gasped.

Caliente asked, "Do you intend, Mr. Cochran, to invoke your Fifth Amendment rights regarding self-incrimination?"

"No, Madam Chairwoman. I just can't think of anything to say in response to Senator Pini's fantasy."

The audience laughed until Caliente banged the gavel.

Pini continued, "Mr. Cochran, do you recall a face-to-face conversation between yourself and Mr. Thomas Macklin, Chief Financial Officer of Bright Cup Incorporated, on the afternoon of August twelfth of this year? The conversation concerned the coffee fungus."

"Not specifically. I've had several conversations a day with Mr. Macklin for most of our careers together. Many of our recent conversations concerned the coffee fungus."

"Then I'll refresh your memory regarding the conversation in question. This is an affidavit from Mr. Macklin." Pini held up a sheet of paper, from which he read. "According to Mr. Macklin, during that conversation on August twelfth, you said to him, quote, 'I wouldn't mind if the fungus made a comeback. Hell, I'd spread it around myself if I could,' unquote." The audience gasped again. "Do you deny making such a statement?"

Cochran covered the microphone. He whispered to Farnsworth, "I did say that, but I meant it facetiously. How should I respond?"

The attorney whispered back, "If you said it, you can't deny it. They'll call Macklin to testify, anyway. But if you acknowledge it, that constitutes self-incrimination, and the burden of proof would be on you to establish your intent at the time. Therefore, I advise you to plead the Fifth."

"No friggin' way," Cochran said, a little too loudly.

Caliente asked, "Is that your response to Senator Pini's question, Mr. Cochran?"

"No, Madam Chairwoman."

"Then what is your answer to his question? I remind you that you are under oath."

Cochran sat silently for half a minute.

"Mr. Cochran, your answer, please."

Cochran finally responded, "I respectfully decline to answer under the rights provided me by the Fifth Amendment..."

÷÷÷÷

Tony Goterrez yelled out to his television set, "Ha, ha, Cochran. A hundred million bucks, here I come."

÷÷÷÷

The next person called to testify was Thomas Macklin, who rolled his wheelchair up to the witness table.

After the swearing in, Caliente announced, "I will note for the record that the Committee has granted this witness immunity from prosecution regarding any self-incriminating statements he might make." Caliente covered the microphone and whispered to Pini, "Go easy on him, Arthur. We don't want the public to think we're badgering a cripple."

÷

After dismissing Macklin, the Committee called Professor Samuel Decker to testify. Decker brought along his attorney, Julie Wells.

Pini asked, "Professor Decker, during your recent engagement as a consultant for the Delcese Agricola corporation of Brazil, did you find evidence that the new coffee fungus may have been genetically engineered or otherwise intentionally created by one or more scientists at that company?"

Decker turned and whispered to Wells, "Technically, my answer to that question should be yes, but that would be a misleading and incomplete characterization of my findings."

Wells whispered back, "Presumably the Senator's intention is to present a misleading and incomplete characterization to the Committee and the public."

Decker sat back for a moment to think, then he leaned forward to the microphone and responded, "My investigation regarding the origin of the fungus was inconclusive, sir."

"My question was not about any conclusion on your part, Mr. Decker. It was about the evidence. Would you like me to repeat the question?"

"That's unnecessary, Senator. To answer your question, I found no evidence regarding the origin of the fungus itself. That is, nothing indicated whether the fungus originally occurred naturally, or whether it was created through crossbreeding or genetic engineering techniques. My investigation did find evidence that the fungus had been *cultivated* by the company's late Chief Scientist, Dr. Paul Mendonça..." Audience murmurs. "...However, such evidence indicated that Dr. Mendonça's intention was to test the fungus in experimental coffee fields isolated from the company's production plantations. The evidence further suggested that the fungus was released accidentally into a production plantation only as a result of the crash of a small airplane which also killed the doctor. Apparently, that crash occurred while Dr. Mendonça was on his way to the experimental fields with a sample of the fungus."

Pini shuffled through papers on the table, then held up a sheet. "This is a summary of a preliminary report by a Lieutenant Oscar Azevedo of Brazil's Department of Federal Police, which describes the crash of the small plane to which you referred, as being the result of poisoning of the plane's pilot, Miguel Silva, with a toxin related to the bacterial infection tetanus. Are you familiar with such findings, Mr. Decker?"

"Yes. In fact, I believe that I was the first person to suggest, in the course of my investigation, that the pilot had been poisoned."

"Then why, Mr. Decker, did you just describe the release of the fungus as accidental?"

"The evidence regarding the pilot suggested that the plane crash may have been instigated deliberately, but no evidence suggested that release of the fungus was an objective of such instigation. Indeed, as best as I could determine, no one other than Dr. Mendonça himself was even aware that he was carrying this fungus on that aircraft on the day of the crash. Release of the fungus appeared to be an unintended consequence."

Pini scratched his head, then he read from the paper in his hand. "According to Lieutenant Azevedo's report, a bioengineer from Delcese Agricola, a Ms. Larissa Junior [he pronounced the woman's last name as though it was merely the converse of *senior*] has been arrested and charged in connection with the incident, including the culturing of the bacteria used to create the toxin which poisoned the pilot. According to the Lieutenant's report, during your own investigation as a consultant to the Delcese corporation, you questioned Ms. Junior, who had ridden in that same airplane earlier on the day of the crash."

"That's correct."

"According to the Lieutenant's report, a Ms. Lucinda Vivan was present during your questioning of Ms. Junior. And Ms. Vivan indicated that during your questioning of Ms. Junior, Ms. Junior said that she saw a container of the fungus in the plane. Is that correct, Mr. Decker?"

"No, that is not correct, Senator. During my questioning of Ms. *Zhoo-nee-or*, she merely said that she saw in the airplane a container— a drink thermos—which conceivably could have contained the fungus. She did not say that she saw the fungus or even that she knew it was present in the plane. As I said before, I found no evidence that anyone other than Dr. Mendonça himself knew of this fungus at the time of the plane crash."

Pini scowled, disappointed that he had been unable to lead the witness to his desired conclusion. The FBI and the CIA, at the direction of the Senator's staff, were still attempting to establish a connection between Júnior and Cochran.

÷

Decker and Wells walked out of the Caucus Room and down one of the twin marble staircases to the floor of the rotunda. A thin man in a dark suit approached them.

"Mr. Decker, I'm Felipe Buarque from the Brazilian Embassy. Come with me, please."

Decker said good-bye to Wells, then Buarque walked him out of the Russell Senate Office Building. A black limousine drove them west to Embassy Row on Massachusetts Avenue. The vehicle pulled into the driveway of the palazzo-style manor known as McCormick House.

"This is the Ambassador's residence," Buarque noted. "That's the chancery." He pointed to another building on adjacent grounds, a glass box raised completely into the air on pillars, which reminded Decker of the Museu de Arte de São Paulo.

Buarque led Decker into McCormick House to a large room where he seated him, then Buarque left the room.

Decker surveyed the decor while he waited, noting the hardwood wainscoting around the lower portion of the walls, topped by an elaborate mural depicting a lush landscape in subdued colors. The neoclassical furnishings were authentic period antiques. *Refined yet restrained elegance*, Decker thought.

Shortly, the Ambassador entered, a tall man with silver hair and a broad nose, who carried himself with a dignity deserving of his position. Decker rose to shake hands.

Aguiar greeted him, "I'm sorry to keep you waiting, Mr. Decker."

Decker responded diplomatically, "But it is I who've been keeping you waiting, Ambassador, while I was occupied with the Senators."

Aguiar directed Decker to sit, then he seated himself opposite.

Before they could begin speaking, the door opened and Buarque reentered. "I'm sorry to disturb you, Ambassador," the attaché said, "but you have an urgent phone call from *Senhor* Costa." He handed over a mobile phone, then left the room.

The Ambassador conversed quietly in Portuguese into the phone. He finished, "*Obrigado*, Ramon," then he set down the phone.

Decker said, "Do you mind if I ask, sir..." He paused, and Aguiar motioned for him to continue. "...How is it that a corporate Chief of

Security has direct access to an Ambassador? I don't know much about diplomacy, but that seems unusual."

Aguiar smiled. "I'll tell you the story only if you promise not to tell Ramon that I told you. He prefers that people not know, and he would never tell the story to anyone himself."

"You have my word, sir."

"Some two decades ago, when I was an energetic and enthusiastic industrialist in São Paulo, I consorted with a veritable who's who of Brazilian society. One year, I threw a party for my cherished daughter and only child, Graciela, on the occasion of her thirteenth birthday. In attendance were many influential people and, of course, their children. It was a lavish affair on the grounds of my estate. Midway through the party, a band of masked gunmen burst into the yard with the intention of taking the children hostage. They immediately shot several of the adults non-fatally. I myself received a bullet wound in the leg." Aguiar pointed to his right calf. "My personal security force subdued most of the gunmen within a few seconds, but one of the criminals eluded their initial fire. That man then ran directly toward my daughter with his gun outstretched, and managed to shoot off one round before being taken down in a hail of bullets from the security guards."

"He shot your daughter?"

Aguiar shook his head. "Ramon Costa was working as a busboy for the caterer that day. He was only sixteen years old at the time. He had been clearing the table where my daughter was seated when the mayhem erupted. As the last gunman ran toward Graciela, Ramon threw her to the ground, covering her with his own body. Ramon took the gunman's bullet in his back." The Ambassador pointed to a spot on his own back near the right shoulder blade.

Decker raised his eyebrows. "Costa saved your daughter's life?"

"Yes, but there's more to the story than that, Mr. Decker. After the incident, Graciela experienced terrible nightmares every night, and she refused to leave the house. She spent all of her time and energy tending to Ramon while he recuperated in a bedroom of my own home upon his release from the hospital. When he was well enough to walk outside, she went with him, the first time in six weeks that she had set foot outdoors. She clutched his arm when they entered the yard where the gunfire had occurred. For the next year, she refused to go anywhere without Ramon by her side. On the eve of her fourteenth birthday, Ramon told me that the whole experience of having her attached to him had helped him because other kids used to make fun of his mark..." Aguiar motioned to the side of his neck where Costa had the port-wine stain. "...But he told me that it was time for him to move on with his own life, to go back to his family and friends. I offered to pay his way through private school and university, then hire him when he was ready for a professional job. He politely declined, and the next day he was gone.

"Graciela was heartbroken, to put it mildly. As she grew up, she hardly dated any boys and never had a real boyfriend. Shortly after she graduated from university, on her twenty-second birthday, nine years to the day after the shooting incident, she saw Ramon's name listed in a news article about the São Paulo State jiu-jitsu championships. She tracked him down through the martial arts school he represented in the tournament, then she knocked on his apartment door. Graciela told Ramon that she loved him. He told her to go away. 'Didn't you love me?' she asked. 'Of course I did,' he replied, 'but you deserve someone from your own wealthy society. A lower class worker like me could never be good enough for you.' 'You are already good enough for me,' she said, 'You have always been good enough for me. And no one else but you could ever be good enough for me. You would have died for me, and now I would die for you.'" The Ambassador clasped his hands together. "Two years later, with my full blessing, Graciela and Ramon were married."

After Decker got over the initial shock, he noted, "I guess that makes you his Ambassador-in-law."

"Indeed, but we digress, Mr. Decker. The reason I requested your presence here today is to tell you that the Federative Republic of Brazil requests your assistance in stopping the fungus that is devastating the world's coffee fields. We wish to hire you as a consultant."

"Why didn't Duarte or Westphal just call me?"

"Delcese's Board of Directors would not allow them to hire you directly."

"But if I accept your offer, I'll need the full cooperation of Delcese to resume my investigation into the fungus. Delcese is where it started, and the solution must lie there."

"This organism must be stopped, Mr. Decker. Whatever it takes." The Ambassador thumped a fist into his own palm. "The coffee crop is too important to Brazil's economy, and as has become evident this week, to the U.S. economy and even the world economy, to let the concerns of one company stand in the way. And from a diplomatic standpoint, the nation of Brazil must appear to be assisting the U.S. and the world in halting the spread of this agricultural epidemic. The Brazilian government has now granted amnesty to the Delcese corporation, such that even if your investigation uncovers incriminating evidence against the company, no one will be able to seek damages against Delcese. Ramon just confirmed that the Board of Directors and *Senhor* Duarte have pledged complete cooperation under such terms."

Decker said, "As we might describe it here in the U.S., you're offering Delcese immunity from prosecution so it can't plead the Fifth Amendment."

Chapter 26

~~~~~

On the obituaries page of Friday's *Miami Herald*, a small item noted the passage two days earlier of Mrs. Isabela Mendonça, aged 92.

÷÷÷÷

The CNN anchorwoman stated, "The NASDAQ composite index closed down again today, bringing its total loss for the week to thirty-eight percent. The Dow is down thirty-one percent on the week. With the coffee fungus continuing to spread unabated, economists have had little hope of imminent recovery, and hopes further worsened today. CNN's Lorenzo Lee reports on a chilling discovery in sunny Mexico."

The video image cut to an aerial scene of several smoldering fires on a mountainside.

A man's voice narrated, "Here at the Finca Irlanda plantation in the southern Mexican state of Chiapas, workers have been burning fungus-infected coffee trees since Wednesday afternoon. Due to interspersing of some of the sprawling plantation's coffee trees among the natural vegetation, workers here must first cut down those coffee trees and haul them to designated fields prior to burning. This morning, workers noticed that some of the fungus-infected trees they were cutting were already coated with traces of ash. Scientists from the local agricultural research station examined the ash, and they've made a disconcerting discovery."

The video image cut to two men standing side by side, one holding a CNN microphone. "I'm here with researcher Hector Barrio. What have you discovered about this ash, Dr. Barrio?"

"We've found that the ash contains fungal spores that are charred on their exteriors but otherwise intact. Apparently, some of the spores on infected coffee plants are not being destroyed by burning. These spores are being carried away whole in the smoke and deposited onto other trees. In fact, the hot air generated by the large-scale burning is creating significant updrafts, which are carrying these spores higher up into the atmosphere, and spreading them faster and farther through the winds aloft than they otherwise would have been spread by the winds near ground level. The burning is accelerating dispersal of the spores and hastening the spread of the coffee fungus."

"Thank you, Dr. Barrio. This is Lorenzo Lee, reporting from Chiapas, Mexico."

The video image returned to the CNN anchorwoman. "In today's Coffee Blotter news segment we have several stories. First, in Palo Alto, California, a software programmer held ten coworkers hostage using a package that he claimed contained plastic explosives. The man demanded that their employer reinstate the recently rescinded policy of unlimited free coffee in the office, saying, quote, 'You'll pry the coffee cup from my cold dead fingers.' Company officials noted that the number of lines of Java program code written per hour had nose-dived since the policy was changed earlier in the week, and they already had been planning to reinstate the old policy. The man then surrendered himself and the package, which turned out to be filled with plastics from the company's recycle bin.

"In Los Angeles, a gang war erupted after two men, reportedly members of rival gangs, fought over the last bag of coffee at a local market. Two bystanders were wounded in the ensuing gun battle.

"And finally today, in New York City, police raided a warehouse and arrested four people for the new crime of coffee counterfeiting. The group had been filling one pound foil bags with dried pinto beans and passing them off as unroasted coffee beans to unsuspecting consumers. NYPD Police Chief Jeremy Jones called the scheme, quote, 'tasteless.'"

÷÷÷÷÷

During the evening rush hour in central San Francisco, protesters amassed on the public plaza at Union Square, prompted by Facebook posts and Twitter tweets in the wake of Cochran pleading the Fifth Amendment at the Senate hearing.

The protesters chanted, "Dump Bright Cup! Dump Bright Cup!..."

When the assemblage reached a critical mass of several hundred people, the crowd overflowed onto Geary St. and began marching down the middle of the road. By the time it got to Market St. two blocks away, the gathering had swollen with passing pedestrians joining the march, and their sheer numbers blocked traffic movement on that major artery.

A driver honked out of frustration at being unable to advance his car. The protesters picked up on the sound and chanted, "Honk for coffee! Honk for coffee!..." Soon the entire Financial District was ringing with a deafening blare of car horns.

The protestors marched onward toward the end of Market St., where they halted in front of the office building housing the corporate headquarters of Bright Cup Incorporated. The street level storefront of the building contained a Bright Cup Café, the interior of which was packed with customers waiting in line to buy coffee. The protesters chanted, "Boycott Bright Cup! Boycott Bright Cup!..."

One protester named Rocco Balducci, a brawny man in a studded leather jacket, used a rolled up newspaper as a megaphone to project epithets in his booming voice at customers in the café. He stopped shouting when he noticed a female barista in a bright yellow apron inside the café, separated from himself only by about 15 feet and an expansive plate glass window. The barista was giving him the finger.

Balducci looked down and saw a loose piece of brick in the walkway. He bent down and with his fingertips pried up the chunk, about one third the size of a full brick. He repeatedly tossed the piece of brick up and down in his right hand while the woman continued to flip him the bird. Then he reared back his right arm, and he rapidly thrust it forward with a follow-through aimed at the employee's head.

÷

Inside the café, the barista cowered in anticipation of shattering glass, but no impact occurred. When she looked back outside, the brick was on the ground beside the protester's feet. Two fingers of his right hand formed a peace sign, and his left hand held up a copy of *The San Francisco Examiner* tabloid newspaper with the headline, "Cochran Arrested On Coffee Grounds."

Part III:
Coffea Gracinha

Chapter 27

"Our LIBERTY, and LIFE is now invaded,
And FREEDOM's brightest Charms are darkly shaded;
But, we will STAND—and think it noble mirth,
To DART the man that dare oppress the Earth."

From the anonymous broadside ballad about the Boston Tea Party,
"Tea, Destroyed by Indians," the title of which satirically misidentifies
the perpetrators by their native disguises, 1773

~~~~~

SEPTEMBER 7

Saturday evening, in the office upstairs at Kraton Kupu Kupu, Zeger was looking over Pukartra's shoulder at a computer monitor.

Pukartra looked back and said, "The economic element of your plan has worked perfectly, Brother Goliath. Worldwide stock markets, especially the American markets, have had their worst week in history. And now that Matthew Cochran is in custody as the mastermind, we may avoid being discovered."

Zeger tapped the fingertips of his hands together. "They'll figure out they have the wrong man when we launch our Sweet Surprise. In the interim, Brother Pyrrhus, we continue to be at risk of discovery in Brazil. And we don't know if Brother Aidea has made Sister Cleobaea extinct yet."

Pukartra checked an email account on the computer. "We still haven't received any new messages from her. Maybe he's succeeded."

"I'm also concerned that we haven't heard from Brother Calanus or Sister Cardui. They may have been netted by the police, who are keeping it under wraps to avoid alerting us."

"Sister Harmonia was with them in Brazil when they sent out the packages the week before. She's already communicated that everything was in order when she left them. We could have her attempt to track their movements afterwards. She could also check into the status of Cleobaea."

Zeger said, "First, we'll try to contact Cleobaea tomorrow at her regular weekly standby location."

÷÷÷÷÷

In Brazil, it was *Dia da Independência*, the national holiday celebrating the country's declaration of its independence from Portugal in 1822. Nevertheless, at Sede de Delcese Agricola, the scientists and lab technicians were on the job, as plantations around the world submitted samples of fungus for testing and comparison with the previous outbreak there.

÷÷÷÷÷

Lucy was waiting for Decker when he emerged through the customs and immigration checkpoints at Guarulhos Airport, and they flew by helicopter out to Sede. Approaching the plantation from the air, Decker got his first encompassing view of the burnt coffee fields.

After a quick freshening up in the Visitor's Residence, Decker proceeded to the Administration Building, where he met in the conference room with the senior scientists, plus Lucy and Duarte. Decker noted with a touch of disappointment that Fabiana Munhoz was not in attendance.

Duarte kicked off the meeting. "I'm pleased that Mr. Decker has agreed to rejoin our effort. Now that the American authorities have the terrorist mastermind in custody, the task of stopping the progress of the fungus and saving the world's arabica crop rests largely in the hands of the people in this room."

Westphal said, "Let's begin by each of us bringing Mr. Decker up to date on what we now know." She motioned to Nestor.

Nestor had a laptop computer connected to the wall-mounted monitor, showing satellite images of Asia, Africa, and South America, with overlaid points indicating infected plantations and farms. "Taking a cue from Mr. Decker's performance on television the other night, I've modeled the progress of the fungus against atmospheric conditions. I found that the path of spread after the initial round of infections is generally following wind patterns. And based on the recent discovery in Mexico, I've confirmed through analysis of smoke direction from burning plantations traceable in the newest satellite imagery provided by the U.S. Government, that at least some of the spreading can now be attributed to spores surviving the burn."

Decker asked, "Why wasn't there accelerated spread from the burning here last month?"

"Winds that week were predominantly from the east-northeast toward stationary low pressure in northern Argentina. The winds would have carried smoke and ash from the burning plantations into Mato Grosso do Sul and part of Paraguay, neither of which are coffee growing regions."

The screen switched to a mosaic of microscopic pictures of the fungus, then to an image of a DNA double helix connected by straight lines representing combinations of base pairs of guanine bonded with cytosine, and adenine bonded with thymine.

Santini said, "Our analysis of fungus samples that arrived this week from plantations around the world confirms that it's the identical species as we experienced here last month. In fact, it doesn't appear to have mutated at all, which would be improbable if it had made it all the way around the globe on its own."

Ribiero added, "I've been attempting to crossbreed the new fungus with more benign fungi, but so far, I haven't had any success."

Tosca said, "I've tested nearly every fungicide known to mankind. The only one that had any impact at all is the extract from *Melaleuca alternifolia*, commonly called tea tree oil. The extract has antifungal properties when applied to human skin for infections such as *pé de atleta*." He pointed a finger down.

Lucy clarified for Decker, "Athlete's foot."

Tosca continued, "Tea tree oil slows down the spread of the coffee fungus on a given plant, but unfortunately, it doesn't kill the fungus."

"That's promising, though," Decker commented.

"Yes and no. Even if it completely destroyed the coffee fungus, tea tree oil wouldn't be a viable fix for the problem. It's about a thousand times more expensive than coffee itself."

Tosca looked to Caison, who continued the train of thinking, "I've been trying to analyze the biological mechanism by which the tea tree oil acts upon the fungus, which might lead us to other approaches that could be implemented more economically. However, I'm not optimistic we can accomplish that in a timely manner."

The screen image shifted to a scatter plot of data points clustered close to a diagonal line. Horton explained, "We've confirmed that the intensity of infection in an arabica field is proportional to the amount of caffeine in the cultivar being grown, as long as the caffeine level is above a certain threshold. We haven't yet figured out why the fungus doesn't infect robusta plants, which is particularly vexing since caffeine content is higher in robusta than in arabica."

Ribiero said, "We should be able to isolate the gene that makes robusta resistant to the fungus, and we might be able to splice just that gene into arabica, but that approach only offers a long-range solution."

Lastly, Manling said, "I've got all the lab staff working overtime on this, Mr. Decker. They're at your disposal. Unfortunately, I'm short two of my best workers. Larissa Júnior is in jail for the tetanus plot, so I don't think she would've been much help to us anyway. And Martina Hasse, the bird lady, is in the hospital."

Decker asked, "What happened to her?"

"Severe allergy of some sort. Her husband said it nearly killed her. By the way, Mr. Decker, *Senhora* Hasse confirmed the presence of a new parrot species in a coffee field here just before the fields were burned down. She even got pictures of it. She was so proud of herself that she snail-mailed me a print from the photo lab. You can have it." Manling slid over a small photo print. "These days, for an amateur birdwatcher to discover a new species, it's the thrill of a lifetime."

Decker didn't bother explaining that Dr. Mendonça must have discovered the parrot prior to Hasse. He put on his reading glasses and examined the image on the print, then he flipped it over. On the back side, two words were neatly handwritten.

The phone on the wall beeped, and Lucy got up to answer it.

Decker asked, "Has anyone been out to Dr. Mendonça's experimental fields west of Fazenda Fiorva?"

Horton responded, "Yes, all the fields there were infected with the new fungus, except for the plot containing the low-caffeine Bourbon cultivar."

Decker said, "Drat."

Westphal asked, "Where do we go from here?"

From across the room, Lucy responded, "I think we go to Paraná. It's *Senhor* Mabro on the phone. He's located Theo, the other worker who was in the field when Dr. Mendonça's plane crashed."

÷÷÷÷÷

Vinícius Búzia rubbed his bloodshot eyes. Since receiving the email from Martelli at NSA on Thursday, he had been staring at the text of the email message from "birdladyofbrazil" to "NaturEd" almost nonstop, in a futile attempt to decipher its meaning. He had slept on a couch in the officer's lounge. He hadn't eaten anything except snacks from the vending machine. And he had consumed enough coffee to have rightfully turned his piss brown. *Maybe Martelli was right*, he thought. *Maybe there's really nothing here. Sometimes an email is just an email.*

Viní drained the remaining tepid coffee from the mug into his mouth, then he got up from his cubicle for another trip to the coffeemaker in the office kitchenette. Holding his mug beneath the spout, he inverted the steel carafe, only to be rewarded with a mere three drops of liquid. *I guess I'll have to make some more.* He opened the cabinet where the pre-measured bags of ground coffee were usually stored. *All gone.* He went to the storage closet where the office manager kept the cases of coffee when they were delivered from the supplier, but no more was there either. Looking at the vacant shelves in the closet, he thought, *Nothing but empty spaces... empty spaces... empty spaces...* Puta merda! *Holy shit! Empty spaces!* He ran back down the hall to his cubicle.

Less than 20 minutes later, he was on the phone. "Oscar, it's Viní. I did it. I decoded the email message..."

A few minutes after that, Azevedo was on the phone with Costa. "Meet me at the DPF in Campinas..."

÷÷÷÷÷

Lucy and Decker rode a cart to the airstrip, where the plane was just pulling up with Carlos the pilot and Mabro inside.

Climbing aboard, Lucy said, "I don't understand why this coffee fungus is such a big deal up in the States, anyway. Why can't everyone there just drink tea?"

÷

The plane landed on the airstrip at Fazenda Madrigal, north of the small city of Maringá in the State of Paraná. A man named Geraldo met them there. Carlos stayed with the plane while Lucy, Decker, and Mabro climbed into Geraldo's 1970s-era Toyota Land Cruiser.

Geraldo explained in Portuguese, which Lucy translated for Decker, "Theo and his wife are staying with his brother, Domingo, who works at Fazenda Madrigal. Geraldo is a supervisor in the processing plant where Domingo runs the bean dryers. Yesterday Geraldo overheard Domingo say something to another worker about his brother who used to work at Fiorva, and how the brother had seen a plane crash there..."

They drove further away from Maringá, and eventually proceeded down a potholed road in the town of Guaraci. They pulled up in front of a tiny single story house, no larger than six by six meters.

Domingo let them inside. Theo and his wife were seated on a tattered couch in the cramped living room.

Mabro asked in Portuguese, "Theo, when the plane crashed at Fiorva, did you see *uma lata*, a metal canister, about this big..." He motioned with his hands. "...inside the airplane?"

Theo shook his head and replied, "*Não.*"

Theo's wife angrily said something to him.

Lucy leaned to Decker and whispered, "She's telling him not to lie now, or else his brother will lose his job, too."

"I'm not lying," Theo responded to Mabro. "I didn't see *uma lata*. I saw *duas latas*."

Mabro held up two fingers. "*Duas latas?*"

"*Sim.*"

Theo's wife pushed him up from the couch. "*Vá buscá-los,*" she said. Go get them.

Theo went into a another room and returned with a dusty canvas knapsack. He unbuckled the top flap, reached in, and pulled out a squat steel canister with biohazard labels on it. Its lid was ajar, and dried red smears were on its exterior. He set it down on a table.

"That would be Dr. Mendonça's cultured fungus," Decker said.

Then Theo reached back in and pulled out another canister, longer and narrower, this one appearing to be a conventional thermos for drinks. Mabro reached for it.

Decker called out, "Be careful of that one. Tell Theo to put it back into the sack."

Mabro asked, "Why? What is it?"

"The drink in that one probably contains the tetanus toxin that poisoned the pilot Miguel."

Mabro relayed the instruction, and Theo put both canisters back in the knapsack.

Decker said, "Ask Theo why he took them from the plane."

Lucy translated the response, "He says that his family is poor, and the canisters looked valuable. He thought he could sell them to make a little extra money."

"Then why does he still have them? Why didn't he sell them?"

Lucy relayed the questions, then the reply. "After he took them, he felt guilty stealing from dead men."

"Please tell him only one of the men is dead. And ask him if we can buy his knapsack for twenty *reais*."

÷÷÷÷÷

In the DPF building in Campinas, Azevedo and Costa entered a holding room where Larissa was seated. Costa remained standing, while Azevedo sat down across from the prisoner.

"*Senhorita* Júnior," Azevedo said, "we now have proof that you were involved in the terrorist plot."

"I want my lawyer here."

"Very well. I just thought you might like to know that we know."

"You can't possibly know anything, because there's nothing to know. I didn't do anything."

"Does the name Goliath ring any bells?"

She looked at him blankly.

"How about Cleobaea?"

"I don't have a clue what you're talking about."

"Don't play dumb with me, *senhorita*. We've decoded your email."

"Email? What email?"

"The one in which you encoded the message."

"What message?"

"The message that says you discovered a new species and that your manager found your jar of toxin in the lab. Ring any bells yet?"

Larissa shook her head.

Azevedo raised his voice. "The email you sent from the business center at the Grande Hotel in Águas de São Pedro..." He pounded a fist on the table. "...where you stayed for more than a week."

"I didn't send any email from the business center at the Grande Hotel... *Jesus Cristo!* I know who you want. It's *Senhora* Hasse."

"Excuse me?"

"*Senhora* Hasse. Martina Hasse. One day while I was staying at the hotel, she was trying to get into the business center, but the door was locked. She said she'd left something in there. I let her in with my room key card. She works in the lab at Delcese."

Azevedo turned to Costa, who nodded that Hasse was indeed a Delcese lab employee.

Azevedo turned back to the prisoner. "We will attempt to verify your claim regarding the email, *Senhorita* Júnior."

÷÷÷÷

A uniformed DPF officer showed an ID photo of Martina Hasse on his mobile phone to the clerk at the Grande Hotel reception desk.

The young man said, "Yes, I've seen her here a few times."

÷÷÷÷

An undercover DPF agent snuck up to the door of the Hasses' apartment. He had planned to pick the lock, but when he tried the knob, it was unlocked. He searched the apartment, being careful to return everything to its original position. He examined and photographed numerous pieces of paper on a small desk in a corner of the bedroom. When he went through the linen closet in the hallway, he briefly looked at the box of Dirt-Away detergent, but he didn't even photograph it when he saw that it was completely sealed. He did, however, photograph the many handwritten notes and lists held in place by magnets on the front of the refrigerator. And in the kitchen cabinets, tucked away in the rear of a top shelf, he discovered the primary incriminating evidence: four small glass jars. The jars were empty, but they all had yellow smiley face labels on their lids.

÷÷÷÷

Azevedo and Costa reentered the holding room at the DPF. This time, Costa was the one who sat down across from the prisoner.

"Larissa," he said, "We believe you about Martina Hasse. The DPF has confirmed that she may be involved. However, in the interests of helping capture the entire terrorist ring, the DPF would like you to remain here a few more days."

She screamed, "What!? You guys arrested an innocent woman, a pregnant one at that, and now you don't want to let her go free?"

Costa nodded to Azevedo, who opened the door. Tulio walked in, and the two others walked out, leaving the couple alone together.

After a few minutes of copious hugging and kissing, Larissa whispered, "Get me the hell out of this place."

Tulio said, "Lari, baby, I love you, I miss you, and I want you out of here as much as you want to get out. But these terrorists already killed *Doutor* Mendonça. They planned to murder many more people with stuff that Hasse was cooking up in the lab. And the coffee disease they spread is destroying Brazil's economy. Azevedo wants the terrorists to keep thinking that the police think you're the one who did it. If you walk out of here, Hasse and the rest of the terrorists will be tipped off. You can help the police catch the bad guys by staying here a few more days. They promise that they'll publicly exonerate you once this thing's over. They'll put it all in writing for your lawyer to approve."

Larissa slapped her hands against the big man's chest several times, then she hugged him.

He said, "You know it's the right thing to do."

"OK. I'll do it. I'll stay here in jail, on one condition."

"What's that?"

"Get me some ice cream."

÷÷÷÷÷

The sun was setting when the plane landed back at Sede.

In the lab, Decker handed over the knapsack with the containers to Westphal and Manling.

"We'll get technicians to work analyzing them," Manling said.

Duarte entered the lab. Decker gave him a brief summary, to which Duarte commented, "Not a bad day's work, Mr. Decker."

"That was the easy part, sir. We still need to stop the fungus. Now, if you folks don't mind, I'd like to grab a bite to eat and get some sleep. I've been awake since yesterday morning."

Westphal pointed to the clock on the wall. "We'll meet in the conference room at nine AM tomorrow."

Decker asked, "Any of you know where Dr. Munhoz is?"

The others all silently looked around at each other, which Decker misinterpreted as meaning that none of them knew.

Duarte put his hand on Decker's shoulder and walked him out of the lab into the hallway. "Sam, she's gone to Miami for a few days... to attend a funeral."

÷÷÷÷÷

Azevedo stood in Captain Ratiba's office at the DPF in Campinas.

"Excellent work identifying Hasse as the terrorist, lieutenant."

"That was the easy part, sir. We still need to identify and capture her co-conspirators here in Brazil. Hasse is currently in the hospital, but she's due to be released tomorrow. We'll closely monitor her upon her release."

Ratiba flipped through a file folder on his desk. "Hasse is a native of Switzerland. She's been living here in Brazil for seven years. She's traveled to eighteen different countries. She could be part of a very broad network. Thankfully, the Americans have the mastermind in custody." He looked in the folder again. "Matthew Cochran has traveled to twenty-two countries, including four times to Brazil and many times to Western Europe. He's even been to Switzerland, although Hasse was here in Brazil at the time. Your next task, lieutenant, is to uncover the connection between Cochran and Hasse."

Chapter 28

"It provides the perfect metaphor, as it entertains the themes of escape and isolation..."

From a review by Allan Schou of a play written by Ingle Knight entitled *The Getaway Bus*, 2003

~~~~~

SEPTEMBER 8

Gunter Hasse supported Martina as she shuffled out the door of Santa Casa de Misericórdia de Piracicaba hospital. He motioned to a waiting taxi, then helped her into the back seat, placing her overnight bag between them. He was about to give the driver the address of their apartment building, but Martina spoke up first.

"Estação Rodoviária de Piracicaba, *por favor.*"

The driver started the meter, then put his hand on the shift lever.

Gunter cried out, "Where? What? Wait! The bus station? Martina, we're going home."

The driver took his hand off the shift lever. As long as the meter was running, he didn't care how long the occupants debated their destination.

Martina said, "I need to go to Campinas first. I'll take the bus."

"Campinas? You just got out of the hospital. We're going home. You need to rest."

"No. I must go to Campinas."

"Why?"

"An old friend is meeting me there."

Gunter looked her squarely in the eyes. "Martina, you almost died a couple of days ago. Your old friend can wait."

"No, he can't." She looked away. "*Por favor,* Estação Rodoviária de Piracicaba."

"Very well," Gunter said. "If you're taking the bus to Campinas. I'm going with you."

"If you insist."

"I insist."

The driver put his hand back on the shift lever.

÷

A silver sedan followed behind the taxi at a discrete distance. When the two occupants of the tailing vehicle realized the taxi was not headed toward the Hasses' apartment, the man in the passenger seat radioed for backup. When the taxi pulled into the bus station, he called into the microphone, "It looks like they're skipping town." When the Cristália bus pulled out of Estação Rodoviária de Piracicaba, the man in the sedan said, "Non-stop to Campinas."

By the time the bus pulled into Campinas at Estação Rodoviária Dr. Barbosa de Barros, two undercover DPF agents were inside, planning to go along for the ride if the suspect boarded another bus, and six more agents waited on the surrounding streets, ready to tail Hasse if she left the station.

÷÷÷÷÷

In the conference room at Sede with the senior scientists present, Westphal nodded to Manling.

The lab manager commenced, "We've confirmed that the canister from the plane crash contains the fungus, lots of it, in an agar-based culture medium."

Caison added, "However, we still don't know where or how Dr. Mendonça originally obtained the fungus."

Manling continued, "Regarding the thermal bottle from the plane crash, it contains brewed coffee..." He cleared his throat. "...plus the tetanospasmin toxin like we found in the jar in the lab refrigerator."

Nestor said, "Larissa gave Miguel a taste of her own toxin."

Decker spoke up. "However, we don't know why."

"It hardly matters at this point."

"I'm not so sure."

÷÷÷÷÷

Gabriel Bonnington boarded the funicular tram in Hong Kong city center. He admired the spectacular receding view of the night skyline on the ride up Victoria Peak, 400 meters above the Harbour. At the terminus of the ride, the tram pulled into the base of Peak Tower, a distinctive structure of concrete, tile, and glass, the upper portion of which was shaped like an immense wok with truncated sides. Hundreds of people milled around inside the lower shopping arcade.

On Level G, near the café aptly named Pacific Coffee Company, Bonnington used a phone card to place a call from a public payphone.

÷÷÷÷÷

Martina and Gunter sat silently in the waiting area of Estação Rodoviária Dr. Barbosa de Barros, refusing to speak to one another.

At the margins of his consciousness, Gunter vaguely heard a page over the public address system. If the page had contained either of the words "Martina" or "Hasse," it undoubtedly would have migrated more to the center of his awareness, but it did not. So, he was surprised when his wife got up and went to the information desk, where the attendant handed her a telephone receiver. He was too far away to make out anything she was saying, as were the undercover DPF agents.

÷

"No, Brother Mariposa," Martina Hasse replied in hushed English, stretching the phone cord as far away from the desk as she could. "I didn't interact with either of them during their trip in Brazil. Brother Calanus and I were initiated into the swarm on the same day, but I've never met Sister Cardui. They must have completed their mission if their target plantations are infected. I wouldn't know what became of them afterwards. You might check with Sister Harmonia. Maybe they were caught by the police."

Bonnington asked, "If they were captured, wouldn't it have been in the news?"

"Unfortunately, I haven't seen much of the news lately. I've been out of commission the past few days. I was ill in the hospital."

"Nothing too serious, I hope."

"It was quite serious. I almost died from a food allergy. In fact, Sister Harmonia and Brother Aidea were there at the time." Martina looked up, thinking, *Harmonia and Aidea were there at the time...* She strained to maintain both her composure and her chipper voice. "Anything else, Brother Mariposa?"

"No. That's all for now."

She hung up. *Why didn't it occur to me before? Goliath must have assigned Harmonia and Aidea to make me extinct. They must have put something in my food. I must flee immediately. But where can I go? I have nowhere to turn. I have nowhere to hide...*

÷

Gunter had looked away at a passing baby boy while Martina was on the phone. When he next looked back at the information desk, she was no longer in sight.

÷

Agent Cabral whispered into his mobile phone, "Subject has boarded a bus for São Paulo city. We'll be on it with her. The husband is still in the station. Repeat, subject bound for São Paulo. Husband remains in station." He nodded to his DPF undercover partner, Agent Matos, and the two headed to buy tickets for the bus.

÷

Gunter went to the information desk. "My wife was just on the phone here. Did you see where she went?"

The woman behind the counter shook her head.

"Any idea who the call was from?"

"It was a man's voice and the conversation was in English, but I'm not too good at that language."

÷

A minute after the husband left the information desk, an under-cover DPF agent showed his badge to the woman behind the counter.

÷÷÷÷

The phone on Lieutenant Azevedo's desk rang.

"This is *Agente* Dourado, sir. The suspect received a phone call in the station, then she boarded a bus for São Paulo."

"How'd she get the call?"

"It came into a line at the information desk. They paged her by the name *Senhora* Cleobaea."

"Good. Now we know for certain she's the one who sent the email from the Grande Hotel. Any info on where the call came from?"

"We're working on that now. I'll get back to you as soon as I have something."

Half an hour later, Azevedo's phone rang again.

"It was an international call, lieutenant, and the routing data from the phone company tracks back to a public payphone in Hong Kong."

"Hong Kong?" Azevedo scanned a printed list of countries on his desk. "Hasse's never been there. Can the Hong Kong police identify the person on the payphone at the time?"

"One of our agents just got off the phone with the police there. The payphone is at a popular tourist destination called The Peak. The place gets over sixteen thousand visitors a day. The police say security camera video shows a guy on the payphone at the time of the call. He's wearing a baseball cap pulled down low. No way they can identify him other than to say he's Caucasian of medium height and medium build with short dark hair."

"Too bad they couldn't get an ID, but good work, agent."

"The Hong Kong police are keeping an eye out for the caller in case he reappears, and they'll tighten up security at The Peak in case the terrorists try anything there. Should we apprehend the suspect's husband, lieutenant? He's still in the bus station."

"Not yet, but keep him under close surveillance."

÷÷÷÷

Gunter wandered around the bus station in Campinas for nearly two hours, during which he had his wife paged repeatedly over the public address system. After failing to get any response, he boarded a bus back to Piracicaba, carrying her overnight bag. *I can't believe it*, he thought. *After all these years, after everything we've been through together, Martina has left me for another man.*

÷÷÷÷÷

At Rodoviária Tietê in São Paulo, to avoid arousing suspicion on the part of the suspect, two new DPF agents, both female, took over the undercover operation. They were prepared to coordinate a team of agents on the streets, assuming Martina Hasse would exit into the city. Instead, the suspect purchased another bus ticket.

Agent Terepa whispered into her mobile phone, "She's headed for Curitiba." Then she turned to her partner and said, "That's over four hundred kilometers from here. She doesn't have any luggage."

Agent Marcela responded, "Neither do we."

÷÷÷÷÷

In the lab at Sede de Delcese Agricola, the scientists and technicians spent the day pouring liquids back and forth in test tubes and twiddling the knobs on microscopes, but they might as well have been banging their heads against the countertops and flagellating themselves with coffee tree branches.

When they finally called it quits for the night, Decker mumbled, "This fungus just won't die."

÷÷÷÷÷

Late that night, in Rodoviária de Curitiba, Agent Terepa whispered into her mobile phone, "Now the suspect has bought a ticket to Foz do Iguaçu." When she hung up the line, she turned to her partner. "That's another five hundred kilometers from here. It's an overnight bus ride. Why didn't she fly to Iguaçu from Campinas or São Paulo?"

"Maybe she's trying to keep a low profile. I'll bet you the price of clean underwear that she's headed to Iguaçu Falls. I think she's planning to meet her accomplices there, where they could all blend in with the tourists."

"You're on for that bet, Marcela. I think the phone call she got at the station in Campinas was a warning to skip out of the country before she's discovered. From Iguaçu, she easily could hop a bus into either Paraguay or Argentina. Day-trippers to the Argentinean side of the Falls can cross the border without a visa. Without any luggage, it would be..." Agent Terepa shifted languages to use an English idiom. "...a piece of cake."

"We'll need to cover all the possibilities. We'll alert the authorities in Argentina and Paraguay. We'll have agents at both the Brazilian and Argentinean sides of the Falls. And we'll have armed officers stationed at all the border checkpoints. If we're lucky, she'll meet up with her gang, and we'll net the bunch of them. In any event, she won't get out of the country unless it's in *um caixão*." A coffin.

Chapter 29

"Crianças de Açúcar" ["Sugar Children"]
"Imagens de Chocolate" ["Pictures of Chocolate"]
"Imagens de Poeira" ["Pictures of Dust"]

Series of works by São Paulo-born artist Vik Muniz (1961-), who photographs creative renderings of common materials

~~~~~

SEPTEMBER 9

Decker awoke hours before sunrise. He tossed and turned in bed, dwelling repeatedly on a question: *How do we stop the spread of a microorganism that just won't die?*

At 7:00AM he headed to the fitness room and plodded on the treadmill for half an hour. *How do we stop the spread of a microorganism that just won't die?*

At 8:00AM he went to the company cafeteria, where he started with a large cup of black coffee. He sat by himself at a table along the windows, contemplating the fungus problem while he sipped the brew. He recognized the taste as Isabela, the cultivar named for the late Dr. Mendonça's now-late mother. *How do we stop the spread of a microorganism that just won't die?*

When he finished the coffee, he went to get a bowl of oatmeal. He returned to the table just as Lucy entered the cafeteria. She picked up a small carton of milk then joined him.

"I thought I'd find you here, Sam."

"You thought right," he said, tasting a spoonful of oatmeal. "I wish I could think right."

She slurped her milk. "What do you mean?"

"I can't come up with a solution to this fungus problem. All morning, I keep thinking the same question over and over: How do we stop the spread of a microorganism that just won't die?" He motioned to the cluster of condiments on her side of the table. "Pass me that jar of molasses, please."

She handed him the jar.

He continued, "With the distribution of this fungus already worldwide, we don't have time to engineer anything as complicated as what I did to stop the cacao fungus." He unscrewed the lid of the molasses. "And we can't even stop this fungus completely by burning the coffee trees." He lifted the jar and tilted it over his bowl of oatmeal. The thick brown syrup oozed out of the jar. "So how do we stop the spread of a microorganism that just won't die?"

Lucy echoed a reply as though his question had been a riddle, "By stopping its spread?"

"And how do we do tha..." Decker's voice trailed off as a series of images flashed through his mind: the duct tape for Hasse to attach the Squawkie bird toy to the coffee tree; Fabiana licking her fingertips after sipping the *caipirinha* drink in *A Cidade Irmã* restaurant; Benito by the pushcart at Instituto Butantan with his ice cream cone covered in chocolate sprinkles; Portinari's painting "The Coffee Worker" at MASP; the tanker truck spraying the road surface on his bus ride from downtown São Paulo to Guarulhos Airport; and lastly, the live image in front of his face of the slow motion pouring molasses. "Lucy, that's it!"

In his excitement, Decker dropped the jar of molasses into his oatmeal, splashing the gloppy brown and tan mixture all over his shirt.

÷÷÷÷÷

Martina Hasse got off the bus at Rodoviária Internacional de Foz do Iguaçu. Waiting for her was another pair of undercover DPF agents, a young man and woman blending in with all the tourists roaming the station. The male agent wore a khaki photojournalist's vest laden with Canon EOS digital SLR camera equipment.

Agent Eliana whispered into her phone as she and Agent Mauricio followed Hasse onto a local bus marked for Parque Nacional.

÷÷÷÷÷

Wearing a clean shirt, Decker clenched his hands behind his back, pacing the conference room while Lucy sat still. The senior scientists filed in and took seats, but Decker remained standing.

Westphal said, "OK, Sam, what's this about?"

"I've been stuck trying to figure out a solution to the fungus problem, but something Lucy said at breakfast in the cafeteria gave me an idea." He straightened himself into his best professorial stance. "Let's assume that we cannot kill this fungus..."

Tosca, the pesticide specialist, protested, "We don't know that."

"Bear with me, please, doctor. Let's assume for the moment that we cannot kill the fungus."

"Then how could we possibly stop it?"

Decker motioned to Lucy. She put up on the table a salt shaker that she had borrowed from the cafeteria, then she slid it to Decker.

He held up a hand. "Let's say that my hand is a leaf on a coffee plant." He picked up the salt shaker and sprinkled white particles into his palm. "And let's say that these salt crystals are fungal spores." He blew into his palm, dispersing the salt into the air. "A little bit of wind, and spores go everywhere. Dr. Nestor confirmed again for us yesterday that spreading of the fungus is coincident with wind patterns."

Nestor asked sarcastically, "Do you propose to stop the wind?"

Decker replied, "Not at all."

Lucy put up on the table a jar of molasses and slid it to Decker. He unscrewed the lid, dipped in a finger, then wiped off the brown goo on the palm of his other hand. He sprinkled on some salt.

Decker held the hand in front of his mouth and blew, but the salt crystals remained in place. He said, "We stop the spores."

"And with what do we do that?"

Decker tilted up the palm of his hand with the salt still attached. "Molasses, of course. It's plentiful. It's inexpensive. And best of all, it's very sticky. We encase the spores in molasses and immobilize them." He posed an open question. "What makes molasses sticky?"

Horton, the biochemist, explained, "The primary component is a long chain glucose polymer, dextran, formed during fermentation of bacterial resin in cane juice during the refining."

"Then all we need to do is get the dextran in molasses onto the spores. Molasses is water soluble, right?"

"Yes."

"We thin the molasses in water, and spray it on the infected coffee plants. When the water evaporates, the spores will be stuck in place."

Tosca spoke up, "There's an obvious problem with that. As soon as it rains, the molasses will dissolve, releasing the spores."

Horton said, "We can get around that problem."

"How?"

"With calcium oxide." Horton turned toward Decker. "We call it *cal*. In English, it's known as lime. The addition of lime to molasses is already in use for industrial applications as an adhesive. When lime is added to molasses, it reacts with residual H_2O, hardening the molasses. The reaction yields calcium sucrate, some of which becomes di-calcium and tri-calcium sucrates, which are effectively insoluble in water. Lime is used in the sugar refining process. Any sugar mill will have loads of both molasses and lime on hand."

Tosca added, "Lime is also used in fertilizers. Coffee farms will have it, too."

Horton drew in a long breath, then she improvised out loud. "The agricultural lime will be hydrated. We'll need the anhydrous type. And we'll have to apply the lime to the plants as a second step after the molasses solution. Because of lime's reaction with H_2O, we can't use water as a liquid carrier to spray it. However, we can use anhydrous ethyl alcohol. Ethanol. In fact, the addition of calcium oxide is a way to remove residual water from distilled ethanol to make it anhydrous, one hundred percent ethanol. We'll just add an excess of calcium oxide. The sugar mill nearby already produces ethanol in volume to make bio-diesel fuel."

÷÷÷÷÷

The tourist bus made numerous stops at hotels along Avenida das Cataratas, but Hasse and her two shadows remained aboard until the stop just before entering Parque Nacional.

When Hasse stepped off the bus, Agent Mauricio watched her direction, then he looked at the tourist brochure. He said to his partner, "She's headed to Parque das Aves."

Agent Eliana replied, "You and I and the dozen other people who got off the bus are all here to see the Bird Park."

÷÷÷÷÷

Technicians ran around the lab with jugs of molasses and ethanol, jars of white powdered calcium oxide, and industrial spray bottles, while the senior scientists did their best to stay out of the way.

Manling came out of the bio-containment area into the main lab. "It works. At least it works *in vitro*. Now we've got to test it *in situ*, on a real field that's infected with the fungus."

Nestor noted, "We burned down the infected fields here at Sede."

Decker asked, "Where's the nearest infected field that hasn't been burned yet?"

At that moment, Duarte was entering the lab. "Fazenda Briole," he replied. "It's not a Delcese plantation, but it's only sixty kilometers from here."

"Lucy, please hail us a bio-bus," Decker said. "We're going on a field trip."

÷÷÷÷÷

The phone rang on Lieutenant Azevedo's desk. "Olá."

"Oscar, it's Viní. I figured out most of the code names in the email message that we deciphered: goliath, cleobaea, and it mentioned a brother aidea. It only took about two seconds on Google. They're all species names. Guess what kind."

"I have no idea, Viní."

"Come on, Oscar. What kind of critter names would a bunch of nature loving terrorists use to symbolize the utmost fragility of the environment?"

÷÷÷÷÷

The DPF agents paid their admissions fees, then they followed a discrete distance behind Hasse as she roamed through Parque das

Aves Foz Tropicana. Hasse's pace was so leisurely that she spent more than two hours at the attraction listed in the tourist brochure as a one hour visit.

Agent Eliana said to her partner, "She's just killing time."

Agent Mauricio zoomed in his camera lens on the suspect. "No, she's studying the birds."

They all strolled along the walkway through the series of aviaries, each featuring a specific natural habitat such as rain forest or swamp inhabited by appropriate bird species. Within the aviaries, the birds flew freely among the visitors. In the enclosure for endangered species, Agent Mauricio watched as a Golden Conure (*Guaruba guarouba*) landed on his partner's head. The bird remained there for a minute while Agent Eliana attempted to look casual with a bright yellow parrot clamped to her hair. A small crowd gathered around them. Hasse walked back in their direction, but she wandered onward when the Golden Conure took off to peck at the fruit of a nearby Wild Papaya tree (*Jacaratia spinosa*).

Hasse then entered the Bird Park's butterfly enclosure, where she spent considerable time amid the colorful flitting. In the enclosure, a female naturalist had a *Danaus plexippus* perched on her fingertip as she explained to visitors—in Portuguese, Spanish, and English—how the park breeds and raises thousands of butterflies a year. "When they reach maturity," she said, "we set them free, to live or die as they were meant to be." She flicked her finger, sending the Monarch to fly away.

÷÷÷÷÷

Azevedo's phone rang again.

"Lieutenant, my name is *Doutora* Humberta Filete. I understand that you're in charge of investigating crimes related to the spread of the coffee fungus."

"Yes. What can I do for you, doctor?"

"Probably nothing, unless you can cure my bursitis. But I may be able to do something for you. I'm the coroner in Belo Horizonte. Last Saturday, a young woman and man were killed when they were struck by a truck while walking along a roadway through the forest near Caratinga."

"How does that relate to the coffee fungus?"

"On the couple's clothing, I noticed traces of red dust. I didn't think anything of it at the time, because it was before all of this week's hoopla about the fungus. But last night, after seeing TV news reports which mentioned that plantations in Minas Gerais and Espírito Santo had been infected, it dawned on me that there could be a connection. When I came into work this morning, I dug out the couple's clothing from storage and examined some of the red dust under a microscope. I'm not an expert in that area of microbiology, but the powder appears to contain fungal spores."

"Can you send down some samples?"

"Certainly. And I'll email you my coroner's report and photos of the deceased right away. By the way, I'm not sure if it's relevant, but the two bodies in the morgue have something interesting in common."

"What's that, doctor?"

"They both have similar tattoos."

"Tattoos?"

"That's right, lieutenant. Care to guess what these tattoos depict?"

"Butterflies."

"How the hell did you know that?"

"Because this must be my lucky day."

÷÷÷÷÷

Eight Delcese scientists, six lab technicians, plus Lucy, Decker, Duarte, and a small load of equipment and containers all got off the bio-bus at Fazenda Briole. A crew of the local farm workers led the team from Delcese to a recently infected field.

For full scale application of the solutions, large plantations would tow sprayers with tanks holding thousands of liters, but for testing purposes, the spraying was done by hand.

Four lab technicians strapped on the backpack-style portable sprayers with plastic tanks. Along the transition line between infected and uninfected trees, the technicians worked in pairs. The first walked along aiming the wand to spray the molasses and water solution on any infected plants, maintaining air pressure in the tank with a hand-operated pump lever. A few minutes later, the second technician came through with the calcium oxide and ethanol hardener.

The technicians returned on the next row in, after which they refilled the sprayer tanks from the half dozen 20-liter containers they had brought with them. The hand spraying continued for eight rows, at which point the technicians ran out of test solutions to spray.

"At the rate this fungus progresses," Caison said, "we'll have a preliminary idea of its effectiveness in a few hours."

Nestor added, "And we'll know for sure by tomorrow morning."

÷÷÷÷÷

Lieutenant Azevedo sat across the table from Larissa in a holding room at the DPF.

"*Senhorita* Júnior, I suspect that two bodies now in the morgue in Belo Horizonte are related to the terrorist distribution of the coffee fungus. I'm trying to establish their connection to *Senhora* Hasse." He opened a file folder and withdrew two photo prints of the corpses' faces. He slid over the photos. "Have you ever seen these two people, perhaps with Hasse?"

She grimaced at the grisly pictures of the banged up faces, then she shook her head. "Sorry." She slid back the prints.

"Thanks, anyway."

Azevedo opened the folder to put away the prints. As he flipped the folder closed, Larissa said, "Let me see those other photos."

"Pardon me?"

"Let me take a look at those other photos."

"They're not pretty pictures."

"I know they're of mangled dead people, lieutenant, but what were those butterflies?"

He reopened the folder and slid over two close-ups of the butterflies. "They're tattoos on the deceased."

"Butterfly tattoos?" Her eyes shot open wide.

"Are you going to tell me that *Senhora* Hasse has a butterfly tattoo?"

Larissa's response came as another question rather than a statement. "Martina Hasse has a butterfly tattoo?"

Momentarily perplexed, Azevedo paused, then he answered, "I haven't seen it, but I now suspect that's the case."

"I've seen a butterfly tattoo on a Delcese worker, but it wasn't Martina Hasse."

÷

A few minutes later, Azevedo telephoned Costa.

"Ramon, I'm headed to Fazenda Fiorva with a bunch of my men for a little harvest."

÷ ÷ ÷ ÷ ÷

When they finally exited the Bird Park, Agent Eliana asked, "Do you think Hasse marked us tailing her in there?"

"No. She was oblivious to everyone and everything except the birds and the butterflies."

A short walk away, a sizable group of people was now assembled at the Centro de Visitantes bus stop, waiting for the special double-decker ride in to see Iguaçu Falls.

Agent Eliana whispered into her phone, "We're on our way in."

Chapter 30

"É melhor morrer do que perder a vida."
["It is better to die than to lose the life."]

Frei Tito de Alencar Lima, a Dominican Order monk who committed suicide in 1974, after having survived torture by the military regime ruling Brazil in the 1960s

~~~~~

In the field at Fazenda Briole, more than 20 people were staring at the branches of coffee trees from mere inches away. The normally dark but translucent molasses had been converted by the calcium oxide into a milky opaque coating.

From the far end of a row, Tosca called out, "It's working. These trees right across from those treated ones show no sign of infection."

Horton studied a few leaves. "I think we can dilute the solutions more. The coating is thicker than it needs to be. We don't want to kill the trees by suffocating them from CO_2."

Decker said, "The infected trees are sacrificial. Our sole objective is to stop the spread of spores into new trees."

Caison remarked, "We appear to have succeeded."

Westphal rounded up everyone. "Good work, people. We'll take back some cuttings to study in the lab. We need a couple of volunteers to stay here to confirm the resistance to water." Two technicians raised their hands, then went with local field workers to fetch sprinklers.

As the rest of the group walked away, Decker paused to admire the coating on the trees, then he sniffed the air. *Smells like somebody put a blowtorch to a case of Snickers bars.*

÷÷÷÷÷

The tourists all filed off the double-decker bus at the stop below Hotel das Cataratas, the only lodging within the Parque Nacional. The throng tramped down the stairway to the trail along the rim of the gaping canyon. Amid the approaching roar, children raced each other to see who would get the first glimpse of the breathtaking Iguaçu Falls. Packs of roving raccoon-like mammals with elongated noses, South American Coatis (*Nasua nasua*), scampered out of the way of passing people, then scampered back onto the path to scavenge for food scraps.

Agents Eliana and Mauricio waited while Hasse lingered near the bus until the crowd thinned, then they followed well behind her as she descended through the lush vegetation along the upper portion of the canyon wall. The agents stared out in wonder at the crescent-shaped complex of waterfalls spanning nearly three kilometers in length, most of which reside in Argentina on the far side of the Rio Iguaçu where the mighty river narrows and drops more than 70 meters in height.

Agent Mauricio said, "I've been here five or six times, and it never ceases to amaze me."

Dazzled by the magnificence, the agents briefly lost sight of the suspect. They sped up their walking pace until they spotted her ahead, where Hasse had stopped to check out two Tufted Capuchin monkeys (*Sapajus apella*) dangling from a tree branch.

For a stretch along the path, Agents Eliana and Mauricio were engulfed by successive swarms of butterflies: black and white spotted Hamadryads (*Tellervo zoilus*); Cramer's "Eighty-eights" (*Diaethria clymena*) with the distinctive numerical-shaped patterns on their wings; Black Swallowtails (*Papilio polyxenes*) like miniature stealth bomber planes; and the most numerous, the iridescent Blue Morphos (*Morpho menelaus*). Wave after wave of delicate color bursts arose from the bushes in meandering flight paths as the agents followed the suspect toward the waterfalls.

The park was not only teeming with wildlife, it was teeming with DPF agents. Agents Eliana and Mauricio recognized two other under-cover agents, and they knew that four more out-of-town agents whom they only had met at that morning's briefing were embedded among the tourists.

÷÷÷÷÷

Sergio was standing in the bay doorway of the maintenance build-ing when he spotted a helicopter above the treetops half a kilometer to the east. He couldn't remember the last time he'd seen a chopper near Fazenda Fiorva, but he did remember the last time he'd seen a black one with yellow and red diagonal stripes across its midsection: on TV news coverage of a massive drug bust the previous year.

÷÷÷÷÷

The DPF helicopter touched down by the hangar at Fazenda Fiorva, and Lieutenant Azevedo and four other DPF officers jumped out. Mabro emerged from the farmhouse and pointed to the mainte-nance building. The DPF men entered with weapons drawn, but the structure was unoccupied.

"Sergio was here a few minutes ago," Mabro said.

Azevedo told his men, "We can't let him get away."

An officer near a rear door pointed to the ground outside. "Tracks go out this way, into the forest."

"You men follow the tracks. I'll search from the copter."

÷÷÷÷÷

Agent Eliana pressed her mobile phone against her ear, straining to hear. She relayed to her partner, "DPF headquarters says that the suspect must be taken alive. Lieutenant Azevedo needs information about the terrorist organization."

Hasse turned off the trail onto the long concrete catwalk over the intermediate cascades, headed to the edge of the falls and the lookout platform that afforded optimal viewing. Spanning the chasm, a bright rainbow hung in the mist. *Garganta do Diabo* (Devil's Throat), the most spectacular of the falls, poured and roared from the Argentinean side into the churning aqueous mass below.

Agents Eliana and Mauricio followed 50 meters behind the suspect, keeping an eye out for other possible terrorists.

"The catwalk is *um beco saído* [a dead end]," Mauricio shouted to Eliana, a necessity to be heard over the intense rumble of the falls. "She's got to return this way." He zoomed in his lens at the lookout platform. "A uniformed Parque Nacional policeman is on the platform. We'll wait here. If she meets with anyone out there, we'll nab them when they come back in."

÷÷÷÷÷

Two minutes after the helicopter took off, the Cessna landed at Fazenda Fiorva. Costa hopped out, and Mabro ran over to fill him in. Costa went straight through the maintenance building and followed the tracks out the back door. In 200 meters he approached the four DPF policemen, who were stopped and looking in all directions.

One of them said, "Captain Costa?"

"Ex-captain. Now I run security for the company that owns this plantation. What have you got?"

"The tracks just end here, sir."

"He might have climbed a tree."

They all looked up, scanning the trees for signs of a man aloft.

"He could've climbed up, then jumped out to break up his tracks."

One of the officers called into his radio, "We've lost his tracks, lieutenant."

He heard a reply, then he pointed and yelled, "The chopper has spotted him from the air."

They sprinted through the jungle for several hundred meters to the place where the helicopter was hovering. Azevedo pointed them that-a-way, then the aircraft moved off, remaining low enough that the air wash of the rotor blew about the canopy of the trees.

The four officers on foot ran ahead, but Costa lingered behind. He caught a glimpse of motion out of the corner of his eye, but when he turned to look, he didn't see anything that seemed out of place. He cocked his head, listening for sounds of human movement, but the noise of the helicopter was too prominent for him to hear anything subtle. He then ran off in the direction of the others.

÷÷÷÷÷

The suspect remained for more than 10 minutes among the tourists at the end of the catwalk on the bulbous platform cantilevered over the lip of the near side falls.

She must be waiting to make her contact, Agent Eliana thought. *Right under the nose of a park policeman. How brazen.*

÷

Hasse stared out at the abyss from behind the waist-high railing. She turned around to survey the dozens of other people on the platform and the catwalk. She glanced at the couple back on the catwalk who had been on the bus all the way from downtown Foz do Iguaçu. She glanced at the uniformed officer nearby. *I have nowhere to run,* she thought, *nowhere to turn.*

She approached the park policeman. "Excuse me, officer," Hasse shouted against the background noise of the falls.

"Yes?"

She motioned for him to bend down so she could speak directly into his ear. She pointed at the couple back on the catwalk.

÷

Agent Mauricio observed through the camera viewfinder a finger pointed at himself. *What the hell is she doing?*

÷

The uniformed officer marched briskly down the catwalk toward the agent couple.

÷

Mauricio lowered the camera to watch the policeman approach. *Does she want to turn herself in?*

Mauricio was taken by surprise when the officer slammed into him, knocking him against the railing.

"This man may be a terrorist!" the officer shouted, wrapping his arms around Mauricio and dragging him to the surface of the catwalk. "His vest might be rigged with explosives."

Due to the sound of the falls, few people actually heard the policeman's words, but the sight of a uniformed officer struggling to subdue a resistant man sparked chaos. Tourists all along the catwalk began screaming. Agent Eliana pounded on the policeman's back, flashing her badge and shouting that the man was an undercover DPF agent. A pair of large men who were also undercover DPF agents jumped in, trying to separate the other two men. Several bystanders assumed that those agents were also bad guys, and attempted to pry them away from the policeman in uniform. Tourists on the far side of the dead end catwalk scrambled to get past the melee, not wanting to be stranded from the safety of land, but they further clogged up the area. Arms and legs flailed left and right, everybody shouting but nobody hearing.

÷÷÷÷÷

Sergio peaked his head up from his position flat on the ground behind a downed tree where he had been tucked underneath several fallen branches. He waited more than a minute after the last man left his field of view before climbing to his feet. He crept in the direction away from the helicopter, slowly at first, picking up speed until he was running at a full sprint. Then, before he realized what was happening, his legs were bound up, and he was prone on the ground. Somehow, someone had caught him from behind and tackled him.

Sergio struggled to free his legs, attempting to roll left and right, but Costa maintained his grasp. Sergio pounded wildly on the other man's head to no effect. A fistful of dirt in the face caused Costa to flinch, and Sergio managed to free one leg. Kicking his heel repeatedly into Costa's back, Sergio believed he was making further progress, but Costa rolled sideways, pinning Sergio's free leg. The trapped man was grasping for another fistful of dirt when he saw the four policemen approach with their pistols drawn. Sergio relaxed his hand, releasing the dirt. Then, he noticed a tiny splotch of bright yellow color on the ground about two meters away.

Costa yelled, "We must take him alive. We need information. Get the cuffs on him."

One of the officers approached with handcuffs. He slapped the metal around one of the prisoner's wrists, but as soon as he did so, Sergio violently swung the cuffed arm, yanking the other cuff out of the officer's hand. The loose end of the handcuffs struck the side of Costa's head, momentarily dazing him.

In a final burst of adrenaline-fueled energy, Sergio flung Costa aside and scrambled toward the spot of yellow. Two officers simultaneously discharged their weapons into Sergio's legs. The big man fell forward, landing, as was his plan, close enough that the Golden Poison Dart Frog (*Phyllobates terribilis*) was within his reach. He swiped at the frog with one hand, and as it jumped, he caught it in mid-air with the other hand.

"I'm sorry to end your life this way," Sergio said to the creature. He stuffed the frog into his mouth, rapidly chewing into its flesh and swallowing as much as he could.

The officers attempted to remove the frog from the prisoner's mouth, but the potent batrachotoxin from the amphibian's skin was already in Sergio's stomach in sufficient quantity to kill dozens of men. Repeated abdominal thrusts to eject the poison were too little too late.

The toxin's action on nerves controlling Sergio's cardiac muscle tissue was fatal before the first aid kit was out of the helicopter. The kit wouldn't have been useful anyway, as it didn't contain ibogaine, the extract of an African plant called Leaf of God (*Tabernanthe iboga*), which could have blocked the ingested frog poison.

Azevedo bent down and tore open the dead man's shirt, exposing the tattoo of the Tropical Leafwing butterfly (*Anaea aidea*) on the left side of the hairy chest, directly over the forever-stilled heart.

÷÷÷÷÷

The fracas on the catwalk at Iguaçu Falls settled down when the uniformed policeman saw that Mauricio's vest contained only camera gear and no explosives. By that time, a solitary woman stood naked on the distant observation platform with a pile of clothes at her feet. A tattoo of the Tiger Queen butterfly (*Lycorea cleobaea*) was exposed on the pale flesh of her left butt cheek.

Hasse climbed over the railing. Facing inward on the outside of the platform with her toes perched on the edge, she took a final breath, then she leaned back and let herself go. Dozens of people watched in horror from as far away as the Argentinean side of the falls as the body plummeted into the raging torrent at the end of the rainbow.

÷÷÷÷÷

On the bio-bus ride back to Sede, the scientists debated the merits of announcing the treatment immediately to save as many coffee trees as possible, versus the risk that the treatment had some unforeseen negative side effects.

As the bus pulled into the entrance road at Sede, Decker argued, "What could be worse than what's already happening to the coffee fields around the world?"

Duarte decided that they would wait until sunset for updates from Fazenda Briole. Lacking contrary news, Delcese would announce in time for treatments to get underway the following morning in the Far East. He headed for Melissa Herrar's office.

÷÷÷÷÷

Azevedo had just returned to his desk when an agent approached carrying an open laptop computer.

The agent said, "Sir, I've got Sergio Moreno's passport records. Other than Brazil, there are only three countries where both he and *Senhora* Hasse have been: Mexico, Costa Rica, and Indonesia."

"Indonesia?"

"That's correct."

"Were they there at the same time?"

"No, sir. A year apart. And those two bodies in the morgue in Belo Horizonte, they've both been to Indonesia, too. And the deceased male was there at the same time as *Senhora* Hasse. Indonesia is the only country other than Brazil where all four of those people have been."

The phone on the desk rang. Azevedo motioned for the agent to wait while he answered it. "Olá."

"Oscar, it's Viní. I found it in the photos from Hasse's kitchen."

"Hang on a minute while I pull up the files on my computer." Azevedo fiddled with the mouse and keyboard. "OK, go ahead."

"Picture eighty-two. It's the stuff on the front of her refrigerator."

Azevedo clicked to open the file. "Got it."

"Look at the slip of yellow paper in the lower left."

Azevedo used the software's magnifying tool to zoom in on the image of the piece of paper. It had one word scrawled on it: *passbird*.

Azevedo asked, "Have you checked the email account yet?"

"Yes. Unfortunately, there are no old messages for us to examine. She was fastidious in cleaning up her email folders. She even emptied her Trash folder. That's the bad news."

"Is there good news?"

"Yes. There's a new message in her Inbox from a couple of days ago. We can't track it back to the sender because her email service strips out IP addresses from incoming message headers. But the message is from Goliath. I've already decoded it. It's asking if she knows the whereabouts of Calanus and Cardui."

"Did you check if those names are butterflies?"

"*Já, já.* The Banded Hairstreak butterfly, *Satyrium calanus*, matches the tattoo on the male in the morgue, and the Painted Lady, *Vanessa cardui*, matches the one on the female."

"Good work, Viní." Azevedo hung up the phone, then he turned to the agent in his office. "Has Matthew Cochran been to Indonesia?"

The agent repeatedly pressed arrow keys on his laptop. "No, sir. And the Americans examined him. He doesn't have any tattoos."

Azevedo furrowed his brow. "Then I don't think Cochran is the mastermind. Indonesia is where we must turn our attention."

"I've already gathered some background info, sir. Indonesia's a huge place. A quarter of a billion people. More than thirteen thousand islands, about half inhabited. Dozens of known terrorist groups, most of them religious extremists."

"We'll need to narrow our search somehow."

"We've already checked Hasse's credit card records from the time she was there. No charges at all. She must have paid cash for everything once she landed."

"How about tattoo parlors?"

"At least ten thousand licensed parlors in Indonesia, and probably thousands more unlicensed."

"I need to get some additional insight," Azevedo said. "I think I'll pay a visit to *Senhora* Hasse's husband. In the meantime, keep confidential the identity of the woman who killed herself at Iguaçu Falls, the usual 'pending notification of next of kin.' Likewise, don't release anything at all about a dead man at Fazenda Fiorva. We don't want the terrorist organization to know that anything has happened." Then he swallowed. *I'll have to tell Senhor Hasse that his wife is dead.*

÷ ÷ ÷ ÷ ÷

"We can organize a huge press conference," Herrar said, waving her hands in wide arcs.

Duarte said, "Just prepare a press release with all the pertinent information, please, Melissa. There'll be plenty of time for press conferences and celebrations in the future, which is already starting to look brighter."

÷ ÷ ÷ ÷ ÷

Azevedo stood outside the door of the Hasses' apartment, along with two uniformed officers and the two undercover agents who had been tailing Gunter. One of the officers was pounding on the door.

"Are you certain he's in there?"

"Yes, lieutenant," an undercover man responded. "He entered the building around noon, and we still saw him in a lounge chair out on the balcony right up until you arrived."

"How long has he been out there?"

"A few hours."

"When's the last time you saw him move?"

"I don't think he has moved."

Azevedo said, "Break down the door."

If they had attempted the doorknob, they would have found it was unlocked, but the two uniformed officers rushed the door, splintering the frame.

From the entryway, the policemen could see the man lying back in the lounge chair on the balcony, unmoved by the loud crack of the forced entry. They ran out through the sliding glass door and huddled around the chair.

An officer checked the pulse and shined a penlight into the man's eyes. "He's dead, sir."

One of the undercover agents held up an empty orange plastic pill vial. The label read "Hydrocodone," a commonly prescribed painkiller.

÷

An hour later, after the other officers had departed with the body and the ambulance crew, Azevedo stood alone on the balcony, staring at the empty lounge chair. He muttered, "*Bolas.* [Balls.] I've reached an impasse."

He balled up a fist, and he drew back his arm. He was about to punch the glass door, which might have caused undue physical harm, perhaps even necessitating a second ambulance, but he stopped himself short. *No,* he thought, *there's always another leaf to turn over.* He lightly tapped the glass with his knuckles. *But where?*

Chapter 31

"Ei! wie schmeckt der Coffee süße,
Lieblicher als tausend Küsse,
Milder als Muskatenwein."

["Mm! how sweet the coffee tastes,
more delicious than a thousand kisses,
mellower than muscatel wine."]

From the libretto by Christian Friedrich Henrici for Bach's
Kaffee Kantate **[Coffee Cantata], 1732**

~~~~~

In the lab at Sede, the mood was celebratory. Staff people were toasting each other with cups of coffee, despite Manling's best efforts to keep the place off limits to food and drink. He finally threw his hands up and said, "What the heck? Give me a cup."

Meanwhile, the senior scientists were seated in the conference room shooting the breeze about the technical details of their solution. They all looked up at the doorway when *Doutora* Helen Strath entered.

Westphal introduced her to Decker, then she gave the doctor the good news. "Mr. Decker and our staff have devised a means of stopping the coffee fungus."

Strath said, "Excellent. I'm still trying to come up with a way to stop the toxin from the new strain of *C. tetani*. That's why I'm here. I heard you retrieved a thermos of the toxin-laced coffee that poisoned the pilot. I'd like to analyze the contents of that thermos to see if the toxin has been chemically altered from prolonged exposure to all the other compounds in coffee. The terrorists might have quantities of bacterial spores or toxin that they're planning to release." She noticed the clipping from a coffee branch on the table. "What's your solution for the coffee fungus?"

Horton explained the chemistry and the application process.

Strath responded, "Molasses and calcium oxide? That combination sounds familiar." She strained her neurons to recall.

Ribiero said, "I vaguely remember something about molasses and calcium oxide from when I was a kid, but I can't recall what. I'll Google it." He pulled out his mobile phone.

Before Ribiero entered anything on his handset, Strath asked him, "Where'd you grow up?"

"In Amazonas."

"Whereabouts?"

"Humaitá. My dad worked on a ranch."

Strath blurted out, "A ranch. That's it."

Decker asked, "That's what?"

"Grass tetany," she said.

"As in tetanus?"

"Sort of." Strath explained, "Grass tetany isn't due to tetanus bacteria, but it produces muscular convulsions similar to tetanus. It isn't from an infection at all. It's from a deficiency of magnesium. In cows."

"Cows?"

"That's right. To prevent it in cattle herds, ranchers can feed the livestock molasses with supplemental magnesium oxide. A deficiency of calcium can exacerbate the problem, so some ranchers add calcium oxide to the mix." Strath said to herself, "Magnesium deficiency." Then she spoke up, "Excuse me, folks. I've got to go to Campinas. I want to test a treatment on your pilot in the hospital down there."

Westphal asked, "What treatment?"

"Some researchers have experimented with magnesium sulfate as a treatment for tetanus infection in humans."

Decker said, "Magnesium sulfate? That's Epsom salt."

"That's correct."

"That's a laxative."

"Correct again," Strath said.

Westphal asked, "Is there a risk to Miguel from this treatment?"

"The only risk is that the orderlies will have to change his bedpan more often."

The phone on the wall rang just as Strath departed.

÷÷÷÷÷

Proofreading the draft press release in English on her computer, Melissa Herrar read from it out loud. "...ingredients: molasses, water, alcohol, and lime," then she said, "That sounds like a recipe for a mixed drink." She deleted and rewrote several sentences.

Duarte came into Herrar's office with his thumbs up. "No further spread at Fazenda Briole. The spores remain fully encapsulated even when the treatment gets soaking wet. Have Wendy review the press release, then put it out there."

÷÷÷÷÷

On her way out of the building, Strath encountered Lieutenant Azevedo on his way in. They met in the vestibule between the inner and outer doors.

"Hello, lieutenant."

"Hello, doctor."

Strath asked, "Did you hear? The scientists here have found a way to stop the coffee fungus."

"I hadn't heard, but that's great news. My news, however, has not been so good."

"Why's that?"

"We've identified four of the terrorists." Azevedo held up four fingers. "But all four of them are now dead." He closed his hand.

"Larissa Júnior is dead?"

"No. Confidentially, *Senhorita* Júnior is not one of the terrorists. In fact, she helped identify two of the actual terrorists for us. But now I'm stumped. One of the terrorists, a Delcese employee named Martina Hasse, went to Indonesia years ago. I came here to find out if anyone knows exactly where she went when she was there."

"Indonesia?"

"Yes. We now know that all the confirmed terrorists have been to Indonesia. We think the group's mastermind is there."

"I thought the mastermind was the coffee business guy in custody in the U.S."

"We no longer believe that *Senhor* Cochran is the mastermind."

"Why not?"

"He's never been to Indonesia, and he doesn't have the tattoo."

"The tattoo?"

"Yes. The other confirmed terrorists have tattoos. Each one is different, but they're all similar. They're all of butterflies."

"Butterfly tattoos? Indonesia?" A wave of lightheadedness overcame Strath, and she staggered forward.

Azevedo caught her by the shoulders. "What is it, *doutora*?"

She blinked her eyes a few times, then she stood upright. "The mastermind, lieutenant. I know who it is."

"Who?"

"His name is Eddy Zeger."

"Who is he? And how do you know it's him?"

"When I was a doctoral student at the University of Melbourne, I spent a year in Panama at the Smithsonian Tropical Research Institute. Zeger was a student there for a semester. He came down from McGill University in Montreal. He was the smartest man I'd ever met, a true genius. I was in love with him. But as we got to know each other better, he began to reveal more of his innermost thoughts and ideas. He viewed all human civilization as a cancer to the earth, destined to ruin the planet's ecosystems and annihilate plant and animal species on a vast scale. Like most twisted geniuses, he was at least partially correct, but the conclusions he drew were misguided. He asked me to join him in an underground group he was organizing, as he put it, 'to take direct action to save the planet.' He said his group was going to make The Monkey Wrench Gang look like a bunch of grade school kids. I thought he was just blowing smoke."

"How do you know he's behind this particular terrorist group?"

"He grew up on Java, one of the major islands in Indonesia. And he had a gigantic tattoo of a butterfly across his back, a Goliath Bird-wing butterfly, one of the world's largest."

Azevedo gasped. "Did you say 'Goliath'?"

Strath nodded. "Last I heard, which must've been ten years ago, Eddy had gone back home and opened one of those touristy butterfly pavilions." She leaned in and put a hand on his shoulder. "It's him, lieutenant. Eddy Zeger has got to be the mastermind. I know it in my heart."

Their faces only inches apart, Azevedo said, "*Doutora* Strath, I could kiss you right now."

She tipped her head forward as though she was about to oblige, but then she turned away. "I must go. I have to get down to the hospital at UNICAMP." Strath opened the door to leave. She paused and turned around. "And lieutenant..."

"Yes, *doutora*?"

"Please don't publicly reveal my identity as the source of that information. I don't need the hassle."

"As you wish."

÷

Fabiana Munhoz got out of her car and walked toward the Administration Building. Approaching the doorway, she greeted the exiting Strath in passing.

"Doctor."

"Doctor."

Munhoz passed Azevedo still standing in the vestibule.

"Lieutenant."

"Doctor."

Upstairs, Munhoz was amazed to see a party going on inside the lab. Among the gathering she saw Westphal and Manling engaged in affectionate embrace.

She made her way over to Duarte. "I take it you've stopped the coffee fungus?"

"Yes," Duarte replied, "and it was Decker's idea. To use molasses."

"Molasses?"

He nodded.

Munhoz glanced around the room. "Where's Sam?"

Duarte looked around. "He was here a little while ago."

She walked out of the lab and toward the light emerging from an office at the far end of the hallway.

÷

Decker was kneeling down with his head practically inside a file cabinet. He was reading the handwritten descriptions on the tabs of manila folders in the bottom drawer.

"It's good to see you again, Sam."

The woman's voice startled him. He jerked up, scraping the top of his head on the handle of the drawer above. "Fabiana." With a hand pressed to his scalp, he stood up. "I heard about Isabela. I'm sorry."

"She lived a long, full life. And from what I hear, her namesake coffee can now live on. Something to do with molasses."

"Yeah, it's a long story."

"I've got all night. Will you join me for dinner?"

"Yes, certainly."

While they stood there, a petite cleaning woman in a blue apron came around the doorway to check the trash can. "*Desculpe* [Excuse me]," she said quietly. When she saw that the can was already empty, she turned around and left.

"What are you up to in here, Sam?"

"I'm searching through the remains of Paul's files. Even though we can now stop the new coffee fungus, a couple key pieces of the puzzle are still missing: the origin of the fungus; and why the pilot was poisoned. Unfortunately, it looks like somebody cleared out most of the files since the last time I was here." He waved a hand around the room. "Oh well. I'll come back tomorrow. Right now, I'm hungry. Let's go eat." With his foot, he pushed the file cabinet drawer closed.

When they turned to head out, the cleaning woman was looking back in the doorway. Fabiana held up a finger and said to her, "*Um momento. Estamos deixando.* [We're leaving.]"

Instead of stepping aside to let them out, in a meager voice the woman asked in Portuguese, "This is the office of the man who died in the plane crash, isn't it?"

"Yes."

"You're his wife, aren't you?"

"Yes, he was my husband."

The cleaning woman looked back and forth several times at Munhoz and Decker. Then she pointed to the bottom drawer of the file cabinet which Decker had just closed. "*Abra. Abra.*"

Decker got the gist of the her request. He bent over and slid open the drawer.

"Tire a gaveta para fora."

Decker looked at Munhoz.

"She wants you to take out the drawer."

He knelt down and fumbled with several possible ways the drawer might be removed, until eventually he lifted the front end and was able to pull it free. Inside the base of the cabinet, underneath the drawer area, were two items. The first was a small foil bag with the letter "G" handwritten on it in black marker. The second was a writing notebook with a black and white speckled cover.

Munhoz and the cleaning woman had a rapid exchange in Portuguese while Decker thumbed through the notebook.

"Her name is Deusinha. She says that several times when she came to empty the trash can, the man was in here with the drawer removed, putting things in or taking them out. He made her promise not to tell anyone, because, he said, it was *uma surpresa gracinha.*"

Decker's eyebrows rose. "Why did she decide to tell us?"

"She says that now that the man is dead, I deserved to know. And, she says..." Fabiana stopped and smiled.

He looked up from the notebook. "What?"

"She says that you look like a good man."

Decker unfolded the foil bag and looked inside. He stood up from the floor. "Tell Deusinha, 'Thank you very much.'" He tipped the opening of the bag toward Fabiana.

She peeked into the bag. *"Muito obrigada."*

Decker stashed the two items in his briefcase, then he and Fabiana stopped in the lab. He made his way to Lucy and told her what he wanted to do the next day.

Lucy smiled and said, "You can't get there from here."

Decker and Fabiana walked back out of the lab.

He asked, "Where to for dinner?"

"My house. I'll cook while you study the notebook."

÷÷÷÷÷

After putting the finishing touches on the press release, Herrar directly emailed it to her own list of over 300 local, national, and international coffee industry journalists and analysts. Then she issued the release globally on Business Wire, reaching more than 30,000 outlets, including newspapers, magazines, online news sites, radio and television stations, brokerage houses, and investment banks.

Chapter 32

"Our enemies have made the mistake that America's enemies always make. They saw liberty and thought they saw weakness. And now, they see defeat."

From a speech commemorating the 9/11 attacks, U.S. President George W. Bush, December 2001

~~~~~

SEPTEMBER 10

Shortly after the morning sun skipped across the rugged surface of the island of Java, Eddy Zeger sat at a table along the west wall in the living room of his home, in a position he was about to find out represented bad *feng shui*. He wore only a pair of shorts and flip-flops, his tattooed back to the door. He was using a laptop computer.

Zeger read the press release from Delcese Agricola. *This is a setback*, he understated to himself. He composed a brief email that he planned to blast out to his entire membership as both instruction and morale booster:

> curators of the earth, operation intended consequence has now concluded. kudos to all our brothers and sisters involved. soon we will unleash operation sweet surprise, and the world will once again feel the flap of our wings. forever yours, goliath

The base text in which he embedded the message was an article about the reconstruction of Rome after the great fire of 64 A.D. He pasted the encoded text into the body of a new email message. He filled in the "Send to:" field with the predefined group name, and on the subject line he entered the word "Reconstruction," followed by the customary exclamation point.

Then the door came crashing in.

Out of the corner of his right eye, Zeger could see two men in black SWAT outfits about five meters away, training handguns at him. The fingers of Zeger's left hand were still positioned over the Shift key and the 1/! key. The base of his right hand was resting on the table with the fingertips protruding onto the laptop's trackpad.

"Put your hands up, right now," a SWAT man commanded.

Zeger did not put up his hands. Instead, he yelled, ""I give up!" loud enough to cover the sound of adding two more exclamation points to the subject line. He nudged the fingertips of his right hand across the trackpad to position the cursor over the "Send" button.

÷

The SWAT marksman had the sights of his Smith & Wesson M&P 9mm pistol lined up on the back of Zeger's right hand, being careful not to put the bullet into the laptop. When the marksman squeezed the trigger, the bullet punched a hole through the metacarpal bones of Zeger's right hand. It also pressed down the hand, sending off the email message. The bullet exited through Zeger's palm, then grazed the front edge of the laptop before passing through the top of the table.

The SWAT team had not cut off Zeger's Internet service because part of the mission was to gain access to his computer while it might be logged on to any accounts. Unbeknownst to the SWAT team, Zeger's important files all resided in encrypted cloud storage, to which he was not logged on at the time. Nevertheless, he was logged on to his email account, and the computer forensics expert who entered next was able to retrieve significant information from that account.

÷÷÷÷÷

Around the world that day, trucks filled with molasses, lime, and ethanol mobilized from sugar mills toward coffee plantations. In some areas, cheering citizens lined the roadways.

÷÷÷÷÷

Around the world that day, members of the Curators Of The Earth scrambled into their emergency plans as they saw the three exclamation points in the subject line of the email from Goliath. Members hastily packed bags, withdrew wads of cash from bank accounts, and in a few cases, kissed unaware spouses and children goodbye for what might turn out to be the last time.

At Kraton Kupu Kupu, Jarma Pukartra disconnected two network storage drives and carried them away, slipping out the back door less than two minutes before the police burst into the building.

÷÷÷÷÷

At sunrise over Fazenda Briole, farm workers trotted out to the treated field and found no new occurrence of fungus.

÷÷÷÷÷

Emerging from a traffic delay at a construction zone in Piracicaba, at Decker's urging, Munhoz drove the car faster than normal.

Decker said, "The plane is scheduled to arrive at eight o'clock from Fiorva with Mr. Mabro." He rubbed the beard stubble on his face and looked down at the clothes he had worn the entire previous day. "I was hoping to get in a quick shower and shave and a change of clothes before heading out in the airplane."

Munhoz checked the clock on the dashboard. "If we're lucky, we'll still get you there in time."

Passing through Águas de São Pedro, a decrepit old Cadillac pulled out from a driveway. Munhoz hit the brakes with time to spare. She waved at the old man driving the other car. "*Bom dia.*"

Munhoz flashed her ID badge at the guard in the shack at the Sede entrance. When the Mercedes came screeching into the parking lot, Lucy was standing on the sidewalk in front of the Administration Building. Munhoz pulled the car up to the curb in front of her, and Decker jumped out.

"Sorry I'm late, Lucy."

"Sam," Lucy said, "I tried to get ahold of you earlier to tell you. I asked at the desk in the Visitor's Residence, but they said you didn't access your room door last night. I should have guessed that you spent the night at Dr. Munhoz's home again."

The front door to the Administration Building opened, and Costa emerged.

Decker said, "I'm having one heck of a *déjà vu.*"

"Come with me please," Costa stated in a manner that did not allow objection. "*Senhor* Duarte would like to speak with you. Now."

Lucy stayed on the sidewalk while Decker followed Costa inside.

÷

"Have a seat please, Mr. Decker." Duarte motioned to the leather-clad guest chair opposite his desk. Costa and a man in a police uniform stood in the office.

"What's happening, Mr. Duarte?"

"Sam, this is Lieutenant Azevedo of the Departamento de Polícia Federal. I'll allow him to explain."

"*Senhor* Decker, Indonesian police have arrested the real mastermind of the terrorist group. Passport records indicate that you traveled to Indonesia three years ago. Why did you go there?"

"That's a personal matter. Are you insinuating that I'm involved with these terrorists?"

Ignoring Decker's question, Azevedo continued, "We now know the name of the terrorist group is Curators Of The Earth. That's C-O-T-E, as in Côte d'Ivoire, where your repeated presence is a matter of public record. We've also noticed that the new coffee fungus has not appeared in the coffee plantations of Côte d'Ivoire. Furthermore, the Departamento de Polícia Federal has cracked a secret code used for email communication among these terrorists. Their messages include species names as code names for members of the group. One of the messages, sent by an employee of Delcese Agricola on August eleventh, several days after your first visit here, refers to encountering a species called *A. deckerii*. We haven't found any actual animal or plant species corresponding to the name, so we believe that this codename might be for a special member of the terrorist group, perhaps even for a mentor of the group's mastermind."

"I don't believe this."

A woman's voice came from the doorway, "What the hell is going on here?"

Duarte responded, "*Doutora* Munhoz, I regret to inform you, but the police have reason to believe that Mr. Decker may be involved with the terrorist group."

Azevedo continued, "*Senhor* Decker, the DPF will need to examine you."

"Examine me?"

"For tattoos."

"Tattoos?"

"Tattoos depicting butterflies, in particular. The members of the terrorist group all have them." Azevedo pointed at Decker, then turned to Munhoz. "This man has been to Indonesia, where the terrorists are headquartered, and he refuses to disclose why he was there."

Munhoz burst out, "You insensitive lout. He went to Bali for his wife to receive an experimental treatment for her advanced Stage Four breast cancer. The treatment failed, and she died there. You should have no problem verifying that from public records."

Decker pointed to his briefcase. "If you don't mind, lieutenant. I'd like to show you something."

Azevedo nodded.

Decker opened the outer flap of his briefcase, and he slipped out a small sheet of thick paper. "This is *Ara deckerii*." He held up the sheet for all to see those two words neatly handwritten on it. He flipped over the sheet to show the photograph of a blue bird. "It's the parrot that Mrs. Hasse found in the coffee field here. She must have named it after me because I gave her the opportunity to go out and look for it again. I assume she was the source of the message you intercepted." Decker pointed to his briefcase. "If you don't mind, lieutenant. I'd like to show you something else." He pulled out a notebook. "Fabiana and I found this yesterday evening in Paul's office, with help from a little angel." He held up the book to show two words written in black marker on the cover: *Surpresa Gracinha*.

Azevedo eyed the cover. "That's like the name of the project the terrorists were preparing to unleash next."

"What?"

"Earlier today, we intercepted and decoded the final message sent by the terrorist leader moments before he was captured. It said that the group was going to refocus its efforts on 'operation sweet surprise.' *Doutor* Mendonça must have been one of the terrorists."

Munhoz yelled, "Nonsense! Paul never had anything to do with terrorists. And he'd never been to Indonesia. And he didn't have any tattoos."

Decker opened the notebook. "If you'll allow me." He flipped the pages, in search of the last one with any notations. He began reading, "Wednesday, July seventeenth." He paused and noted, "That's the day before the plane crash," then he continued reading. "Came into lab at six o'clock this morning to get head start on preparations for field test tomorrow. Surprised to find Mrs. Hasse already hard at work. She had little jar with smiley face on it and clear liquid inside. When I asked why she was in so early, she said she was working on *uma surpresa doce*, a sweet surprise. Funny she used almost the same project name as mine. Can't imagine what she was doing. Something odd going on. Will have to look into her project when I have time." Decker closed the notebook. "The obvious implication is that Mrs. Hasse, not Larissa Júnior, was the one who cultured the tetanus bacteria in the lab here."

Azevedo snorted, "We already know that." He lowered his voice. "But it's not public information yet."

Decker continued, "And if Larissa Júnior wasn't involved, then the farmhand Sergio must have been the one who poisoned the coffee ingested by Miguel the pilot, causing the plane crash which took Paul's life. Sergio also must be one of the terrorists."

"We already know that, as well. Sergio Moreno is now dead, as is *Senhora* Hasse."

"They must have conspired to kill Paul after he stumbled onto Hasse in the lab. They must have known it wouldn't take long for Paul to discover the true nature of her extracurricular work."

Munhoz added, "They must have expected Paul to drink the poisoned coffee, too. But they didn't know that he would only drink Gracinha."

"Speaking of Gracinha..." Decker reached into his briefcase again and pulled out the foil bag from Mendonça's office. "This is Paul's surprise." He handed the bag to Duarte. "Have Manling run chemical analyses on it. I think you'll find the results quite interesting." He handed over the notebook. "And I think you'll find that quite interesting as well."

Costa spoke for the first time. "We've made a major mistake."

"No apologies necessary."

"That's not what I meant, Mr. Decker. Something else is wrong." Everyone turned toward Costa, awaiting his further explanation. "If we've already stopped the development of the tetanus bacteria in the lab here, why was the terrorist mastermind still planning to unleash 'operation sweet surprise'? The terrorists have no chance of getting it into the coffee supply now. Even if they're also developing the bacteria elsewhere, they must know that the entire world's coffee supply will be under close scrutiny."

Munhoz was the first to have her light bulb switch on. "What if the coffee supply isn't the target of the tetanus bacteria? What if the coffee supply never was the target of the tetanus bacteria?"

Decker said, "*Surpresa doce.* Sweet surprise." He turned and pointed out the window.

Duarte stood up from behind the desk and looked out the window at the vast fields of sugarcane. "But *Doutora* Strath had told us that the tetanus spores wouldn't survive the sugar refining process."

"That's true," Munhoz noted, "but she also said the spores could be added effectively after the sugar goes through the mill."

Lieutenant Azevedo moved toward the window. "At that time, we had no idea that an extensive terrorist network was involved. It hadn't occurred to us that it might also involve someone at..."

"...a sugar mill," Costa finished his sentence.

Decker said, "While you men pursue that plot, I've got a different plot, an agricultural one, to investigate. And I'm late for my plane."

÷÷÷÷÷

The CNN anchorman reported, "Stocks opened sharply higher today on news of a successful treatment to halt the spread of the coffee fungus. Financial industry analysts were characteristically cautiously optimistic, but individual investors have taken the news as a harbinger of recovery and have unleashed a stock buying spree."

÷÷÷÷÷

The Cessna buzzed over the isolated hectare plots west of Fazenda Fiorva. Decker was in the co-pilot's seat, with Lucy and Mabro in back. Decker pointed to a specific field. Carlos made a flyby low over the field, after which Decker pointed straight down.

When they climbed out of the plane on the dirt airstrip, Lucy asked Decker, "Why that field?"

He replied, "You'll see."

Carlos stayed with the plane, while Lucy, Decker, and Mabro hiked off along a dirt trail.

÷÷÷÷÷

Azevedo drove his DPF-issued black SUV with the lights flashing and the siren blaring.

Costa said, "It feels good to be in a cruiser again."

"Oh? You thinkin' about rejoining the force, Ramon?"

"Hell no. I'd be a dead man."

"What do you mean? You're still tough enough to hold your own."

"It's not the crooks who'd kill me. It's my wife, Graciela."

They entered a long approach road, headed toward a tall smoke stack from which arose a thin white plume. The enormous complex of the sugar mill was nearly a square kilometer in size, with an expansive array of buildings and storage tanks of various vintages spanning more than 70 years of cumulative development, decay, and redevelopment.

"The smell of industry," Costa said when they got out of the SUV.

Azevedo flashed his badge at the receptionist in the office building and asked to see the General Manager. A few minutes later, a stout man with a pencil-thin moustache greeted them in the lobby.

"I'm Jusco Portelino, the Chief of Operations here. How may I assist the Federal Police, lieutenant?"

"We're investigating terrorist activities related to the coffee fungus. We'd like to ask you a few questions." Azevedo took out his mobile phone and pulled up photographs of the butterfly tattoos from the bodies at the morgue in Belo Horizonte. "Do any of your employees have tattoos of butterflies, such as these?"

Portelino gave them a puzzled look.

Azevedo added, "I can assure you, *Senhor* Portelino, this matter is of utmost importance to national security."

The receptionist coughed.

Portelino responded, "I wish I could be of assistance, *senhors*, but I have over one thousand six hundred employees here. I'm not privy to all their body art."

"Perhaps we could speak to your Personnel Manager?"

The receptionist coughed more loudly, then she said, "Pardon me, for eavesdropping."

Portelino asked, "What is it, *senhora*?"

"Gilberta in Accounting, she's got one. A tattoo of a butterfly." The receptionist pointed to the back of her own left shoulder. "You can see it peeking out when she wears a sleeveless top. Personally, I think it looks tacky on a woman who is well past her optimum ripeness date."

÷

In the Accounting Department at the sugar mill, Azevedo, Costa, and Portelino stood in front of the Controller, Cesar Ronha.

"Yes," Ronha said, "I believe that Gilberta Faria does indeed have a tattoo of a butterfly."

Azevedo asked, "Can we speak with her?"

"She didn't show up for work today."

Portelino asked, "Did she call in sick?"

"No, she just didn't show up. That's unlike her, though. She's been working here for eight years, and I can't recall her ever not showing up without calling first. Perhaps her mother has taken a sudden turn for the worse. The old lady had some kind of major surgery a few weeks ago. Gilberta took off two whole weeks to tend to her up north."

Costa and Azevedo looked at each other.

The policeman asked, "Where up north?"

"In Manaus."

÷

Portelino and Ronha observed while the other two men examined the contents of Gilberta's desk, but they found nothing unusual.

Costa looked at the calculator on the desk. "Something doesn't add up here. A terrorist group wanting to contaminate tons of sugar at a mill wouldn't do it through the Accounting Department."

Azevedo said, "But that group might want to fund its operations through some creative accounting."

Portelino turned to the Controller. "*Senhor* Ronha, launch an audit of every *real* that Gilberta Faria might have accessed."

Costa asked Portelino, "Hypothetically, if you wanted to contaminate the sugar coming out of this mill, where would you do it?"

"Follow me to Production. Nobody's going to sour our sugar."

÷÷÷÷÷

As the trio approached the experimental farm plot, Mabro threw his arms up in the air and ran ahead. When he reached the edge of the coffee field, he called out, "The trees are infected with the red fungus, but they're not only alive, they're thriving."

When the other two caught up to Mabro, Lucy asked, "What is this field?"

Decker pulled out a piece of paper from his pants pocket, the printout of the plot map he had made weeks earlier on Dr. Mendonça's home computer. On the map, he pointed to the plot where they stood, then he slid his finger to the single word alongside it: Gracinha.

Mabro noted, "These trees have mature cherries. They weren't due to bear fruit for another year."

Decker responded, "Another of the many surprises Dr. Mendonça found here."

While they were gathering samples to bring back to Sede, Mabro shouted out, "*Olha!* Look!" He pointed just above the tree tops. "There. In that tree." Five meters away, a blue parrot was perched on a branch.

Lucy said, "You saw that parrot from the plane, didn't you, Mr. Decker?"

"My eyesight isn't that good, Lucy. But get your camera ready." Decker walked past the other two, who fell in line to follow. Another 20 meters into the field, he stopped and pointed, "*That's* what I saw from the airplane."

One entire coffee tree was enmeshed in a massive bird's nest, at least two meters wide and three meters high. A beak poked out from a hole near the base of the nest, and they watched in wonder as one bird emerged, followed by another.

Lucy raised a camera to her eye, and she pressed a button. The device beeped, and a bird responded with a mimicking call. Within a minute, the three people were inundated with squawks from a dozen members of the species *Ara deckerii*.

÷÷÷÷÷

Portelino walked Azevedo and Costa outside and across to one of the production buildings at the sugar mill.

Inside, pipes snaked between tanks of assorted shapes and sizes. The hum of pumps and motors droned in the background, and brief hisses sent blasts of steam into the air above the workers.

Portelino explained, "This time of year, we run three shifts around the clock, churning out a million and a half kilograms a day." Toward the far end of building, a series of pipes emerged from the conglomeration of equipment. "Those pipes carry sugar syrup to another building where it's further refined and packaged into white sugar for domestic consumption."

"And for international consumption?"

Portelino walked them further to a set of broad conveyor belts that carried away a continuous stream of light brown crystals at high speed. "Crystallized raw sugar goes on these conveyors into the bulk storage shed where it's held until it's loaded onto rail cars for transport to the Port of Santos and shipment overseas."

Azevedo and Costa both pointed in the direction of the conveyors. The three men followed the conveyors into the adjoining structure, an enormous shed hundreds of meters long, the far half of which was filled with a heap of raw sugar large enough to fulfill the sweet tooth fantasies of a medium-sized nation. Several workers in hard hats monitored the conveyors which rose overhead into the rafters to dump their loads at the active drop point.

Costa looked out a glass panel in an exterior door. "If someone wanted to contaminate the sugar at this mill, they'd have to store the contaminant somewhere. What are those tall white tanks outside?"

"They're for storage of white sugar prior to bagging. They're in constant use, so I don't think anyone could store anything improper there. However..." Portelino turned around and marched them back into the processing area. He pointed to three vertical tanks, each three meters in diameter and five meters high. Their steel exteriors were pocked with surface rust. "Since a plant retrofitting years ago, we don't use these older tanks anymore."

Costa rapped his knuckles on the first tank. The thick metal rang back with a hollow reverberation.

Portelino knocked on the second tank, with a similar result.

Azevedo knocked on the third tank, but the response was dulled. "This one's not empty."

÷÷÷÷÷

When the plane returned to Sede, Decker and Lucy proceeded to the lab, where they handed off cuttings to Manling for analysis. In return, Manling handed over a small bag.

Decker and Lucy walked down the hall to the cupping room. They watched from the observation window as *Senhor* Mosta slurped and drooled a round of coffee cups. When he was finished, they entered.

Decker showed *Senhor* Mosta the red-coated contents of the Gracinha bag.

Lucy explained, "We'd like you to taste these beans."

One of the world's foremost coffee cupping experts shook his head emphatically. "That's *uma abominação*. And you've only got enough beans for a few cups. I can't perform a proper cupping with so little. And the beans are already roasted. I only cup fresh-roasted."

"But you *must* taste it, *Senhor* Mosta," Lucy pleaded on Decker's behalf. "We need to know if it was worth what happened to Dr. Mendonça." She added, "Pretty please with sugar on top."

Mosta reluctantly took the bag, then ordered them back out to the far side of the observation window.

Mosta ground the beans—fungus and all—and placed the resultant powder into three cups. The master seated himself at the table as Decker and Lucy eagerly looked on. Mosta poured in the hot water. After a brief pause for steeping, he dipped a spoon into the first cup and raised it to his lips.

When Mosta tasted a spoonful from the second cup, Decker noted, "He didn't spit it out. He swallowed it."

After the abbreviated cupping session was complete, Mosta went out to them and spoke in Portuguese. Lucy translated for Decker, "He says, 'Now my career has been made complete. I have at long last tasted the perfect cup of coffee.'"

Fabiana came walking down the hall. "I was looking for you, Sam. I got a call from Dr. Barada at UNICAMP hospital. Let's take a ride."

÷÷÷÷÷

In the yard adjacent to the sugar mill buildings, all the production employees had been sequestered with armed DPF men standing guard. Male employees had their shirts off, and the mill's staff physician was checking them for obvious tattoos, although more thorough examinations would be performed later.

Portelino walked over from the office building and said to Costa and Azevedo, "One production worker failed to show up without calling in sick."

Inside the mill building Emílio Melan consulted in muffled tones with two technicians in HAZMAT suits.

Melan went to the holding area outside and approached Azevedo. "The tank definitely contains massive quantities of bacteria and spores that look like *C. tetani*. We'll have to wait for the lab tests to confirm if it's *Senhora* Hasse's baby, but I'd lay odds we've got enough of the new tetanus in there to kill millions of people."

Azevedo asked, "How the hell does someone make that much of a deadly bacteria without anybody noticing? And how do they do it without killing themselves in the process?"

"We may never know for sure, lieutenant, but here's my guess. Tetanus bacteria are anaerobes. Throw some starter spores in an airtight tank such as the one here. Then add an organic growth medium, a palladium catalyst, and a carbon dioxide and hydrogen chemical generator to suck up all the oxygen. You add some water to activate the chemical generator, and you seal the tank. Then you just sit back and wait. When you eventually reopen the tank, the oxygen kills off the live bacteria, but the dormant spores remain intact and relatively safe to handle with proper precautions. The color of the tetanus spores even blends in nicely with raw sugar."

Azevedo said, "A small group of determined people almost pulled off the most deadly terrorist plot in history."

÷÷÷÷÷

In Hospital das Clinicas at UNICAMP, Barada, Munhoz, and Decker stood around a bed in which the patient was awake and relaxed. Miguel's wife and young daughter were there, too.

"As you can see," Barada said, "Miguel has responded remarkably well to the new treatment. As suggested by *Doutora* Strath, we added magnesium sulfate to his feeding solution last night. When a nurse checked on him a few hours later, he was wide awake."

Miguel pointed to Decker and asked a question in Portuguese.

"He wants to know why you examined his feet when you were here before."

Decker shook his head. "How could he know I did that? He was in a coma."

Barada responded, "Like I said before, medical science doesn't understand comas very well."

"Tell Miguel, I wanted to know if he had stepped on a rusty nail. My mother always told me that's how people got tetanus."

They were all chatting and laughing when *Doutora* Strath entered the hospital room.

After the obligatory congratulations, Strath told them, "Today, I made another important discovery about the effect of magnesium sulfate on this new strain of *C. tetani*. I found that the presence of magnesium sulfate blocks the spores from germinating into active bacteria. If spores from this strain ever get out into the population at large, all that would be necessary to prevent a massive tetanus outbreak is a spoonful of Epsom salt with every meal."

Munhoz said, "People worldwide will breath more freely knowing that this new bacteria can be stopped so easily."

Decker added, "If people worldwide are consuming Epsom salt, breathing isn't the only thing they'll be doing more freely."

Chapter 33

~~~~~

SEPTEMBER 11

The senior scientists plus Munhoz, Decker, Lucy, and Duarte, sat in the conference room at Sede. Manling held a glass beaker containing coffee cherries coated with fungus. Several tree clippings were on the table.

Decker put on his reading glasses and opened Dr. Mendonça's notebook. He began reading aloud, "May thirtieth. My analysis of the wild Gracinha cherries in one of the bags indicates that they have been infected by a fungus. Have checked the two remaining bags of cherries from wild Gracinha trees, but neither showed fungal infections. Therefore, this bag must be the prime. Conceivable that a single spore from the wild was original source of contamination." Decker flipped pages as he changed dates.

"May thirty-first. Visited Gracinha experimental plot for first time in months. No sign of fungus, but discovered two surprises. First, the trees all have cherries. They're bearing fruit a year before anticipated. Second, a massive bird nest with blue parrots...

"June fifth. Fungus does not match any known species. Possibly a mutation of *Corticium salmonicolor*, or a crossbreed of that species with *Hemileia vastatrix*...

"June tenth. Inside fungus-infected Gracinha cherries, reddish crystalline substance on surface of silverskin and endosperm...

"June eleventh. Analysis of the red crystals indicates they contain monosaccharide galactose and amino acid L-theanine...

"June thirteenth. Galactose appears to be a product of fungal metabolism. Will hand separate and dry small batch of these infected beans...

"June eighteenth. Research from Japan indicates that theanine naturally occurring in green tea blocks bitter tastes. Gracinha beans not infected by fungus contain traces of theanine, but concentration in infected beans is more than twelve X higher...

317

"June nineteenth. Discovered that infected beans have little caffeine remaining. Apparently, the fungus also metabolizes caffeine from endosperm and produces theanine...

"June twenty-first. Waited until *Senhor* Mosta went home for day. In cupping room, roasted batch of beans including red powder from fungus. Taste is marvelous, even better than uninfected Gracinha. Could be *Santo Graal*, Holy Grail of coffee taste, with built-in sweetener and no bitterness. And it's all naturally produced on the bean...

"June twenty-fifth. Have searched for prior references to parrot in Gracinha field, but found none. Perhaps I've discovered new species...

"June twenty-seventh. Took small sample of fungus to Gracinha experimental plot to test on live trees. Applied to three trees in center of field...

"July first. Back to Gracinha plot. Can't believe how fast fungus has spread. About half of field infected...

"July fourth. Entire Gracinha plot is now infected. Discovered probable mechanism of rapid spread: the parrots. Birds observed carrying whole cherries and eating beans. They could spread seeds for Gracinha trees far and wide. Wouldn't that be great? Wonderful new species of coffee plant, made even better by new fungus, spread by new species of parrot. A three-way symbiosis of new species. Would be unprecedented. Fabiana would love it, but I won't tell her yet. Keeping it secret until further tests. It will be a truly sweet surprise for her. *Uma surpresa gracinha.* Only pilot Miguel knows about it, and I have sworn him to secrecy...

"July eighth. Must determine if fungus has similar effects on arabica cultivars. In lab, applied fungus directly onto Typica and Isabela sample beans...

"July ninth. Fungus effects are different on other beans in lab. On the arabica beans, fungus drawing moisture out of beans and replicating itself faster. Perhaps lab conditions are not correct. Applied fungus to Gracinha beans in lab...

"July tenth. Arabica beans infected in lab are desiccated, and fungus not growing at all on Gracinha beans. A crucial element must be missing. Or perhaps incorrect lab conditions? Must test fungus in field conditions. Began cultivating fungus in lab incubator...

"July twelfth. Going out to north experimental fields next week for salicin project with Larissa. Will test application of fungus on another of west fields that day. Isolated enough that should be safe if anything goes horribly wrong..."

Decker closed the notebook and set it on the table. "I believe we already know many things went horribly wrong after that."

Everyone looked around at each other for a few moments, then Munhoz said, "I don't understand why the fungus didn't spread to other fields sooner. If the Gracinha field was already infected, why didn't the spores get around everywhere?"

Decker picked up a branch clipping from the table. "When the fungus infects arabica cultivars like Isabela, it draws moisture quite strongly, even away from its own spores. The surface of the spores dries out rapidly, and they readily drop off. But on Gracinha..." He waved the clipping around. "...it doesn't draw the moisture out of the plant so quickly, and the fungus retains a surface tackiness, keeping the spores in place."

Lucy said, "Like the molasses."

Duarte asked, "But why didn't the fungus grow on Gracinha beans in the lab? It apparently grew on Gracinha in the foil bag."

Manling said, "I can answer that. On arabica trees and beans, the effect of the fungus is self-initiating. In the case of Gracinha, however..." He raised up the beaker he had been holding. "The fungus on these infected Gracinha cherries contains traces of uric acid. It acts as a catalyst needed to kick off the metabolic process of the fungus."

Decker commented, "I guess the symbiosis was more involved than Paul thought. The parrots weren't just physically carrying the fungus, they were chemically enabling it."

The scientists all laughed.

Lucy and Duarte looked at each other, then she asked, "What's so funny about that?"

Munhoz explained, "In avians, uric acid forms a white pasty substance."

"*Cocô de pássaro*," Nestor said.

"Bird poop!" a voice called out. Everyone looked up to see Larissa in the doorway with a huge grin on her face and Tulio at her back.

After exchanges of greetings, Westphal said to Larissa, "Regrettably, Dr. Mendonça, the discoverer of this fungus, can't partake of a traditional privilege. In recognition of the time you spent in jail falsely accused, we've all agreed that you should have the honor of formally naming the new fungus. We've determined that it's genus *Hemileia*. You get to choose the species name."

Without hesitation, Larissa said, "In memory of Dr. Mendonça, and in honor of this region of Brazil, I name it *Hemileia paulista*."

÷

Later that day, Lieutenant Azevedo visited Larissa Júnior's apartment to inform her that she would be receiving a reward of one million *reais* from the Brazilian government for her help identifying two of the terrorists. She pointed out to him that the amount was the same as the bail she hadn't been able to post.

÷÷÷÷÷

U.S. Secretary of Homeland Security, Roland Fiske, appeared in a televised press conference. He pointed to a reporter.

"Mr. Fiske, are you certain that Eddy Zeger, the man arrested in Indonesia, is the head of the terrorist group responsible for spreading the coffee fungus?"

"Yes. His email account is a smoking weapon of mass destruction." Fiske pointed again.

"How was Zeger discovered to be the mastermind of this group?"

"In order to protect our sources, I can't disclose that information."

"Will anyone receive the one hundred million dollar reward?"

"Sorry, I can't comment." Fiske pointed to another reporter.

"Will the Indonesian government extradite Zeger for prosecution in other countries?"

"Brazil is first in line for any extradition, but Zeger will remain in Indonesia for the foreseeable future. He infected his own country's plantations, and the Indonesians intend to prosecute him themselves. They won't be inclined toward leniency. Coffee is that country's largest agricultural export."

"Have other members of Zeger's group been identified? And have any of them been apprehended?"

"A suspected cohort who worked at Zeger's business in Indonesia has disappeared. Another is—or at least was—in Hong Kong, and we have security camera images of him, but he is yet to be identified. Six more of the terrorists have been positively identified in Brazil. Four of those are already dead, two in a traffic accident, and two by suicides. The whereabouts of the other two in Brazil are unknown. We will continue to work with the Brazilian authorities, the Indonesians, and others to identify and apprehend more of the terrorists."

"How much of a threat does the remainder of the terrorist group pose?"

"Practically speaking, the terrorist group known as Curators Of The Earth is now history. A few dozen of them may still be out there lying low, but they are now headless. Zeger is a uniquely charismatic individual. New heads such as his don't just come crawling out of the woodwork."

÷÷÷÷÷

Matthew Cochran and his lawyer emerged from the Russell Senate Office Building. A crowd of reporters mobbed them.

"Mr. Cochran, what are your plans now?"

"I'm going back to San Francisco to carry on with my business. This whole experience has given me great ideas for new products, new marketing methods, and new ways to take Bright Cup to the top." He pointed straight up. "For starters, we've just signed an agreement to upgrade the coffee services in the Congressional offices..."

÷÷÷÷÷

That evening, inside a nightclub called *O Cisne Dourado* (The Golden Swan), Decker and Munhoz sipped a new mixed drink named *semente grudenta* (sticky seed), consisting of *cachaça*, molasses, lime, and soda water.

Among a crowd half their age, they slow danced to a classic 1970s Brazilian rock ballad by Erasmo Carlos, *"Sou Uma Criança, Não Entendo Nada"* ("I'm A Child, I Don't Understand Anything"). When the song ended, Decker took Munhoz by the hand and led her off the dance floor. They stood at a tall pedestal table.

"Fabiana," he said, "if you ever come up to Boston, please look me up." He gentlemanly kissed her hand.

"I certainly will, Sam."

SEPTEMBER 12

Eddy Zeger lay in bed at Bethesda Hospital Yogyakarta. His left ankle was shackled to the bed frame. After surgery to repair damaged tendons in his palm and reconstruct the second and third metacarpal bones that had been shattered by the bullet, his right forearm and hand were encased in a fiberglass cast suspended by a sling from a bedside pole.

Two armed policemen were stationed outside Zeger's hospital room door at all times. The Indonesian authorities denied Zeger access to any electronic communications such as telephone, Internet, and even television, despite protests of his lawyer. The lawyer was permitted in the hospital room without a policeman present, although he was searched before entering, and he was forced to surrender his mobile phone and any other electronic devices while inside.

Zeger was allowed to see one daily newspaper, but another means of comprehending his state of affairs was simply by listening to the muffled sounds of conversations that took place in the hallway.

On this particular day, he overheard the two policemen outside his door. One of them asked, "Is anyone gonna get the big reward money for this Zeger guy?"

The other replied, "Good question."

Yes, that's a very good question, Zeger thought. *How did the police connect me to the plot? None of my group's communications were traceable to me or to Kraton Kupu Kupu. Someone must have tipped them off. But who? None of the swarm had been captured alive. And I can't believe that any of the members would have ratted me out at the peak of our success.*

I was always so careful about choosing the people I approached to tell of my group. And of those people, only a handful didn't join. The two that threatened to tell the police are long dead. Of the few others, how would they have known that I was behind the recent events?

He lifted his head off the pillow. *There's only one person I can think of who might have been smart enough to figure it out.* He let his head fall back into the pillow. *I knew I should have done her in. I shouldn't have let my emotions get in the way. But how would she have connected me to this whole affair? I haven't had any contact with her in ten years. I should have kept track of her after we parted ways. I wonder what became of her.*

He looked up at his arm suspended in the sling. *I'd give my right arm for some Internet access right now.*

I have no idea where she is, not even what country she lives in. I'm not even sure if she's still alive.

Epilogue

~~~~~

At the moment of the autumnal equinox, the sun's motion as seen from earth appears to cross the equator from the Northern Hemisphere into the Southern. However, the day of the autumnal equinox (September 22nd in 2013) is not the day in which there are closest to being exactly 12 hours between the times of sunrise and sunset, due to refraction of the earth's atmosphere and the amount of time it takes the sun to cross the horizon line. The 24-hour period in which the forces of light and dark are best in balance is known as the *equilux*, and it's timing varies slightly depending on one's location on the earth's surface.

In 2013 in the Washington D.C. area, the autumnal equilux began at sunrise on September 25th, with its midpoint occurring at sunset that day, which was within a few seconds of being on the dot at 7:00PM Eastern Daylight Time.

SEPTEMBER 25

In the Oval Office of the White House, President Bates checked the time on the desk clock. At precisely 5:00PM, he said, "Send her in."

Secretary Fiske motioned to a Secret Service agent at the door, who admitted Dr. Helen Strath.

Dressed in a conservative business suit, Strath shook hands first with Fiske, then with Bates, who needed to reach upward to greet the woman nearly five inches taller than himself.

She said, "I'm pleased to meet you, Mister President."

"The pleasure is mine, Dr. Strath. You've done the world a great service on multiple levels. And for that, you truly deserve this. Still don't want any public ceremony?"

"For my personal safety, Mr. President, I'd prefer not to have my face plastered across the worldwide news. I appreciate that your government has honored the request to keep my identity secret."

"It's the least we could do. Fortunately, the news media and even contributing foreign governments have acquiesced to our statements about not wanting to compromise our intelligence sources. Brazilian officials are the only others who know your identity."

Fiske commented, "You're wise in that regard, Dr. Strath, considering that the dregs of a terrorist group might not be too happy with your actions. We'll keep you informed in the event there's a resurgence of that group."

Strath interlocked her thumbs and flapped her hands. "Like a butterfly rising from the ashes?"

Fiske replied, "Not likely, but you never know."

Bates added, "Besides the terrorists, there are many unscrupulous people who'd like to get their hands on a piece of your newfound wealth. I know a thing or two about that. There's no shortage of bloodsuckers in the world."

Strath nodded. "Another group I'd like to avoid."

Bates straighten up his stance, cleared his throat, and announced, "Dr. Helen Strath, on behalf of the government of the United States of America, as well as the contributing governments of Brazil and the European Union, plus a consortium of coffee industry corporations, for your invaluable information leading to the identification and arrest of the terrorist mastermind, Eddy Zeger, I hereby award you one hundred million U.S. dollars." Bates vigorously shook Strath's hand. He lowered his voice. "As of two minutes ago, we've wired the money to your account."

"Thank you, Mister President."

"You're most welcome. And thank you for your development of the prophylactic treatment to ward off the new strain of tetanus bacteria."

Strath said, "Hopefully we'll never have to find out how well that works."

Bates turned to Fiske. "Did we deduct any federal income tax out of that reward?"

Fiske shook his head. "Sorry, Mister President. The doctor is not a U.S. citizen, and her work related to this incident was conducted entirely outside of our country."

Seeing her to the door, Bates asked, "What will you do with the money, Dr. Strath?"

"I think the more important question, Mister President, is: What will I do with my life?"

"You now have the luxury of deciding that for yourself in a manner which few people get to enjoy."

÷÷÷÷÷

At 7:00PM that evening in Washington D.C., Dr. Helen Strath emerged in casual attire from the doorway of the elegant Fairmont Hotel. She paused while she tucked most of her lengthy red hair under her black beret. Walking toward the Georgetown section of the city, she wondered, *What will I do with my life?* She chuckled to herself. *Anything I want to do.*

As twilight dwindled into darkness, Strath strolled along the brick sidewalks of M Street, admiring the trendy boutiques, the nouvelle cuisine restaurants, the chic art galleries, and the stylish people out on the town. *I can use the money to open my own research institute, although it would be hard to top the one where I already work. Or I can retire and travel the world, see the great wonders. Or I can become an artist, learn to paint, maybe make music. Or I can become a philanthropist. I can use the money to do good in the world. But what really constitutes doing good?*

She crossed the street to get a closer look at a particular shop in a brick building. She gazed at the rows of colorful designs in the storefront window under a sign reading "Jinx Proof." *Too bad about Eddy. He had a few good ideas.* She opened the door and walked into the shop. *And he's still the smartest man I've ever known. But after all, he's only a man.*

A shaved-headed woman in a chocolate leather vest sat on a stool behind the counter. She craned her neck to look up at the tall customer and asked, "What can we do for you this evening, big sister?"

Strath smiled and replied to the tattoo artist, "I'd like something in the way of a snake..."

THE END
(FORWARD VERSION)

[CONTINUED BELOW]

ALTERNATE ENDING
(BACKWARD VERSION)

÷÷÷÷÷

At 7:00PM that evening in Washington D.C., Dr. Helen Strath lay in the Jacuzzi in the bathroom of the elegant Georgetown Suite at the Fairmont Hotel. Twilight dwindled into darkness outside her room's windows.

Letting the water jets soothe her muscles, Strath wondered, *What will I do with my life? I can use the money to open my own research institute, although it would be hard to top the one where I already work. Or I can retire and travel the world, see the great wonders. Or I can become an artist, learn to paint, maybe make music. Or I can become a philanthropist. I can use the money to do good in the world. But what really constitutes doing good?*

She turned off the water jets.

Too bad about Eddy. He had a few good ideas. And he's still the smartest man I've ever known. But after all, he's only a man.

She stood up, and when she stepped out of the tub, she smiled as she caught a glimpse in the mirror of the tattoo on her own back, the Queen Alexandra's Birdwing (*Ornithoptera alexandrae*), the only butterfly in the world larger than the Goliath Birdwing.

THE END
###

Vote for your preferred ending at www.stevehoffenberg.com

"Like" the book at www.facebook.com/coffeecrash
Twitter follow the author @SteveHoffenberg
Tweet about *Coffee Crash* with hashtag #CoffeeCrash

www.ingramcontent.com/pod-product-compliance
Lightning Source LLC
Chambersburg PA
CBHW070805180626
46818CB00001B/108